Her Unexpected Adventure

Her Unexpected Adventure

Cheryl A. Hunter

Cheryl A. Hunter

© 2021 by Cheryl A. Hunter

Grand Owl Publishing

cherylahunter.com

Artwork by Cheryl A. Hunter

ISBN: 978-1-7328351-6-0

Chapter 1

Heavy, wet snowflakes fell in clumps and began to accumulate on the
roads and sidewalks as Athena Romano made her way to her travel agency.
The weather was not unusual for Falmouth, Massachusetts at the end of
February, but it was cold, and she wished she had taken a vacation to a
warmer place if only for a week. She parked her car and stepped out. The
wind blew her hair around her face, and snow melted on top of her head.
As she looked at her reflection in the car window, she gathered up her
long, light brown hair, twisted it behind her, and put it down inside the
fluffy, white, knitted scarf she had around her neck. She felt fortunate that
at forty five years old, she did not have any gray hair. She tucked the ends
of the scarf down the front of her bright red, wool coat, which was a little
long on her slender, only five foot four inch tall body, but in this weather,
covering more of her legs helped keep her warm. Athena adjusted the strap
of the quilted messenger style bag she carried containing her laptop and
papers. She shifted her two small tote bags to one arm, and then she turned
and quickly walked a few blocks to her travel agency.

Her Unexpected Adventure

Athena's business was in a block with two other store fronts. She and her now ex-husband James purchased the building twelve years earlier, and despite the divorce, they still owned and managed the building together. He was a realtor, and he believed purchasing the building was a good financial investment. At that time, the neighborhood was fairly run down, and many of the buildings needed repairs, but new businesses were moving in. They renovated the inside, put on new vinyl siding, and updated the electrical and plumbing systems. As a result, the property value steadily rose.

When Athena opened the door of her agency, a blast of noise assaulted her ears. The phones were ringing, and the three people in the room were typing away on their computers assisting customers with travel plans. The flashing light indicated that other callers were waiting to talk to an agent. It was organized chaos. Athena closed the door, went over to the first empty desk she came to, and picked up the ringing telephone. "Fantasy Get Away Travel Agency," she said happily into the receiver. While she talked to a customer, she slipped off her snow boots and put on the low-heeled black pumps she had in one of her bags. She then logged into the computer and began a chat with another customer. She took notes on a legal pad and assured the caller that the vacation would be spectacular all while she typed a message to the other customer. It seemed they were making more and more online bookings in recent months.

Two hours later, when the calls finally slowed down, Athena gathered her things, went to her own office, and closed the door. Her assistant came in with a large cup of tea. "Good morning."

"Thank you, Holly." Athena looked at her watch. "It's barely morning," she said with a sigh.

2

"I guess it's the cold and dreary weather. Everyone is looking to get out of town," Holly said with a chuckle. She handed Athena the day's mail and closed the door as she left the office.

Athena drank her tea while she opened the stack of mail on her desk which consisted primarily of monthly bills. She then checked email. She had another email from Ellen, her editor, wondering when she planned to finish her manuscript. Athena took a folder of notes out of her computer bag and set them on her desk. She was almost finished incorporating the material into the last chapters of the manuscript, and she knew if she could just get a few uninterrupted weeks to work on it, she could finish the draft. However, that was not going to happen right now because she simply had too much to do. She had students taking exams in her online Travel Agency Operations and Administration class. The travel agency was busy because people were tired of the cold weather, and tax refunds were starting to come in. She had not updated her travel blog in a week either. She sighed deeply, and the phone rang. "Fantasy Get Away Travel Agency," she said brightly into the phone.

About two o'clock in the afternoon, Holly, came into her office with a stack of bookings. "It seems the Bahamas is a favorite destination today."

Athena looked out the window at the snow. At least six more inches of snow accumulated since she arrived at the agency that morning. "It will be a tough ride home. Holly, do you need to pick up the kids?"

"Yes, they didn't cancel school, but the after-school program was cancelled, so I am heading out now."

Athena nodded. "Ok, drive safe." She began looking over the bookings.

An hour later, Athena's twenty four year old daughter, Aria, who taught eighth grade science at the middle school down the street, came into her office. "Hi Mom," Aria said as she set down a cup of tea. She took off her camel wool coat and unwrapped the white scarf from around her neck. Her very long honey blonde hair was in a low ponytail and fell almost to her waist. Her black pants were tucked into knee high black boots that had a four inch heel and made her six feet tall. She sat down in front of her mother's desk and stretched her long legs out in front of her.

Athena leaned back in her chair, "Hi, honey."

"Afternoon activities were cancelled because of the snow, so no Math Meet."

"How was teaching today?"

"Good. We did some hands-on activities with prisms after the review today since it's Friday, and there's an exam next week." Aria took a sip of her tea. "Busy today?"

"Extremely. Everyone wants to go somewhere warm," Athena sighed. "Including me."

"And me," she added with a laugh.

"Well, speaking of warm places," Aria paused. She was not certain how her mother was going to take her suggestion for the upcoming Easter holiday, but she had to ask.

Athena looked up at her daughter. "What's wrong, Aria?"

"Nothing is wrong." She took a deep breath. "Trevor has asked me to go to Texas for the Easter holiday to meet his family."

Athena smiled. She approved of Trevor Young. He was smart, kind, and completely in love with her daughter. "I think you should go to Texas."

"There's more," Aria said softly. Athena raised her eyebrows. "We want you to come with us."

Athena looked at her daughter and smiled. Clearly, Aria worried about her being alone on a holiday. "You don't have to worry about me," she assured her daughter. She leaned over and put her hand on Aria's hand. "I will be fine. It will give me a chance to write. My deadline is looming."

Aria looked crestfallen. "Mom, you don't understand," she said very quietly. "We want you to come to Texas with us, and his family wants to meet both of us."

"Oh." Athena thought for a moment. "Are you two planning to marry soon?"

"The subject has come up quite a bit recently." Aria smiled and leaned toward her mother. She continued, "The Young family is very close, and they want both of us to visit for Easter. It would be nice to have a big family holiday, don't you think?"

Holidays had become very small. Athena and Aria were both only children. She and James divorced, and then both her parents passed away. They had some extended family members, but they lived in other states. Holidays were just the two of them in recent years, and it was why they often went overseas for holidays. Athena could tell this meant a lot to her daughter. "Yes, it would be nice," she finally said. Aria breathed a sigh of relief. Athena continued, "I will work on the flights and hotel reservations."

"Oh, no hotels needed. Trevor's family has guest cabins on the ranch. So, just flights."

"Ok. Well, that is easy enough to do."

"Have you ever been to Texas, Mom?"

"Does an overnight at the Dallas airport count?"

"No," Aria laughed.

Athena stacked up a few papers on her desk and closed the lid on her laptop. She picked up the notes for her manuscript and put them and the laptop in her bag. Unfortunately, she did not have time to work on the manuscript today. "What should we have for dinner?"

"Mexican?" Aria suggested.

"Definitely. I am always in the mood for burritos."

The restaurant was not crowded, but because it was still snowing, they ordered the food to go and headed home. When they arrived home, the driveway was plowed and the walk to the front door was cleared. "David did a good job, as always," Athena said as they got out of the car.

"I think he spends extra time clearing snow here," Aria said, and she smiled at her mother. "I think he wants to keep you happy."

"Oh Aria," Athena laughed, "David and I have known each other forever."

"I know, but he is definitely interested in you."

"No. There is nothing romantic between us. We are just friends," Athena reminded her daughter. She unlocked the front door, and they went inside. They took off their coats and boots, went upstairs to their rooms to change into comfortable clothes, and returned to the kitchen to eat.

Later that evening, Aria said good night and went in her room to talk to Trevor, and Athena sat up in bed updating her travel blog. Tonight's post: 'Traveling with young children part three'. Her blog did very well. She had doubts about its profitability when she first started it, but she found she enjoyed writing the blog, and it actually made money. The blog was one of the reasons her first book was published. She incorporated many expanded blog posts into the book on family friendly vacations. The book she worked on now was more specific as it focused just on traveling to London. It was nearly completed; she just needed to sit and write without distractions. However, distractions were piling up.

Athena felt a sense of accomplishment as she hit Post. She pulled out her calendar. Tomorrow she had to book flights to Texas. There were four weeks until Easter, and her deadline for the manuscript was three weeks later. She knew she had to make a writing schedule. However, it was almost one am, so she placed her laptop on the nightstand and slid down under the covers and went to sleep.

The next morning, Athena got up, put on her robe, and went downstairs to the kitchen. Aria was already dressed and eating breakfast. "Good morning." Athena said. She gave her daughter a kiss on the head.

"The water just boiled," Aria told her mother. Athena nodded. "Trevor will be here soon." She continued to eat her cereal. "What do you have planned for the weekend, Mom?"

"I will book our flights to Texas, and then I need to set up a writing schedule and do some writing. Tomorrow morning, I may meet Jasmine at the bookstore for breakfast."

"She's back?" Aria asked. "How did she like Iceland?"

"She loved it. She has pictures of the aurora."

Aria got up and put her cereal bowl in the sink. She wore a tight pink fluffy sweater over skinny black jeans, and she slipped on her knee-high boots. "Trevor thought we could fly to Texas on the Wednesday before Easter and return on Monday. I am on April vacation the week before Easter, and I plan to take a personal day on Monday."

"That sounds good. The weather should be nice. Much warmer than here."

"Trevor says the wildflowers will be in bloom, so it should be beautiful."

Athena poured herself a cup of tea, brought it to the table, and started dunking her tea bag. She yawned.

"Why don't you go back to bed." Aria suggested.

"No, I'm up. Just not fully awake."

The doorbell rang. "That's Trevor." Aria jumped up to open the door. Athena heard them saying hello and obviously kissing before they came into the kitchen.

"Good morning, Athena," Trevor said cheerfully. Unlike Athena, Trevor was a morning person. He stood six foot two inches tall, lean, and muscular. He worked out at the gym often, and he and Aria skied and skated in the winter. He had dark eyes and a big smile. His black hair was short and slightly curly but not overly so. During the week, Trevor wore suits to the office, but today, he wore blue jeans, a plaid flannel shirt, and cowboy boots as he often did on weekends.

"Good morning," Athena replied. "Would you like some coffee or something to eat?"

"No thanks," he replied.

"How was the conference?" She took a long drink of tea.

"It had its ups and downs like most conferences," he chuckled. Athena nodded. She knew what he meant.

"Well, Mom, we are going to head out."

Trevor picked up Aria's weekender bag and her skating bag, and they walked to the door.

"Ok." Athena got up. "Have fun." She hugged and kissed her daughter. "Text me."

"I will. I love you."

"I love you too." Athena watched them get into Trevor's car, and she waved as they pulled out of the driveway and onto the street. She closed the door and returned to the kitchen. She put water on for another large cup of tea and put a bagel in the toaster for breakfast.

She sat at the island in the kitchen and looked outside while she ate. There was very little wind, and the sun was shining. Athena drank down the rest of the tea and put her plate in the dishwasher. She had work to do, but it was a good morning for a walk on the beach. She bundled into her coat, put on a hat and mittens, and picked up her beach pail. She might find large shells washed up on shore after yesterday's storm. She locked up her home and walked the short distance to the beach.

Chapter 2

The days leading up to the trip to Texas were stressful. Aria and Athena went shopping and purchased some new clothes for the trip. Trevor said to bring swimsuits, so they purchased new ones. They hoped for a few warm days in the sun because this year was exceptionally cold and snowy on the East coast. There was over two feet of snow the first couple days of April. It seemed to Athena that the seasons were shifting. Spring temperatures were colder, and fall temperatures were warmer in recent years.

On the plane, Athena, Aria, and Trevor were seated three across in the center row. They had complimentary alcohol on the flight, and they decided to have Bloody Marys with breakfast which Athena hoped would calm Aria's nerves. They were fortunate to have a direct flight from Boston to Austin, so after breakfast, Athena closed her eyes and took a nap.

The flight landed at Austin's airport just before eleven o'clock on the Wednesday before Easter. After they retrieved their luggage, Aria wanted to stop at the ladies' room before exiting the terminal. "I'll just be a minute," she said to Trevor. "Mom? Ladies' room?" She inclined her head in the direction of the restrooms. Athena pulled her bags over to Trevor and joined her daughter "Trevor says it is an hour plus ride to the ranch."

"Aria, are you ok?" Athena asked when they were out of Trevor's ear shot. "You look nervous."

"I am," she replied. "I didn't sleep at all on the plane. I hope his mother likes me."

"Why wouldn't she like you? You are kind, intelligent, pretty, and you have a cheerful personality."

"You are biased, Mom."

"Yes, I am, but you are still all of those things."

The ladies' room was packed with women as restrooms always are at any public venue, and while waiting for her mother, Aria squeezed between two women at the mirror to brush her hair and freshen her makeup. Athena washed her hands and then brushed her hair. "We need a tan," she laughed as she lightly applied a bronzer to the apples of her cheeks.

"Well, it is warm and sunny in Texas, so maybe we can get a little tan." Aria did a last check of her hair in the mirror.

"Oh, I hope so. I need to soak up some sun rays. It has been a long winter." Athena was happy to see her daughter smiling as they walked over to where Trevor stood waiting.

"The family is waiting right outside the doors," he announced as they picked up their bags.

Aria turned her head sharply and looked panic stricken again. "The family? The whole family is here? I thought just your brother was picking us up?"

"They were anxious to meet the both of you, so they all came." He smiled at them.

Athena gave a weak smile back and looked at her daughter.

Aria put her hand over her stomach which was doing a flip flop. She took a deep calming breath, held it, and picked up her suitcases ready to face Trevor's family. She looked at her mother and mouthed 'here we go' as they went through the doors.

Amongst the large crowd waiting for passengers were Trevor's mother, father, and two brothers. They all smiled and waved as Trevor, Aria, and Athena approached.

"Oh, it is good to see you!" Trevor's mother, Maria, pulled him into a tight embrace and kissed him.

"Mom," Trevor said with a sigh, but his eyes were smiling as he held onto her and kissed her cheek. She wiped her eyes and stood back while Trevor began the introductions. "This is Aria, my girlfriend, and this is Athena, her mother."

Maria was sixty eight according to Trevor. She stood about five feet three inches tall and had a heavy medium build. Her shoulder length brown hair was streaked with grey, and her rugged face was very tan. She wore a blue and white checkered shirt tucked into a pair of dark blue jeans, and she wore fancy engraved cowboy boots.

Maria smiled at them. "It is so very nice to meet you both." She pulled first Aria and then Athena into a tight hug.

Trevor's father, John, was seventy-one and a very strong and rugged looking man. He stood just over six feet tall. He wore jeans and a plaid shirt. His hair was entirely grey, and his face was deeply tanned and weathered from many years out in the blazing Texas sun.

"Nice to meet y'all," he said. In one hand, he held a cowboy hat, and with the other, he shook Aria's and then Athena's hand, and they felt the callouses and strength of hands that worked a ranch.

Trevor jerked a finger at the two men who stood holding onto their hats. "And these two are my brothers, Troy and Dan."

Troy was forty seven, and his brother Dan was forty four. They were as handsome as Trevor. Troy had a full head of wavy, black hair. Dan's hair was shorter but straight and styled. They were both six feet two or three inches tall. They were dressed nearly identically in dark blue jeans and crisp white button-down shirts that set off their deeply tanned skin. Athena's gaze lingered over them longer than it should have, and she started to blush. These two were real men: handsome, strong, and confident. They smiled and shook hands with the women. Aria also blushed, and Trevor put a protective arm around her. Although he trusted his brothers, he was suddenly aware of how handsome and fit they looked. He spent more time sitting behind a desk than on a horse, and he decided that he needed to start spending more time at the gym.

"Let me get that bag for you," Dan said taking Athena's large, wheeled suitcase.

"Oh, thank you," she squeaked. Her voice sounded higher than normal to her, and she cleared her throat. Troy took Aria's suitcase, and they all made their way out of the terminal.

"Are you certain you can fit everyone and the luggage in your vehicle?" Athena asked as they walked through the parking lot.

"We have a ranch vehicle. It seats nine," John explained as he led the way to a large white vehicle. He opened the doors, and Troy and Dan loaded in the luggage.

It was early in the day, and it was already quite warm. She took off her jacket and folded it over her arm before she pulled herself up into the vehicle. She, Aria and Trevor sat in the middle row, and Troy and Dan sat in the back row with the luggage. John and Maria sat up front.

"I'll have the air on in a minute," John called as he started the vehicle.

Maria turned and looked at them. "You three look wilted already."

"It's quite a change in temperature from New England," Athena explained. "It was thirty one degrees when we left this morning.

Maria shivered, "Oh that is cold."

"Have you two ever been to Texas," Dan asked.

"No," Aria replied.

"Athena, you own a travel agency?" Troy asked her.

"I do."

"So, you travel a lot but have never been to Texas?"

She gave him a forced smile. "Well, until now there hasn't been a compelling reason to come to Texas." The man started to grate on her nerves already. "I do a great deal of traveling in Europe."

Aria looked at her mother with wide pleading eyes. She knew her mother could be witty and sarcastic at times, especially if someone questioned her or seemed to disapprove of her actions. She decided to steer the conversation off its current path. "It is amazing how distant the horizon is here. It is so flat, and it's such a clear day."

Athena smiled at her daughter. She wanted to make the visit as pleasant as possible. After all, it looked like these people were going to be her daughter's in-laws one day.

"Austin looks like a nice city," Aria commented as she looked out the window. They were on the top level of Route 35 heading North, and it afforded them an opportunity to see the university and the city laid out before them.

"Austin is a fun city," Trevor said to Aria. "We need to come for a longer visit, so we can see Austin, and San Antonio, and New Braunfels too."

"Wurstfest," Troy and Dan said together.

Trevor laughed. "The beer festival in New Braunfels in October," he explained to Aria and Athena.

"Yes, Trevor," Maria agreed. "Y'all should come back for a longer visit. There is so much to see."

They drove out of Austin and past Round Rock. The sides of the roads bloomed with wildflowers. Vast areas of colorful flowers blanketed the sides of the roadway and extended beyond. "The wildflowers are gorgeous," Athena said as they passed field after field of colorful blooms.

"The planting of wildflowers all began with Lady Bird Johnson, wife of President Lyndon Johnson of Texas," Maria informed them proudly.

"Wow, I did not know that!" Aria exclaimed.

Maria continued, "Yes, she pushed for a law to control outdoor advertising and encourage enhancement and roadside development to make the country's roads more scenic. So, wildflowers were planted alongside roads. And this is the result."

"Well, it is beautiful," Aria said, and Athena nodded her agreement.

They exited the highway and headed west. There were still areas of wildflowers, but the landscape looked drier the further west they traveled. Athena looked out the window to the distant horizon. The trees were small and there were large expanses of yellow grassland. A short while later, John turned down a gravel driveway and slowed down. Even at a slow speed, a cloud of dust rose behind the vehicle as they drove along. Up ahead, the house, stable, and several other buildings came into view. A split rail fence lined this part of the driveway leading up to the large two story older wooden home painted dark grey with white trim. A set of wooden steps led up to an expansive front porch with several rocking chairs, other assorted chairs, and four small tables. The original building had been expanded at various times with additions on the back and on the side of the house. A small vegetable garden grew off to the left side, and next to it was a small flower garden. Across the driveway was the stable. This building and two smaller buildings were painted light grey with dark grey trim.

John turned the corner and parked the vehicle along the edge of the driveway. There were two trees on the side of the house and across the narrow driveway there were three cabins. Each cabin had a small porch and was painted a shade of grey with white trim. Athena looked down the driveway, past a few more trees, and saw another house at the far end of the driveway.

"Here we are," John said as he turned off the vehicle. They opened the car doors, and hot dry air rushed in and tickled their noses.

"The first two cabins are prepared for y'all," Maria said as she slid out of the vehicle. The first cabin was closest to the road. The other was set slightly back.

Troy and Dan pulled the luggage out of the back of the vehicle. Dan took Athena's bags and brought them to the first cabin. She opened the door and held it for him so he could bring the bags inside.

"Oh, this is very cozy." Athena entered the main room which had a sitting area with a sofa, end table, and a TV. There was a bistro table and chairs and a kitchenette off to the side. The kitchenette had a half stove, a microwave, and a refrigerator. Next to the window sat a desk and chair. A door at the back lead to a bedroom with a queen size bed, a dresser, and two nightstands. The small but adequate bathroom was off another door from the main room. The rooms were painted a light cream color with white trim, and the sofa and bed linens were in shades of cream and yellow. On the walls were Texas landscape paintings, and the lamp overhead was made of antlers. "I will be very comfortable in here," she smiled at Dan.

He nodded and brought the bags into the bedroom then came back into the main room and sat down at the table. "The cabins are comfortable." He stretched out his legs and leaned back in the chair. "We occasionally rent them out, but mostly they are for family and guests."

Athena opened the refrigerator and saw that it contained cans of seltzer, a small bottle of milk, and a small bottle of cream. On the counter were two kinds of tea bags, regular and peach. "How did Maria know I drink seltzer and tea?"

Dan laughed. "Mom has been grilling Trevor for information on what you and Aria like since he told her you were coming to visit."

"Oh." She put her hand to her mouth. "I did not want Maria to go through that much fuss."

"It's ok," Dan said waving his hand dismissively. "Mom likes to make sure everything is perfect."

Athena nodded. "Well, I certainly appreciate it."

Maria poked her head in the door. "Is everything ok?" she asked.

"Yes, everything is wonderful. Maria, thank you for the amenities. You really make me feel so at home." Athena smiled at her.

She came in and pat Athena's arm. "Good. When you are settled, come to the main house for lunch."

"I will. Thank you."

Maria turned to leave then looked over at her son. "Dan, I need your help."

"Ok, Mom." He got to his feet. "See you soon, Athena."

"I won't be long getting settled," she replied with a smile.

Dan left the cabin, and Athena went into the bedroom. She put the suitcase on the bed and took out the dresses, sweaters, and slacks she brought and hung them in the small closet, and then she placed her assorted shoes and flip flops on the closet floor. She shook out several dressy shirts and hug them up, and she put the rest of her clothes in the dresser drawers. She stowed the suitcases under the bed.

The bathroom had a sink, shower, and toilet. Athena placed her toiletries on the countertop. She washed up and brushed her teeth and hair, and she changed into shorts and a tank top. Trevor was right when he said to bring mostly warm weather clothes. She probably did not need the light sweaters she brought. Athena went back into the main room, took out her laptop, and placed it on the desk. She pulled out the plastic envelope with her notes and set it on the desk. She hoped to find the time and inspiration to write. She sat down on the desk chair to put on her sandals. A light breeze came in through the screen door. Athena noticed how quiet it was on the ranch. At her home on Cape Cod, she often heard the dull roar of cars as people drove along the beach road. There were also the sounds of neighbors coming and going, children playing, and dogs barking. She closed her eyes and listened. All she heard was the wind blowing. It was oddly peaceful.

"Mom?" Aria called breaking Athena out of her thoughts.

"Aria? Is everything ok?"

"Yes. Are you ok?"

Athena laughed. "Yes, I was just listening to the quiet."

Chapter 3

Very early Thursday morning, Troy got up, dressed, and walked up to the main house. He was so accustomed to getting up early, he could not sleep in even after staying up until past midnight talking and playing cards. Normally, he ate breakfast at his house. He lived alone and enjoyed his freedom, but this weekend, he wanted to spend time with the family. The image of Athena swam before his eyes. He shook his head and went in the large country kitchen to make a pot of coffee.

The rising sun cast a pinkish glow over the landscape, and he stood in the kitchen and looked out the window at the cabins while he drank a cup of coffee. One of the cabin doors open, and Trevor emerged, closed the door behind him, and walked up to the house. Troy chuckled to himself. Trevor had always been a stringy boy that followed him and Dan around the ranch. He always tried to lift more than he was capable of and work as hard as his two older brothers. Troy was old enough to be Trevor's father, and he helped raise Trevor, so naturally he thought of him as a child. However, Aria certainly did not think of Trevor as a child. Troy could tell that she adored his brother, and she saw him for the confident and capable man he was today. He decided to speak to Dan. It was time they stopped ribbing Trevor and started treating him as an equal. He did not want to do anything to undermine the confidence Aria had in Trevor. But, since she was not around right now, Troy decided to have a little fun with his baby brother.

Trevor quietly opened the front door and started to tip toe up the stairs.

"Good morning," Troy drawled.

Trevor stopped dead mid-step and turned to look at Troy. The two brothers stared at one another for a few seconds. There was no point in denying he came from Aria's cabin, and why should he? He was not a child. He was a successful, albeit junior, financial planner. He provided for himself, and he and Aria practically lived together. Finally, Trevor straightened up. "Good morning," he said with confidence. "Is the coffee ready?"

Troy nodded. "It is."

"Good." Trevor walked into the kitchen, took a mug out of the cabinet, and poured himself a cup.

Troy followed him and sat down at the kitchen table. "Aria is a wonderful woman," he said to his brother. He almost said girl, but he wanted to show his brother he did not think of him as a boy anymore.

"She is. She is smart, pretty, and she keeps me on my toes," Trevor laughed.

Troy nodded his agreement. "I can understand that. Aria and her mother are a little … intense." Trevor raised his eyebrows at Troy. "No offense, but man they talk really fast. I had trouble keeping up with the conversation last night."

Trevor burst out laughing. "Oh, no offense taken." He picked up his coffee cup. "In fact, last night, Athena and Aria both said they worried they scared the family." He reached into the cookie jar on the table. He offered one.

Troy shook his head no. "I guess people talk faster back East. I noticed you talk faster than you use to."

"Yeah, I guess so."

"The only place back East I ever visited was Connecticut when you graduated."

"You should visit me sometime."

Troy looked uncertain, "I don't know."

"Really, we could take a trip to New York City too. It is an exciting place. The city that never sleeps."

Troy shifted uncomfortably in his seat. "Do they sleep on Cape Cod?"

"Why do you ask?"

Troy took a deep breath. "Well, I woke up about 2:30 am and went in the kitchen for a glass of water, and I saw lights on in Athena's cabin. I thought she might be sick. You know traveling and the time change," Troy added quickly. "Anyway, I went to the cabin just to see if she was ok. I could see her inside. She was on her computer, typing. She had headphones on, and she moved to music while she typed."

"Did you knock on the door?" Trevor asked.

Troy looked shocked. "Of course not!" he exclaimed. He shook his head in disbelief. "I didn't want her to think I was a Peeping Tom."

"But you were a Peeping Tom," Trevor suppressed a laugh behind his coffee cup.

Troy narrowed his eyes and looked at his brother. "I told you, I worried that she was ill."

"Did I hear someone was a Peeping Tom?" Dan said as he came in the kitchen. He took a mug out of the cabinet, poured himself a cup of coffee, and sat down at the table with his brothers.

"Troy," Trevor said emphatically.

"I was not a Peeping Tom," Troy said firmly. Dan looked at his brother and waited for an explanation. Troy sighed and continued in an exasperated tone, "I saw Athena's light on during the night and thought she might be ill."

"Was she ok?" Dan sat up straighter. "What did she say when you asked?"

"She didn't say anything," Trevor laughed. "He just looked in her window."

Dan slouched back in his chair and laughed, "So he's the Peeping Tom."

Troy shoulders sagged, and he let out a very deep sigh.

"Good morning." Maria came bustling into the kitchen. "Oh, it is so nice to see my three boys in my kitchen." She kissed each of them on the cheek. "What are you boys talking about?"

"Just talking," they replied almost in unison.

Maria looked at them and then went over to the refrigerator and began taking out items for breakfast. "Trevor, do Athena and Aria eat bacon?"

"Aria does. I told her we smoke our own bacon, and she is excited to try it."

"Athena doesn't eat bacon?" Troy asked in disbelief.

Trevor shook his head. "I'm not really sure. I've never seen her eat it, and she never serves it when I have been over for breakfast."

Maria stopped putting bacon in the fry pan. She turned to him with narrowed eyes then decided not to ask how often he has been over for breakfast.

John came into the kitchen carrying a basket of fresh eggs. "Mornin' boys," he said cheerfully. He set the eggs on the granite countertop.

"Do they both eat eggs?" Maria asked.

"Who?" John asked.

Maria took a breath and let it out. "Athena and Aria. I asked Trevor if they both eat eggs."

"Yes, they do," Trevor replied.

Soon the delicious smell of bacon filled the kitchen. John put on a fan to blow heat out of the already warm room.

"Good morning. Oh, that smells so good, Mrs. Young." Aria came into the kitchen. She wore a pair of pink shorts with a pink and white floral top, and she cradled a large mug of tea. Trevor jumped up and gave her his seat.

"Oh, call me Maria, Aria. No need to be so formal." She bustled around and then went to the stove and flipped the bacon "Do you like scrambled or over medium eggs, dear."

"Either are fine. Whatever is easiest," Aria smiled at Maria. She liked Trevor's mother. She was down to earth, but Aria worried she was also old fashioned. She suggested Trevor go back to his room in the main house, but he wanted to spend the night with her. She hoped he got back before his mother noticed he was not in his room.

Maria started to whip up a dozen eggs and some milk in a large bowl. "Aria, is your mother up?"

"She just finished showering. She said she needed to send an email, and then she would be right over. Apparently, she did quite a bit of writing last night."

"Oh, did she stay up late last night?" Dan asked with a nod to Troy who walked behind Aria and glared at his brother.

"Oh, yes. She is working on her second travel book. Her editor has been bugging her to get writing, but Mom has been stuck."

John brought in a few chairs from the dining room. "Should we eat in here this morning? It's less formal than the dining room."

Aria nodded yes. "This is a big country kitchen. I love it." Trevor pulled up a chair and sat down next to her.

"Good morning," Athena said as she entered the kitchen.

"Good morning," Maria replied cheerfully and gawked at her sons as both Troy and Dan jumped up and offered her his seat.

Athena smiled and sat in Dan's seat which was next to Aria. She wore khaki shorts and a short-sleeved white blouse with tiny pink and blue flowers. She took a long drink of tea from the mug she brought in with her. "The bacon smells delicious, Maria."

Aria looked at her mother. She could not remember the last time she saw her eat bacon.

Athena drank more tea and then stood up. "Let me help you."

"No. No," Maria replied. "You are a guest, and I have everything under control."

"I can set the table then," Athena suggested.

"Yes, dishes are in that cabinet."

The kitchen had tall wood cabinets and granite countertops. Athena opened the cabinet door, stretched, and stood on her tip toes to reach the

24

plates, and then she set them around the table. She set a paper napkin by each plate, and she placed a fork on each napkin.

"What else can I do?" Athena asked.

Maria noticed Dan and Troy both intently watched her every move, but she smiled at Athena. "You can start toasting biscuits."

Dan stood up quickly. "I'll help you, Athena." He went into the pantry and came back with a colorful straw basket full of biscuits. Together they sliced the biscuits and put them in the toaster. When the biscuits popped out of the toaster, they put them back into the basket, and covered them to keep them warm.

Athena examined the basket. "This is a unique basket, Maria. I've never seen one like it."

"It's a tortilla basket," Maria replied.

"Where can I get one?"

"This one is from the Mercado in San Antonio, but you might find one at the country store in town."

While Athena and Dan finished toasting biscuits, Trevor got up and put a kettle of water on the stove to boil. He knew Aria and Athena needed more tea. Soon everything was ready. The table was laden with an overflowing basket of biscuits, several bowls of scrambled eggs, and a mound of bacon on a platter. It was tight, but they sat around the kitchen table and began eating breakfast.

Aria ate several pieces of bacon, a large scoop of eggs, and two biscuits. Athena, on the other hand, only had a small slice of bacon. She did have a good-sized portion of scrambled eggs, but she did not have a biscuit.

Troy noticed that last night Athena did not have a dinner roll either. "Would you like to try a biscuit?" he asked Athena.

"No, thank you," she replied.

"Afraid you will get fat?" he asked and then gasped. Everyone stopped talking. Aria looked at her mother and then at Troy. She hoped her mother did not get mad or have a sarcastic reply. "Sorry," he meekly whispered.

Athena stared at Troy, reached into the basket, took out half a biscuit, buttered it, and took a bite. "They are delicious," she said taking another bite. Trevor and Aria both breathed a sigh of relief.

John cleared his throat. "Have either of you ladies ever ridden a horse?" he asked.

"I took a pony ride at the state fair a few times," Aria said.

Trevor put his hand over hers. "Our horses are a bit bigger, but I think you will have fun," he assured her.

"I can't wait," she said, and she leaned over and gave Trevor a little kiss which surprised Maria.

"There are hats in the hall for you ladies to wear. Neither of you have a hat, right?" Maria asked.

"I haven't owned a cowboy hat in years," Athena remarked. She took another drink of tea.

"Have you ever been on a horse, Athena?" Troy asked with a sarcastic tone of voice. Maria glared at her son. She did not understand why he was antagonizing that woman.

"Don't worry, riding a horse is easy," Dan said to Athena. "I will teach you."

Athena picked up her mug of tea and took a long drink. "I haven't been on a horse in a long time, but when I was a teenager, I barrel raced." She hid a smile behind her tea mug.

"Really?" Dan sounded impressed.

"Yes, she even won some ribbons," Aria informed them.

"Of course, that was a number of years ago. I hope it's like a bicycle, and you never forget how to ride." Athena took another long drink of tea. She raised her eyebrows at Troy. His mouth fell open in surprise, and she hid her laugh.

After breakfast, Athena and Aria returned to their cabins. Aria was not sure what to wear. It was warm, but she wanted to be appropriately dressed for horseback riding. 'Mom, what are you wearing?' Aria texted to her mother in the next cabin.

Athena left her cabin dressed in jeans, a white cotton shirt over a black tank top, and sneakers. "This is what I'm wearing," she said as she knocked on the door and then walked in her daughter's cabin. She looked around the room. The cabin was very similar to her cabin except the walls were light blue and the furnishings and linens were in shades of blue.

Aria looked at her mother, "Ok, I think I will wear something similar."

Athena rolled up the sleeves of the cotton shirt. "Do you have an extra belt? I can't believe I forgot to pack one."

"In that suitcase," Aria pointed to a mostly empty suitcase on the floor in the main room as she rummaged through her other suitcase in the bedroom which she had not yet unpacked. A few minutes later, she walked into the main room. "How's this?" She wore a pair of jeans and a short sleeved red cotton top. "I have this plaid long sleeved shirt. Do you think it is ok?"

"Absolutely," Athena replied. "You look nice."

Trevor knocked on the door. "Are you two ready?"

Aria tucked the shirt into her pants and fastened the belt on her jeans. "Is this ok?"

"You are beautiful," Trevor replied. He walked over and slid his hands up and down her arms.

"I meant is this appropriate for riding?"

"It is." Trevor smiled. "Let's go."

The three of them walked to the stable. Troy and Dan had the horses ready. Aria approached one of the horses apprehensively, as Trevor came up beside her. "Wow these horses are tall." Her voice shook and her were wide.

Trevor instructed her to put her left foot in the stirrup, pull herself up, and swing her right leg over the horse. Aria tried to lift herself up, but she did not make it. "Try again and this time I will give you a boost." The boost did it, and Aria was perched up on top of the horse. Her back was stiff and straight, and she gripped the reins tightly with both hands.

Athena looked at her horse. She hoped she could get up on the horse gracefully. Dan came over and offered his assistance. She smiled at him. "Let me try myself first." Troy smirked, and she was determined to get up on that horse on her own. She put her foot in the stirrup, took a deep breath, and pulled herself up onto the horse and into the saddle on the first try and without assistance. Dan smiled at her then he mounted his own horse.

Troy watched his brother with narrowed eyes. Dan was being obvious, but he doubted Athena was interested in him. Why would she be interested? They were very different people. She was successful and smart, and although he loved his brother, Dan was a bit of a loafer. Still, he felt a weird twinge when she smiled at Dan. Was it a pang of jealousy? He shook his head no. He was not interested in Athena. She was too high strung for his taste. He turned his attention to riding. "These horses know the trail well," he explained to Aria and Athena. "Relax and let the horse pick its own way." He went first, and they followed him out of the stable and made their way to the trail.

Athena realized that riding a horse was like riding a bicycle; you never forget. Soon, she felt very comfortable riding. She enjoyed the slight bounce as the horse walked along, the wind in her hair, and the view from on top of the horse's back.

They entered a small field, and Dan pulled his horse right along-side hers. "You are looking really relaxed and comfortable."

"I am. I just was thinking about when I led trail rides," Athena told him.

"You barrel raced and led trail rides?" Dan asked.

"Yes, the country club where I rode and took lessons offered trail rides to guests. The club had conference rooms and was often rented out by companies for functions. I remember a company in Boston rented the club for its annual company retreat one year. None of them had ever ridden a horse," she recalled with a laugh.

"Oh, that must have been something to see," Dan laughed.

"Why did you stop riding? Got bored," Troy asked. His tone was harsh. He always seemed to be abrupt and antagonistic with her. "Sorry," he said quietly.

Athena glared at him. She took a deep breath. She refused to let him get to her. "No, the country club decided keeping horses was too expensive. They stopped the riding program," she told him in a most pleasant voice.

"There was no place else to ride?"

Athena shook her head no. "Not in the area. It was also the Spring of my senior year in high school when they closed. I was going away to college anyway."

"It sounds like you enjoyed riding," Dan said. He shook his head at his brother, and he hoped Troy did not say anything to put a damper on the mood.

"I did," Athena smiled. "I loved riding, Buttercup. She was my favorite horse." Athena nudged her horse, and he started to trot.

Dan caught up to her. "I guess it is coming back to you."

Athena smiled at him, "It is."

After passing through a cluster of live oak trees, they came into a field. "Follow me," Dan said to Athena. He nudged his horse and started to gallop across the open expanse.

Athena nudged her horse and followed him. The wind blew her hair back, and she felt so light as they moved swiftly across the open field. She pulled back on the reins and slowed her horse as she reached Dan then came to a stop next to him. "Oh, that was exhilarating!" Athena looked back and saw Troy, Trevor, and Aria slowly making their way across the field.

"Race you back," she called over her shoulder to Dan as she urged her horse forward and galloped back. It caught Dan off guard, and although he knew he could catch her, he intentionally held back.

"Mom, that was amazing," Aria said when her mother reached her.

"Do you want to try to go a little faster?" Trevor asked Aria.

"No," Aria said at once. She tightened her grip on the reins, and with her other hand, she held onto the saddle horn.

They turned the horses around and started to head back to the stable at a slow even pace.

"We can ride again tomorrow," Dan said as they clopped along.

Athena raised her eyebrows. "It will depend on whether or not I am sore tomorrow."

"True," Dan laughed.

"Sore?" Aria questioned.

"Riding a horse uses muscles you normally do not use," Athena informed her daughter.

"Oh." Aria stretched her back which already hurt.

Trevor pulled his horse alongside her horse. "Don't worry, Aria," he said. Then he leaned over and whispered something in her ear that made her smile and blush.

Chapter 4

Athena stretched and looked out the window at the stars twinkling in the dark sky. She looked at her watch. It was three am. There were sounds made by frogs and crickets, but no road noise at all. The quiet unnerved her at first, but she was becoming accustomed to it. She leaned on the window ledge. A gentle breeze blew in the open window. She thought about going outside to sit on the porch, but she was afraid of bats, snakes, animals. The screen on the window offered a little protection from what lurked out there.

She found the quiet opened her mind, and she wrote more in the past couple days than she did in the weeks prior to coming to Texas. Perhaps inspiration came from the change of scenery. She thought she might go somewhere and write when they returned home. Things were quieting down at the agency. By April, most of the summer travel was already booked. She thought she might go to Florida to write and soak up the sun. She turned back to her computer and reread Ellen's email. 'Glad you are writing again. Please try to finish by the deadline.' Athena knew publishing practically closed down during the Summer months. She needed to keep writing, but right now she needed to sleep. She closed the laptop and got into bed.

It seemed to Athena that she just closed her eyes when the brilliant sun started came in the window and woke her. She picked up her phone which lay on the nightstand charging. "8:00," she groaned. She lay there for a few minutes. She heard Aria and Trevor talking and laughing. It sounded like they were sitting on the porch of Aria's cabin. Athena got out of bed and went to the bathroom to take a quick shower. She dressed in a pair of denim shorts and a blue floral blouse then went outside. "Good morning," she called to them.

"Morning, Mom," Aria called. "Did you sleep well?"

"I did, once I got in bed," Athena replied. "I stayed up until about three o'clock writing. I was on a roll."

"We know. That's why we didn't wake you," they said together.

"How did you know?"

"Troy saw your cabin lights on when he got up during the night," Trevor replied as he suppressed a laugh. It seemed his big brother was up a lot during the night too.

"I'm glad you are unstuck," Aria said.

"I think I just needed a change in scenery." Athena took the towel off her head. She looked at Aria. Her daughter wore a pair of cut off jean shorts and a red and white top she never saw before.

"I have hot water in a kettle. Would you like a cup of tea, Mom?" Aria asked.

"I'd love one."

Aria stood up and went inside her cabin to get her mother a cup of tea. Trevor took a chair and walked over to the porch on Athena's cabin. "I am glad you like it here, Athena," he said as he sat down and stretched out his legs. He wore a worn pair of blue jeans, a plaid western shirt, and of course, cowboy boots. He crossed his feet.

"It is so peaceful here. Thank you for inviting me." Athena went inside and combed out her long brown hair.

"It seems that Texas has been inspiring for your writing," he called to her.

"Yes, it seems to be."

"Aria and I were talking. We know you have a deadline coming up. Why don't you stay longer and finish your manuscript?"

Aria returned carrying her cup of tea and a cup for her mother. She sat down next to Trevor.

Athena went out on the porch and looked at Trevor and Aria. "Stay longer?' She shook her head. "No, I could not impose on your family."

"It is not an imposition," Trevor said. "After the weekend, everyone will go back to their normal routine. Dad is busy on the ranch all day, Mom works a few hours a day cooking lunch at the local elementary school, Dan is either working on the ranch or at his part-time job, and Troy and his business partner are building houses nearby. You can stay and write."

"You have the kitchenette to cook, and when we go to the airport on Monday, you can pick up a rental car," Aria suggested.

Athena thought for a few moments. It was a good idea. She liked the ranch and Trevor's family. Even Troy when he refrained from making comments. "I insist on paying to rent the cabin. Let me think about it."

"Want some breakfast while you think?" Aria asked. "We ate earlier."

Athena looked around. The three of them were alone. "Where is everyone?"

"Maria went to town, Troy is at a job site, John is doing horses, and Dan is picking up Danny for the weekend. Maria said to tell you there are fresh eggs in the kitchen and bacon in the refrigerator," Aria explained.

34

Athena stood up. "Breakfast sounds good. I am actually starving. It must be the fresh air," she laughed. The three of them walked to the house and went in the kitchen. Athena held up an egg. "Fresh eggs really do taste better." She cracked two eggs into a bowl, added some milk, salt and pepper, and whipped them up with a fork. She put the eggs in a pan on the stove.

"No bacon?" Trevor asked.

"Not this morning, but I think I will have a biscuit. They are delicious."

Maria returned a short time later, and Trevor went out to the car and helped carry in her shopping bags. "How are you doing today?" she asked Athena.

"Great, thank you. I wrote two full chapters last night. Ellen, my editor, is very happy."

"Good. Well, it is quiet here. Have you thought about staying longer? We would love to have you." Maria started to put the groceries away.

"Are you sure it is not an inconvenience?" Athena asked.

"No inconvenience at all."

"I also need to make sure my assistant will be ok before deciding, but if I stay, I insist on renting the cabin."

"Oh no, no," Maria replied.

"Yes," Athena said. "It's only fair. If I went to a hotel, I would pay for the room, and you are feeding me too."

"I'm sure we can work something out. You really do not eat much, dear," she said. "Oh, Athena, Aria, do you two eat steak?"

"Yes, we do," they replied together.

"Good. We will have grilled steaks tonight."

"That sounds good," Athena replied. "What can I do to help?" The two women made potato salad and rubbed down the steaks. Trevor and Aria sat at the kitchen table and filled plastic eggs with candy, money, and small toys for the egg hunt on Sunday.

"Mom is all this for Danny?" Trevor asked. He and Aria had filled over three dozen plastic eggs and they were not finished yet.

"No, Mandy and Ronnie down the road are coming over too."

John came in the kitchen and sat down. Maria poured him a cup of hot coffee, and he watched as Trevor and Aria continued filling eggs.

"Aria, would you like some iced tea?" Trevor asked when they finished their task.

"Yes, thank you," she smiled at him, and Trevor got up and poured them each a glass of tea.

"When are Dan and Danny due?" John asked.

"Dan texted me, and they should be here any minute. I have cold cuts for lunch." Maria took a platter out of the cabinet. A rumbling noise grew louder. "Oh, that must be them." She bustled out to the porch. John followed her.

"How old is Danny?" Athena asked.

"He's six," Trevor replied. Trevor, Aria, and Athena followed them outside.

Dan stopped the car. Immediately, the passenger door swung opened, and Danny emerged. He was a lanky boy, and he wore jeans, a plaid shirt, and cowboy boots just like his father, uncles, and grandfather. His had dark and wavy hair and deep, dark, brown eyes.

"Oh," Maria squealed as she embraced the boy. "I missed you." She hugged him tight and kissed the top of his head.

"Good to see you, Danny," John said as he tried to hug his grandson, but Maria was not ready to release him. Finally, she let him go, and he was able to say hello and hug the rest of his family.

"Danny, this is Aria and her mother Athena," Trevor said.

"Aria is Uncle Trevor's girlfriend," Dan explained.

"I have heard a lot about you, Danny," Aria told him.

"It's nice to meet you, Danny," Athena said.

"Hi," Danny said. He smiled and stared at Aria and Athena.

"Well, come on y'all. Let's go in and have lunch," Maria said as she ushered everyone inside.

Athena helped Maria set out the cold cuts, rolls, and fixings. She passed on a roll and had a meat roll and iced tea. Danny talked about school and playing baseball. He asked plenty of questions too. He was interested in where Athena and Aria lived, what they did for work, and the things they liked to do.

"Danny, slow down on the questions," Dan laughed. "They will be here all weekend."

Athena looked at her daughter. Aria sat in a chair next to Trevor and leaned into him. He had his arm around the back of her chair, and he occasionally rubbed her shoulder. A few minutes later, Athena saw Trevor get up and make a couple sandwiches. No one else paid any attention to him because everyone listened intently to Danny. Athena watched Trevor out of the corner of her eye as he went over to the pantry and put the sandwiches, a plastic container from the refrigerator, and a thermos into a duffel bag.

Trevor walked over to Aria and put his hands on her shoulders. "Well, Aria and I are going to go for a walk," he announced, and he took Aria's hand.

She stood up and looked at her mother. "Do you mind, Mom?"

Athena smiled at her daughter. "No, I do not mind at all." She turned to Maria. "Actually Maria, I was wondering if I could get a ride to town? I need to pick up a few things."

"Well…" Maria started to say.

Dan interrupted her. "I'm taking Danny to Austin this afternoon to get sneakers at the mall. Perhaps you would like to join us, Athena?"

"I don't know. Are you sure I would not be infringing on your time alone with Danny?"

Dan laughed. "Believe me, it is no infringement."

"Then I would love to go to Austin." Athena replied.

"We will see y'all later," Trevor said as he picked up the duffel bag.

Athena stood up and hugged her daughter. "Be careful. There are snakes here," she whispered.

"Don't worry, Mom. I'll be with Trevor," Aria replied quietly. She kissed her mother then took Trevor's hand, and they left the kitchen.

"When are you leaving?" Athena asked Dan.

"Thirty minutes sound ok?"

"Yes, it will give me time to check my email and change my clothes."

"Check your email?" Dan made a face. "You are on vacation."

She laughed. "I am never totally on vacation." She gave a wave and headed out the door.

As she left, Troy was coming up the walk. "Hi." He ignored the way his heart seemed to skip a beat when he saw her. Yes, she was pretty, but he reminded himself that he did not need a girlfriend.

"Hi, Troy."

"Are you leaving?"

"I'm going to my cabin to check email and get dressed. I'm going to Austin with Dan and Danny this afternoon."

"Austin? Yeah, Austin sounds fun. I think I will go too," he said.

"Good. See you soon." Athena started to walk back to her cabin.

Troy watched her as she went down the stairs. She walked very quickly and stayed in the center of the driveway. She practically pranced, and her head looked quickly from side to side. He shook his head and walked in the kitchen.

Danny ran to him. "Hi, Uncle Troy!"

Troy hugged his nephew. "You are getting big."

"Would you like lunch, Troy?" Maria asked.

"I'll have something in a minute." He looked at Dan. "I heard you are going to Austin." Dan nodded yes. "I think I will come with y'all."

"Ok," Dan replied.

Troy looked down at his tee shirt and dusty jeans. "I better clean up and change my clothes. I will hurry back." He headed out the kitchen's back door and walked to his home.

A half an hour later, Dan, Danny, Troy, and Athena were in Dan's car headed to Austin. Athena insisted on sitting in back with Danny. "I'm smaller," she said when Dan suggested she sit up front. Danny kept up a running conversation with Athena. He asked her about her travel agency, her book, and places she visited.

"Greece sounds fun," Danny said.

"It is. And it is full of history."

"You do a lot of foreign travel," Troy observed. Athena sat behind the driver's seat, and he turned to look at her.

"Yes, I have always loved to travel. Aria and I have spent most holidays overseas the past three years."

"Do you travel in the U.S. much?" Dan asked.

"A little, mostly on the East Coast and Chicago. I've actually never been to California, and this is my first trip to Texas."

"There is a lot more to see in Texas," Troy said.

"Like San Antonio," Dan added.

"From pictures I saw of San Antonio, it does look like a fun town. So much culture."

"Here we are." Dan parked the car in the crowded mall parking lot. They got out of the car and walked toward the mall entrance. Athena put on her sunglasses.

"Can I visit the arcade," Danny asked excitedly.

"After we get your sneakers," Dan told his son.

"And Bee's?" Danny said. He bounced up and down as he walked alongside his father.

"What is Bee's, Danny?" Athena asked.

"A candy store!"

"Oh, I want to stop there too," Athena replied.

"You eat candy?" Troy asked sarcastically.

Athena glared at him. "I do occasionally have a piece or two of candy," she replied with a fake smile. She walked ahead, and Dan looked back at Troy and shook his head.

"Athena," Danny called as he hurried to her and took her hand. "Do you want to come help me pick out sneakers? Then we can go get some candy. They always give out free samples."

"Sounds fun," Athena replied with a genuine smile for Danny.

"Are you coming too, Uncle Troy?" Danny called as he pulled Athena to the shoe store.

40

"Sure," Troy replied. He pulled Dan's arm to hold him back from catching up to Athena and Danny. "Just what are you doing?" he asked his brother now that Danny and Athena were out of ear shot.

"What do you mean?"

"Using the kid to get to know Athena."

"I am not. I said nothing to Danny. And I resent you thinking I would ever use my kid like that." At first, Dan felt angry, but then he smiled. "Why, do you like her?" he laughed.

Troy looked flustered. "She's probably going to be Trevor's mother-in-law."

"So, what? Are you interested in her?"

"What makes you think I might be interested?"

"So, you aren't interested. Then what does it matter to you if Danny and I talk to her?" Dan yanked his arm free and walked ahead. He did not look back at his brother.

Troy grumbled and set his jaw. When he caught up to the others in the children's shoe department, he sat down heavily in one of the chairs and watched as Danny tried on several pairs of sneakers. The sales lady checked the fit of each pair, and Danny walked, actually ran, back and forth to try out the sneakers. He settled on a superhero pair.

"Kid's shoes have gone up in price since Aria was Danny's age," Athena commented as Dan went to the cash register and paid.

"Everything has gone up in price," Troy replied.

Danny took Athena's hand. "Let's go to the candy store."

"Lead the way," she smiled and skipped along next to him.

At the entrance to the store, a woman wearing a white apron handed out candy samples. Athena took one, unwrapped it, and took a bite. "Umm, this is good chocolate," she said as she put the remainder of the candy in her mouth. Danny nodded his head because his mouth was full of candy. Athena selected several boxes of candy. She bought chocolate for Aria and Trevor and added a big chocolate bunny to her order for Danny when he was not looking. "Double bag the bunny please, so he doesn't see it," she said to the sales lady who smiled and nodded.

There were craft vendors in the mall for the holiday weekend, and the four of them took their time looking at the various carts. Athena went to a cart with cacti arrangements. "These are cool," she said. "I can grow cacti."

She selected a small cactus. "If I am careful, I think I can get this home safely."

"Where do you live, Ma'am?" the vendor asked in a very deep drawl. He was short, had grey hair, and was deeply tanned. He also wore a plaid shirt, jeans, and of course, cowboy boots.

"I live on Cape Cod," she replied. He gave her a quizzical look. "In Massachusetts. South of Boston."

"Ah. I thought so by your accent."

"Dan?" Athena called. Dan walked over to her. She looked at a larger garden of assorted succulents. "Do you think Maria and John would like this?"

Dan nodded, "Yes, Mom loves plants. That is a good gift for them." Athena decided to get it.

The vendor packed up the garden and the small cactus separately. "I gave you a baggie of my cactus soil mix and another of decorative sand in case your cactus spills on your way home."

Athena smiled at him. "Thank you. That is very nice."

"I have also included my card with my website. I ship all over the country, Ma'am."

"I will definitely check out your website."

"Thank you, and Happy Easter."

"Athena, let me help you carry something," Dan said.

"Thanks." She smiled at Dan, and he took the box with the garden.

"Oh, Athena?" Troy called in a sing song voice from the next aisle. She looked over at him. He held up a colorful straw tortilla basket.

"Perfect," she replied as she walked over to the vendor's booth. She selected two baskets, one for her and one for Aria.

"I need to stop and get Danny an Easter basket," Dan whispered to Athena while she made her purchase.

"I bought him a chocolate bunny," she whispered. "I need to get a few more things."

"I have an idea," Dan whispered. Danny was on the other side of Athena, so Dan dropped back and found his brother who stood at another booth looking at several wooden items. "I need to get an Easter basket for Danny."

"Ok," Troy replied.

"Can you take Danny to the arcade, so I can get some stuff?"

"Sure." Troy looked over at Athena. "What is Athena going to do?"

"She's coming with me," Dan smirked. "She wants to get some things too. We will come to the arcade when we finish shopping."

Troy grunted again. He did not know why it bothered him that Athena was going with Dan. She was definitely not his type. She lived on the East Coast, and she was intense. But as he watched her looking at items, she tossed her hair back over her shoulder, and he felt an odd sensation.

Danny broke him out of his thoughts. "Come on, Uncle Troy, let's go to the arcade." Danny took his uncle's hand and pulled him in the other direction. Troy looked back and watched as Athena and his brother talked as they walked away. Athena put her hand on Dan's shoulder for just a brief second, and Troy felt a pit in his stomach.

Danny fell asleep before they were out of the city. He had his head on Athena's shoulder. She yawned, leaned her head back, and closed her eyes. Dan and Troy drove in silence. Troy looked over his shoulder at Danny and Athena. He did not know exactly how he felt about Athena or even why he thought he had any feelings for her. Troy saw his brother looking at him. "Danny had a lot of fun at the mall today."

"I think we all did," Dan replied.

Troy continued to look at Athena and Danny. He pursed his lips. "Danny likes Athena."

"I think we all do." Dan smiled, and Troy turned his head and glared at him, but he did not respond.

Athena woke up when the car decelerated getting off the highway. She sat up. "I guess I was tired," she laughed. "What did I miss?"

"Not much," Troy replied. He did not turn around to look at her.

Danny started to wake up too. "Are we at grandma's yet," he muttered half asleep.

"Almost," Dan replied.

When they pulled in by the house, it looked like no one was home at first, but then Maria came out on the porch. "Hi. How was the mall?"

"Great," Danny replied as he got out of the car.

"Did you get new sneakers?"

"Yep." Dan gave the sneakers to Danny, and he went on the porch to show his grandmother.

Athena looked around. "Where is Aria?" she asked Maria.

"They aren't back yet," Maria said casually as she looked at Danny's new sneakers.

"Do you think they are ok?"

Maria looked up at her. "Yes, I am sure they are fine."

"Let me help you to your cabin, Athena." Dan looped the candy bag on his arm and picked up the two boxes containing the plants and walked toward her cabin. Athena followed him, but she craned her neck to see if Aria and Trevor were coming up the road that went away from the stable. They were nowhere in sight.

Troy stood with his arms crossed as he watched Athena and Dan walk away then he walked up onto the porch and went inside the main house muttering to himself. Maria shook her head as she watched Troy start up the stairs, turn around, leave the house, and head toward his own home.

Chapter 5

Despite reassurances from Dan that Trevor was perfectly capable of taking care of Aria, Athena worried. She almost called her daughter's cell phone when she saw Aria and Trevor walking slowly, hand in hand, toward the cabins. Her daughter looked so happy. Both of them had wet hair and their clothes looked damp. She wondered what they did all afternoon.

Athena decided not to say hi and disturb them. She went into the bathroom and freshened up. She brushed her hair and dressed. She put on sandals, and then she grabbed her white bolero sweater for when the sun went down. and the temperature dropped. She closed the cabin door and walked to the house to help Maria prepare dinner.

Dan put bottles of beer in the cooler outside. He looked up as Athena approached. "Wow! That is a nice dress," he commented as she walked by.

"Thank you."

Troy brought out a platter of steaks, and he stopped and looked at her. Unlike his brother, he just said, "Good evening," but he could not take his eyes off her.

"Good evening. Your hands are full; let me get the door for you," Athena held open the screen door. Troy still did not move. "Are you going out, Troy?" she asked.

He recovered and stuttered, "yes, yes," and walked outside.

"Hi Athena!" Danny called.

"Hi Danny. Hi Maria. Let me get the dishes." She walked over and took the stack of plates off the table. She put the silverware caddy and napkin holder on top of the plates and went outside. Danny followed her.

Maria watched as Athena and Danny set the table. Dan and Troy were also watching Athena. She wanted to say something to both her sons, but she did not want to escalate a rivalry between them. "Dan," she called.

"Yes, Mom?"

"Bring out the glasses and the water cooler, please."

"Sure." Dan glanced back at Athena one more time and went inside to get the items.

Aria and Trevor came out of her cabin and walked over to the main house. Everyone bustled around the kitchen and outside getting dinner ready.

"Hi, Mom," Aria called.

"Hi, honey." she replied with a wave.

The two women looked at one another and laughed. They were wearing similar yellow dresses. "I guess we had the same idea about what to wear tonight, Mom."

"I guess so," Athena laughed. "How was your day?"

"Fantastic," Aria replied, and she blushed a very dark shade of pink.

Trevor leaned over and kissed her cheek. "I'm going to go upstairs and clean up. I'll be right back."

Aria watched him walk up the stairs then she turned toward her mother, "So how was the mall?"

"A lot of fun. I bought us each a tortilla basket."

"Oh, thanks."

"Look. Aria. I got new sneakers." Danny held up one of his feet, so she could see his sneakers better.

"Those are cool sneakers, Danny."

"The grill is ready for the steaks," John called.

Maria came out with a bowl of potato salad. "The rest of the food and condiments are on the counter in the kitchen." Athena, Dan, and Aria all nodded and went inside.

"Your mother really can cook." Aria looked at the abundance of food. They each took items and carried them outside. Soon, the table brimmed with potato salad, leafy salad, corn on the cob, rolls, butter, green beans, watermelon, strawberries, and assorted condiments.

Trevor joined them. "Looks good." He rolled up his shirt sleeves. "I'm starved."

"Trevor, please light the torches," Maria called to him.

Troy and John manned the grill, and the air was filled with the delicious aroma of grilling meat.

"Steaks are ready," John called a short while later as he brought the steaks over to the table.

Aria looked at her mother. The steaks were very large, and she knew she could not eat a whole one. "Should we split one?" she asked, and Athena agreed.

They filled their plates and ate. The sounds of crickets and frogs grew louder as the sun set, and the sky darkened. There were few bugs, but several large moths were attracted to the torch flames.

Danny told everyone about the arcade at the mall. "I beat Uncle Troy on the pinball machine!" he exclaimed happily.

Dan chuckled. "Well, Uncle Troy doesn't practice as much as you do." He turned to Athena and Aria. "Danny goes to the arcade near our place almost every week with his friends," he stuttered, "that is the apartment where he lives with his mother." Athena and Aria both smiled and nodded.

"Dinner was delicious," Athena said. "I can't remember the last time I had steak."

"Really?" Troy asked.

John laughed, "Well, here we eat steak quite a lot." He went over and scraped the grill while the others cleaned up.

After dinner, they sat around the fire pit, and Maria brought out marshmallows, chocolate bars, graham crackers, and long skewers. "Oh, I love smores," Aria said as she took a couple of marshmallows, skewered them, and put them over the fire to toast.

Danny had two marshmallows in his mouth, and Dan helped him put two on a skewer. "Not too close to the flame, or they will catch fire," Dan warned.

"Mom, do you remember when we made smores in Girl Scouts?" Aria asked.

"Oh, I do. It was so much fun."

"You were in Girl Scouts?" Trevor asked.

Aria nodded yes. "Mom, was a troop leader."

"You were?" Troy said to Athena. He found it hard to imagine Athena out in the woods. She was always dressed in fine clothes and looked neat as a pin.

She laughed. "Yes, believe it or not, I was a troop leader."

"Remember when that skunk walked through our troop's tent, Mom?"

"Oh my god, how can I forget."

"Did it spray you?" Danny asked.

"No, it just walked through, but we never went camping again," Aria laughed. "I think making smores was the best thing about Girl Scouts." Aria placed a piece of chocolate bar on top of a graham cracker. She topped it with two hot toasted marshmallows, placed another graham cracker on top of the marshmallows, and smooched it all together. She took a bite. "This is so good," she sighed. She offered Trevor a bite of her smore.

"Troy, why don't you play for us," Maria suggested.

Troy reached down next to him and pulled up a guitar case. He removed his guitar, tuned it, and then he started to play a lively song. The family joined in, even Trevor.

"I didn't know you could sing," Aria said to Trevor, and he laughed.

"Here's one you may know, Athena." Troy started to play *Country Roads*, and to everyone's surprise, Athena began to sing along with the others.

From there, Troy played *The Yellow Rose of Texas*. Athena and Aria knew the tune but not the words.

"Oh, that was good," John said. He got up. "Anyone want a beer?"

"I'll have one," Dan said.

"Athena? Aria?" John asked.

"Yes, thank you," they both replied.

"I'll have one too," Trevor added.

John opened a bottle of Corona for Troy and set it next to him. Troy continued to play, stopping occasionally to have a drink. Aria sat close to Trevor. She had her arm around his, and she often put her head on his shoulder. Danny sat in Maria's lap and fell asleep. She pushed his hair back and hummed along to the song Troy played. The fire crackled, and John put a few more pieces of dry wood on to keep it burning.

"Dan, carry Danny up to bed," Maria whispered.

Dan got up and picked up his son. Danny did not even stir. "Well, I might as well turn in too. Night y'all."

"Night," they replied.

Aria yawned.

"Tired, babe?" Trevor asked her. She nodded. He took her hand, and they got up.

"Do you want to go back to the cabins, Mom?"

Athena nodded and started to get up.

"You can stay, Athena," Troy said. "I will walk you back to your cabin."

Athena looked at Troy. Sitting in front of the fire was very relaxing. "Oh. Ok. Thank you."

"Good night, Mom. Don't stay up too late writing." Aria bent down and hugged her mother.

"Good night, honey. Sleep well."

Troy continued to play a soft slow tune. John tapped to the music and then he yawned. It had been a long and busy day on the ranch. "Well, I think it's time to turn in. I've a few things to do in the morning'." He stood up and stretched. "Maria, are you 'bout ready for bed?"

Maria looked at Athena and Troy. "I guess so," she said as she slowly stood up. She was tired, but she also did not want to leave the two of them alone.

"Good night," Athena said.

"Night, Mom, Dad," Troy said.

"Troy, make sure the fire is out before you turn in," John reminded his son.

"I will, Dad." He continued to play softly.

Troy and Athena sat outside for quite some time. They did not talk much, and Athena thought it felt nice just to sit and relax. It seemed that lately she did not have time to just relax. As the fire started to die down, Athena leaned back in her chair and looked up at the stars. Troy put his guitar back in its case and sat down next to her.

"The stars are so beautiful here," she said. "There are so many of them. Where I live, there is so much light pollution that only the brightest stars are visible."

"A shooting star!" Troy exclaimed and pointed. "Make a wish."

Athena smiled, closed her eyes, and made a wish. She pulled her sweater closer to her body. The fire had almost died out, and it was getting chilly. "Well, I think it's time to go back to my cabin," she said.

"Hang on. Let me make sure this fire is out."

Athena felt very nervous about walking back to her cabin in the dark. She took her phone out while she waited for Troy.

"All set," he said. Athena pushed the flashlight icon on her phone, and a bright light illuminated the area. "You can turn that off," Troy said in a clearly annoyed tone. "I know the way."

"There might be snakes," Athena blurted out as she looked around.

So that is what she is afraid of, Troy thought to himself. "Snakes usually do not come this close to the house. You will be fine. Take my hand."

Athena turned off the light, put her phone back into her pocket, and took Troy's extended hand. He carried his guitar in his other hand, and they started to walk toward her cabin. "Isn't this better? We can still see the stars, and they light the way." They made the short walk to her cabin, and Troy took her right to the door. "Good night, Athena," he said with a nod of his head.

"Good night, Troy. Thank you for walking me back." She opened the door and went inside.

Troy stepped off the porch and started to walk down the driveway to his home.

Athena locked the cabin door, turned on the small lamp on the end table, and went into her bedroom to slip into something warmer and more comfortable. She did not feel very tired, so she took her laptop and sat on the sofa. She checked her blog statistics, and then checked her school email. She did not expect a student to email when no big assignments were due, and it was a holiday weekend. She opened the manuscript document and did some writing.

About 1:30 am, she closed the laptop and turned off the small light. She let her eyes adjust to the darkness again, and then she sat by the window and looked out at the stars. She saw a dim light go on in Troy's home way down at the end of the driveway and then it went off. She yawned. She was tired, so she checked to make certain she locked the cabin door and went to bed.

Chapter 6

Early the next morning, Athena stretched and looked out her window. Saturday was another beautiful day, bright and sunny. The weather is certainly nicer than New England, Athena thought to herself. Despite the cool nights, the daytime temperatures were quite warm.

"Mom, are you up?" Aria called from the porch.

Athena got up and opened the door. "Good morning, honey."

"Morning." Aria looked around the cabin. She wondered if maybe Troy was there with her mother, but he was not. "Trevor is taking me into town this morning. Do you want to come? Danny and Dan are going with us. And we will ask Troy too."

"Yes. I want to pick up fruit for dinner tomorrow and something for dessert tonight. Maria has been cooking for days. I told her last night that I wanted to help. Let me hop in a quick shower."

"Do you want breakfast? Maria is making bacon and eggs."

"No, thanks. I think I will have tea and a bowl of fruit this morning. I have cantaloupe in my refrigerator. You go have breakfast."

"Ok." Aria headed out the door.

Athena locked the door and went in the bathroom. She took a quick shower and washed her hair. She put on a kettle of water and went in the bedroom to dress. She decided to wear a pair of blue jeans, a striped blue and white blouse with lace trim at the neckline, and a pair of sandals. By the time she finished dressing, the tea water boiled. She drank her cup of tea while she ate fruit and a yogurt she also had in the refrigerator. She rinsed the tea mug and cleaned up the kitchenette. By the time she finished, her hair was nearly dry, so she finished drying it, put on some mascara and lip gloss, picked up her purse, and headed to the main house.

The kitchen was noisy when Athena walked in. Troy and Dan were in a conversation about housing prices with Trevor. As a financial planner, he thought it best to buy a house early to build a foundation for the future. Danny was showing Aria his video game. Maria stood at the stove cooking more bacon, and John sat quietly behind his morning newspaper.

"Good morning," she said.

Everyone stopped talking. "Morning," they replied, and then they resumed their conversations.

"Would you like some bacon?" Maria asked.

"No thank you. I had fruit and yogurt in my cabin."

"Ok." Maria put the bacon on a platter.

Once the others finished eating, they piled into the car. Trevor wanted to drive, but Troy took the keys. Dan sat up front with him. Athena and Danny sat in the middle row of seats, and Aria and Trevor sat in the back row.

"I have to warn you," Trevor said, "this town isn't big. There's a department store, a gas station, a convenience store, and a couple of places to eat."

"Actually, a small strip mall has opened since you were last here little brother," Dan said.

"Really?"

"Yeah, we have a phone store, another pizza place, a mattress shop, and an eyeglasses place."

"And more is scheduled to go up," Troy added.

"We are becoming a real city," Trevor laughed.

"Can we get an ice cream?" Danny asked. Everyone smiled and looked hopefully at Dan.

"Yes, if you are good," Dan replied.

Troy turned into the crowded parking lot and parked the car. As they started to walk to the store entrance, Athena's phone rang.

"Oh, it's Holly. Sorry, I must take this call. I will meet you inside," she said to the others.

"Oh course," Troy replied, and they continued toward the door.

Dan walked next to Troy. "She works a lot," he said as he glanced back over his shoulder and shook his head. "Doesn't she ever take a break?"

"She has a business to run. She has a lot of responsibilities," Troy told his brother. "Being responsible is not a bad thing."

"It's a holiday weekend, and she's on vacation. No one needs to work all the time."

"Being on vacation doesn't matter. The business takes priority. That is something you have never understood." Troy shook his head at Dan, pushed past him, and caught up to Trevor, Aria, and Danny.

The parking lot was very busy, so Aria and Trevor had Danny between them, and they held his hands.

The store was very crowded. Aria wanted to get cards and candy for Danny, so she and Trevor went to the seasonal section while Dan took Danny to the boy's department. Danny was growing very quickly, and Dan wanted to get his son a couple pairs of jeans. Dan noticed that Troy hung

56

around in the front of the store pretending to look at the fruit, but he kept glancing at the door. Dan had a feeling his brother was waiting for Athena because he liked her. He did not think Troy had any more of a chance with Athena than he did. She was very different from the women they dated. Yes, she was pretty, but she talked fast, was very intense, and lived in a city a long way from Texas.

Athena finished her call with Holly and then walked to the store entrance. Holly felt confident she could handle everything at the agency while Athena finished her manuscript. Athena had been undecided about staying in Texas, but after hearing Holly's confidence, she was leaning toward staying. She walked into the store and saw Troy. "Hi," she called to him.

"Is everything ok at your agency?" he asked.

"Yes. I wanted to talk with my assistant about extending my stay here to work on my manuscript." She took a deep breath. "Holly is confident she can handle everything while I am away."

"You know, if you finish early, you might even have time to see more of Texas."

"Maybe." Athena picked up two large packages of strawberries. "Do you like chocolate covered strawberries?"

"I guess so," he replied. "I like strawberries, and I like chocolate."

"You must have had chocolate covered strawberries before."

"Yeah, I think so. It's just not something I eat a lot."

Athena put the strawberries in the shopping cart. Troy walked around the produce department with her as she bought a fresh pineapple, a cantaloupe, and two packages of microwavable dipping chocolate for the fruit platter she was making for Easter Sunday.

"I told Maria I would pick up pies for dessert tonight," Athena said as she walked over to a table laden with assorted pies.

"Pie, I love," he replied.

"Great. What kind?"

He gave her a blank stare. "Pecan."

"Ok, what else?"

"Pecan."

"You do not like any other kind of pie?" Athena asked with a sigh.

"There are other kinds of pie?" Troy laughed.

Athena rolled her eyes at him and put three pecan pies in her cart. She picked up a key lime pie, her and Aria's favorite type of pie, and she selected a classic lemon meringue pie.

"I have a short list of things Mom needs." Troy took the list out of his pocket, and he picked up a shopping basket. "Mom needs coconut, confectioner's sugar, and Ritz crackers." They found the items and then started to look around for the others.

Danny saw them and ran over. "Dad bought me new jeans," he told Athena and Troy.

"You probably outgrow them very quickly," Athena said.

"We should get Mom flowers, Troy," Dan said.

The four of them started to walk toward the garden center. As they passed the seasonal section, Athena stopped. "I need to get a couple cards."

"Ok," Dan replied, "Troy and I will go on ahead."

"Can I stay with Athena?" Danny asked.

Dan looked at Athena; he did not want to impose his son on her.

"Of course, you can," she said with a smile, so the two men left.

Athena picked out a few cards. "Danny," she said, "Let's get a few bags of snacks too." They walked over to the snack aisle and were selecting bags of chips and popcorn when a police officer approached them.

"Hi, Danny," he said.

"Hi."

"Who is your friend? Where is your dad?"

"This is Athena," Danny told him. "Dad's getting flowers for grandma."

The officer looked at Athena. She extended her hand. "Hi. I'm Trevor's girlfriend's mother Athena." She shook her head and laughed. "Wow, that was a mouthful."

Suddenly he smiled and extended his hand. "From back East. Yes, I remember Maria saying Trevor was bringing his girlfriend and her mother home. Sorry, I was suspicious. It's just I saw Danny with a stranger."

"No need to apologize," Athena replied with a wave of her hand.

Troy and Dan approached them. They each had a potted plant. "Hey, Kevin," they greeted him at once.

"Hi, y'all." The guys shook hands.

"I see you met Athena," Dan said.

"Hey, Kevin. How are you?" Trevor called as he and Aria joined the group. The two shook hands. "This is my girlfriend Aria, and I guess you have already met her mother."

"Nice to meet you," he shook Aria's hand. "It's good to see you, Trevor."

Kevin asked Trevor about work. He asked Aria and Athena a few questions too, but since he was on duty, he had to leave fairly quickly. "I should head out," he said, "I was finishing up a call about a potential shop lifter when I saw Danny." Kevin turned to leave. "Happy Easter, y'all."

"Happy Easter," they replied together, and they walked toward the front of the store.

Athena looked in Aria's basket. In it were two dozen white eggs and an egg coloring kit. "I guess you plan to color eggs."

"Yay, I want to color eggs!" Danny exclaimed.

"It will be fun," Aria said.

Trevor took the pot of pink tulips out of the cart. "I want to get Mom something else. You shop with your mom, and I'll meet you at the front of the store." He kissed Aria on the cheek.

She smiled at him. "No problem." Aria and Athena finished shopping and then went to check out. "Oh, I didn't get a gift bag." Aria sighed because she just finished paying for her items.

"I bought several, so you can have one," Athena replied.

"Oh, a key lime pie, yummy."

"I have a feeling it will be all for us."

"Oh good."

On the drive back to the ranch, they stopped for ice cream. The ice cream stand was very busy, and Danny changed his mind on what he wanted at least three times before they made it to the front of the line. He decided he wanted a hot fudge sundae.

"That will ruin your lunch," Dan said, but he ordered it anyway. "A small hot fudge sundae," he said to the young cashier who smiled at him and Troy.

"Hi Troy," she said with a big smile. "How are you doing today?"

"Hi, Carrie," Troy replied.

"It is nice to see you," she said batting her eyes at him. Athena glared at the cashier as she flirted with Troy.

Dan turned to the others, "What do y'all want?"

Trevor ordered a large chocolate cone dipped in chocolate sprinkles, Troy and Aria each ordered a medium hot fudge and peanut butter sundae, Dan ordered a banana split. "Athena, your turn," Dan called to her as the others stepped aside.

Athena looked up at the board, "I'll have a kiddie size cup of chocolate and vanilla twist," she said to the cashier.

Everyone looked at her. "That's what you are ordering?" Troy asked in disbelief voicing what the others were thinking.

"Yes," Athena squeaked out in reply.

"Well, we know one thing," Dan said to Troy, "she's a cheap date." Troy nodded, and the cashier suppressed a laugh. Trevor started to laugh, but Aria nudged him hard in his side. Aria cringed anticipating that her mother 's snappy and probably sarcastic remark.

However, once again, Athena just smiled. "Let me pitch in some money to pay for the ice cream," she said as she took out her wallet.

An hour later, Maria fluttered around the kitchen. "I'm going to pack up sandwiches for y'all to take. You might get hungry after swimming."

Dan nodded to her and called to Danny, "Let's get you in your swimsuit." Danny ran upstairs, and Dan followed him.

Aria and Athena put the food they purchased away. "It's so hot." Aria fanned herself.

"We aren't used to the heat," Athena reminded her.

"Swimming will feel good."

"I'll change and come to your cabin," Trevor said to Aria as she and Athena walked out of the kitchen.

John looked out the window and watched them walk back to their cabins to change into their swimsuits. "Troy," he called before Troy walked out the back door. "Y'all are going to the Pool?"

Troy turned toward his father. "We are."

John took a deep breath. "You keep a close eye on them, Troy. Those two women are city girls."

Troy burst out laughing. "They certainly are." Still laughing, he left the kitchen and went to his place to change.

Everyone talked excitedly on the drive to the Pool. "You are going to love this place," Troy said to Aria and Athena. "It is a natural pool, and there is a waterfall. In the summer, the park is packed with people and reservations are required. Normally, no reservations are needed this time of year, but it's a holiday weekend, so I made reservations just in case of a crowd." Troy added.

"We have been coming here since we were kids and very few people knew about the Pool," Dan said. "Now everyone wants to visit."

They pulled in the parking area and got out of the car. To their surprise, there were only fifteen other vehicles in the lot. Troy picked up one cooler, and Dan picked up the other. Athena and Aria carried the bags with the towels, and they walked to the trail head with Danny in the lead. It was a quarter mile hike to the Pool on a well-marked path. There were no clouds in the blue sky. It was hot, but the gentle breeze cooled them, and the fragrance of wildflowers filled the air.

"This was once an underground grotto, but the dome collapsed. You can see remnants of the dome," Troy explained. Since the brothers had been there many times, even Danny had been there before, they let Aria and Athena emerge from the path and view the Pool first. The two women gasped at the beauty in front of them.

"This is amazing!" Aria exclaimed. She looked around trying to take in everything.

"I have never seen anything like this," Athena whispered. She took out her camera and began taking pictures.

At the far end of the grotto, a small waterfall fell fifty feet into the jade-green pool of water. The edge of the Pool was surrounded by limestone bedrock, and they could clearly see the remains of the dome that once enclosed this wonder. "The water level is about the same throughout the year," Troy explained. "The water is chili at this time of year, but we can swim."

They put their belongings on the small sandy beach, took off the clothes they wore over their swimsuits, and then walked to the edge of the water. Troy was right, the water was quite cool, but since the temperature neared ninety degrees it also felt refreshing, in a way.

Athena looked at the three brothers. "They are wearing almost identical swim trucks," she whispered to her daughter.

Aria laughed. "They are. I bet Maria buys a lot of their clothes, including John's, and she buys in bulk."

Athena looked at her swimsuit and then at her daughter. Both of their suits were a tropical hibiscus print on a black background. "You do realize we have on almost identical swimsuits except mine is a one piece and yours is a bikini."

Aria laughed. "That is so true."

They walked in a little further. Now they stood in water up to their thighs.

Danny plowed into the water and started swimming. Dan stayed right beside him. Trevor and then Troy plunged in.

"There are probably fish in here," Aria leaned over and whispered to her mother.

"I'm not worried about fish," Athena whispered back. She looked at Aria. "Snakes." Aria's eyes went wide.

Trevor swam over and then stood up. Aria grabbed Trevor's arm and slowly walked into deeper water. She shivered a little. "I guess we should just go under," Aria called back to her mother.

"You first," Athena called.

Aria took a deep breath and sank under the water's surface. She came up quickly. "It's refreshing," she laughed.

Trevor wrapped his arms around her waist. "I'll keep you warm," he said softly, and Aria turned around and kissed him. They slid back under the water and moved away.

"Are you getting in or are you just going to stand there?" Troy asked with a bit of annoyance in his voice as he swam by.

"I'm working up to it," Athena replied with just as much sarcasm.

Troy floated by on his back. "Just get in."

Athena took a deep breath and dove under the water. She surfaced, flipped over, and floated on her back.

Troy swam by. "That wasn't too bad was it. It is nice here, isn't it?"

"The water is cool, but nice," she said. The water was cold, and she knew she would not stay in long.

Athena scanned the water for Aria. She and Trevor were swimming toward the waterfall. Danny swam out in pretty deep water, but he had on a life vest, and Dan swam alongside him. She floated a bit. When she looked up again, Aria waved to her and beckoned her to come out to the waterfall.

Athena's teeth were chattering. Even though she lived on the Atlantic Ocean, she did not like cold water.

Dan and Danny were heading toward the beach. "We are walking over to the waterfall. Want to come?" Dan called to Athena.

"I prefer walking to swimming," Athena called back as she walked out of the water. She wrapped a towel around her body, but she was already warming up under the warm Texas sun. Troy came out of the water and dried off too.

"Are you walking too?" Dan asked, and Troy nodded.

Athena put a couple towels and Aria's and Trevor's sneakers in her bag. Then she put on her sneakers. She put her cell phone in a waterproof plastic bag, so she could take pictures but protect the phone.

Dan struggled to get Danny's sneakers on his feet. Once they all were mostly dry and had shoes on, they started walking around the pool.

In a few places, there were man-made walkways, but primarily they walked on the natural rock. They took their time and eventually made it around the edge of the pool and stopped on the path near the waterfall. The water fell from the cliff above them, and the air felt cooler.

Aria and Trevor stood on the rock under the main waterfall. "The water is pretty cool, but come under it, Mom," Aria called as she stepped away from the water.

Troy, Dan, Danny, and Athena left the path and climbed to a nearby rock. Troy took off his shoes then jumped to the next rock and stood under the waterfall. "Whoot," he yelled as the water bounced up and around him, and he shook his head.

Athena looked up and watched the water as it tumbled over the edge of the rock fifty feet above her. The sun glittered off the falling water.

Athena handed her phone to Aria. She took off her shoes and tentatively walked up to the rock. The water bounced off it and splashed her. It was cooler this close to the falling water. Troy stretched out his hand to her, and she tentatively took it. She was not sure she really wanted to do this.

Troy shook his head at her indecisiveness. He preferred action. He reached out, grabbed Athena's hand, and pulled her under the falling water.

She gasped, but then she laughed and gathered up her hair and pulled it to one side as the water beat down upon her shoulders. Aria took some pictures. "Ok that was fun," Athena said as she moved out from under the water. Aria handed her the phone.

Danny scrambled over the rock and got under the waterfall, and Athena took some pictures of him. Then she stood at the edge where the water hit the rock and took a picture as the water fell from the cliff above. She saw a rainbow in the mist, and she snapped several pictures.

Troy looked over her shoulder. "That is a great shot," he said. Aria and Trevor looked over and agreed.

Aria and Athena posed with the water falling behind them for a selfie, and then Trevor took the camera and took several pictures of them together under the waterfall. Athena continued to snap pictures. They tried posing for a group selfie, but they were having trouble getting everyone in. Finally, a couple walked by and offered to take a group picture.

"We can post these when we have service," Aria said, and Athena nodded yes.

Aria and Trevor dried off and decided to walk back. "Thanks for thinking to bring our sneakers," Aria whispered to her mother.

"I figured you might not want to swim back," Athena replied.

Together, they walked around the rest of the pool and back to the beach.

"I'm hungry," Danny said when they sat down on the sand. Dan opened the cooler, pulled out a sandwich, and handed it to Danny. "Anyone else want one? Mom made a lot of sandwiches."

Everyone, including Athena, reached for one. Troy watched as she unwrapped a sandwich and took a bite. He opened the other cooler and pulled out several water bottles and cups. A metal bottle was marked adults. Athena looked at the bottle and then at Troy. He smiled and poured her a cupful. Athena looked at the greenish yellow liquid in her cup, smiled, and drank down the margarita.

Chapter 7

The spacious kitchen bustled with activity Saturday evening. Aria, Trevor, and Danny colored hard-boiled eggs. Danny carefully applied stickers to one of his eggs. Aria put together a little paper board egg stand, set an egg in it, and then started decorating another egg. Trevor mostly watched the two of them as they intently worked.

Athena cut up the fruit, melted chocolate, and dipped the fruit. Maria grated cheese for macaroni and cheese, peeling potatoes, cleaning vegetables, and making biscuits.

"I'm going to go upstairs and check my email," Trevor said as he kissed Aria lightly on the cheek. "I'll be right back." He also wanted to put Aria's Easter present together while he was upstairs.

She smiled up at him. "Ok."

Athena drizzled some white chocolate over the strawberries and set them on the countertop in the pantry to cool. Maria leaned over the sink peeling a couple dozen of eggs.

"You are going to be exhausted," Athena said as she watched Maria work.

"Oh, I cook this much all the time. I enjoy cooking big meals for the family, and I cook at the elementary school every day during the school year." She made quick work of the eggs and then bustled around the kitchen preparing more food. "Oh, Athena, have you decided if you will stay longer? We really would love to have you stay."

"Thank you," Athena looked up from cutting up fruit and smiled at Maria. "Yes, I decided I will stay. I talked to my assistant Holly this morning. She is rebooking my return flight, and she feels certain she can handle the agency while I am away."

"Of course, Holly can take care of the agency," Aria said in an offhanded way. "She could be the office manager if you let her."

Athena stopped cutting up fruit and looked at Aria. "Do you think Holly wants a promotion?"

Aria looked up from decorating an egg. "I am sure she does. She is more than your assistant. She runs the office and takes care of things when you are away." Aria slid another hardboiled egg into the cup of bright pink food coloring.

Athena thought for a moment. She hired Holly when she opened the business, and she was very competent. Holly worked with her from the start and knew the business inside and out, but she still was not convinced. A business was very personal, almost like a child, and you had to be careful who you let take care of your business. "True, but usually my trips are scheduled, and I get things in order before I leave. This is impromptu," Athena pointed out.

"This could be a good test then," Aria added.

Athena went back to preparing the fruit, but she thought about Aria's comments. Athena trusted Holly completely, and if things went well, maybe she should promote Holly and give her more duties. It would free up time for writing.

"The bar-be-que smells delicious," Aria said a short while later. She took a deep breath and breathed in the delicious, sweet yet smoky aroma.

"You are going to love it," Trevor told her as he sat back down next to her and leaned over to give her a peck on the lips. "There is nothing like Texas bar be que."

When the eggs were colored and on display on the table, Aria cleaned up the egg coloring mess and helped Danny wash his hands in the sink. "Your fingers are blue," she laughed as she soaped up his hands again.

The meat was ready, so Troy and John began to slice it up and place it on platters. Outside, on the buffet table, were bowls of corn on the cob, salad, potato salad, fresh fruit, and rolls. Maria set out a stack of heavy paper plates, thick dinner napkins, and cutlery while Athena and Dan carried out pitchers of iced tea and lemonade and bottles of Corona and set them on the table. Danny ran outside and jumped up on a chair. He picked up a fork and eagerly waited for his dinner.

"Ok, everybody, dinner is ready," Maria called.

Troy set a plate of bar-be-que down in front of Danny. "Thanks, Uncle Troy," he said as he stuffed a forkful of meat in his mouth.

Troy ruffled his nephew's hair. Although he never thought about having children of his own, he enjoyed being with Danny.

Everyone lined up and walked around the buffet table filling their plates then sat at another table to eat.

The sun was setting, and the whole sky was ablaze with color. "The sky is so big here. You can see a long way in every direction," Athena commented. She leaned her head back and looks at the streaks of bright red and orange that filled the sky and stretched along the distant horizon. She planned to write about that beautiful sky on her blog tonight.

"I was thinking the same thing." Aria took a bite of her sandwich and savored the tangy bar-be-que sauce. "This is so delicious." She closed her eyes and took another big bite.

"It really is delicious," Athena added returning her attention to her meal.

"Oh, I missed this," Trevor said as he added more bar-be-que sauce to his sandwich to enhance the flavor. "There is nothing like it, back East."

Everyone was so engrossed in eating that the conversation was sparse. The sound of chirping crickets grew louder as darkness began to fall. Some fireflies flickered in the distance, and the croaking frogs seemed louder than the evening before. John lit the tiki torches that were placed around the patio area, and they cast a soft glow over everything.

One by one, everyone went back for seconds, even Athena. She put more meat on her plate. "Maybe we should get a smoker," she said to Aria who made another sandwich. "This is really good."

"Trevor would like that." Aria poured bar-be-que sauce on the sandwich.

When everyone finished eating, Maria and Athena did most of the easy clean-up. They wrapped up and put the leftovers into the refrigerator. Maria put on a pot of coffee, and Athena put a tea kettle of water on the stove to boil.

"The pies look good," Maria said. "Oh, you got lemon meringue. That's John's favorite."

Troy came into the kitchen and asked if he could help. He watched Athena take the pies out of the packaging and set each one on a serving plate.

"Can you carry out two pecan pies, please," Athena asked.

"Gladly," he replied. "I'll just set one right by me."

Maria took the third pecan pie, and Athena picked up the lemon meringue and the key lime pies and carried them out. They set the pies on the table, and Maria went back in for the coffee pot, and Athena made cups of tea for her and Aria.

Everyone was full, but as John said, "never too full for dessert." He put a large slice of lemon meringue pie on his plate and began eating it. "This is delicious."

Aria took a slice of key lime pie, and Trevor took a slice of lemon meringue and a slice of pecan. Maria gave Troy, Dan, and Danny each a slice of pecan pie. She served herself a slice too and then sat down. As Maria started to eat her pie, she stopped and stared as Athena picked up a piece of her key lime pie with a fork and held it up to Troy.

"Try this," Athena said. Troy looked at the pie, opened his mouth, and she fed him the pie.

He chewed and smiled. "Humm. It's really good. Tangy. I like it."

"See, I told you there were other kinds of pie." Athena picked up another piece with the fork and fed him again.

Maria looked around at the others. No one else seemed to notice Athena and Troy. They were all busy eating and talking. She shook her head and sighed as she took a bite of pecan pie.

Easter morning dawned bright and sunny. I could get used to this weather, Athena thought to herself as she combed out her wet hair. She applied some eyeliner and mascara. She looked at her skin. Only a few days in the Texas sun and she already had the start of a golden tan. All she needed was a little lip gloss. She put on her dress and slipped her feet into white sandals. She looked out the window and saw Troy walking up the driveway toward the house carrying a box.

"Good morning," she called to him.

Troy looked at her and smiled. He stared maybe a little too long at her. The white dress with embroidered black flowers she wore showed off her figure well. "Good morning." He walked up to her cabin. "You are up early."

"The sun coming in the window woke me, but I love the early morning glow. It is tranquil here in the morning."

Troy could see a basket and several gift bags on the kitchenette counter. "It looks like you have a few Easter things."

"Could you help me carry them? I do not want to tilt the cactus garden.

"I have an idea," he said. "I will be right back." Troy walked quickly to the house. He set the box he carried on the kitchen table, and then he went to the shed behind the house.

Athena tidied up the cabin and kept watch for Troy. Soon she saw him approach the cabin pulling a child's red wagon. He wore a tight-fitting white dress shirt with dark blue pin stripes, dark blue jeans, boots, and of course a cowboy hat. He looked like a picture perfect cowboy.

"That's a great idea." She said as she carried out the basket and placed it in the wagon. She went back in and brought out the gift bag with the cactus garden then brought out the other bags. Once they put everything in the wagon, Troy pulled it, and they made their way back to the house.

"Are you hungry," Troy asked.

"After all I ate last night, no," Athena said with a smile. "That bar-be-que really was delicious." She looked around. "Are we the only ones up?"

"No, Dad saddled up and went out earlier to do his morning check of the ranch. Mom usually sleeps in on Sunday, but she may be up by now.

Danny is here, and the neighbor children will be coming over for the egg hunt this morning."

"I used to set eggs out for Aria when she was young. Unfortunately, many years it was too cold and rainy or snowy to hunt eggs outside." Athena looked around and made a face. "Isn't it dangerous doing an egg hunt here?"

Troy stopped. "What do you mean?"

"Well, you put eggs under bushes and in the grass. Don't you worry about snakes?"

Troy looked at her and chuckled. "You really are afraid of snakes."

"Not normal snakes, just poisonous snakes," she clarified.

"Well, we don't have a problem with snakes near the house, and once we have walked around and placed eggs, it is safe for the kids. Snakes are afraid of people and don't hang out around them."

Athena pursed her lips. She still was not sure it was safe, but she did not say anything.

Troy knew he should not be watching her, but he could not help it. He found himself drawn to her in a way he never felt with another woman. He often sat outside late at night. He enjoyed listening to the night sounds and looking up at the stars. Athena stayed up and worked after everyone went to bed again last night. He realized then that he never saw her sit on the porch at night. "What else are you afraid of?" he asked. She looked startled. Troy quickly added, "I just noticed that you do not go outside alone much especially at night."

She looked at him. Was he watching what she did? Was he interested in what she did, or was he looking for something else to comment on? "I sat outside with you and the family at night," she replied.

"True, but you always stay close to people." He looked away and took a breath. "Ok," he said, "I saw you leaning on the windowsill a couple times when you were up writing late at night."

"Oh," she gasped.

"I wasn't spying on you," he added quickly. "I just noticed when I was getting a drink or sitting out on my porch at night. With the light on, it is easy to see inside your cabin."

Athena nodded. "To be honest, I am afraid to go outside alone especially at night."

"Why?"

"Why? Bats, snakes, animals, bats."

"You said bats twice."

"I'm especially afraid of bats, and Texas has a lot of bats. I saw some flying around the first night I stayed here."

"There are bats in New England."

"Not as many varieties, and they hibernate in winter. I live in a city so there are fewer bats, and the bat population is also down in our area because of white nose syndrome that is killing off bats."

Wow, Troy thought and shook his head. She really was afraid.

They went inside the house, and Athena placed the basket for Danny next to two other baskets on the table. "It looks like the Easter bunny has been good to Danny," she said with a chuckle.

"He's going to have a lot of candy." They walked into the kitchen. Troy put on a pot of coffee, Athena put on water for tea, and then they sat down at the kitchen table and talked until everyone else came in for breakfast.

"You two are up early," Maria said as she came into the kitchen. Dan came downstairs a few minutes later followed closely by Danny.

"Wow, the Easter bunny came," Danny said when he went into the dining room.

"Wait for your mother before you open them, ok Danny?"

"Ok," Danny replied reluctantly.

"His mother is coming?" Athena whispered to Troy.

Troy nodded. "Shelby's parents live down by the border. She took Danny down last weekend for an early Easter with her parents and stayed for a few days because he is on school vacation this week. So, she is coming here for the egg hunt and Easter dinner."

"It's nice that they still get along for Danny's sake."

"If Dan used his head, he would go back to Shelby, and make it work. He just doesn't want to grow up."

Dan came in, and they stopped their conversation. He looked at Athena and his brother sitting at the table. He definitely likes her, he thought to himself. "Good morning," he said out loud. "Oh, good. Coffee." He poured himself a cup. "Mom, Shelby texted and said she is on her way."

Maria had bacon frying on the griddle and eggs cooking in a large skillet.

"I'll toast the biscuits," Athena said. She got up and went to the pantry to get them.

John walked in. "Mornin'." He sat down, and Maria placed a cup of coffee in front of him.

Shelby arrived just before Trevor and Aria. Danny ran out to greet her. "Mom look; the Easter bunny came," he said as he pulled his mother inside. She looked at the baskets on the table and smiled.

"Can I open them?"

"Let's wait until after the egg hunt, ok."

"Ok," Danny said grumpily.

Shelby and Danny came into the kitchen. "Shelby this is Athena," Dan introduced the two women who said hi. "And this is Aria," Dan added as she and Trevor came into the kitchen.

Shelby was young. Athena estimated she might be a year or two older than Aria. She was a pretty woman with blonde curly hair and green eyes. She wore a sun dress and sandals. Dan was a lot older than Shelby, yet Shelby seemed more mature. Men always go for younger women, Athena thought to herself.

The doorbell rang, and Danny ran to the door and let Mandy, Ronnie, and their mother, Candace, in. After quick introductions, everyone went outside for the egg hunt.

"Ok, you guys stay in here, and no peeking," Dan said as he and Troy went outside.

They each took a basket of plastic eggs and started to hide them. Athena went outside to watch. Troy handed her a few eggs. "Here you go," he said, "you can help hide eggs." She took the eggs and went to find good hiding places for them.

Once all the eggs were hidden, Troy called the others outside. The kids ran out and stood at the bottom of the steps looking eager to get started. "One golden egg each," Troy reminded them. "If you find a second one, leave it for someone else."

They nodded, and Maria handed each child a basket. The hunt began. The kids scrambled over items in the yard and looked under every shrub. Mandy found a golden egg first. The adults cheered as the kids ran around searching for eggs. It took some time to find them all, but once all the eggs were found, the kids ran to the kitchen table and started to open them.

Inside they found candy, small toys, and coins. Each child also had a golden egg which contained a chocolate bunny and a $5.00 bill.

When Mandy, Ronnie, and Candace left, Shelby told Danny he could open his baskets. Danny stood on a chair and tore back the plastic coverings. Each basket was full of candy, small cars, and other toys. Maria opened the cards from her three sons, and John read them over her shoulder. She opened the bag with the cactus garden from Athena, and the box from Aria and Trevor with a necklace inside. For Aria and Trevor, Athena placed two chocolate bunnies nose to nose in a basket, so it looked like they were kissing. She surrounded them with assorted candies and tucked in a gift card to their favorite restaurant back home. She also had a box of chocolates each for Troy and Dan. She wished she knew Shelby would be there because she could have gotten her something too, but Shelby seemed happy to open the chocolates Dan received and have a piece of candy.

Athena received a bracelet from Aria and Trevor. She smiled when Dan gave her a chocolate bunny. She opened a gift bag from Troy and gasped. Inside was a yellow miniature rose plant.

"A yellow rose of Texas," he said to her, "to remember your visit."

"It's beautiful, Troy." She smiled at him. "This is so thoughtful. Thank you."

Trevor waited until everyone finished opening gifts before he handed Aria her egg. She gave him a little kiss and untied the ribbon. She opened the egg and looked inside. She opened the card. It had four words written inside, 'Will you marry me?' Aria looked at Trevor. Her hands trembled as she opened the small black box tucked among the chocolates. Her breath caught and her eyes widened as she stared at the pave diamond engagement ring. The room went quiet. She looked up at Trevor. "Yes!"

she exclaimed. She jumped up and threw her arms around him, and they kissed. He put the ring on her finger and kissed her again.

It took a few moments for everyone to realize what happened. "Congratulations!" they shouted and gathered around the couple.

Aria showed off the ring.

Athena cried as she hugged Aria, then Trevor, then Aria again. Maria cried too as she hugged them. Trevor's brothers and father shook his hand and hugged Aria.

Shelby gave Aria a hug. "I can give you lots of wedding planning advice. I love weddings."

"Thanks."

Danny looked at the ring then at Aria. "You are going to be my aunt?"

"I am," Aria replied, and she hugged him. "And you can be the ring bearer when we get married."

"What's a ring bearer?" he asked.

"The ring bearer has an important job. He carries the rings for the bride and groom," Aria explained.

"Cool," Danny said.

"Is this why you bought champagne yesterday?" Maria asked. "You said it was for mimosas."

"That was the excuse," Trevor said with a laugh.

"I will get the champagne." Troy took four glasses out of Maria's hutch. "Athena, can you help me?"

"Absolutely," she replied and took the glasses he handed to her. He took out four more glasses, and Athena followed him into the kitchen.

Troy took two bottles of champagne out of the refrigerator and popped the corks. Athena carefully poured the champagne into the glasses.

Troy got a large tray from the pantry, and Athena set the glasses on it. "Did you know," he asked her.

"No," she shook her head. "I am as surprised as everyone."

Troy touched her arm and looked into her eyes. "Are you ok?" He knew Athena and Aria were very close, so even if Athena was happy, she might also be a little sad. He thought he wanted to always see her happy. He stopped. The thought surprised him.

Athena smiled at him. "Thanks for asking." She placed her hand on his. "There will be changes, but I like Trevor, and I am ok."

"Good." Troy picked up the tray and carried it into the dining room. Athena filled a glass with grape juice for Danny and followed Troy in. They each took a glass. "To Aria and Trevor. Congratulations, and may you have many happy years together," Troy said.

"Cheers!" They drank then started asking about wedding plans.

"We just got engaged," Aria said to everyone with a big sigh. "We haven't set a date."

"We will let y'all know as soon as we decide," Trevor said, and he leaned over and kissed Aria again.

Chapter 8

The sun had long set, and Aria and Athena watched as Dan and Troy packed up Shelby's car. John carried Danny outside. Danny was exhausted. John set him down, and Maria hugged him again. "I love you."

"I love you, Grammy."

Aria hugged Danny. "It was nice meeting you, Danny." She gave him a kiss on the cheek.

Athena bent down and hugged Danny. "Will you be here when I come visit?" he asked.

"I plan to be," Athena said. Danny staggered over to Dan who picked him up and put him in his car seat.

"It was nice meeting you, Shelby," Aria and Athena said.

"Let me know if I can help with the wedding planning," Shelby said with a smile. "I love weddings. Well, see ya." She waved and got in the car.

"Danny and Amber are the same age," Aria said to her mother. "They will look cute as the flower girl and ring bearer." Athena nodded yes. "Mom, are you ok with all this?"

Athena put her hand on her daughter's shoulder. "Absolutely. I am fine. And Amber is your half-sister; she should be in the wedding party."

"That's not exactly what I mean."

Athena smiled at her daughter. "I'm fine."

They waved goodbye as Shelby turned the car around and drove down the driveway.

They all went in the house and into the dining room, but Troy went in the kitchen.

"It has been an eventful day." Maria gave Aria a hug. "Good night, dear." She turned to Athena. "I'm glad you are staying longer. We have some planning to do." Athena nodded her agreement. "Well, good night y'all."

"Good night," they responded.

"Night." John took Maria's hand as they went upstairs together.

"I'm heading up to bed too. Night," Dan said.

"Trevor took Aria's hand. "I'll walk you back to the cabin."

"Mom, are you ready to head back?" Aria asked.

Athena started to say yes, but Troy came out of the kitchen holding a bottle of wine. "Would you like a glass of wine and star gazing, Athena?" he asked.

She did not immediately reply. She looked at Troy. He was a very handsome man, and when he was not annoying her, he was rather nice. "Sure. Wine sounds good." Athena gave her daughter a hug. "You two go on ahead."

"Mom, are you sure you will be ok getting back to the cabin by yourself?"

"Yes, I'm sure."

"Don't worry, Aria. I will walk her back, so a bat doesn't get her," Troy said with a laugh. Athena rolled her eyes at him.

"Ok. Good night," Aria said as she stifled a laugh. Trevor covered his mouth to keep from laughing and started to walk outside, and Aria followed.

"Good night," Athena and Troy called to them. She and Troy walked out on the porch, and Athena sat down in one of the rocking chairs. She watched as Aria and Trevor walked hand in hand down the stairs and toward Aria's cabin. She knew they were keeping in a laugh until they were out of ear shot, and she shook her head, but she could not be mad.

Troy poured them each a glass of wine. "It's been a long day," he groaned as he handed Athena a glass and sat down in the other rocking chair. She smiled at him as she took the glass, and Troy thought how pretty she looked when she smiled. He was attracted to her, but the attraction went beyond her looks. She was…unexpected.

"Thank you. It certainly has been a long day. Cheers." She touched her glass to his.

"Cheers," he toasted. They sat in the rocking chairs, drank wine, and listened to the night sounds around them. Athena's eyes became accustomed to the darkness, and the stars became more visible.

"Trevor's not coming back to the house, is he?" Athena remarked.

"He hasn't slept all night in his room yet this trip," Troy replied. He poured them each more wine. "Aria lives with you, doesn't she?"

"Sort of," Athena replied. "She spends a great deal of time at Trevor's place too."

"And you were surprised by the engagement?"

"Yes and no. I asked Aria if they were planning on getting married when she asked me to come to Texas and meet the family. She said they talked about it, but she did not say it was imminent. So, I knew they were discussing the possibility of marriage, but I did not know Trevor purchased a ring. Apparently, Aria did not know either."

They finished a second glass of wine, and then Troy stood up and held out his hand. "Want to do some star gazing?"

Athena stood up and took his hand. "Sure," she said hesitantly.

He led her down the stairs, and they started walking toward her cabin. Up ahead she saw Troy's truck. He led her over to it. He took a milk crate out of the back and placed it on the ground. "Climb on this and get in the bed of the truck."

Athena looked at him. He waited. Finally, she stepped onto the crate, and he helped her climb in. To her surprise there were blankets and pillows in the truck bed. Troy pulled himself in. "Well, what do you think?"

"This is amazing. What a great idea."

"Lie back on a pillow," Troy suggested.

Athena leaned against the pillow and looked up at the star filled sky. "The stars are beautiful, and there are so many of them."

"They are beautiful." Troy laid down next to her. "This is what I call comfortable star gazing." He pulled a blanket over himself and Athena.

Athena relaxed and gazed up at the stars. "It certainly is comfortable."

Trevor left Aria's cabin at three am. He quietly stepped off the porch and started walking back to the main house. He was surprised to see Troy's truck still parked near the cabins. As he walked by, he casually glanced in the truck bed, and then he stopped dead in his tracks. He turned and looked again. Troy and Athena were asleep under a blanket in the bed of the truck. He was not sure what to do. Should he wake them? Should he go back and wake Aria? Should he forget what he saw? He stood there for several minutes trying to decide what to do. He decided to gently nudge Troy. He poked him several times, but Troy continued to sleep. The stars were out, so there was no chance of rain. They looked warm. Trevor shrugged his shoulders, poked Troy one more time with no response, and continued to the house and his bed.

Just as the sky started to get light, Athena woke up. She bolted upright and looked around. Troy woke up. "Good morning," he said in a lazy drawl. Athena did not respond. Troy sat up. Athena's eyes were wide, and her breathing was fast and shallow. "Are you ok?"

"I don't know. We must have fallen asleep and stayed out here all night."

"We were dressed the entire time," Troy said with a laugh. "It's not a big deal."

"We slept outside in the open all night!"

Troy caught on. "You have never slept out under the stars before?" He could not believe it. Sleeping under the stars especially on a beautiful night was something he did regularly since he was a child. He knew she grew up in a house with a yard. Surely, there were opportunities to camp in the back yard.

"No!" Athena exclaimed. "I have never stayed outside all night." She clutched the front of her shirt and looked around wildly.

"Well, now you have." Troy stood up in the bed of the truck and hopped down. He reached up to take Athena's hand and help her down. Her hands were clammy, her face was white, and she was unsteady on her feet. "Athena, you are ok. I was right beside you."

"I'm ok," she said taking a deep breath to calm herself down. "I just felt a bit disorientated. Really, I'm ok."

He walked her up to her cabin door. Her hands were still shaking. "Maybe you should lie down."

"I'll take a shower and make a cup of tea." She looked at him and took another deep breath and let it out. "Thank you for a night of star gazing. They really were fantastic."

He let go of her hand. "Do you still want me to come to the airport with you?"

She gave him a puzzled look. "Yes," she paused. "Unless you have work to do," she added quickly.

"No, I planned to take the day off to see my brother before he flies out. I will clean up and see you later."

"Ok." Athena opened the door and went inside. She put water on for tea, locked the door, and went in the bathroom for a quick shower. She let the warm water run over her then she washed and conditioned her hair. She soaped up and was rinsing off when she heard the tea kettle whistle. She got out of the shower, wrapped a towel around her body, and went to the kitchenette to pour a cup of tea. She dunked the tea bag a few times and then finished drying off and got dressed in a tee shirt and a pair of shorts.

Aria knocked on the door about fifteen minutes later. "Good morning, Mom. Are you up?"

"Come on in."

"I thought we should talk before going to the house for breakfast."

"Good idea." Athena came out of the bedroom. "How are you doing?"

"Good. Not in the mood to go back to work tomorrow." Aria said. "Did you get any writing done last night?"

"Oh. No. No. I did some star gazing with Troy. He set up blankets and pillows in the bed of his truck, so we could relax and look at the stars."

"That sounds like fun," Aria said. "I have to tell Trevor we need to do that too."

Athena was not sure if she should tell Aria that she and Troy slept outside all night. Honestly, it was not a big deal, she tried to convince herself. She decided not to mention it. "So now that it is just us, do you two plan a long or short engagement? Tea?"

"Yes, to tea," Aria said. "I don't think we will wait too long. There really isn't a point to wait, is there?"

"It is up to you two. Have you given any thought to where you want to get married and how big a wedding?"

"Actually, I'm thinking a winter wedding. What do you think?"

"At a ski resort? A destination wedding?"

"No, just at wintertime. I thought velvet dresses for the girls, maybe little white fur bolero jackets, or maybe a muff."

"I like that idea," Athena said. "When you get back, make sure you go over and tell your father. It's best to tell him in person."

"I thought the same thing. I messaged him this morning and said Trevor and I will stop by after work tomorrow."

"Good." Athena took two mugs out of a cabinet. "How many attendants do you want?"

"Amber and Danny for flower girl and ring bearer. I'm thinking Brittany as maid of honor and three or four bridesmaids."

Athena poured two mugs of tea. "I think a rental or extended stay hotel would be good for the family when they come up for the wedding."

"Trevor mentioned that as well. Maybe Dad could find something. I'll ask him." They drank their tea, and Athena washed the rest of the strawberries for them to eat. "Mom, are you set to pick up the rental car at the airport today?"

Athena nodded. "All set, and my flight home is booked. Ellen is happy that I'm taking some time off from other things to finish the book."

"Are you driving back here alone?"

"No, Troy and Dan are going to keep me company."

"Troy is a nice guy," Aria said. "I wasn't sure if you two were going to get along a couple days ago though." She gave a little laugh.

"He can be blunt and annoying sometimes," Athena added, but she also smiled.

Trevor knocked on the door. "Good morning."

"Good morning," they replied together.

"Come on in," Athena said.

Trevor walked in. He carried a covered platter. "Mom sent over some eggs and bacon. She figured you two wanted to talk alone this morning."

"That's nice of her," Athena said. She handed Aria a plate and a fork.

"It smells good," Aria said. She scooped eggs onto her plate and took a few pieces of bacon. "Are you having any, Mom?"

"I will just have eggs." She looked at the bacon. "Ok. And a piece of bacon or two." She laughed. "And a biscuit."

After they talked and ate, Aria went back to her cabin to pack. Athena decided to check email again, and then she started writing. The words were flowing easily, and she had some phrasing and ideas to get down on paper while it was fresh in her mind. She could hear Aria and Trevor laughing in the next cabin. They were so in love, and it made her happy that her daughter found such a kind and respectful man. The whole family was nice. She thought about Troy. Aria said that Troy was a nice guy. Was Aria encouraging her to see Troy? Athena did not know what to think. She took a deep breath. No, she thought to herself. There is no time for a romance right now. Athena shook her head and looked at her watch. They were going to leave for the airport about noon. She closed her laptop and went into the bedroom. She changed into a pair of jeans, a short sleeved floral blouse, and a pair of sneakers. She put on some eyeliner and mascara and spritzed on some perfume. She put a few things in a tote bag and went to Aria's cabin.

Aria was all packed, so Trevor took her suitcases and headed to the car. Athena gave her daughter a tight hug. "I will miss you."

"I'll miss you too, Mom."

They arrived at the airport and Aria and Trevor checked their bags. They had some time, so Aria and Athena went to the newsstand. Aria bought a pack of gum, and she decided to pick up a bride magazine to read on the plane. She stared at the cover. "Wow, there is a lot to wedding planning." She flipped through the magazine and read some of the article titles then looked up at her mother.

"A wedding is a big event, but you will not have to do it alone," Athena assured her.

They all walked over to the security check in and said good-bye. Maria had tears in her eyes when she hugged Trevor.

"Text me when you are on the plane and then when you land," Athena said to Aria. There were thunderstorms in the area, and many flights were already delayed, and a few were cancelled. "We will stay at the airport until the plane takes off."

Once Aria and Trevor were through security, Athena went to the car rental counter and picked up her rental car. She received a message on her phone. "Aria and Trevor's flight is delayed for twenty minutes," she said to John and Maria. "I'm all set with the car if you want to head back."

"Yes, I think we will head back," Maria said. "Dan, are you staying or coming back with us?"

Dan put his phone back in his pocket. "I'm going to go back with you and Dad. I got a call to work tonight." Dan looked at Troy and Athena. "You two going to be alright?"

"Of course," Troy replied with a tone of sarcasm. "We definitely don't need you. Go to work."

Maria did not think leaving Troy and Athena alone was a good idea, but unfortunately, she did not have a choice. "Ok, be careful. We will see you two when you get back." She, John, and Dan started to walk away. Maria glanced back at Troy and Athena and shook her head. She hoped they knew what they were doing.

Athena and Troy first went to the café and got tea and coffee, and then they found a couple of empty seats and sat down to wait until the plane took off. Athena flipped through her to do list on her tablet. "I need to stop at a department store for a few things," she said to Troy. "I didn't plan to extend my stay, and it is much warmer than I thought it would be at this time of year."

Troy nodded. "It is warmer than normal. And drier. We can stop at the small store close to the ranch, or we can stop at a bigger department store here in town." He paused then added, "Or we can go to the mall."

Athena thought for a moment. "Let's stop at the bigger store here," she said as she added a few additional items to her list. After an additional five-minute delay, Aria texted that they were boarding the plane. Finally, after yet another short delay, the plane took off, so Athena and Troy left the airport. Troy gave Athena directions and soon they arrived at the department store.

"I need a few clothes and some toiletries," Athena said as they walked in the store. "Did you want to look around and meet up in say twenty minutes?"

90

"I don't mind shopping with you. I'm not in a rush, so take your time," Troy replied.

"Ok, thanks." Athena was surprised he wanted to shop with her, but she took a shopping cart, and they went to the ladies' department. First, she picked up a couple of sleeveless shirts and a pair of shorts. She saw a dressy pair of shorts, but she needed to try them on, so she selected two different sizes. Troy pushed the cart and offered his opinion on colors and styles as they walked through the department. Athena saw a rack of dresses and flipped through them. She selected a white lace dress that she thought was quite beautiful, and a blue sleeveless dress that she also liked. The dresses could be either casual or dressy depending on the accessories she selected.

Athena added a couple more items to the cart, and they walked over to the fitting room. "This is nice," she said. "There is a bench near the fitting room for you to sit down while I try things on." She started to head in the fitting room.

Troy nodded and sat down to wait. "Will you come out and show me the clothes?"

Athena stopped, turned, and looked at Troy. She was surprised he was so interested, but she smiled and nodded yes. First, she tried on the shorts and shirts. She went out and showed Troy the outfit. She was happy that the smaller size shorts fit. Next, she tried on the dresses.

I like the white one better," Troy said. "It looks good with your tan."

Athena looked at herself in the three-way mirror. "I think you are right. The white one it is. I'll be out in a minute."

Troy watched her go back in the dressing room. Normally, he did not like shopping, but he found he did not mind it with Athena. He shook his head. She was so different than the other women he dated. The truth was, he enjoyed being with her doing ordinary everyday things, like shopping.

Athena came out of the fitting room a few minutes later, gave the items she did not want to the attendant, and put the rest in her cart. She went to a table and selected two cotton short sleeved shirts. Athena was hesitant to pick up panties with Troy, but she really needed to get a package, so she headed in that direction.

On the way, they passed a rack of straw cowboy hats. Troy stopped and took one off the display. "Try this," he said. Athena took the hat and tried it on. "It looks good on you," Troy said.

Athena looked in a small mirror on the hat display and smiled. "I like it," she said to Troy. "I haven't owned a cowboy hat in many years."

"Good," he said, "I will get it for you. You need your own hat if you are going to ride."

"Thank you." Athena smiled at Troy.

They continued shopping, and Athena selected a package of lace panties. She did not look at Troy or ask his opinion. She simply put the package in the cart. Troy smiled. He would love to see those panties on her, but of course he did not say that to her, and he looked away as if he did not notice.

Athena moved on to the health and beauty section of the store for shampoo, conditioner, and a few other items. In the grocery section of the store, she picked up two bags of popcorn, several bottles of seltzer water, and a few other snack items. She was not one for many treats, but she often wanted a snack when she stayed up late at night writing. Once she had everything on her list, they went to the cash registers to check out.

From the parking lot, they saw heavy traffic. Athena looked at her watch. It was rush hour, and the traffic moved slowly on the highway.

"Do you like Mexican food," Troy asked.

"I love it."

"Let's go have drinks and dinner while we wait for the traffic to ease up."

"That is a good idea. There is no point in sitting in a back-up. I do that all the time at home."

"Is there a lot of traffic where you live?"

"Yes, it is continuous. I get so tired of rolling along the highway sometimes."

They got in the car, and Athena pulled out in traffic. Troy texted Maria that they planned to wait until after the traffic subsided to head back to the ranch and that they would eat out tonight.

Troy directed Athena, and fortunately, she was able to find a parking space about two blocks from the restaurant he had in mind for dinner. They walked to the restaurant. For a Monday evening, the restaurants and bars were busy, so while they waited for a table, Troy ordered them margaritas.

"They will only serve a person two margaritas," Troy informed Athena as he handed her a glass. "They are made with Everclear."

Athena took a sip and puckered her lips. "Wow! That is a strong drink." She took another sip. "But really good."

Troy nodded and took a drink. "We will walk around after dinner before driving back."

"Absolutely."

They brought their drinks to the table when they were seated. Athena looked over the menu. "What is good here?"

"Everything," Troy replied. "I have never been disappointed here. I particularly like the Enchilada plate. They have chicken, beef, or vegetarian enchiladas. You get two enchiladas, refried beans, Spanish rice, and warm flour tortillas."

"Sounds good. I will try the chicken enchiladas."

The waitress came to take their order and brought salsa and corn tortilla chips for an appetizer. Athena dipped a chip in the salsa and took a bite. "Hot." She waved her hand in front of her mouth.

"And that's the mild salsa," Troy informed her as he dipped a chip in the salsa and put it in his mouth.

The vibrant restaurant was decorated with colorful flowers, woven tablecloths, and placemats. Art prints of southwest dessert scenes covered the walls. A mariachi band played traditional music, and Athena looked around took in the sights and sounds. The atmosphere was lively, and a wide variety of people dined at the restaurant. At the next table were two college students obviously on a date, a few tables over a family with four children ate tacos, and there were several older couples sipping drinks.

Athena's eyes opened wide when the waitress brought their dinners. The platters overflowed with food. She took a few pictures and planned to post them to her travel blog later.

Troy took a warm flour tortilla out of one of the baskets and dipped it in the cheese and refried bean mixture. "Dig in," he said as he took a bite.

Melted orange cheese covered everything on the plate. It contrasted with the golden corn tortilla and the dark red enchilada sauce. The gooey cheese oozed as Athena cut into the enchilada, and she took a bite. She expected it to be spicy and hot, but it was slightly sweet and tangy. "Oh, this is so good. So cheesy and delicious."

"I bet you never had enchiladas like this before."

Athena shook her head no. "This is amazing."

"I'm glad you like it." Troy called the waitress over. "Two more margaritas, please," he said to her. She nodded and left. "You don't want water with spicy food," he said to Athena. "It makes it spicier."

"The margaritas go down so well with the spicy food," Athena said as she finished her first drink.

Troy ate his entire meal including four flour tortillas and the remainder of the chips. Athena struggled, but she finished majority of it. She enjoyed the flour tortilla dipped in the cheesy refried bean mixture. She felt very full when the waitress came to wrap up the leftover tortillas. Troy insisted on paying for dinner, but Athena left the tip.

They left the restaurant and started to slowly walk down the street.

"At certain times of year, the city blocks this street off for a street festival," Troy told her. They stopped to watch a street performer then continued walking. "There's a gelato shop up ahead. Should we split a cup?"

Athena nodded her head yes. "Sounds good after the spicy meal."

"What flavor?" Troy asked as they waited for their turn.

"Chocolate?"

Troy smiled, "Chocolate it is."

They ate gelato and then continued walking up the street. "Why are all those people lined up near the bridge?" Athena asked.

"Over a million bats come out from under that bridge every night," Troy told Athena.

She stopped abruptly and looked at Troy. "Bats!?"

"Maybe we should head the other way," Troy suggested. Athena nodded yes.

The night air felt cool, so they stopped at a coffee shop for coffee and tea before going back to the car. "Should we sit outside?" Troy asked as they picked up their order.

"Yes. It is a beautiful night." Athena had a pashmina in her bag, so she pulled it out and wrapped it around her shoulders. She watched Troy as he drank his coffee. He was a very good looking man, and despite their rocky beginning, now the conversation flowed so easily. Athena chalked it up to how wrong first impressions could be.

As they enjoyed their coffee and tea, Troy watched as Athena's hair moved slightly in the light breeze. She was quite stunning, but she was more than beautiful. She was smart. He leaned back in his chair and listened to Athena tell him about her business. He appreciated the amount of work she put in because he too put in long days. However, he found that in the past year, he wanted to take a step back. He was financially comfortable, and he wanted to spend more time doing cabinetry and enjoying life. "So, you run a travel agency, have a profitable blog, teach classes, and are writing your second book." Troy was truly astonished by Athena's ambition.

"It sounds much worse than it is," she laughed. "It is a lot, but being a single mom, I guess I felt I needed to set an example for Aria. A woman needs to make her own money and be able to provide for herself."

Troy nodded. He was not someone who believed the man needed to be the provider in the family. He believed a successful marriage had to be an equal marriage, and with equality came equal responsibility. "I agree." He looked at this confident and accomplished woman sitting next to him. She knew what she wanted, and he had no doubt she could get anything she wanted. She worked hard to be successful. "But Aria is out of college and has a career of her own now," he said out loud, but he thought to himself, not to mention she is going to be married soon.

"True." Athena thought a moment. "I guess I like what I do."

"Liking what you do is very important. I just wonder if you would be happier if you didn't work as much. Take time to enjoy the fruits of your labors."

"Ironically, I have been thinking about work lately." She leaned back and looked at Troy sitting opposite her. He was an observant and thoughtful man. He spoke his mind which was good and bad. She continued, "I do want to spend more time writing. It is where my passion lies." She drank some of her chai tea. "My ex-husband John and I talked before I left for Texas. I thought about expanding and opening another agency, but he pointed out that more and more of my business is Internet bookings. It makes sense to increase staff but not to open a second location."

Troy nodded. "Brick and mortar stores are going out of business every day."

"Exactly."

They finished their beverages and started to walk again. A small crowd of people stood on the sidewalk in front of one bar, so they stopped and listened to the band. Eventually, they made their way back to the car, and Athena drove back to the ranch.

Chapter 9

Early the next morning, Troy ate breakfast and headed to the job site. He drove slowly by Athena's cabin. It did not look like she was up yet. When he went to bed, he looked out, and saw her light was still on. She was writing. He stopped at the convenience store not far from the ranch and gassed up his truck. He went inside and saw Kevin getting a cup of coffee. The two men shook hands.

"Have Trevor and the ladies gone back East?" Kevin asked.

Troy poured coffee in a large cup and put a lid on it. "Trevor and Aria went back yesterday, but Athena is staying longer to work on her book."

Kevin's eyes lit up. "Really? I might stop by and say hello."

"Why?" Troy asked sharply.

"Why not? She seems like a nice woman, and I would not mind getting to know her."

"She's busy working. You shouldn't bother her." Troy walked up to the counter. The young woman smiled at him and said hi, but he paid no attention to her. "Athena doesn't want any distractions." Troy glared at Kevin.

"She can't write all the time. She must take a break."

"I am just saying, she stayed here because she needs to work without distractions. She has a deadline, and people need to leave her alone." Troy paid the woman for his coffee and started for the door. Kevin shook his head in wonder and watched him leave without another word.

Athena woke up and felt energized. She put water on for tea and washed some strawberries for breakfast. She had a very productive night writing, and as soon as she washed up and poured a large cup of tea, she got right back to work. She wrote steadily for several hours, getting up only for short bathroom breaks and to get more tea.

About 12:30 pm, she stood up and stretched. It was hot in the cabin even though she had the air conditioner on. She went out on the porch and broke into a sweat. She reloaded the weather app on her phone. It was ninety degrees. She looked around and took in the quiet of the ranch. Everyone was at work, and the quiet unnerved her a little. She felt very much alone, and for some reason, it unsettled her. It occurred to her that if something happened, no one would hear her scream.

Maria told her there were cold cuts and salads in the refrigerator for lunch, so she walked to the house. The door was unlocked. Athena shook her head. She could not leave her cabin door unlocked especially when she slept. She grew up in a city, and no one left the doors unlocked unless they want to be robbed. She went in the kitchen and made herself a few meat rolls for lunch and poured herself a cold glass of iced tea. She turned on the TV in the kitchen for some company while she ate. The weather report came on, and the words tornado watch caught her attention. She turned up the volume and listened to the weatherman outline the forecast. Thunderstorms tonight with a chance for hail and a tornado watch.

"Terrific", she said out loud to the TV. It was one o'clock, and Maria said she came home about 2:30 pm, so Athena went back to her cabin to write.

The writing went well again, and she did not take a break until after 4:30 pm when she heard John outside talking to Maria who picked vegetables in the garden. Athena walked outside and looked up. Big black clouds, some with a touch of green, swirled overhead, and the wind blew harder than before. Dan drove in and waved.

"How are you doing today?" he asked Athena.

"I am doing well. I got a lot of work done."

"Did you get outside at all?"

"Just to go to the house for lunch." While Dan parked his car, Athena joined Maria in the garden.

"I'm picking the ripe tomatoes. Looks like a storm tonight," Maria said.

"Yes, I watched the news at lunch time, and they said storms." Athena paused. "Maria?" Maria looked up at her because of the nervous tone of Athena's voice. Athena continued, "what do I do in case of a tornado?"

Maria stood up. "I guess you don't have tornadoes back East."

"They are extremely rare."

"I need to show you the cellar." Maria picked up her basket of tomatoes and led the way to the bulkhead not far from the house. She pulled open the door and motioned for Athena to follow her. She went down the steps and opened a door. Inside was a small room. "This is the storm cellar," Maria said. She showed Athena the lantern and the supplies. "Make sure you close and lock the bulkhead and then latch the inner door."

"Showing her the cellar," Dan called down. Athena gave a little scream. "Sorry to scare you," he said apologetically.

"How will I know when to come down here?" Athena asked.

100

"There's a siren. If you hear it, come straight here. Move quickly. You will only have a few minutes to get to safety," Maria said.

"Don't worry." Dan put his hand on Athena's shoulder. "Tornadoes rarely hit this area."

"There's a tornado watch," Athena said. She walked back up the stairs. Maria followed closing the doors behind her.

"There are a lot of watches, but few actual tornadoes," Dan explained.

Troy drove by the house and turned toward his home. He stopped when he saw Maria, Dan, and Athena come out of the cellar. "Evening."

"You better clean up, Troy. Dinner will be in half an hour," Maria said as she walked past them and into the house.

"Were they showing you the cellar?" Troy asked. Athena nodded. "Don't worry. We don't get a lot of tornadoes here."

"That's what I told her," Dan said.

"I'll get cleaned up and be back in a few minutes." Troy drove on.

"Let's go inside," Dan said, and Athena followed him in the house. John sat in the front room. He had the weather on. The announcer talked about a line of thunderstorms advancing through the area. Dan sat down to watch too, but Athena went into the kitchen. She did not want to watch the weather. However, Maria also watched the weather on the TV in there.

"Hi there. Would you make the salad please, Athena?"

"Certainly," Athena started to tear up the lettuce and slice the cucumbers and tomatoes.

"Now that I had feta in a salad, I really like it," Maria said as she continuously stirred the white gravy as it thickened.

"I am glad you like it," Athena said. "I tend to put feta on everything," she laughed. "Even watermelon."

Maria looked at her. "On watermelon?"

Athena nodded. "I will make watermelon and feta for you to try. I think you will like it."

Troy came in. "Mom, the fryer is to temperature."

"What are we having tonight?" Athena asked.

"Chicken fried steak," Maria said.

"What is that?"

"It is steak that is pounded very thin, battered with egg and flour, and then deep fried like chicken," Maria explained.

"It sounds good."

"I think you will like it," Troy said.

Maria pulled a platter of prepared steaks from the refrigerator, and Troy took them outside. She followed him and carefully placed the steaks in a basket and lowered it into the hot oil. She set a timer and went back in the kitchen. She stirred the white gravy again, and then she poured it into a gravy boat. She emptied a pot of mashed potatoes into a large serving bowl.

Athena made the salad, and then she helped Maria put everything on the kitchen table.

When the chicken fried steaks were ready, Troy carried in the platter, and everyone sat down to dinner. Maria set a chicken fried steak and a scoop of mashed potatoes on a plate, and she covered it all in thick white gravy. She handed the plate to John. She then filled another for Dan and then one for Troy. "Are you ready to try chicken fried steak?" she asked Athena.

"I'm ready."

Maria filled a plate and set it before Athena and then filled a plate for herself. "Dig in everybody," she said.

Athena picked up a fork and a knife and cut a couple of pieces of steak. She put a piece in her mouth. "This is delicious," she said. She picked up another piece and ate it too. She next tried the steak with some mashed potatoes. "I'm not a huge fan of mashed potatoes, but these are so tasty with the white gravy." The others nodded, and all continued to eat.

Despite the forecast, it barely sprinkled that evening, and it did nothing to cool the temperature. Athena looked at the thermometer that hung on the porch. It was still eighty degrees and oppressively hot for nine o'clock at night. She walked quickly and returned to her cabin to video chat with Aria.

She set up her computer and connected. "Hi, Aria. How are you doing? I miss you."

"It was a tough day back," Aria replied.

"How did your father take the engagement news?" Athena asked.

"Better than I thought he would. Brook is excited and so is Amber. I told Amber she could be a flower girl."

"She will be so cute."

"Do you think we can have the wedding in December? Is that too soon?"

"I think a wedding can be planned in eight months provided you can get the venue you want. Where are you thinking of getting married?"

"Dad suggested The Castle. What do you think?"

The Castle was a Medieval-style castle and museum right on the ocean north of Boston. It was a very romantic setting that suited Aria's taste. "It's a wonderful idea," Athena replied enthusiastically. "You can get married in the Chapel and have the reception in the Great Hall. The wedding will be beautiful there."

"Yes. Dad said he can rent it for the evening. We are thinking of Saturday December 30th."

"You can either stay around for New Year's Eve or leave on your honeymoon."

"Exactly, we haven't decided yet. I'm glad you agree on the venue. The Castle will set the tone for the wedding. I am thinking a Medieval style gown with lots of lace."

"You need a very long train. You should start looking at wedding gown styles," Athena suggested.

"Oh I am. I bought several more bridal magazines, and I am on the Internet."

"Actually, me too. I have been looking at wedding ideas when I take a break," Athena laughed.

"Did you get a lot of work done?"

"I did. But the ranch is so quiet when everyone is out."

"You wanted quiet," Aria said with an exasperated tone.

"True. But it is really quiet here. Too quiet in some ways, and there was a tornado watch today."

"Are you sorry you stayed?"

"No, not at all."

"Well, everything is fine here. I took in the mail, and I will water the plants tomorrow."

"Thanks."

After she chatted with her daughter, Athena poured herself a glass of white wine and set to work.

The phone rang very early the next morning. "Hi James," Athena said groggily into her phone.

"Athena, glad I caught you." She looked at her watch. It read 7:30 am. "Aria and Trevor came over last night to tell us the happy news and show us the ring."

"Yes, I spoke to Aria last night."

"I like Trevor," he said. "He's smart and will be a good provider."

Athena was going to say that Aria did not need a provider. She needed someone to love and support her, but she knew it would be wasted breath. James was ten years her senior, and he believed it was the man's responsibility to support the family. That was one of the reasons their marriage broke up. As Athena's business grew, he became more distant because she became more independent.

"Athena? Are you there?"

"Oh, yes. Yes, I am here. I'm just not awake yet."

"Oh, sorry. I forgot it was an hour earlier there." She doubted that but decided not to say anything. They got along well, better actually than most divorced couples, and she did not want to argue with him right now.

"Aria said you are staying another couple of weeks and writing. How is it going?'

"Very well, thanks."

"We should probably have lunch when you get back."

"Why?"

"To discuss the wedding. Amber was very excited that her big sister is getting married."

"Half-sister," Athena mumbled under her breath.

"Trevor says his nephew is six, so they will be flower girl and ring bearer."

"Yes."

"I told Aria to start looking at wedding gowns. Do you think five thousand dollars is enough for a gown? I want her to have a fancy gown."

Athena's eyes went wide. "I hope that is enough. That is a lot of money."

"Are you planning on going overseas this year?"

"Maybe at some point," she said. "I don't have firm plans just yet. With the wedding in December and all the planning, I just do not know if I will have the time. I will decide once I finish this manuscript and start to plan the wedding with Aria."

"Well, I'll let you go. Call me when you get back, so we can have lunch and talk."

"Ok, bye," Athena hung up the phone and sighed. She put water on for tea and laid on the couch. She did not get to sleep until almost three am. She yawned then got up, turned off the burner, and went back to bed.

She woke up a couple hours later feeling much better. She turned on the air conditioner and started the tea water again. She turned on her laptop and read email while she waited for the water to boil. A noise outside caught her attention, and she went to the window and looked out. John sat up on a horse talking to three men. He pointed Westward and then the four men trotted off on their horses.

Athena had a handful of strawberries and a yogurt for breakfast and settled down to serious writing. About one o'clock, she took a break and stretched. She was not hungry, but she knew she should have something to eat, so she went to the house and took the egg salad out of the refrigerator. She put some in a small bowl and went back to her cabin, opened a bag of popcorn, and poured a glass of flavored seltzer water then wrote for the rest of the afternoon.

Dan knocked on her door about 4:30 pm. "Athena?"

She opened the door. "Hi."

"Did you just unlock the door?"

"Yes."

"Athena, you don't have to lock doors here. It's safe," he said.

"Habit," she replied.

"How are you doing?"

"Good. Is it dinner time already?"

"Just about. Do you eat tacos?"

"Yes." Athena walked over to her computer and saved her work then she picked up the cleaned bowl from lunch. "I'm all set." They talked about their day as they walked up to the house. She looked around and did not see Troy or his truck. They went inside, and she helped Maria finish preparing dinner.

"Should I set the table?" Athena asked.

"Please, the plates are on the counter."

Athena picked up the plates. There were only four. "Is Troy coming for dinner?" she asked Maria.

"No, he's working late. They must put the final touches on the house. The closing is on Monday." Athena nodded. "Do you want hard or soft tacos?" Maria asked.

"Soft please." They sat down to dinner, and Athena realized she was suddenly very hungry. John sat quietly as always, but Dan kept her engaged in conversation.

"I talked to Trevor this afternoon," Maria said suddenly. "He said they went to Aria's father's house last night for dinner and told him they are engaged."

Athena nodded. "Yes, James called me early this morning."

"Trevor said he is very excited about the upcoming wedding. He told Aria he's giving her five thousand dollars for her gown."

Athena smiled. "Yes, he likes to pamper Aria."

"They are thinking of having a December wedding?" Maria paused. Athena nodded yes. "At a castle?"

"The Castle is a museum that can be rented for weddings and parties. It's located on the North shore." To clarify, she quickly added, "North of Boston. Along the coast."

Maria nodded. "Trevor said the wedding would be back East."

"We should discuss guests, lodging, and other details while I am here," Athena suggested.

"Yes, we should," she paused again. "James sounds like a good provider." Maria filled her second taco and took a bite.

Athena raised her eyebrows at Maria's tone. "Yes, he needs to be the provider," she stated.

"Most women want that in a man," Maria replied as she spooned Spanish rice onto her plate.

John and Dan stopped eating and looked up at Maria and then over at Athena.

Athena smiled and spooned some rice onto her plate. "Being a good provider does not make a man a good husband. There's more to life than money."

"True," Maria agreed, and John and Dan went back to their tacos.

After dinner, Dan said he was going to the local bar. "Interested in a drink, Athena?" he asked as they left the house.

"Thanks, Dan, but not tonight. Aria and I are video chatting in forty five minutes. Good night." As she went back to her cabin, she looked down the driveway. Troy's house was still dark. She went inside, locked the door, and poured a glass of wine.

Athena did a great deal of writing, and the manuscript was taking shape quickly. On Friday morning, she had a video conference with Ellen, her editor. "I think what you have so far is great. Start doing a comprehensive revision," Ellen said. "I knew you just needed to get free of distractions." Ellen paused. "Maybe you should consider cutting back on other things and focus on your writing?"

Athena nodded. "I am considering it."

Her statement shocked Ellen, and she looked carefully at Athena. She was Athena's editor, but she was also a close friend. "You have been working hard, but you look rested." She was amazed how good Athena looked. Not that she looked bad, but now Athena's skin was a golden color, she did not have bags under her eyes, and she smiled. A lot. "Take the weekend off and have some fun. You deserve it."

"I think I will. The weather here is gorgeous. Hot and so sunny."

"Well, enjoy it because it's cold and rainy here. Call me next week."

"I will. Bye."

Athena worked until 1:30 pm and then had a yogurt for lunch. She checked email while she ate. She had an email from Jasmine wanting to know how things were going in Texas. Athena sent her back a short reply.

Since she told Maria she planned to cook dinner, Athena used her GPS and drove to the store. She decided to make meatball subs, salad, broccoli, and something for dessert. She also bought a box of ice cream sandwiches because Danny was coming for the weekend, and he told her he liked them. As she pushed her cart out of the store, she recognized Kevin.

"Hello, Athena" he called cheerfully as he waved and walked toward her.

"Hello, are you here on official business again?"

"Yes, I am, but this time an alarm had accidently been triggered." He looked at her cart. "Doing some shopping I see. Taking a break from writing?" Athena looked at him. How did he know she was here writing? But before she could ask, he said, "I saw Troy earlier in the week, and he said you were staying here to work on your book."

She nodded. "Yes, I have a manuscript deadline, and I needed a place to write. The ranch is perfect because it's very quiet and free of distractions."

"I hope it isn't all work and no play," he said.

She knew that look he gave her. He was going to ask her out. He seemed nice, but she was not interested in dating him. For one thing, he was not really her type. However, more importantly, she was not sure she needed the distraction of a relationship, especially a long distance one, right now.

She knew she had to discourage him. "I'm afraid that it is primarily work. I have a very tight writing schedule."

His face fell. "Oh ok. Too bad. Maybe next time you visit you will get a chance to see some of the things this area has to offer."

She only gave him a very small smile. "Maybe. I'm sure I will be back. You have heard the news that Trevor and Aria are engaged."

"No! I had not heard. That's wonderful."

Athena was quite surprised Kevin did not know about the engagement because he just told her that he spoke to Troy earlier in the week. Why didn't Troy mention the engagement? Maybe he was not happy about it?

Troy told him she stayed here to work on her manuscript, but he did not tell Kevin about Aria and Trevor. That seemed very odd.

"I'm sure you'll be back to visit then." Kevin looked at his watch. "Well, I better be going. It was very nice to see you again, Athena."

She wheeled the cart to her car and put the bags in the trunk. Kevin got in his cruiser and rolled down his window as he slowly drove by. "Hopefully, you will make time to see the game tomorrow, and I will see you there. The whole town is going. You really should make the time." He waved and drove out of the parking lot.

"Game? What game?" Athena said out loud. She shrugged and got into her car.

When she arrived back at the ranch, Danny and Maria were sitting on the porch. "Hi Athena," Danny called. He jumped off the rocking chair, and he ran up to her.

"Hi, Danny. How was your week at school?"

"Not bad."

"Did you do anything exciting?"

"We played kick ball during recess."

"That sounds like fun."

Danny helped Athena carry some of the groceries, and they went into the house. While she cooked, Danny told her about kick ball, school, and boy scouts. Athena made the tomato sauce and let it simmer. She mixed breadcrumbs, cheese, onions, garlic, spices, and eggs into the hamburger meat and set the bowl in the refrigerator. She cleaned and cut up the broccoli then put it in a steamer basket, but she did not turn on the burner just yet. She started making the salad; she cut up tomatoes and cucumbers and added them to a bowl containing shredded lettuce.

She handed Danny a couple of cucumber slices for him to munch on. Danny heard Dan and John walking up the porch stairs, and he ran out to say hi.

"Oh, I wish I had that much energy," Maria said as she came in the kitchen.

"Oh, me too," Athena laughed. She opened a can of olives and continued to prepare dinner.

"I'll set the table and get the drinks," Maria said. "Troy should be here in about ten minutes."

Athena decided not to ask Troy why he did not tell Kevin about the engagement. It did not matter one way or the other if he approved, and perhaps there was a reason he did not tell Kevin. Texas and Massachusetts were a long way apart. Immediate family would likely attend wherever the wedding took place, but not friends.

She started the broccoli and was tossing the salad when Troy arrived. He came into the kitchen and smiled at her. She was barefoot and dressed in a skimpy tank top and shorts. "Good evening."

Athena looked up. "Hi, Troy." He offered to help, and he stayed in the kitchen while she finished preparing the meal. He carried the salad and dressings to the dining room table.

Next, Athena handed him a bowl of olives. "There are olives in the salad," he said.

"In an Italian house, we always have an extra bowl of black olives." Troy shrugged his shoulders and brought the bowl of olives to the table.

Athena stood by the stove and watched the meatballs cook in the hot oil. They came out crispy on the outside and tender on the inside. She put most of them in the sauce, but she left some without sauce.

Danny came in, and she gave him one of the cooler un-sauced meatballs on a fork to eat. "This is really good," he said. Athena had him carry the sliced sub rolls to the dining room when he finished eating.

When the broccoli was ready, Athena tossed it with butter and garlic, and Troy set the bowl on the table. She then put the sauced meatballs in one bowl and the plain ones in another. She put extra tomato sauce in a bowl with a small ladle. Once everything was on the table, Troy poured wine for the adults and a glass of grape juice for Danny, and everyone started to eat.

"Athena, this is delicious," Maria said. She finished her sub and ate a sauced meatball. "It is authentic Italian food."

John, Dan, and Troy agreed with Maria. "The meat is seasoned very well," Troy said.

"Yes," Maria agreed. "It is delicious."

"Thanks," Athena said. "I am glad you like it."

Clean up took time because of the various pots and pans. Maria put on coffee, and a kettle of water for tea. Once the dishes were washed and coffee and tea were ready, they sat down to pistachio cake and ice cream.

When Danny finished eating, he asked Dan if he could watch a movie.

"How long is it? You have to get up early for your game tomorrow."

Danny showed him the back of the DVD.

"It's ninety minutes. Ok, go ahead." Dan turned to Athena, "You should come to Danny's game tomorrow. It will be fun."

"Game?"

"Danny plays baseball. Tomorrow is a big game. Everyone in town will be there. You should come."

"Oh, that's the game Kevin was talking about," she said with a laugh.

Troy sat straight up in his chair. "You saw Kevin today?"

"Yes, when I shopped at the store earlier. He was there responding to an alarm."

"What else did he say?" Troy asked. The others stopped talking and looked at Troy.

"Not much," Athena replied with a shrug. "Why?"

"Just wondering."

Dan chuckled. Troy acted jealous of Athena talking to Kevin. It was an interesting development, and he could not resist stirring the pot just a little. He had to get Athena to go to the game. "So, Athena, what do you say. Going to come to the game tomorrow? Everyone in town will be there, and it is going to be fun."

Athena nodded her head. "Sure, I will go. It does sound like fun."

Chapter 10

The next morning, John finished breakfast and sat quietly in the kitchen reading the newspaper and having his coffee. "John," Maria said, "I think we should all go in our car." She put more bacon in the fry pan.

"Where are we going?" he asked.

Maria put her hands on her hips. "To Danny's game," she said in an exasperated voice.

John looked up from his paper. "Why do we all have to go together?"

"Because I think it is best. We can keep an eye on everyone." She went back to cooking the bacon.

John stared at his wife for a couple moments. "Maria what is going on?"

"Nothing," she quickly replied.

"Yes, there is something."

"It's just a feeling. I think Dan and Troy both like Athena and maybe Kevin too." Maria let out a deep breath. "You know what happened in the past. Troy liked someone, and Dan intentionally took the girl away from him. And Kevin was always in the mix somehow."

"Maria, they aren't teenagers anymore. They are all grown adults."

"But I see it all happening again, John." She gave an exasperated sigh. "I just don't want anyone to get hurt."

"I think you should stay out of it. They are not kids. Besides, Dan is still married to Shelby, and Kevin has an ex-wife." He put his paper down. "And what makes you think they are interested in Athena, or she is interested in one of them. They live here, and her life is on the East Coast."

Maria glared at John and stood with her hands on her hips. "I just know." She turned away from him.

"Good morning," Troy said as he walked in the kitchen.

Maria fussed with her apron. "Breakfast, Troy?"

"No thank you, Mom. I ate at my place."

Danny came running in the kitchen dressed in his baseball uniform. "I'm starving."

"Sit down, honey." Maria set a plate of eggs and bacon in front of him and poured him a glass of milk.

"Morning," Dan said as he came in the kitchen. He got himself a scoop of scrambled eggs and several pieces of bacon and sat down to eat.

While Maria served herself eggs and bacon, she looked long at her sons. They both had on new blue jeans. Troy wore a white collared shirt with the sleeves rolled up, and Dan wore a blue tee shirt. Both men were clean shaven and wore cologne. Maria looked at John, but he had returned to reading his paper.

"Good morning," Athena said when she entered the kitchen carrying a travel mug of tea.

"Good morning. Would you like some breakfast?" Maria asked.

"No thank you. I had breakfast in my cabin this morning."

"Good morning," Troy looked at Athena and smiled. She wore a pair of blue dressy shorts, a floral short sleeved blouse, and a new pair of slip

116

on dark blue shoes. He liked that she wore just a little make up around her eyes to accentuate them. He breathed in, and he could smell the light rose scent of her perfume.

Maria wrapped up the leftovers while Dan rinsed the plates and put them in the dishwasher. "Should we all go to the game together?" Maria asked cheerfully. John looked up over his glasses at her.

Dan and Troy looked at each other. "Sure," they said at the same time.

Maria looked at Athena. She shrugged. "Sounds good to me. I don't know where anything is around here."

They all piled into the car, and John drove to the ball field. When they arrived, Danny said good-bye and ran off to join his teammates, and the family went to find seats in the bleachers. Shelby was up in the bleachers already. She waved to them.

"Shelby's saving us seats," Dan said.

By late morning, the sun was hot, and Athena was thirsty from all the cheering. She looked over at the concession stand. The line was finally short. Troy also watched the line. "Thirsty?" he asked. Athena nodded.

"I'm hungry," Shelby said. "Dan, let's go get something to eat while the other team is at bat."

Dan got up and followed her down the bleachers. Athena and Troy stood up, and Athena started to make her way down too.

"Mom, Dad, do you want anything from the concession stand?" Troy asked.

"I'll take a beer," John replied.

"If they have any lemonade, I'll take one. If not, an iced tea. Thank you, dear."

Troy caught up to the others. While they waited in line, Kevin approached. "Hi y'all."

"Hi," they replied. The guys shook hands.

Kevin stood next to Athena. "I see you are here, Athena. Glad you are taking a break." He smiled at her and then looked over at Troy. "Oh, Athena told me yesterday that Trevor and Aria are engaged. That's fantastic."

"Yes, it is," Troy replied. "Aria is a wonderful woman."

Athena smiled at him. So, he did approve of Aria.

"You two talked quite a bit then yesterday," Troy said sounding slightly annoyed.

Kevin smiled broadly. "Yes, we had a nice long conversation. Didn't we, Athena?"

Athena looked from Troy to Kevin. "It wasn't that long." she said, and she blushed.

Kevin stood very tall in his uniform, and Troy edged his way between him and Athena. Troy, Athena, and Kevin stood there looking at one another not saying anything.

Dan shook his head. "You going to order, or should we?"

Athena looked up at the board. Troy glared at Kevin then turned to place an order. To Troy's dismay, Kevin helped carry the food and drinks back to the bleachers. Troy handed his mother an iced tea.

"Thank you." Maria looked at the group and let out a very deep sigh.

John took the beer Troy handed him and avoided looking at Maria.

Troy motioned for Athena to sit next to Shelby, and he sat next to her. Kevin sat down on the other side of him. "Aren't you on duty?" Troy asked Kevin.

Kevin shook his head no. "Just got off. I thought I'd come see how Craig is doing."

"Oh, is your son playing too, Kevin?" Athena leaned past Troy and asked.

"No, my son is the assistant coach. That's him there at third base. He's actually getting married in August."

"Oh, congratulations," Athena replied.

Troy offered Athena the bag of popcorn. She reached in the bag, and she moved closer to him. Troy looked down and saw a woman standing at the bottom of the bleachers trying to get Kevin's attention. "Kevin, you are being summoned," Troy said with a triumphant smile.

Kevin looked annoyed. "Well, I have to go. Looks like Katherine wants to talk."

"Your wife?" Athena asked.

"My ex-wife," Kevin replied. He gave a long suffering sigh. "Katherine probably needs money. See y'all later."

"Bye," they replied.

Danny's team won, and they piled in the car to drive to the ice cream place for a celebration. "I don't think I have ever eaten this much ice cream," Athena said as they walked up to the counter to order. She ordered a kiddie size twist in a cup again.

"It's hot here. You need ice cream," Troy replied, and he ordered a banana split.

Danny sat with his teammates, and they talked excitedly about the game. Dan sat next to Shelby with some of the other parents. At one point, he put his arm around her, but he withdrew it quickly.

A short while later, Kevin and Dan walked over to where John, Maria, Troy, and Athena sat. "Danny's team is going to the dive-in tonight. Shelby and I are going too of course. Y'all want to go?" Dan asked.

"A drive-in!" Athena exclaimed. "I used to love the drive-in, but I haven't been to one in years. They all closed where I live."

"What's playing?" John asked.

"A dinosaur action movie," Dan replied.

"That's supposed to be really good," Athena said.

"Have you seen the others?" Kevin asked.

"Oh yes," Athena replied. "I love the whole series."

"Then you want to go?" Kevin asked excitedly.

However, before Kevin could say anything more, Troy leaned close to Athena blocking her view of Kevin. "You like action movies?" he asked with a slight tone of sarcasm. "I thought you were more the chick-flick type."

Athena gave Troy a smirk and leaned toward him. "For your information, Aria and I have seen all the new superhero movies, and I am a huge sci-fi and fantasy fan."

"I would not have thought," Troy commented. He moved a little closer to her.

"There's a lot you do not know about me," Athena replied smugly.

"I'm beginning to realize that," Troy replied as he stared at Athena. Neither of them broke eye contact.

Dan and Kevin just looked at them. Dan shook his head. Finally, he asked, "So, who is going to the movie? And who wants to drive?"

"No, thank you," John said. "Y'all have fun."

Troy and Athena continued to stare at one another. Troy took a deep breath. "So, Athena," he paused, "do you want to go with me … to the drive-in … in my truck?"

Athena did not respond immediately. She continued to study Troy then nodded her head ever so slightly yes.

Troy looked up at Dan. "Athena and I will go in my truck."

Kevin let out a sad sigh, and Maria shook her head and gave John an 'I told you so' look.

Later that afternoon, John came back from his ride around the ranch and sat on the porch when Athena walked up the stairs. "Hi John."

"How are you doing, Athena?" he asked in his slow drawl.

"I'm doing well, thanks."

"Sit down, relax." John motioned to the rocking chair.

Athena sat down on the rocking chair, closed her eyes, and started to gently rock back and forth. Maria heard Athena's voice and went out on the porch and sat in the other rocking chair. Athena opened her eyes. "Hi Maria," she said. "This rocking chair is so relaxing. I have to look for one when I get home."

"Do you have a porch on your house back East?"

"No, I have a very small porch, but I am thinking of getting a rocking chair for my attic room."

"Attic room?"

"Yes, I have an office/sitting room in the attic. From the window I can see the ocean." Athena closed her eyes and thought about that view she loved and missed so much.

"I bet you miss your home, Athena," Maria said. Athena nodded yes. "I am sure you are anxious to return."

Athena did not reply, she just smiled and nodded.

Danny came downstairs looking for Dan. Maria picked him up and set him on her lap. "Daddy has gone to pick up your Mommy, so we can all have dinner, and you can go to the drive-in," Maria explained to him.

He laid his head on her shoulder. "What are we having for dinner?" Danny asked.

"I am thinking cheeseburgers," Maria replied. "Would you like a cheeseburger?" Danny nodded, yes.

"I will make salad, Maria," Athena said.

"Thank you."

Dan and Shelby drove up, and Danny jumped up to say hi.

"John, can you start the grill?" Maria asked. "I think they want to leave in an hour or so."

John got up and went out back. Troy already started the grill. "Thanks, Troy."

Troy took a deep breath. "Dad, what do you think of Athena?" he asked quietly.

"She is a fine woman. Independent, smart, pretty."

"She's surprising," Troy added.

"How so?"

Troy thought for a moment. He thought he knew the type of woman she was, but then she did something that proved him wrong. "The more I get to know her," he paused and looked at his father and shrugged, "the more I realize I don't know her."

John recognized the look on Troy's face. His son had feelings for Athena. John put his hand on Troy's shoulder. "She keeps you guessing, and she is unpredictable."

Troy nodded. "Yes, she surprises me all the time."

"That's a good quality in a woman," John looked back through the kitchen door. Maria and Athena were in the kitchen preparing dinner. John patted his son's shoulder. "Take it slow, Troy. Like a filly, I think she spooks easily."

When the cheeseburgers were ready, everyone sat down to eat. Athena decided to just have a salad for dinner. Troy leaned over and whispered, "afraid you will get fat?"

She rolled her eyes at him and whispered back, "No. I am saving room for drive-in food." Troy raised his eyebrows.

After dinner, Athena got in Troy's truck. "Troy, I think we should stop for popcorn and candy since those things were expensive at the drive-in."

"Good idea." He preferred to let the others go ahead and get places, so he could park on the outside edge of the group and not in the middle. Troy pulled up to Dan's car. "Y'all go ahead," he said to Dan. "Athena and I are stopping for popcorn."

Athena bought four large tubes of popcorn and a variety of bags of candy. Troy bought two six packs of Coronas and put them in the cooler full of ice in the bed of his truck. When they arrived at the drive-in, Kevin flagged them over. To Troy's dismay, he saved them a spot.

Troy pulled out two chairs from the bed of his truck and set them in front of the vehicle. Athena sat down, and Kevin brought over his chair and sat down on the other side of her. Troy lit a citronella candle to keep the bugs away, and he opened the cooler and passed around Coronas. Athena passed around the popcorn and the candy.

The great thing about a drive-in is it is outdoors. The kids run around and play while the adults sit, drink, and talk. A group of teenagers played frisbee and another group, mostly girls, walked around.

The sky slowly darkened, and the cricket chirps became louder. Athena got up to get her jacket. When the previews came on, Troy took a large blanket out of his truck. He moved his chair closer to Athena, sat down, and placed the blanket around them. She moved even closer to him, so she was wrapped up fully in the blanket. Kevin gave Troy a scowl, but Troy just smiled.

The movie was quite scary, and several times they all jumped when a dinosaur jumped out of hiding. At one point, Athena wrapped her arm around Troy's arm and squeezed it. Danny and his friends screamed at times, but when the movie ended, everyone clapped. They got up and stretched at intermission. The kids were showing signs of fatigue and some were falling asleep in their chairs. Shelby walked over. "Ladies' room, Athena?"

"Yes, maybe if we hurry, we can beat the mob." They ran off. The guys took their time knowing that the line for the women was much longer than for them, and they would have to wait. Finally, Shelby and Athena joined the men in front of the concession stand.

"Are you hungry, Danny?" Dan asked. Danny shook his head no. He looked tired, and Dan picked him up and carried him.

"I'm hungry," Shelby said to Dan.

"What would you like?" he asked. She looked up at the board and they placed their order.

Athena turned to Troy. "I'm going to get a cheeseburger. Would you like anything?"

"I'll have a hotdog. He started to get out his wallet, but Athena already had her wallet out of her purse.

"I'll get this," she said. Troy just stared at her. "Curly fries?" she asked. He did not answer. "Troy, curly fries or maybe onion rings?"

"Umm fries," Troy finally replied.

They carried the food back to their chairs, and Troy opened a couple of Coronas. Athena unwrapped her cheeseburger and took a bite. "Yum," she said. "I love cheeseburgers at the drive-in." She took another bite. "I think it's the foil wrapper." She laughed, and Troy shook his head.

Part way through the second movie, which was an older movie, most of the kids fell asleep. It was colder, so everyone retreated to their vehicles. Several people left including Kevin. Danny was asleep, and Dan laid him down on the back seat of his car. He and Shelby sat very close together on the front seats.

Troy's truck had a bench seat. He pushed the seat back so they could stretch out, and Athena took off her shoes. Troy put a blanket over them, and she slid close to him. He wanted to put his arm around her, but he was not sure if he should. Instead, he decided to move closer to her, so their arms touched. He hoped she would hook her arm in his and then he would know it was ok to put his arm around her, but she didn't.

Early the next morning, Troy knocked on Athena's cabin door. "Are you ready?"

She hung her camera around her neck and put on her cowboy hat. "I am."

They walked to the stables. John was already up on his horse. Troy and Athena mounted their horses, and John led the way out of the building. The sun was rising, and John headed east so they had a stellar view of the sunrise.

"Wow, I just cannot get over how big and beautiful the sky is here." Athena took a few pictures of the sunrise. She planned to post several pictures of Texas to her travel blog later in the day. She looked around at the gorgeous scenery. She planned to write about this area in the future after she researched and visited more places.

John, Troy, and Athena continued their slow leisurely ride around the ranch. They rode along the south perimeter fence, and John made note of an area of fencing that needed to be repaired. This area was fairly green. "The herd needs to be moved to the next field this week," John said as he surveyed the fields.

"I have time tomorrow afternoon," Troy replied.

"That's good. Dan will be here too, and we will have plenty of help. Athena, would you also like to help?"

"Oh yes. I would love it."

John sped up a little, and Troy and Athena followed. "Looks like we have a new calf," he called to them.

Athena gasped. There in front of her, a very young calf stood on wobbly legs next to its mother. The mother munched on some vegetation, and the calf looked around nervously. Athena snapped some pictures.

Troy sat back in his saddle and watched Athena as she took pictures and marveled at the sights, that to be honest, he often took for granted. She wore the cowboy hat he bought for her, a pair of jeans, and a tight-fitting peach colored tank top. The color looked good against her tan skin. Her hair was caught in a low ponytail and it flowed down her back. Troy noticed that her hair was getting lighter from the sun.

They rode on for only a few minutes when John stopped again. Up ahead they saw another mother and calf. This calf stood on steadier legs and bent its head to nibble some grass. Athena took more pictures and made some notes on her phone. She was nearly giddy with excitement, and when she turned and looked at Troy and smiled, his heart seemed to skip a beat.

They were fairly close to the ranch now, and while they were stopped, Troy received a text from Maria. "Athena, Mom is making pancakes for breakfast this morning, do you eat pancakes?" He started to text no to his mother anticipating that she wanted fruit or yogurt instead.

"Oh, that sounds good. I am starving," Athena replied enthusiastically. Troy looked up at her, shook his head, and texted his mother that they all wanted pancakes.

They returned to the stable and took care of the horses before going to the house for breakfast. "Did you have a nice ride?" Maria asked as Athena entered the kitchen. Dan and Shelby were having coffee, and Danny was eating a pancake.

Athena smiled at them. "Good morning." She took off her camera and her hat and then went to the sink to wash her hands. "It was a great ride. The sunrise was spectacular, and we saw a couple of new-born calves." She beamed with excitement as she washed and then dried her hands.

"That's so cool," Danny said between bites of pancake. "Dad, can we go see the new calves?"

"Sure, we can."

"Good morning," Troy said as he entered the kitchen and went to the sink and washed his hands.

After cleaning up, John came into the kitchen. "Mornin' y'all." He poured a cup of coffee then sat down next to Dan. Maria set a plate of eggs, bacon, and pancakes in front of him. She was about to ask Athena and Troy what they wanted for breakfast when she realized they were already fixing their own plates. Maria sat down at the table and watched the scene unfolding in front of her.

First, Athena poured herself a cup of tea, then she poured a cup of coffee, and she set the mugs on the table. Next, she went to the sink and washed and cut up some strawberries.

Troy added eggs to two plates. "Athena would you like bacon," he asked.

"One piece, thanks,"

Troy added a piece of bacon to one of the plates, and he added several pieces of bacon to the second plate. "Pancakes?"

Athena looked over at the size of the pancakes. "Yes, one please."

Troy added a pancake to one plate and several pancakes to the second plate.

Athena set the bowl of strawberries on the table between the two mugs. She took two napkins, placed them on the table, and set a fork on each one. Troy walked over and set the plates down-side by side. "Thank you," Athena replied with a smile as she sat down.

"Thank you." Troy smiled as he sat down next to her.

Athena picked up the creamer and poured some cream into her mug. "Cream?" she asked. Troy nodded yes, and she poured some cream into his mug too. Athena put strawberries on her plate, and then she passed the bowl to Troy. He put a few berries on his plate. Troy poured syrup over his pancakes and passed the syrup to Athena, and they both started to eat.

Maria just shook her head, closed her eyes, and sighed.

Chapter 11

Having a productive day was becoming the norm now for Athena. She also felt more relaxed than she had been in a very long time. She attributed it to sunshine and fresh air. At this point in her life, she was fairly comfortable financially. Well, she would never feel totally comfortable financially. When she married Aria's father, she was young. James offered stability, but at a price. Oh, he encouraged her to finish school, and he never put restrictions on her, but he had to be the provider. As her business grew, their relationship fell apart. Still, he was not a bad man. He loved his daughter, and he did give sound financial advice whenever she asked him for it; and when she didn't ask.

After lunch, Athena went to the stable and pet a few of the horses. She walked around the garden and up the driveway then picked a few wildflowers that grew by the fence. She went in the house but could not find a vase, so she put the flowers in a mason jar and carried them to her cabin.

She placed the flowers on the counter and went in the bathroom to wash up. As she dried her hands, movement caught her eye. Carefully, she looked out the window, and she saw…a road runner. Athena blinked and then stared at it as it pecked at the ground. Finally, she carefully backed away from the window and went to get her camera. She turned the camera on and very very slowly approached the window. The bird was still there, and she snapped a few pictures of it. A few seconds later, the bird took off and was quickly out of sight. Athena looked at the pictures and decided to post a couple to her blog before getting back to the manuscript.

When the family returned from work, Athena put on her flip flops and went to the house to help with dinner preparations. As she walked, she twisted her hair and put it up with a clip. She looked at the thermometer that hung on the porch post. It read ninety three degrees.

Dan worked late, and Maria, John, Troy, and Athena ate an easy dinner of cheeseburgers and hotdogs outside on the patio. Athena noticed that Troy was wearing a tight black tee shirt instead of the normal shirts he usually wore. She liked the look.

After dinner, she thought about going back to her cabin and putting on a movie when Troy approached her. "What are you planning to do tonight, Athena? Writing?" Troy asked.

"I'm thinking of watching a movie tonight. Would you like to watch something together?"

"Actually, I wanted to ask if you would like to go to Cruise Night at the ice cream place."

"Old cars?"

"Vintage cars," he said emphasizing the word vintage. "Is that something you might be interested in doing with me?"

"Sure, why not," she said without hesitation. "What time are we leaving?"

"Ten minutes too soon," he asked.

"I can be ready in ten minutes." Athena walked to her cabin to change clothes and get ready.

Maria came into the kitchen. "I heard you ask Athena to Cruise Night."

"I thought she might want a night off," Troy replied. Maria saw the hope in Troy's eyes. She wanted to warn him to be careful. She did not think Athena would intentionally hurt her son, but they were such opposite people. However, Maria decided not to say anything.

"Well, good night, Mom." Troy gave his mother a kiss on the cheek and went outside.

Athena came back to the house a few minutes later. She wore a denim skirt, a blue floral off the shoulder blouse, and blue slip on shoes. She carried a tote bag and a wristlet.

"Is this ok for the Cruise Night?" she asked. She spread her arms wide and turned around.

Troy smiled. Bare shoulders were very sexy in his opinion. "It is. You look very pretty."

Athena blushed. "Thank you."

Maria appeared in the doorway. "Have fun," she called.

"Good night," Athena gave a wave as she climbed up into Troy's truck. She placed the tote bag at her feet and put on her seat belt.

Maria watched as Troy drove down the driveway. She hoped the two of them knew what they were doing.

"Have you ever been to a Cruise Night?" Troy asked as he turned out on the main road and sped up.

"No. One of the ice cream places near my house has one during the summer. I think it is on Tuesday evening, but I have never been to it."

"Then you are in for a treat."

When they arrived, there were already about fifty cars in the back parking lot. Troy parked and came around to help Athena down. He put his hands at her waist, lifted her up, and set her gently on the ground. Their bodies were so close. Troy felt Athena's quick intake of air, and she stared up into his eyes. He wanted to kiss her. He leaned close. "Thank you," she breathed. Her cheeks turned pink, and she looked down.

"You are welcome," he replied softly. "Ready?" Athena nodded yes.

As they walked, Troy resisted the urge to put his hand at the small of her back. He was afraid of being too forward, but he ached to feel her in his arms. Her skin would be soft and silky beneath his hands. He imagined running is fingers through her hair then bringing his mouth to hers in a kiss.

The vintage cars were in the adjacent parking lot, and people moved around looking at them and talking to the owners. They walked up to a small MG.

"Would you like to sit inside?" the owner asked Athena. He opened the door, and she sat down on the soft, tan, leather seat. "This is very comfortable," she said as she ran her hand along the seat.

"Custom upholstery," the owner said proudly.

They continued, stopping here and there. Athena was not sure she was going to have fun at basically a car show, but she was enjoying herself. She looked at Troy as they walked. Maybe I just enjoy his company, Athena thought to herself. She watched him as he leaned in a car to look at the dashboard. His body was lean and hard, and she wondered how it would feel to have his arms wrapped around her.

"Would you like an ice cream?" Troy asked when they made it to the ice cream stand.

"A kid sized, chocolate and vanilla twist cup, please."

"Your usual." Troy replied with a laugh as he walked up to the window to order. The young woman behind the counter smiled at him, "Hi Troy," she said with a smile. "You look good."

"Hi Carrie," he replied. Troy ordered the cup and a twist cone for himself.

"Oh, you aren't alone tonight," Carrie replied. She smiled, but she also looked around the room to see who accompanied him.

Athena watched the young woman flirt with Troy, and even though he did not flirt back, Athena still felt uneasy. Troy handed her the ice cream. "Thank you."

"You're welcome." He took Athena's other hand and walked toward the door. "Come on. We need to get a good spot." As Troy led her away, Athena glanced over her shoulder at the woman behind the counter. She did not look happy, and that made Athena smile.

"They are going to start cruising around in a few minutes," Troy told Athena as they walked outside. They found a spot along the fence and then started eating their ice cream. Soon the cars started to drive by very slowly. Some of the drivers revved the engine or tooted the horn to the roar of the crowd.

"Oh, I like that Mustang." Athena pointed at a canary yellow convertible as it drove by. "My parents had one of those."

"Classic car," Troy replied.

"Oh wow!" Athena exclaimed as a cherry red Corvette rolled past.

"I've always liked a Stingray, but in black," Troy remarked.

It was quite a parade of cars. Sometime later, when they returned to Troy's truck, Athena pulled out the jacket she had in her tote bag and started to put it on. Troy started the truck and looked over at her. "You don't need a jacket. I'll put on the heat." Athena nodded and returned the jacket to the tote bag. "Feel like a ride?"

"Sure." Athena sent a quick text to Aria that she was out and would chat with her tomorrow, and then she settled back in the seat as Troy pulled out onto the road.

Troy returned from the jobsite around noon on Tuesday. He took his hat off and wiped his brow. The driveway was dusty because of the extended drought the area was experiencing. They had not had significant rain in weeks. As he drove down the driveway toward his home, he saw Athena sitting on her porch. She waved. She was barefooted and dressed in shorts and a tank top. She had her hair twisted and held up by a big clip in a messy and loose bun at the back of her head. Her laptop sat on a small table in front of her, and a tall glass of iced tea sat on the other small table next to her.

"Hi," Troy said as he stopped the truck and rolled down his window. He noticed Athena had a fan blowing on her.

"Hi. You are home early."

"How is the writing going?'

"Really well. I am working on a revision," Athena replied. "But right now, I am just doing some email."

"Have you had lunch?" Troy asked.

"Not yet."

"I have some cold watermelon and chicken salad in my refrigerator if you are hungry."

"That would be nice," Athena replied. "I'll walk over."

"I'll wait."

Athena closed her laptop and put it and the fan inside then closed the door. She carried her flip flops and climbed up into the truck. Troy could not help but look at her tan legs as she sat down. His eyes continued down to her pink painted toenails. He smiled at her, put the truck in gear, and drove the very short distance to his home at the end of the driveway.

He opened the door to the house, and they went inside. "Would you like a tour?"

"Absolutely," Athena replied.

The home had two bedrooms, a full bath, a half bath, a large country kitchen, a small den, and a very large grand room with a high ceiling and a fireplace.

"This is a beautiful home, Troy," Athena said as she looked around.

"Thank you. It is comfortable."

It was definitely a man's home. The den was set up as a workout room with weights and a complicated looking exercise machine. Over the mantle in the grand room was a deer head, and on the wall with the fireplace hung several stuffed birds including a pheasant, a quail, and a woodcock. Most of the walls were painted a neutral light cream color, and the trim was dark stained wood. At the ceiling peak was a fan and several lights hung down as well. There was a large desk that held a laptop and had a comfortable looking leather desk chair in front of it. Next to the desk were two bookcases of books and assorted items, and in a corner were two filing cabinets. On another wall was a bar with three bar stools. A large flat screen TV was on the wall to one side of the fireplace and there was a leather sectional sofa and two leather easy chairs placed in front of it.

They went back into the kitchen. The open concept design made for easy conversation. "Sit down." Troy pointed to a stool in front of the kitchen island. Athena pulled herself up and continued to look around. The

135

cabinets in the kitchen were made of honey colored wood with contrasting door pulls. Some of the cabinets had glass doors, something Athena always wanted to have in her kitchen to display fine glassware. Inside one cabinet, Athena could see beer steins. She smiled; several said Wurstfest.

Troy brought out a bowl of chicken salad, a bowl of potato salad, a large bowl of watermelon, some rolls, lettuce, tomato, and pickles. He set out two plates, two forks, and two glasses, and he set a large pitcher of iced tea on the countertop then he sat down next to Athena. "Oh, forgot chips." He got up and took corn chips and tortilla chips out of a cabinet then returned to his seat.

Athena poured them each a tall glass of iced tea. "This looks good," she said as they each made a chicken salad sandwich and began to eat. "You are working nearby right now?"

"This area is growing quickly. The school system is good, and people are moving in with families."

"Do you do a lot of the construction work?"

"I am mostly a project manager," Troy said between bites. "My business partner and I subcontract majority of the work. I do some of the finish work and make some of the cabinets if it is a custom home."

"You make cabinets?"

"Yes. In fact, I made all the cabinets in this kitchen."

"Wow, they are gorgeous!" Athena appreciated the craftsmanship of the cabinetry even more now that she knew Troy made them.

"I want to concentrate on making custom cabinets in the future. I like being a project manager, and my partner and I are making a lot of money building homes, but I want to slow down and savor more of what life has to offer."

Suddenly, Troy saw himself walking in the kitchen for a drink after working outside in his shop. He poured a tall glass of iced tea, and then sat on the end of Athena's fancy desk. She looked up from working on her latest manuscript and pulled him down to her to give him a good afternoon kiss. He shook his head and cleared the vision then took a deep breath.

After they cleaned up from lunch, they took their iced teas and went out on the porch. The light breeze did little to cool them. "Would you like to go for a swim and cool off?" Troy asked.

"Yes!" Athena replied quickly. She was just thinking she needed to take another shower to cool off.

"Give me a few minutes." Troy went inside and began putting some things in a bag.

Athena opened the door and called in to him. "Troy?"

Troy looked up. "Almost ready."

"Why don't I go back to my cabin and put my suit on."

"Ok, I'll meet you there in a few minutes."

Athena closed the door, put on her flip flops, and walked up the driveway to her cabin. She quickly shaved her legs and put on her swimsuit. She did not have a cover up, so she put her shorts and tank top on over her suit. She put a hairbrush and a towel in a tote bag. She decided to wear sneakers. She did not know where they were going, but since it involved some walking, sneakers were safer than sandals.

Troy knocked on her cabin door. "Ready?"

"I'm ready."

Troy had a bag and a cooler in his hands. "Let's go." They walked up the driveway toward the stable, turned right, and headed down the trail. They walked through some trees and then came out in a field. Athena could hear water up ahead. She stayed close to Troy. She was very nervous walking through brush and high grass even if they were on a path. As they went around a large rock, something made a noise, and Athena jumped and gave a squeal.

"Are you ok?" Troy asked.

"Yeah. I'm just a little jumpy. I thought I heard a snake."

"Rattle snakes make a distinctive rattling sound," Troy said as they continued walking.

Just before they reached the river, Athena heard another rustling noise, and she instinctively grabbed Troy's arm. "Sorry," she said meekly looking up at him.

"That's ok." He smiled.

"Do you always carry a gun with you, Troy?"

"You are afraid of snakes. What are you going to do if you see one? Running won't help." Athena did not say anything. "Have you ever shot a gun?" Troy asked. Athena shook her head no.

They rounded a bend, and up ahead was a small stream. "Well, here we are." Troy put down the bag and the cooler on the small sandy area alongside the stream.

Athena looked around. She was hot, and a refreshing swim sounded good at the time. However, now, she had reservations and thought swimming might not be a great idea. Why did she agree to come?

Troy sensed her apprehension. "It's safe, Athena. We swim here all the time."

Athena watched intently as Troy took off his boots and stripped off his clothes down to his swim trunks. He was a very good-looking man. He was deeply tanned and very muscular from working construction and on the ranch. Troy noticed she watched him undress, and he smiled at her, but Athena quickly looked away.

138

She took off her sneakers, shorts, and tank top. She exercised regularly, but she was somewhat self-conscious of her body. She looked up, and Troy was smiling at her. He reached out his hand. She took it, and he led her to the water's edge. The water felt refreshingly cool, but not cold, and they slowly walked in deeper. When she was about waist deep, Troy let go of her hand and did a shallow dive under the water. Athena looked around to make sure nothing was in the area, and then she sank down, so the water covered her shoulders. She bobbed up and down in the water for a few minutes while Troy splashed around, and then finally, she went under the cool refreshing water.

She surfaced. "Ah, this feels so good." She unclipped her hair and let it fan out and float around her.

"Nothing like a swim on a hot day."

"I checked the average temperature before we left, and it has been much warmer."

"This area is in a severe drought," Troy explained. "Many ranches are suffering."

Once they were cooled off, they got out of the water, dried off, and sat down on towels at the water's edge. Troy reached into the cooler, took the cap off a Corona, popped in a lime wedge, and handed one to Athena.

"Thank you."

"You're welcome." Troy leaned back on his elbow and took a drink of his Corona. "Are you glad you stayed?"

"Yes," Athena replied. "Not only am I getting a great deal of writing done, but I am having a lot of fun." She looked at her arm. "And getting a great start on my tan."

They stretched out on the little beach and talked. They sometimes were serious and sometimes they laughed as the conversation moved from topic to topic. They talked about their childhood and shared stories about things they experienced in life.

"The ranch is beautiful, Troy."

"A few years back, we decided to reduce the number of cattle on the ranch," he explained. "The water table dropped because of the frequent droughts, and there just wasn't sufficient water. We want to keep all the land, so now we are also going to diversify."

"Diversify?"

"We're planning to lease some of the land for wind turbines."

Athena nodded. "Windfarms are clean renewable energy. Although there was controversy over proposed windfarms in my area, but more turbines are going up all the time. And if it will enable the family to keep the land, well, that is very important. I know Trevor misses being on the ranch."

"Yes, we were surprised when he decided not to go to a Texas school and go to an eastern school. But it seems to have worked out well for him."

"Have you ever been to Boston or New York?"

Troy shook his head no. "We went to his graduation in Connecticut but did not go anywhere else."

"You should visit sometime," Athena suggested.

Troy looked at her. There was a reason to visit now. "I think I will."

They wiled away the afternoon talking and occasionally taking a dip in the cool water. It was nearly six o'clock when they walked back to the house. Maria was busy in the kitchen preparing dinner. She looked up from cleaning a bunch leaf lettuce from her garden and saw Troy and Athena walking up the trail. Troy was shirtless and wearing swimming trunks, and Athena had on a pair of shorts over her swimsuit. Her hair was casually up in a ponytail. Maria saw Athena laugh at something and take Troy's arm.

She shook her head. She liked Athena, but she wondered how two very different people who lived on opposite ends of the country could possibly make a relationship work. However, she had not seen Troy look so happy in a long time, and his happiness was important to her.

She continued to watch them as they turned and went toward Athena's cabin. Would Troy go in the cabin? She was not sure she wanted to know, but she kept watching. They approached the cabin. Maria leaned closer to the window. She held her breath. Athena stepped up on the porch. And Troy kept walking toward his home. Maria breathed a sigh of relief.

"What are you looking at?' John asked.

Maria screamed and jumped. "Don't sneak up on me like that," she said in a breathless voice.

John looked at his wife. "Didn't you hear me come in the front door?"

"No, I didn't." She went back to washing the vegetables.

John shook his head and left the kitchen.

Chapter 12

"Good morning," Athena greeted Maria as she entered the kitchen.

"Good morning. Have you had breakfast?" Maria sat at the kitchen table having coffee before going to work.

Athena blushed. "Actually, Troy brought me a breakfast sandwich this morning."

"Oh, how nice of him."

"Yes, it was a surprise. He said he was making breakfast, and when he looked out his window, he saw me sitting on the porch drinking tea. So, he brought over breakfast sandwiches, and we ate, and watched the sunrise."

"You were up early then."

"I fell asleep earlier than normal last night, so I woke up early this morning." Maria nodded her head. "Troy seems to get up very early." Athena felt uncharacteristically nervous.

"Yes, construction starts early because of the afternoon heat." She saw Athena had a bag of laundry in her hand. "Did you want to use the washing machine?"

"Yes, thank you."

Maria stood up and took a load of clothes out of the dryer. "It is all yours."

"Thank you."

Maria went back to her coffee, and Athena put the clothes in the machine and started it. When she went back in the kitchen, Maria stood at the sink washing out her coffee mug. "Well, I am off to the school in a few minutes. There are some ripe tomatoes on the vine if you want to pick them for lunch," Maria suggested.

"Your tomatoes are delicious, Maria. Thank you."

"You have a good day, Athena."

"You too, Maria. Thanks again." Athena went back to her cabin. She planned to take the clothes out of the washer and hang them to dry after her shower, and then she planned to write the rest of the morning.

About noon, Athena stood up and stretched. She completed some revisions, updated her blog, and responded to student emails. She walked out on the porch and looked around, mostly for Troy's truck. She hoped he would come home soon. They had a relaxing and enjoyable afternoon yesterday, and part of her thrilled to the idea of doing something this afternoon too. She felt very comfortable with Troy, and she found him interesting and very different than what she expected the first time she met him.

She put on her flip flops and walked over to the house to get her dry laundry. She returned to her cabin and folded and put away the clothes then went to her kitchenette and cut up a couple fresh tomatoes from Maria's garden. They were vine ripened and dark red and juicy, perfect for a salad. She cut up a cucumber and added it to the bowl then added some black olives and chopped red onion. She topped it with a liberal amount of feta cheese and sprinkled on some salt, pepper, olive oil, and a dash of vinegar. She spooned salad into a small bowl, poured a tall glass of iced tea, and went out to the porch to eat.

A few minutes later, Troy pulled in the driveway. He hoped Athena would not be busy this afternoon. He wanted to get out of work earlier, but there were a few details to go over at the job site. Athena heard the truck and looked up. "Hi," she said with a smile when he stopped in front of her cabin.

"Hi, taking a break?" Troy looked at her and smiled. She had her bare feet up on one of the chairs, and she wore short shorts and an off the shoulder white top that set off her tan and showed off her smooth bare shoulders. She was getting quite tan from the Texas sun, and her skin had a healthy sun kissed glow.

She nodded yes. "Would you like a bowl of salad? I also have some cold cuts for a sandwich."

"Sure, thanks. A salad and sandwich sound good." He turned off the truck and got out.

"Come inside," she said. He watched her walk as he followed her in the cabin.

"Would you like a turkey sandwich? I have a roll."

"Thanks." Troy smiled. He knew Athena rarely ate rolls. She must have gotten one from the house in anticipation of him stopping by for lunch, and this pleased him immensely. He liked spending time with her, and the more he got to know her, the more interested he became in her. She was accomplished, competent, and fun to be with when she let herself relax and enjoy the moment.

"You can wash up in the bathroom while I prepare a sandwich." He went into the bathroom and washed his hands and face. "Mayo, lettuce, and tomato on your sandwich?" Athena called to him.

Troy leaned out the bathroom door. "Yes, please."

Athena prepared a turkey and cheese sandwich, and she put salad in a bowl for Troy. She refilled her bowl with salad and poured two glasses of iced tea.

Troy came out of the bathroom. "It looks good. I'm starving."

"Shall we eat in here or out on the porch?"

"The porch." He helped her carry everything out to the small tables.

"Busy day at the job site today?" Athena asked as they ate.

"It certainly was. We can go weeks without a problem and then something will come up. We need to get this house finished. It's already sold." Troy took a bite of his sandwich. "This is good."

Athena smiled. "You recently closed on a house, and you have another sold already?"

"Yes, this one is due to close the end of May."

While they talked, Maria drove up the driveway and came to a stop in front of the main house. She looked over and saw Troy and Athena sitting on Athena's cabin porch. They were so deeply involved in their conversation with one another that they did not notice her. She stared at them for a few minutes. She was not sure how she felt about them spending so much time together, but she decided not to call to them and carried in her bag of groceries.

Troy helped Athena bring in the dishes and wrap up the left-over salad. She put it in her little refrigerator. He leaned on the counter as she washed the dishes. "Do you feel like going for a ride?'

"Where?"

"Just around."

"Ok. Is what I am wearing ok, or should I change clothes?'

"You should put on a short-sleeved shirt, pants, and sneakers. I'll go change and be right back."

145

"Ok." She wondered where he planned to take her. Athena went into the bathroom and washed up, brushed her teeth, and combed her hair. She twisted her hair up and secured it with a big clip. She put a white long-sleeved shirt into her tote bag with her wristlet. She slipped into a pair of jeans and put on a light pink tee shirt then she put on socks and sneakers. She applied some mascara and lip gloss, picked up her cowboy hat and her tote bag, closed the door, and sat on the porch to wait for Troy. He pulled up alongside her cabin and opened the passenger door. She pulled herself up into the truck. She had to stretch to close the door, then she put on her seat belt as he drove down the driveway and out onto the road.

Maria looked out when she heard the truck and saw Troy and Athena driving off. She hoped they knew what they were doing. "Hi Mom," Dan called as he came into the kitchen. "I just saw Troy and Athena driving out. Where are they going?"

"I don't know," Maria replied curtly.

"They sure are spending a lot of time together. I'm going to change and head to work at the lumber yard."

"Ok," Maria grunted then let out a sigh.

"So where are we going?" Athena asked.

"You will see," Troy replied with a grin. He wore a dark blue tee shirt that stretched snuggly over his arms and chest. Athena could see his muscles flexing as he drove, and she caught herself staring at him as he reached over to adjust the radio. She turned her head and looked straight ahead. Troy noticed her watching him and smiled to himself as he turned on the radio. "My guess is you don't listen to country music," he said as he went through the radio stations.

"Not usually."

146

"What about classic rock?"

"I listen to a classic rock station at home."

They drove for about forty-five minutes then Troy turned onto another road. Athena looked at the road sign, and then she looked again. "RM? What does that mean? Is that a road name?"

"RM stands for Ranch to Market." Troy explained. "There are also RR, Ranch to Ranch, and FM Farm to Market roads. They are typically narrower and windier roads that are primarily in the rural areas."

"That is interesting.'"

Next, Troy turned off the Ranch to Market road and onto a long and narrower road that said, 'Private Way Keep Out'.

Athena looked around. The land was flat and aside from a few isolated buildings, there did not seem to be anything in sight. "Where are we?" she asked.

"You will see in a moment."

Up ahead she could see a house, and she could hear gun shots. Troy pulled in the parking lot behind the larger building. "Want to learn to shoot?"

Athena opened her mouth to speak then closed it. Finally, she squeaked out, "Ok."

"Great." Troy got out of the truck and hurried around to the passenger's side to help Athena out. He moved the seat forward and took out a gun case and a bag. Athena was a little apprehensive, but she was willing to try it.

"Hey, Troy," a tall, skinny, younger man with blonde hair said as they went inside the club house.

"Brandon, how are you, man?" They shook hands. "This is Athena. I'm going to teach her to shoot."

Athena and Brandon shook hands. "Nice to meet you, Ma'am," he said.

"Nice to meet you," Athena replied.

Brandon looked at Troy and then at Athena. "Where are you from Ma'am?"

"It's that obvious?' Athena laughed.

"It is as soon as you speak," Troy laughed.

Brandon looked a little uncomfortable. "I'm from Massachusetts," she told him with a smile. She did not want him to think she was upset that he asked where she lived.

"Is anyone on field one?"

"No, it's a slow day. It's all yours," Brandon replied.

"Great," Troy looked at Athena. "Are you ready?'"

She took a deep breath. "As ready as I will ever be," she replied as she followed him outside.

"Good luck," Brandon called to her, and she waved.

"I'm going to have you shoot at some clay targets," Troy explained. He took the shotgun out of the case and set in on the gun rack. He took glasses, a package of foam ear plugs, and a shooting vest out of another bag. "Put this on," he said to her as he handed her the vest.

Athena put it on, but it was very big on her body. Troy took binder clips out of the bag. He went behind her, pulled back the extra material and fastened it with the clips. She put on the glasses, and she put the ear plugs in her ears. Troy also put on glasses and ear plugs then he picked up a box of shot gun shells and led her to the middle of the field.

"Ok. First, I will demonstrate how to hold the gun, and then I am going to have you just shoot the gun, so you can get a feel for it. This is a 20-gauge shot gun. The recoil is pretty light."

Athena nodded and watched. Troy opened the gun, inserted two shells, closed the gun, and put it to his shoulder. He pulled the trigger twice.

"Ok your turn." Without any ammunition in the gun, he first showed her how to hold it. The gun was not too heavy, but her arms did get tired. She shook them out.

"Are you ready to try shooting it?"

"I think so," Athena replied hesitantly.

Troy went behind her. She opened the gun and he dropped in one shell. "Now keep your finger away from the trigger until you are ready," he explained.

Athena put the gun to her shoulder. "Ok, now put your finger on the trigger, take a breath, and then squeeze the trigger." Athena did as he instructed. Bang. She lowered the gun and looked at him. Her heart was beating fast.

"Want to do it again?"

"Absolutely." She shot the gun several more times.

"Ok. Are you ready to try to hit a clay target?"

She nodded yes. "I will try."

Troy led her over to the building on the right side of the field. "We are on a Skeet field and this is station seven. There are seven stations in a semicircle and one at the half-way point between stations one and seven. A person shoots at targets thrown from the two houses at either end. Station seven low house is fairly easy, so we will start there." Troy picked up a black cord and handed it to Athena. When I say pull, I want you to push this button, and a target will come out of the house." He pushed it to show her.

"Ok, simple enough."

Troy got into position, loaded a shell into the gun, and said, 'Pull'. Athena pushed the button, and the target came flying out. Troy shot and broke it.

"So, when the target comes out, you move the gun up slightly until the target looks like it is sitting on the end of the gun barrel then you pull the trigger." He demonstrated again. "Your turn."

Athena stepped into the station. Troy released a target for her to see. She took a deep breath. She opened the gun and dropped in a shell, closed the gun, and brought it to her shoulder. She called pull, and the target flew out. She quickly pulled the trigger and missed the target.

"That's ok," Troy said. "I did not expect you to hit it the first time. Try again."

Athena nodded and repeated the process. By the fourth try, she hit the target. She watched it break into several pieces. "I can't believe I hit it," she said to Troy as she lowered the gun.

"Try again."

Athena hit the target a couple more times, but her arms were getting tired, so she handed the gun to Troy. "You know, this is a lot of fun."

"I'm glad you enjoyed it." They walked back to the gun rack, and Troy packed everything up. Athena looked around and took some pictures. There were people shooting on the next field, and she watched as one of them shot and broke targets.

"You know, Skeet shooting originated in Massachusetts," Troy commented as they walked toward the club house.

"It did?" Athena asked, and Troy nodded yes.

They went inside. "How did you like it?" Brandon asked Athena. "I saw you hit a couple targets."

"I really enjoyed shooting. I didn't think I would enjoy it, but I did," she said with a chuckle.

"Maybe you will come back and shoot again," Brandon said.

"I would like to come back." Athena smiled at him then she went to the ladies' room, washed her hands, and splashed water on her face to cool off.

When she came out, Troy was talking to Brandon and the people she saw shooting. Troy introduced her to the other men.

"We are always happy to have a new shooter," one of the older men said as he shook her hand. "Come back again."

"Thank you."

"Are you ready?" Troy asked.

"Yes." Athena waved to Brandon and the others. "It was nice to meet you."

"Good-bye." Brandon waved.

They left the building and went back to the truck. Troy loaded the gear in behind the seat and helped Athena up. He got in and started the truck. "I'm really glad you had fun," he said as he drove down the private road and then back onto the Ranch to Market road.

"I really liked it. Thank you."

"Would you like an ice cream?"

"I would," Athena laughed.

Troy pulled into a Dairy Bar, and they went inside. He ordered a large hot fudge sundae with nuts, and Athena got a small hot fudge sundae without nuts. "Wow, expanding your menu," he said with a bit a sarcasm, but Athena just rolled her eyes at him.

"I'm actually hungry," she said.

They got back in the truck and drove back to the ranch. Athena looked at her phone, it was almost seven o'clock. "Oh, we should have called your mother. She might be holding dinner."

"I did," Troy replied. "When you were in the ladies' room at the club."

"Oh good," Athena said in relief. She could imagine Maria pacing the kitchen and wondering where they were.

"Are you still hungry?"

"That was a big ice cream, but I am hungry." She laughed. "It must be all the fresh air.

"I'll put some cheeseburgers on the grill. How does that sound?"

"That sounds good." Athena looked at Troy as he drove. She could imagine herself with him. They got along so well and being with Troy felt easy.

Troy drove past the main house. No one was outside. He pulled up to his house and went around to help Athena down.

They worked together to prepare dinner. Athena made a salad and sliced up tomatoes for the hamburgers. Troy took chips and hamburger buns out of the cabinet. He opened a can of ranch beans.

Athena looked at the can. "I have never had these beans."

"They are good. I think you will like them. The beans are in a tangy tomato based sauce." He put them in a container and microwaved them.

Athena took mayonnaise and mustard out of the refrigerator.

"Corona?" he asked.

"Yes, thank you."

They brought everything outside. Athena set the table while Troy started to grill the meat.

When the meat was cooked, they sat down to dinner. There was a very gentle breeze, and the ranch was quiet. It seemed like they were alone in the world as they sat side by side and watched the sunset.

Troy looked over at Athena. The slanting rays of the sun shone on her hair and face. She certainly was beautiful, but she was also smart, confident, adventurous, and absolutely everything he wanted in a woman.

Chapter 13

The weekend arrived, and Athena felt energized, relaxed, and very happy. She saw Troy walking toward her cabin from the stable. They had been spending quite a bit of time together. She liked him … a lot. But she still worried because he was going to be Aria's brother-in-law. She sighed, it wasn't only that, it was the distance, and she just had too much going on right now for a romance.

"Morning Athena" he said as he approached her.

Still, all concerns seemed to disappear when she heard his deep voice say her name. "Good morning." She smiled at him.

Troy smiled too. Athena leaned back in the chair on the porch. Her hair was up in a bun on her head. Tendrils of hair escaped the large clip and fell softly on her shoulders. Her skin was golden, and she wore a very skimpy spaghetti strap top and shorts.

"Have you had your breakfast?"

Athena shook her head no. "Not yet."

"Are you hungry?" Troy asked.

"Actually, I am," she laughed.

Troy stepped up on the porch. "What are you going to eat? There's bacon in the kitchen."

"I think I will have a bowl of cereal."

He held out his hand, and she took it. He pulled her up, and Athena slipped her feet into her flip flops. "Have you finished the book?" Troy asked as they walked to the main house.

"Yes," Athena said with a big sigh. "I emailed the manuscript off late last night," she paused, "actually, early this morning."

"Your editor won't get it until Monday."

Athena laughed. "You don't know Ellen. She's probably reading it already."

"She works on Saturday?"

"She works all the time." Athena took the box of fruity cereal out of the pantry. She poured herself a bowl. "Would you like a bowl, Troy?"

"No thanks."

Athena poured in the cold fresh farm milk and started to eat. "Fresh, full fat milk makes such a difference," she said between bites.

Troy nodded. "Since you're finished writing, I thought you might like to go for a horseback ride today."

Athena smiled. "Yes, I would love a ride."

"Good." Troy went to the refrigerator, took out a package of lunch meat, and made sandwiches. "I thought we would also have a picnic."

"That sounds fun." Athena finished her cereal and went to the sink to clean the bowl and put it in the dishwasher. "I will make a salad." She took a fresh tomato out of the bowl on the counter. "I'm really going to miss these tomatoes. We won't have garden fresh tomatoes for a couple of months."

They worked side by side preparing a picnic lunch. Troy went to the stable and brought back two saddle bags. They put the food and some ice packs inside one bag. Troy added some bottles of Corona to a small soft sided cooler and put it inside the other saddle bag.

"I'll go get dressed for riding," Athena said.

"I'll get the horses ready and meet you at the stable."

Athena hurried back to her cabin and put on jeans and a tank top. To protect her arms, she also put on a long-sleeved shirt. She wished she had cowboy boots, but she had not owned cowboy boots in years. She put on her sneakers, and then she brushed her hair and put it in a ponytail. She washed her face, and she brushed her teeth. She looked in the mirror, at her lovely golden brown tan and decided she did not need any make up She put her phone in her pants pocket, picked up her camera bag and her hat, and walked to the stable to meet Troy.

He had the horses ready when she arrived, so they mounted the horses and slowly made their way out of the stable. They followed the trail through the low growing Live Oak trees that surrounded the area by the main house and other buildings. It was cooler on the trail thru the trees, but then Troy veered off onto a smaller trail that went due West. "Remember I said we were branching out and leasing land?"

"Yes," Athena replied.

"I'm going to show you where the wind turbines will be located."

They rode for some time. The trail disappeared, and the landscape grew increasingly barren. The trees were gone, and there was mostly scrub brush. The horses plod along carefully sometimes kicking up loose rocks as they walked. The land started to rise up a small hill. It was rocky and there was just a little dry grass blowing in the hot wind. "Here we are," Troy said. "Dad took the owners up here a couple weeks ago, and they approved the site."

Athena nodded. She remembered seeing John and some men riding off together. It was hot. Athena took off her hat and wiped her brow with a tissue. She squinted and looked out over the arid landscape. There were a few yucca plants, but primarily the vegetation consisted of prickly pear cacti and dry scrub bush. There were several tiny dust devils swirling nearby. The dryness tickled her nose, and when she licked her lips to wet them, she tasted dust.

"There will be a number of wind turbines up on this hill." Troy settled in his saddle and waved his arm wide.

Athena shielded her eyes and looked out over the desolate landscape. Not that far above them a turkey vulture scanned the land in search of food.

"The family is relying on its success to enable us to keep this part of the ranch." He sighed and shook his head. "I would hate to see condos and shopping malls here."

"You said the town is growing," Athena commented. "Is there any industry besides ranching?"

"No, people commute to work around here, but they want to live in the country and raise their children," Troy explained. "Most of this part of Texas has been ranch country since Texas was a territory, and at one time, we ran cattle here. However, with the extended drought, there isn't enough for them to eat or enough water to drink."

The wind whistled as it blew across the hill. Movement caught Athena's eye, and she turned to see a jack rabbit emerge from a hole. She quickly snapped a few pictures before it hopped away. Troy turned his horse, and Athena followed. As they rode, the grass became greener and there were larger shrubs. Athena realized they circled around and were at the stream where they swam. She recognized the large Live Oak tree and the sandy beach area. They led the horses to the water, so they could drink.

"Are you hungry?" Troy asked.

"Starved!"

They got down off the horses, and Troy undid the saddles and put them on the ground. He tied the horses under a tree and took the saddle bags over to a shady spot by the stream. Athena spread out several towels. She peeled off the long-sleeved shirt she had over the tank top, removed her shoes, and rolled up her jeans to her knees. Troy took off his shirt. They sat down on the towels, and he started to take out the food and the drinks.

Athena watched him and smiled at how comfortable they were together in such a short period of time. It felt as if they knew each other for years. She originally thought they were very different people, but as they talked, she realized they shared many of the same values and ideas. Troy passed her a sandwich and a Corona.

"The water should be much deeper at this time of year. We didn't get Spring rains yet again." He took a bite of his sandwich.

"The weather is certainly changing. We are seeing stronger and more frequent storms in the Northeast."

"Is your house on the water?"

"No, it's a couple blocks from the ocean. People who own homes on the shoreline have been struggling with storm surge damage and general erosion."

They ate sandwiches and salad, then leaned back and finished their Coronas. They were quiet and listened to the sound of the water. It was peaceful, and Athena lazily pushed her toes into the sand and daydreamed.

"Want to take a dip?" Troy asked.

"I didn't wear a suit." Athena sounded disappointed. The sun reflected off the water, and it looked so inviting.

"Neither did I." Troy took off his hat and boots. Then he stood up and unbuckled his jeans. Athena just stared at him in wonder. "Underwear is like a bathing suit," he said as he stepped out of his jeans and ran into the stream. "Refreshing!" he exclaimed as he slid under the water. He swam around, and she sat there watching him. "Are you coming in?" he called.

Athena thought about it. She felt extremely hot, and the water looked delightfully cool. She reasoned with herself that a tank top and panties was sort of like a swimsuit. She slipped her bra off without taking off her tank top. She stood up and took off her jeans. She wore lacy panties that left little to the imagination, so she pulled the tank top down as far as possible, then she walked into the water. This time, she went right under the water to cool off. "Oh, this feels so good."

The water twinkled with sunlight, and there was the faintest hint of a breeze. What Athena marveled at the most was the quiet. She closed her eyes, and the only sounds she heard was the moving water and an occasional bird call. No noise of people, cars, or airplanes. Just nature.

They bobbed and swam around for a while. When she started to get cold, Athena walked out of the water, and laid on one of the towels. Troy walked up and laid down on a towel next to her. They closed their eyes, relished the warmth of the sun, and just listened to the sound of the moving water. Troy took more Coronas out of the cooler and passed one to Athena. It was a pleasant way to spend the day.

When they were mostly dry, Troy saddled the horses, and they rode back toward the stable.

"Would you like to go out to dinner with me tonight, Athena?" Troy asked.

Athena looked at him. Was he asking her out on a date? They had been spending a lot of time together, but this felt like he was asking her on

159

a real date. She should say no. This was not going to work she reasoned with herself. "I'd love to," she replied despite her doubts.

"Six o'clock?" Troy asked. Athena nodded, yes. "I will let Mom know we will be out for dinner."

When they reached the stable, Athena helped Troy hang up the gear, and then went back to her cabin and took a quick shower. She decided to wear the white lacy dress. She dressed it up with gold hoop earrings and a plain gold chain, and she changed her purse to the dressy one she brought with her for Easter. She had limited accessories with her, but when she looked in the mirror, she smiled at herself. She took her white bolero sweater with her in case the restaurant was cold.

Then she heard Troy's truck stop in front of her cabin. She heard him get out of his truck and walk up on the porch. Athena had butterflies in her stomach, and she checked her appearance again in the mirror.

Troy knocked on the door. She took a deep breath and let it out slowly, and then she opened the door and smiled. He wore a grey suit and a white shirt, and he looked so very handsome.

"You look beautiful," Troy said to Athena. He could not help but stare at her. He had never met anyone like her before. Troy extended his hand, Athena took it, and they left the cabin. He helped her up into the truck then went around to the driver's side, got in, and started it up. As they drove by the house, they waved good-bye to Maria and Dan who were sitting on the porch.

"Hey, Mom. Where's Troy and Athena going now?" Dan asked.

"He's taking Athena out to dinner," she replied without looking at him.

"He was wearing a suit!" Dan shook his head. "He must really be trying to impress her." Maria stood up and went into the kitchen. Dan followed her. She started putting dinner on the table.

John came in the kitchen. "I just saw Troy and Athena. They goin' out to dinner?"

Maria nodded and did not look up.

"He's all dressed up for his city girl," Dan laughed.

John gave his son a stern look, and Dan's smile faded. John rarely got angry with his sons. They were grown men, and he did not like to interfere. "I think that's enough," John said firmly.

Maria let out a deep sigh.

Dan looked from his father to his mother. "Mom," he said, "Don't worry about Troy. He will be fine. You know I was just joking around."

Maria did not reply. She put sausages on a platter. Dan took the platter of sausages from her and set it on the table. He joked and liked to tease Troy, but he was also worried about him getting hurt. Athena was a nice woman, and he did not think she would intentionally hurt his brother, but she was not a country girl, and she lived a long way from Texas.

Chapter 14

"I made reservations at a restaurant on the lake," Troy said as he drove. He wanted to get out of town where they could relax and not run into anyone. He had a feeling Dan might come look for them or worse Kevin.

"It is a nice evening for a drive," Athena added.

Troy turned on the radio, and they chatted as he drove. Finally, he slowed down and turned right down a driveway. "I think you will like this restaurant. It has grown in recent years, so it is a little touristy, but the food is good, the drinks are strong, and the view is," he paused, "well, you will see the view."

Troy pulled into the valet parking area. He took the card the attendant handed him and went around the truck and took Athena's hand. The entrance was crowded with people waiting for a table. Troy gave the hostess his name, and she said the table would be available in ten minutes. They walked to the bar to get drinks while they waited. The bar was long and wide, and it had a stone façade. Across from the bar were two comfortable looking chairs placed in front of the stone hearth, but no fire burned on this warm night.

"What would you like?" Troy asked.

"What are you having?"

"Margarita."

"Sounds good." Athena looked around the spacious bar packed with patrons, mostly couples and several groups of college students. Some people were dressed up, but many wore jeans or shorts and a shirt. A few minutes later, the hostess called Troy's name, and then she led them to their table. The décor of the restaurant was rustic with a variety of stone accents. They walked out on the patio, and Athena's eyes widened, and her breath caught. She looked up and down, left, and right, and everywhere she looked, she saw decks with a great many people on each one. The restaurant was built into the side of a cliff high up over the lake. The sun was beginning to set, and it reflected off the water. "The view is breathtaking," Athena whispered.

Troy pulled the chairs around, so they could sit side by side and look at the sunset. They sat, sipping margaritas, and admiring the view for some time.

"Everything I have seen go by looks and smells so delicious," Athena said. "What do you recommend?"

"Should we order a couple different things and share?" Troy asked. Athena nodded yes, so Troy placed their order.

The waitress brought another round of margaritas, and she set down a bowl of tortilla chips and a bowl of salsa. Troy and Athena dipped a chip each in the salsa and took a bite. "Wow, that's hot," Athena said, but she dipped another chip into the salsa.

The sunset deepened with dark red and orange, and the water and the surroundings reflected the fiery intense color. Athena took out her phone and took a couple pictures. "Excuse me," she said as she stood up and went over to the rail to take more pictures.

She returned to the table and sat down. "Thank you," she said to Troy as she placed her hand on his. "This is so beautiful."

Troy looked into Athena's eyes. He longed to kiss her. He thought this might be the right time, and he started to lean toward her. She leaned toward him, but before they kissed, their dinner arrived.

The waitstaff set bowls of food on the table. There was a large platter of spiced chicken which was steaming and smelled delicious. There were bowls of refried beans, guacamole, onions, shredded cheese, and chopped lettuce and tomato. There were also two tortilla baskets of soft, warm, flour tortillas, and there was a large platter of grilled Cajun shrimp.

"Wow," was all Athena could say. She took a few pictures of the food. Troy opened one of the tortilla baskets, and Athena took out a tortilla. Troy took one, and they started to fill their tortilla with beans, meat, cheese, and condiments. Athena added just a little bit of salsa and rolled up her tortilla. She took a bite and sighed. "This is so good."

"I am glad you like it," Troy said as he took another bite of his tortilla.

Athena had a second tortilla, and she lost count of how many shrimp she ate.

As the sky began to darken, the staff lit torches to supplement the soft lighting. The waitress brought another round of margaritas. "They have delicious desserts here," Troy said as he leaned back.

Athena shook her head no. "Not for me."

"Me neither." Troy smiled at her. "We will have to come back another time and just get dessert."

"I would like that very much."

After dinner, they took their drinks and sat at the bar. A band played country music, and they talked and occasionally danced. It was well after midnight when they got back to the ranch. Troy parked the truck and walked Athena to her cabin.

"I had a wonderful time today," Athena said. "Thank you for dinner."

"I had a great time too."

She opened the cabin door and turned to him. Troy leaned toward her, and finally they kissed. They kissed again. And again. Athena wrapped her arms around Troy's neck, and he lifted her up and deepened the kiss. Troy held her tight as they continued to devour one another.

Finally, Athena leaned back, and Troy set her feet on the floor. "Good night," she said softly. She turned and went inside her cabin.

"Good night." Troy smiled as he walked off the porch.

Late Sunday afternoon, Athena noticed that once again a very gentle breeze blew easing the temperature. The quiet surrounded her, and the only sound was of a bee buzzing at a nearby flower. John and Maria went to the store, Dan went home with Shelby and Danny to eat dinner, and Troy was at his home down the end of the driveway. They all had lunch, and then they took Danny out for ice cream. Athena enjoyed being in Texas. It was definitely the change and the serenity she needed to finish the manuscript, but she also felt oddly at home here. She was also extremely conflicted in her feelings for Troy. She enjoyed being with him, but there were so many complications.

She put on her flip flops and went outside. She shook her hair and let the light breeze catch it, then she started to walk around the garden and continued to think about Troy. They spent a lot of time together the past couple of weeks, but part of her was afraid of a relationship with him. He was going to be her daughter's brother-in-law, and they lived on opposite ends of the country. A relationship was simply not practical she told herself over and over again, yet a relationship was what she wanted.

Troy saw Athena walking around outside. He stood and watched her for a while. He admitted to himself that he liked her. He let out a breath. Who was he kidding, he more than liked her. He wanted her, and he could see himself with her long into the future. He enjoyed spending time with her and talking to her. He knew she enjoyed his company, but something held her back; he felt the hesitancy. He gazed at her and thought how he did not want to say good-bye to her when she returned home in a couple days.

He watched Athena walk over to the Mesquite tree and sit down on the swing that hung from one of its thick branches. She looked deep in thought as she started to swing a little higher. She wore short black shorts and the white off the shoulder shirt he liked so much. Her hair was down, and it flowed behind her and fluttered in the breeze as she swung back and forth. Her flip flops fell from her feet, and she continued to swing.

Athena felt so happy and so carefree as she swung back and forth. As a child she loved to swing on the swing set in her back yard, and this brought back many fond memories of carefree childhood days. Finally, she jumped off the swing, landed on the ground, and screamed.

Troy jumped. He ran out of the house to her. Athena sat on the ground holding her foot. "What happened? Did you hurt your ankle?" Troy called as he ran up to her.

She shook her head no. "I stepped on something." There were tears running down her face. "It really hurts."

Troy reached her and looked at the bottom of her foot. "It's a mesquite thorn." He helped her stand on one foot, and then he picked her up in one easy motion. "Hang on. I will get it out and make sure the puncture is clean. Mesquite thorns are fibrous." Athena wrapped her arms around his neck as he hurried toward his home.

Troy opened the door and brought Athena inside. He carried her to the kitchen table and set her down. "Stay right there. I'm going to get tweezers and peroxide."

Athena's foot burned and hurt. She nodded and closed her eyes. Troy returned quickly. He put peroxide on a gauze pad then grasped the thorn and pulled it out of her foot. Athena gasped, but pulling the thorn relieved the pressure and burning sensation, so it actually felt better. She let out a sigh.

Troy picked up an eye loop. "Lean back so I can lift your leg. I have to make sure all of the thorn is out." Athena leaned back, and Troy checked her foot. He pulled out a few fibers with the tweezers and then cleaned the puncture wound with the peroxide. "It's all out," he announced.

Athena looked at the thorn on the gauze pad. "That is some thorn."

"Mesquite thorns are tough and sharp, needle-like."

Troy helped her down off the table. Her foot was tender, so he pulled out a chair for her to sit down.

"Thanks for helping me," Athena said.

"Anytime. Have you eaten dinner?"

She shook her head, no. "Not yet. I was going to make a salad."

"I was going to make a cheeseburger. Want one?"

"Yes. Thank you. Can I help?" She started to stand up, but she wobbled a bit.

"You sit," Troy said. "Your foot is sensitive."

Athena sat down and watched him. He took hamburger patties out of the refrigerator, and then he went out on the porch and turned on the grill. He came back in and took out mayonnaise, mustard, and lettuce. He took a

167

tomato out of the bowl on the counter. "You can slice the tomato," he said to Athena. He set the tomato, a cutting board, and a knife on the table near her. He went back outside, put the meat on the grill, and set a timer.

Troy took a bag of potato chips out of a cabinet and set it on the table. Athena looked at the name on the bag and then looked at Troy. "Mesquite bar-be-que?" she said with a note of sarcasm.

"Ironic," Troy replied with a smile. He put cheese on the meat, toasted the buns, and brought them to the table. He took two Coronas out of the refrigerator, opened the bottles, popped in lime wedges, and handled one to Athena. "Cheers," he said.

"Cheers." They touched bottles and drank.

"These burgers are delicious." Athena smiled at Troy. "I like a man who can bar-be-que."

"Thank you."

After dinner, Troy suggested a movie. Athena hobbled over to look at his movie collection. He had a lot of action and sci-fi movies. She selected, Rogue One, one of the Star Wars movies.

"Good choice." Troy set a bowl of popcorn and two more beers on the coffee table. They settled side by side on the couch, ate popcorn, and watched the movie. Then they put on a second movie. They both fell asleep while watching the third movie.

Troy woke up and looked around. Athena was fast asleep next to him. Her head rested lightly on his shoulder. Her breathing was even, and she looked content and stunningly beautiful. He wanted to kiss her so badly. He smoothed back her hair, and she opened her eyes and smiled at him.

"We fell asleep again," she said.

"We did." Troy continued to smooth her hair. "At least we are inside this time." He looked into her dark brown eyes and leaned closer to her seeking her permission. He wanted her so badly. He never wanted a woman as he did Athena.

She leaned toward him and lifted her chin. She watched his face as he pulled her close. She felt the warmth of his body, and she could see the need in his eyes. As his lips met hers, she closed her eyes. He kissed her softly then kissed her again. Her lips parted slightly, and he deepened the kiss.

Athena reached up, pulled Troy to her, and kissed him back. There was fire in the kiss, and he responded with a sense of urgency. Troy wrapped his arms around her. He ran his hands up and down her back. His touch sent tiny shock waves through her body.

They continued to kiss for quite some time touching and caressing one another as their needs and desires took over. Each kiss held more passionate than the one before. Athena tilted her head back, and Troy kissed his way down her neck as he removed her shirt and bra. He kissed her breasts, and she moaned softly.

Athena unbuttoned Troy's shirt and slid it off him. Her hands roamed over his strong muscular back, and her body molded to his.

Troy's hands found the button of her shorts, and he slowly undressed her as he kissed his way down her body. With effort, he controlled the burning desire within him. He wanted to be slow and gentle with Athena despite his raging needs. His hands caressed her body, and soon she was moaning and twisting beneath him. Athena closed her eyes, ran her fingers through his hair, and enjoyed the sensations. Her breathing was as ragged as his.

He stood up and finished undressing as she watched. He could see the desire in her eyes. He carefully positioned himself above her and kissed her. She whispered his name as she ran her hands over his chest and around his back drawing him down to her. Troy slid his hands underneath her slender body and kissed her passionately. A sigh escaped them both as their bodies joined and became one.

They made love and explored one another's body both finding pleasure and release. He whispered passionate words in her ear as their breathing returned to normal.

Troy kissed Athena softly, smoothed her hair back off her face, and looked deep into her eyes. He never felt like this about anyone before. In one swift movement, he stood up, picked her up off the couch, and carried her into his bedroom. He laid her gently on the bed, and she reached up for him.

"I want you, Troy," she whispered. That was all he needed to hear, and his mouth devoured hers. This time he let his urgent desire for her take control. Athena's body felt tingly, and she moaned softly as they lost themselves in their passion for one another once again.

The aroma of cooking bacon woke Athena. She looked around. She was in Troy's bed. She smiled as she remembered how they made love, and then fell asleep in each other's arms. Part of her wondered what she was doing, and the other part of her did not care because being with Troy made her so very happy.

Troy heard her stir, and he looked in the bedroom door. "Good morning. Hungry?"

"Very hungry," Athena said with a laugh.

"Breakfast is almost ready. There are fresh towels in the cabinet in the bathroom if you want to freshen up."

Athena sat up, took a deep breath, and then stood up carefully.

"How is your foot feeling?"

"It's ok, but still a bit tender."

Troy went back into the kitchen. Athena walked carefully to the bathroom. She washed up and looked in the mirror. She ran her fingers through her hair. "What am I doing?" she asked herself out loud. She took a deep breath and let it out slowly.

It was a cool morning, and as she walked out of the bathroom, she reached for Troy's shirt that hung on the back of a chair. She put the shirt on, rolled up the sleeves, slid on her panties, and went in the kitchen.

Troy wore lounge pants and was shirtless while he stood by the stove scrambling up eggs. There was a pile of bacon on a platter on the table. He even made her a cup of tea.

"It smells good in here."

Troy turned around and looked at Athena standing in his kitchen dressed in his shirt. She looked so sexy. I can get used to this, he thought to himself. He smiled and stared a bit too long, then he composed himself, put the eggs into a bowl, and put the bowl on the table.

They sat down, and Troy opened the tortilla basket. Athena reached in and took out a warm flour tortilla. "I have never eaten so many tortillas as I have since I have been here. But these are so much better than the ones I get at home." Athena scooped up some eggs and put them on the tortilla, sprinkled on shredded cheddar cheese, added a spoonful of salsa, and laid three slices of bacon on top. She rolled up the tortilla and took a bite. She sighed. "Delicious."

"I'm glad you like the bacon," Troy said as he finished rolling up his tortilla.

They ate quietly. Neither seemed to know what to say. They had a wonderful night together, but Troy sensed that Athena was anxious. They finished eating, and he suggested they finish their tea and coffee on his back deck, so they went outside and sat down. Athena looked out across the field behind Troy's home. A hawk lazily circled overhead looking for food.

"Today is your last day here," Troy said softly.

Athena nodded. "It is."

"I guess you cannot extend your stay again," he said sadly.

"No. I have a meeting on Thursday morning in New York City with my editor, and Aria has a bridal appointment in the afternoon." Bridal appointment. Her daughter was marrying Troy's brother. Athena felt her face flush, and her heartbeat quickened. What am I doing, she thought to herself? She took a long drink of tea so she could regain control.

Troy took a deep breath. He had to know what she was thinking. "This does not have to be good-bye, Athena. I want to continue to see you."

Athena dreaded this conversation, but it had to happen. "Troy, we live on opposite ends of the country."

"I know. But I feel we have something, Athena. I want to explore this relationship further. I think you do too. I know you feel the connection between us. Don't let it end."

Athena looked at him. There were tears in her eyes. "I don't know what to do, or what to say." She closed her eyes to keep the tears back.

"Don't say anything." Troy feared if she thought too much about it or said anything, her answer would be no, and he desperately wanted to pursue a relationship with her. "Let's just keep in touch and see what happens. We don't have to make a decision now, do we?"

Athena gave a tiny smile, "We definitely don't need to make a decision now. Let's keep in touch and see what happens." Troy put his hand over hers, looked into her eyes, and smiled at her. She gave him a weak smile back.

Later in the day, Troy was outside raking up the area under the Mesquite tree and around the swing so no one would get hurt again. Inside her cabin, Athena packed her suitcase. She was leaving the next morning. She looked out the window at Troy. He wore only boots, jeans, and a hat. His arm and chest muscles moved as he raked up the debris under the tree, and she watched him for a long time remembering their night together.

Her attention was snapped by Maria who brought Troy out a glass of iced tea and a large paper lawn bag. He stopped, drank down the tea, and continued raking. Athena went back to her packing. When she looked out again, the lawn bag was full, but Troy was not outside.

Troy went into the house. He washed his hands and poured himself another glass of tea. Maria and John were in the front room, and Dan casually leaned back in a chair at the kitchen table. "So, what happened last night?" he asked Troy.

"Athena stepped on a Mesquite thorn." He drank down the tea and set the glass on the countertop.

Dan stood up and rinsed his glass. He turned around and leaned against the sink. "So, did you sleep with her?"

Troy glared at his brother. "That is none of your business," he said firmly. He turned away from Dan and started to walk out of the kitchen.

Dan laughed, "I don't think there's a mother of the bride and brother of the groom dance, but hey, we could start a new tradition."

Troy turned back toward his brother. "That's not funny," he said, but Dan just grinned at him.

Troy stared intently at Dan, and then without any warning, Troy hit him.

Dan yelled, and Troy turned and left the house. Maria came running in to see what was going on. Dan held his hand to his nose to stem the flow of blood.

"Did Troy?" she stuttered. She was at a loss for words.

Dan nodded his head yes. He took a paper towel off the roll and held it to his face.

"Why?" Maria finally asked.

"I think he's in love."

Chapter 15

Troy drove to the jobsite in the morning and got out of his truck. He had not spent much time here the past couple of weeks and that was fine. Things were moving along smoothly, and he kept updated each night with his partner, Carlos.

"How's it goin, Troy?" Matt, one of the subcontractors they used for finish trim work, called to him. "I haven't seen you in a few weeks."

"I'm good. How are you, Matt?"

"Last time we talked, you said your brother was bringing his girlfriend home. How did it go?"

"She's Trevor's fiancé now," Troy informed him.

"Trevor's engaged! Wow."

"He surprised everyone on Easter Sunday. He hid the ring in a plastic egg."

Matt scrubbed his hand over his face. "She's from back East right?"

"Falmouth, Massachusetts."

"Hum. I guess he won't be moving back here then."

Troy sipped his coffee and studied Matt. "His job is in Massachusetts. I don't think he had plans to come back anytime soon."

"Maybe not, but she is not going to want to move here." He finished his coffee and toss the empty cup in the trash barrel. "See ya later, Troy."

"See you." Troy stared off into space. He wanted a relationship with Athena, but was it possible? She lived on the other end of the country, and she would not want to leave her home and Aria and move to Texas. At least not permanently. He looked around at the work going on around him. He could scale back. It was something he was already considering before he met Athena. He could be a financial partner instead of a working partner. But the ranch. He may not be needed there all the time, but the ranch was his home just like the house on Cape Cod was Athena's home. He kicked a few loose rocks and started to walk while he thought.

They could split their time at each house. He had never been to her house on Cape Cod, but he lived simply and could live anywhere. Athena enjoyed the ranch. She liked riding the horses, and she certainly worked hard and enjoyed helping when they moved the cattle. She could work from almost anywhere. But would she? Would she be willing to be so far away from Aria for a month or two? She was already pulling away from him. He kicked a large rock and it rolled down the dirt road. He needed to talk to her. She was a smart, reasonable woman. He was certain they would be able to work it out. Troy walked down the road to the house that was closing next week and started his inspection.

That evening, Athena talked to Aria and then made herself a cup of tea even though it was very warm. She sat down at the kitchenette table and took small sips of the tea. She let out a deep sigh. She did not know what to do. The wedding was coming, and how was she going to carry on a long-distance relationship with the groom's brother no less. She shook her head. No, I must end this. It will not work, she decided. I am the mother of the bride, not the sister of the bride. She took another deep breath.

She did not know if Troy planned to come to her cabin, but she felt ready if he did. She simply needed to explain that the distance was too great and that it was inappropriate for the bride's mother and the groom's brother to pursue a romantic relationship. They really had no choice but to just be friends.

Athena closed her eyes, remembered the previous night, and smiled. When she was with him, Troy made her feel like she was the center of his world. Even their banter was enjoyable. She hit her hand on the table. "No!" she said out loud. "We cannot have a relationship." She resolved to insist they just be friends.

There was a gentle tap on the door. Athena broke out in a cold sweat. It was him. "Yes," she said though the door.

"Can we talk?" Troy asked.

"Of course," she replied as she opened the door and let him in. They stood in the kitchenette area.

"You were very quiet at dinner. Are you ok?" Troy asked.

"Oh yes," Athena replied with a fake smile. "Just thinking about everything I have to do when I get home tomorrow." She did not look at him. She could not look into his deep brown eyes for fear she would lose her resolve. She took a breath. "Thank you for making my stay here very pleasant. I really had a good time."

Troy was quiet, so Athena continued. "I will keep Maria informed as we get the arrangements settled for the wedding." Troy said nothing. Athena was getting nervous because of his silence, but she continued. "Well, it is getting late. I should finish my packing. Let's keep in touch," she stammered. Her voice sounded especially high to her.

Troy continued to stare at her and not speak. Despite her resistance, she had to look at him, and when she did, she melted. She knew she was falling in love with him. No. Think of Aria. You cannot let this go any further, she thought silently to herself. She moved toward the door.

Troy stared at her. This was not what he wanted. This morning, he was certain they would come to an arrangement. He knew she had to return to Massachusetts, and he had commitments here in Texas, but she wasn't trying to work things out. She was telling him she just wanted to be friends. "Athena, Trevor and Aria marrying does not make us family."

"Oh, yes. I know," she squeaked.

"I think we should talk about us," he said softly.

She smiled at him. "There's nothing to talk about. We had some very special times together that I will always cherish. But we are very different people, we live thousands of miles apart, and we will be in-laws soon."

Troy took a deep breath and let it out slowly. "And that is your decision?"

"Yes," Athena said. "We are friends. Good friends."

"If that is what you want," he replied sadly. "Good night." He walked past her, opened the door, and left closing the door behind him. Athena went to the window and carefully looked out so he could not see her watching. He walked to his house. Athena turned away from the window and wiped the tears from her eyes.

The next morning, Athena got up very early and cleaned the cabin. She took the sheets off the bed and brought them to the house to wash. She returned to her cabin, packed up the last-minute items, and then showered. She stood in the shower and let the cool water flow over her, and she began to cry again. She needed to leave the ranch quickly before she lost her resolve. She turned off the water, dried off, and got dressed. Troy wanted to take her to the airport, but Athena insisted on going alone. She had to return the rental car, and she did not think she would be able to say good-bye to him there alone in the airport. She was heading back to Massachusetts and to her life.

Fortunately, she had to leave by nine am to get to the airport on time. Troy knocked on the door. "Come on in," Athena called to him. She zippered her suitcase.

"Are you certain you do not want me to come to the airport with you?" he asked.

"I think it is best this way." She smiled weakly.

Troy did not think it was best, but he accepted her decision. Emotionally, she pulled away from him, and there was nothing he could do to change her mind right now. He knew if he pushed, she would back further away. He loaded her suitcases into the car and then went back inside.

"Thank you again for a wonderful time," Athena said.

"I am happy you stayed." Troy leaned down to her and kissed her lightly on the cheek.

When they went outside, Dan, Maria, and John were walking over to say good-bye. "Are you sure you will be ok going to the airport alone?" Maria asked.

"Oh, yes,' Athena replied. "I travel alone a lot." She hugged Maria, John, and then Dan. She gave Troy one more hug and then got in her car. "Thank you all again for everything. Maria, I will talk to you soon. Good-bye."

"Good-bye," they said together.

"Have a good flight," Troy said.

They waved as she drove down the driveway. Maria went to the house, and John walked over to the stable.

"Is that it?" Dan asked Troy. "Are you just going to let her leave?"

"I can't stop her," Troy said sadly. "She's afraid."

"Of what?" Dan snapped.

"She's afraid that Aria and Trevor would feel uncomfortable if we were in a relationship. She is also afraid of the distance."

"Both of which are not issues and can be worked out," Dan replied heatedly. He did not want to see his brother get hurt.

Troy let out a long breath. "I know, but she won't give us a chance to try and work it out." He watched the car turn onto the main road. "I hope she will reconsider after her book is published and the wedding planning is finished."

Dan shook his head and put his hand on his brother's shoulder. He just did not know what to say.

Athena's plane landed in Boston. She was still conflicted, but she needed to pull herself together because Aria was picking her up at the airport. What was she going to say to her daughter? Did she need to say anything? She went to the ladies' room and freshened up then went to the baggage claim area. Her bag came around on the conveyor belt, and she pulled it off. When she exited the baggage area, Aria stood there waiting for her.

"Hi, Mom." Seeing her daughter made Athena feel better about her decision. After all, she was the mother of the bride, and there was no place in her life right now for a relationship with the groom's brother on the other end of the country.

"Hi!" She smiled and waved.

180

Aria kissed her mother and helped her load the bags in the car. They got in, and Aria pulled away from the curb. Fortunately, it was after rush hour, so traffic was not bad. "So, how was the visit?"

"Good," Athena said. "It was good. Did lots of work."

"Good." Aria was not sure, but something did not seem right with her mother. When she talked to her yesterday, she seemed nervous and that was not normal. "So, you got to see some of Texas too and had some fun with Trevor's family."

"What? Oh, yes, I had fun too." Now Aria knew something was wrong. "It's good to be back," Athena said as Aria drove out of Boston toward home. "It was very hot in Texas."

"Trevor said that Maria told him you were a little freaked out about the tornado watch."

"Yes, it was scary." Athena looked at her daughter. Was it possible that Aria knew about her and Troy? Trevor obviously talked to Maria often. She was not sure if Maria approved of her, and that was yet another factor holding her back from getting involved with Troy.

"Are you tired, Mom?"

"Not really."

"Should we stop for something to eat? Mexican? Or are you Mexicaned out?"

"I did eat a lot of bar-be-que and Tex-Mex. I also had delicious grilled shrimp when Troy took me to dinner Saturday night."

Aria looked at her mother. "Sounds like you and Troy had a good time together." To Aria's surprise, her mother blushed.

"Yes, he is a nice guy when you get to know him."

"So, what did you guys do?" Aria asked.

Athena felt her face get hot. "Oh, nothing much. Mostly, we just hung out. Should we go to Sam's for dinner? I would like sea food tonight."

Aria nodded her agreement. She had the feeling that more went on than just hanging out. However, she did not ask more questions.

Athena kept the conversation light. She asked about the house and the wedding plans. Finally, they drove over the Bourne Bridge, and Athena felt more relaxed. She was home. A short while later, Aria pulled in the restaurant's parking lot. It was cool out, so Athena put on a jacket and they went inside and walked up to the counter. Athena ordered scallops, and by the time she finished her dinner, she felt like she was back to normal.

Aria drove home and helped bring in the suitcases. "You seem to be walking ok. Is your foot better?" she asked.

Athena's mouth dropped. "What?"

"Your foot. Why didn't you tell me you got hurt? Trevor said Maria told him you stepped on a Mesquite thorn, and it went right into your foot." Aria looked at her mother. "Mom, are you sure you are ok?"

Athena's face was flush, and she was taking shallow breaths. "Yes, yes. I am fine. Glad to be home." She took a can of seltzer out of the refrigerator, and they sat down on the couch in the living room. Athena looked at the bowls of seashells on the mantle and smiled. It really was good to be home.

Aria shook her head. She had a feeling her mother was keeping something from her. She knew she would find out eventually, so she changed the subject. "I have Thursday off. I realized I had another personal day, so I put in for it. Saves me calling out sick."

"Oh great," Athena replied. "Is Brittany coming to New York too?"

"She is. We are going to go to Macy's and do some shopping while you are in your meeting."

"Good." Athena smiled. "How is the house hunting going?"

"Tiring."

Athena nodded. "I know, but when you and Trevor are in your own home, it will be worth it." Athena hugged her daughter. "I missed you."

"I missed you too, Mom."

In the morning, Athena yawned and shuffled into the kitchen when Aria was getting ready for work. She put on a kettle of water for tea and turned on the news. She watered her plants and opened the curtains to let the sunlight in. She texted Maria and Troy when she returned last night. She expected Troy would try to persuade her to reconsider her decision about their relationship, but he did not. She was not sure how she felt about it. She expected him to fight more for their relationship.

"What time are you going to work?" Aria asked breaking Athena out of her thoughts.

"I plan to get in around noon. I'm going to walk the beach this morning." Athena really missed the beach while she was away and needed a morning walking on the sand and breathing in the salt air. This time of year was perfect for beach combing. The water was still cold, but the sun was warm. Few people would be on the beach, and low tide was in the morning, so she might find some driftwood, big seashells, or other items while she walked.

Aria looked at her mother. "You aren't going in early?"

"No, there's no rush," Athena replied. She was pleased with the work Holly did during her absence. She felt comfortable leaving Holly in charge now, and Athena planned to give Holly more responsibilities to free up time so she could do other things.

Aria shook her head. "Ok," she said with some hesitation. "Have a good day, Mom."

Athena kissed her daughter on the cheek "Thanks, you too."

Aria gathered her bags and headed out the door. Athena watched as Aria got in her car and drove away. Aria was getting married, and life was changing.

Chapter 16

Brittany slept over because they needed to be at South Station at five o'clock in the morning on Thursday to catch the train to New York City. Athena drove, and the girls slept in the back seat. She parked the car, and the three of them went in the station.

Brittany was a tall girl with shoulder length red hair and a big smile. She and Aria were college roommates. Aria and Brittany wore nearly identical outfits, black leggings, a short-sleeved shirt, and sneakers. Athena wore a pair of black slacks, a turquoise blouse, and a black jacket. She wore a pair of black pumps for her meeting, but she had a pair of sneakers in her bag for later when she had to do a lot of walking.

The three women boarded the train. Athena booked them seats that faced one another with a table between them. Once the train was underway, they went to the dining car and bought breakfast sandwiches then settled in for the ride to the city.

Athena worked on her computer making a few revisions and listing questions for Ellen while Aria and Brittany looked at gown styles on their tablets. Before they reached the station, Athena checked her email. She was disappointed that Troy had not emailed her. She thought he might email to say good luck knowing she was meeting with her editor and shopping with Aria. She closed the laptop and put it in her bag.

The train station bustled with people. They walked across the lobby and exited the station onto the bright crowded street. It was a beautiful day in New York. The sky was clear, and the flowers were in bloom. The temperature was warm, but a fairly strong breeze blew off the water to cool them. They walked along the streets looking in the store windows. They did not have far to walk because the publisher's office was close to the train station. They entered the building and took the elevator up to the fifty sixth floor to Ellen's office.

The office assistant, Sharon, was a short older woman with short grey hair. She dressed in a tailored blue suit, and she smiled when they got off the elevator. "Let me see the ring, Aria," she said as she bustled up to them.

"Hi, Sharon. This is my friend Brittany," Aria said as she held out her left hand.

"He has good taste," Sharon said. "Go right in. Ellen is waiting."

Ellen heard them in the outer office, and she got up to greet them. "Hi," Ellen said excitedly. Ellen was in her mid-fifties. She had light brown, medium length hair, and she always wore eclectic outfits that looked like she just stepped out of the seventies. Today, she wore a long dark maxi skirt, a gauzy white blouse, and several long necklaces. "Let me see the ring!" she exclaimed. Aria held up her hand, and Ellen nodded her approval.

"This is my maid of honor, Brittany. Brittany this is my mother's editor, Ellen Blake." The two women smiled and said hello.

"So what time is the bridal appointment?" Ellen asked as they all stepped into her office. The office was spacious. There were bookshelves full of books along one wall. There was a sitting area with a love seat and two soft comfortable looking chairs arranged around a coffee table. Ellen's desk faced away from the window, and there were several silk flower arrangements and lots of pictures scattered throughout the office.

"1:30," Aria replied. "We are going to Macy's to shop first."

"Tea or coffee, anyone?" Sharon asked.

"Tea please, Sharon," Athena said.

"No thanks, Sharon. Brittany and I are heading out. I just wanted to come in and say hi." Sharon nodded and left the office.

Athena hugged her daughter. "You two be careful. I will meet you at the bridal salon at 1:30."

"We will be careful. And I will text you if we find something good," Aria said. "Bye, Ellen."

"Bye. Have fun," Ellen replied.

As they walked out, Sharon walked in. She handed a cup of tea to Athena and then left the office and closed the door.

Athena sat down on one of the black leather chairs in front of Ellen's long wooden desk. "So, what do you think about the manuscript?" She took a drink of tea.

Ellen sat down. "The manuscript is great. As always, your work needs little editing." Ellen looked at Athena then leaned forward across her desk. "What I want to know about is Troy. When are you seeing him again?"

Athena looked sad, and she took a deep breath. Ellen looked at her. "You aren't seeing him again?"

Athena shrugged her shoulders. "I don't know."

"What is there not to know?" Ellen said. "You looked so happy when we chatted when you were in Texas." She paused. "And so relaxed, I might add."

"I know. I like him. I like him a lot. But."

"But what? He is gorgeous. He makes you very happy. What is holding you back?"

"The wedding. The fact that he is Trevor's brother. He lives two thousand plus miles away. I am not sure his mother likes me. Take your pick. There are a lot of complications."

"You aren't going to try and see if anything develops?" Ellen shook her head. This was not like Athena who was an I can do anything person. "Does Aria know?"

"No!" Athena said firmly. "Aria has enough to think about right now. She does not need me to complicate matters. I think it is for the best if Troy and I do not pursue a relationship."

Ellen did not agree, but she did not say anything more. Athena's mind was made up, and at this point, nothing she said would change Athena's mind. Ellen decided it was best to get to the discussion of the manuscript.

Athena and Ellen had a very productive meeting and a relaxing lunch in the office. Aria texted that she and Brittany had lunch and were on their way to the bridal salon.

"I will be in touch," Ellen said as Athena put her laptop in her bag and prepared to leave.

"I'll make the revisions and send it to you in the next couple of weeks."

"Great, you take care." Ellen and Sharon watched as Athena walked to the elevator. "Have fun bridal gown shopping," Ellen called.

"Thanks." Athena waved and got in the elevator. She decided to hail a cab to take her to the bridal salon instead of walking.

Aria and Brittany waited on the sidewalk outside the salon. They looked at the manikins in the window that were dressed in very elaborate wedding gowns full of lace and sparkling jewels. "Ready?" Athena asked. Aria and Brittany nodded, and they walked in together. They checked in and were soon greeted by a very enthusiastic bridal consultant.

"Hi, my name is Charlotte, and who is my bride?" she asked. Aria waved. The consultant brought them to a sofa, and they all sat down. "Ok, so tell me about the groom, your venue, and what kind of wedding you are having."

Aria answered her questions. "Trevor is from Texas, and he is a financial planner. We are getting married in December at a castle near Boston. I am having a Medieval and masquerade theme. I am thinking lace, possibly long sleeves, sweetheart neckline."

Charlotte nodded. "Budget?"

"Around five thousand." Aria replied.

"Ok, let's go shopping." Charlotte led them to the racks to look at dress possibilities. After selecting six dresses, the consultant brought Aria to a dressing room, and Athena and Brittany sat on the sofa and waited.

"This is overwhelming," Brittany said as she looked around the salon.

"It certainly is," Athena agreed. She texted James on their progress. "I think James should have come along."

Brittany looked around. There were only a couple of men in the salon. "Do father's usually go dress shopping?"

"I don't know if they usually do, but I think he should be with us. When I got married, my mother, maid of honor, and I narrowed the dresses down, and then I brought my father with us to make the final selection."

"I can't imagine making a decision on a dress in one day." Brittany looked around. "There are so many different types of gowns."

Aria came out of the dressing room in the first gown. "What do you think?" she asked as she stepped up on the podium. The dress was beautiful. It was a fit to flare style with long sleeves and an illusion sweetheart neckline. Brittany and Athena nodded and waited for Aria's opinion. "I'm not sure I like the sleeves," Aria said.

She turned around so they could see the front. Aria pulled at the neckline.

"The illusion netting looks like it is very high on your neck. Is it comfortable?" Athena asked.

"Not really."

"Ok, well this is just the first dress. Let's try on another," Charlotte said, and she led Aria back to the dressing room.

Two hours later, they had several possibilities. Athena took pictures of each of the possible dresses, so Aria could look at them later. Charlotte explained that most dresses needed six months for delivery, so Aria needed to decide soon.

They left the store and stopped for hotdogs at a street vendor close to the salon. "I learned a lot today," Aria said, "I don't think I want sleeves even though I thought I did." She paused and looked at her mother. "I was thinking should we have Dad come to the appointments?" Aria took a drink of soda. "It felt weird not having him with us. He was there when I picked out my prom dress, and my dress for the sorority formal."

"I thought the same thing." Athena finished her hotdog and tossed the holder in the trash can.

"I also know I want a cathedral length veil."

"Definitely a long veil," Brittany said. "I didn't like that little one Charlotte suggested."

"No, I didn't like it either, and it wouldn't fit with the Medieval theme at all," Aria agreed.

"Ellen told me today that she booked me at a travel conference in Rome in September. We could get the veil in Italy and get wedding favors," Athena suggested.

"Oh, could we go to Venice for the masks for the masquerade?" Aria asked. Athena nodded, yes.

It was a long day of shopping, and on the train ride back to Boston, Aria and Brittany both fell asleep quickly. Athena checked her email. She smiled. She had an email from Troy. He sent her several pictures he took of her on horseback. He also asked how the meeting went with her editor and how dress shopping went. She composed an email back to him. She already missed him, their conversations, just sitting and watching the sun set together. She stared at the pictures he sent, and they brought him back to her. She shook her head. She could not allow herself to get distracted. There was too much to do. She put the photos in a folder on her desktop. A text from James came in, so she texted him back and confirmed lunch with him the next day then she leaned back and closed her eyes.

Athena entered the restaurant and looked around for James. He was dressed in a suit. He was a good-looking man in his mid-fifties with close cut, mostly grey hair.

He saw her walk in and waved. "Hi." James stood up and held the chair for Athena. "Wow, you are tan."

"Thanks." She intentionally wore a white v neck shirt to show off her tan. She always dressed up when she saw James. They were divorced ten years ago, and his new wife of seven years, Brook, was much younger. Athena actually liked Brook and sometimes baby sat for their daughter,

Amber, but Athena wanted to make certain she looked good when she saw him. The waitress came right over to refill James' coffee and to take their order. James ordered a hamburger, and Athena ordered a Reuben. "Iced tea, unsweetened," Athena said, and the waitress nodded.

"So how was dress shopping?" James asked.

"Aria has a better idea of what style she would like." Athena told James everything she and Aria had discussed. James nodded and agreed with her. One nice thing about James was that he usually was agreeable, especially when something involved Aria.

"How much do you need?" he asked when she finished.

"I'm adding everything up. Aria wants you to come to the bridal gown appointments. She missed your input," Athena said.

"I can't wait. She texted me the days and times. She said she needs to select a gown soon."

"Yes, gown orders need six months or more lead time."

"So, I should be ready to put down the deposit at one of the appointments?"

"Yes."

"I already put the deposit on the venue to reserve it."

"Great. Aria wants to have a masquerade, so I think we will pick up masks and the veil in Italy."

"Why don't I write you a check for six thousand. Just let me know when you need more." He obviously planned it because he slid an envelope over to Athena. The food arrived, and Athena put the envelope in her purse. "So how was Texas?" he asked.

"I finished the manuscript."

"That's fantastic. What are Trevor's parents and brothers like?"

192

"They are all very nice. They have a cattle ranch, and they are branching out and leasing to a wind farm. Maria and John are older. Trevor's brothers are in their forties."

"And Trevor's brothers work the ranch?"

Athena nodded. "Yes, but Dan also works at a lumber yard, and Troy is co-owner of a construction company."

"What else did you do while you were there? Aria said you all went horse-back riding."

"I enjoyed riding the horses. It has been a long time since I rode."

"You rode more than once?"

"Oh yes, Troy took me riding a couple times." James saw Athena blush slightly when she talked about Troy. He rarely saw her blush, and he knew there was more to the story.

Dress shopping turned out to be more difficult than any of them imagined. Aria looked through every bridal magazine available. She tried on dresses at a second shop and then a third and then a fourth. It was now mid-June, so the pressure was on to find a gown. Aria stood on the podium and looked at herself in the mirror. The dress was fitted and had cap sleeves. "What do you think?" she asked her mother, father, and Brittany who sat on the couch.

"Very pretty," they all said.

"Do you like the cap sleeves?" Aria asked.

They nodded yes. "It looks Medieval," Brittany said.

"I like this silky material," Aria said.

"Me too," Athena agreed.

"Dad?" Aria said.

James looked at his daughter. She looked beautiful in everything. It started to sink in that she was getting married. "I like this one quite a lot."

"It is a contender," Aria said. Athena took a picture, and the consultant looked at the tag and made notes. "I think I am finished for today."

"I have the dress information. Let's get you out of it," the consultant said as she helped Aria off the podium and then back to the dressing room.

"She's having trouble making a decision," James said to Athena.

"She has a lot on her mind with the wedding planning, looking at houses, and now she has the college job interview next week." Athena replied.

"Well, I think the sellers will accept their offer on the house on Blueberry Lane," James told Athena. "I am meeting with the seller's realtor tomorrow."

"I hope so. They really like the house," Athena said. "And getting the house will ease a great deal of the stress they are both feeling."

A week later, Aria got up and went downstairs for breakfast even though she did not think she could eat anything. She really wanted to work full time at the community college, and she would hear one way or the other today. She set up her laptop and checked her email.

"The college won't contact you by email, will they?" Athena asked.

"No, they said they would call," Aria picked at her scrambled eggs and toast.

"Would you like to walk the beach after breakfast?" Athena wanted to distract Aria to make the waiting bearable. Aria nodded yes.

A short while later, the two women picked up their sand pails and beach bags and walked to the beach. They kicked off their sandals, set down their towels and other items, and took off their swimsuit coverups.

"I don't want to miss a call," Aria said as she put her phone in a waterproof bag. She carried the bag, and they each carried a sand pail as they walked to the water's edge.

They quietly walked along the beach collecting shells. Athena saw a crab shell and bent down to pick it up. "This one is almost entirely intact," she said as she added it to her pail. All around her home, Athena had bowls and bowls of shells, rocks, driftwood, and other items she found on her walks along the beach. She liked crab shells and now had a collection of them lined up on a shelf in her kitchen.

It was early morning, so it was not too warm yet. People were setting up along the beach. Umbrellas were popping up and children splashed in the water.

"I'm going to take a dip," Athena said when they returned to their spot. She set her pail down and went back to the water. Slowly, Athena walked in until the water was over her knees. Still carrying her phone in its waterproof bag, Aria walked in until she was waist deep, and then she dived into an oncoming wave. They swam around, but Athena could not stay in the cold water long. "I am going to lay in the sun," she told Aria.

"Me too."

They tanned and ate the strawberries they brought with them. Aria's phone rang, but it was Trevor asking if she heard anything. She told him no, and then Athena heard Troy's name. She did not look up from her book, but she strained her ears and shifted a little closer to Aria to try and hear what was being said.

"That is so generous of your parents. I will call your mom and thank her," Aria said to Trevor. "When is he coming up?" Aria listened to what Trevor was saying, and then she said good-bye and hung up.

Now, Athena looked up from her book. "What is going on?" she asked in as casual a tone as she could manage.

"Maria is giving us some family heirlooms. Troy is going to drive a truck up with the furniture and stay and help Trevor remodel after we close on the house in September."

Athena was happy that Aria and Trevor purchased a home only a short distance from her own. It was a big house, but it needed updating, especially the kitchen. "That is very nice." Athena dabbed her forehead with a towel which did not escape Aria's notice.

"It will be good to have Troy's help," Aria commented.

Athena nodded nervously. "When is Trevor moving into the house?"

"His lease is up at the end of October, so he will start to move in right after we close, but I think it is best if I move my things in gradually." Aria rolled onto her stomach and began flipping through a bridal magazine.

Athena took out a writing magazine and started flipping through the pages. "Business at the travel agency is slowing down. People are booking online more and more often."

"There are so many travel websites and APPs."

"Yes, my website traffic has increased dramatically these past six months. I am so glad I listened to your father and did not try to open a second travel agency location." Athena set down her magazine. "I think I want to spend more time traveling and writing."

"That is a great idea. You really will enjoy that," Aria replied seriously. "You seem to enjoy writing more than anything."

They soaked up the sun and then went back in the ocean. Aria swam back and forth parallel to the shore, and Athena stood in waist deep water. She heard her name. She turned around and saw her friend David running up the beach.

"Hi, David," she called.

He stopped running and walked up to her. He splashed himself with some water. "Are you fully going in?"

"Maybe?" She laughed. "Are you on vacation?"

"Just between jobs. I have a project starting up next week." Athena nodded. "What about you?"

"It's a slow time of year. Everyone is actually traveling," Athena replied.

Aria swam toward them. "Hi, David," she said. She stood up and pulled back her hair.

"Hi, Aria. How is the wedding planning going?"

"Really well, thanks."

"Well, I better get back to my run. You ladies have a great day. Nice to see you, Athena."

"Have a good run," they replied together as he walked out of the water.

"He likes you," Aria said as they went back to their blanket and laid down.

"We have known each other since we were kids."

"And he has liked you since you were kids."

"We never dated."

"That doesn't matter." Athena gave Aria a smirk. "You should date more often, Mom."

"I'm too busy to date." Athena picked up her magazine again and began to read. The truth was, since being with Troy, she did not have any interest in anyone else. It was true she was the one who said they should be friends and picked up and left Texas, but he was not exactly pursuing her. On one hand, it made her sad, but maybe it was for the best she told herself.

About 2:30 pm, they decided to head back to the house. Just as they were walking up the front steps, Aria's phone rang. They both stopped walking. Aria looked at her phone and nodded her head. "It's them," she whispered to her mother. "Hello," she said happily into the phone. A huge smile broke out on Aria's face, and Athena knew it was good news. "Thank you. Thank you very much." She ended the call. "I got it!" she screamed.

"Congratulations!" Athena hugged Aria. "I think we need to celebrate tonight."

"Yes, we do!" Aria called Trevor. "I got the job!" she exclaimed as they went inside.

Athena was right, once Aria received the call that she had the position, she narrowed down the choices. They just finished back to back appointments at two shops. Aria tried on each dress at least twice, but she narrowed the choice to two dresses in the same shop. The next appointment should be the last. Athena went inside her home, hung up her keys, and went to the refrigerator for a glass of iced peach tea. She was exhausted.

The attendant's dresses needed to be ordered soon. Brittany was the maid of honor, and Aria asked three of her friends to be bridesmaids. Amber was the flower girl, and they all needed dresses. Getting all of them to agree was going to be a challenge. James also suggested that Athena and Brook look for dresses while they shopped for the attendant's dresses because he wanted to buy all the dresses.

Athena checked her voicemail, and there was a message from Shelby. She and Maria were planning the rehearsal dinner, and they decided on a restaurant James suggested. Athena called Maria back to go over the details.

"I reserved for up to fifty people. Is that enough?" Maria asked.

Athena did a quick count in her head. "Yes, that should be fine."

"How is everything coming along?"

Athena filled her in on the latest happenings. "The guys have it easy," she laughed, "just a basic tux."

"I wanted to ask you what color you plan to wear, Athena. As mother of the bride, you get first choice."

"Thanks, Maria. I don't know yet. I have not had any time to look at dresses for myself. Did you have a color in mind for yourself?"

Maria hesitated. She did not want to limit Athena's selection, but she really liked the dress. "Well, I actually saw a nice green dress at a shop in Austin," she replied.

"Great. I definitely will not be wearing green, so get the dress."

Maria breathed a sigh of relief. "Thank you. It really is a nice dress. Are you sure you won't pick a green dress?"

"Green really isn't my color," Athena replied. "So," she paused, "how is everyone there?" she asked as casually as she could.

Maria sighed. "Everyone is good. They are all out on the ranch now."

"Well, say hello to everyone for me." Athena was disappointed. "Bye." She hung up the phone.

The dress selection for the attendants did not take as long as Athena feared. They only needed two appointments to select and order gowns. Since it was a Christmas time wedding, Aria wanted the maid of honor and bridesmaids to wear dark red velvet dresses. The rich color also worked with the Medieval theme of the wedding. As the maid of honor, Brittany selected her gown first. She tried on several styles, and finally, she selected a modified mermaid strapless gown with a sweetheart neckline. The dress was fitted to the mid-thigh and then it flared out to a ruffled bottom. The dress had a crystal embellished belt at the natural waist.

The bridesmaid dresses were made of the same dark red velvet material. Their dresses were all the same style and had strapless sweetheart necklines. These gowns were in fit to flare style, so the dresses were fitted to the natural waist where there was a single strand of rhinestones, and then the dresses flared out and flowed to the ground.

Amber's flower girl dress was very easy to find. Her dress was a floor length white chiffon dress with puffy cap sleeves. It was a communion dress, so she could wear it again.

Athena was having trouble deciding on a color and a style. She tried on floor length gowns, short dresses, and tea length dresses in a variety of colors. Some of the dresses were very embellished and some were not. She tried on satin, chiffon, taffeta, and so far, all she decided was she did not like taffeta.

Brook, however, despite not really looking because she hesitated to look for a dress until Athena selected one, found a beautiful light blue dress at one of the shops. It was tea length and had a handkerchief hem. It had some beading, but it was not overly flashy. Brook stood and looked at herself in the three-way mirror. She moved right then left then right again.

"You look very good in that dress, and it is obvious you really like it," Athena said to Brook when they returned to the dressing room. "You should purchase it."

"Are you sure," Brook asked with a pained expression because she really did not want to infringe on Athena's choices for a dress.

"Absolutely. The dress is perfect for you. Get it."

"What if you find a light blue dress?"

"I won't. The odds are not good that I will find the perfect dress in light blue," Athena said. "Get the dress."

"Thanks, I really like it, and it looks good on."

Athena nodded her agreement and set the dress she was trying on back on the rack.

So, everyone's dress was selected except for the mother of the bride.

Chapter 17

Aria and Athena made several shopping trips to look for a dress for Athena. However, she still did not have a dress for the wedding.

"I will find something eventually," Athena told Aria at breakfast one morning.

"I hope you find something soon," Aria said. She was getting worried. It was not like her mother to be so indecisive. She had been acting a bit off since her return from Texas, and Aria hoped it was not because of her upcoming marriage.

Athena changed the subject. "Ellen emailed me this morning. Remember the sweets section she told me to cut from the manuscript?" Aria nodded. "Well, now Ellen said it should be added back in and expanded. I have to go back to London the first week in August to do a little more research."

"How long will you be gone?" Aria asked.

"Probably four, maybe five days. It will be a short trip. Want to come along?" Athena nudged her daughter. She hoped Aria wanted to go to London with her. It was a quick trip, but it would give her and Aria a chance to be together before the fall semester began and the wedding drew nearer.

"You know, I am pretty sure Trevor will be at a conference the first week in August," Aria said.

"Good, then you can come with me to London. There is no point in staying here alone."

Aria nodded, yes. "I agree, and London is so much fun." She looked at Athena and smiled, "And who knows, Mom, maybe over there we can find you a dress for the wedding. You have exhausted the stores here," Aria said with a laugh.

Athena shrugged, "Maybe. Who knows," she laughed.

In early August, Athena and Aria flew to London. The temperature was hot and somewhat humid for England. They made their way to Athena's favorite hotel right near King's Cross Station. The central location was ideal for business trips because of easy access to the Tube and to St. Pancres for International travel.

Before doing anything personal, Athena had work to do. Since they flew overnight, they dropped their bags at the hotel, and then they set out to visit several sweetshops in London for inclusion in Athena's book. This involved tasting a variety of macrons including ice cream macrons which were Aria's favorite.

"I am happy to help with this kind of research," Aria said as she bit into a macron. "This is so good." Athena made some notes and talked to several shop owners.

At 4:30 pm, they decided to pick up dinner in King's Cross Station and bring it back to their hotel room across the street. The time change had caught up to them. They changed into comfortable clothes and watched TV while they ate, and they went to sleep early.

The second day of sweets research went well. Athena took notes and photographed some displays of the confections then interviewed the shop owner. She rejoined Aria at a small bistro table outside the shop and took a bite of a macron. "Wow. These are very good," she said as she finished the cookie then started looking over her notes and filling them in.

Aria texted Trevor several times, and then she leaned back and watched people as they passed by while her mother wrote. London was one of her favorite cities. She remembered the first time she came to London when she was ten. They stayed for a week and visited Buckingham Palace, Westminster Abby, and saw a play at the Globe Theater. Now that she thought about it, it was one of the last vacations she and her parents took together.

"Well, I think I have enough material," Athena said. She put her notebook and pen into her tote bag and finished her cup of tea. "Should we shop?"

"Yes!"

As they walked, Aria twisted her hair up and secured it with a large hair clip. Since it was nearly five o'clock, they walked to the Tube station, and they took the underground to Covent Garden for dinner and shopping.

"I need real food," Athena said as they made their way through the crowd on their way to a restaurant. "I have eaten entirely too much sugar over the past two days." They stood in line and read the menu. When they reached the counter, they each ordered a crispy chicken sandwich on a buttermilk bun, and they decided to split an order of curly fries. They found seats in the eating area and waited for their food. Aria ordered a strawberry milkshake with her dinner. Whipped cream was piled high on top, and she scooped some off with her straw. "This is really good. Would you like a taste?"

"No thanks," Athena replied. Their number was called, and Aria went up to get their food.

"There's a bookstore down the street that I want to stop at later," Athena said between bites of chicken sandwich. "I should look in some shops for a dress too." Now that the work was completed, she felt she could spend the remainder of the trip shopping for a dress and enjoying the city.

"I need to stop in the perfume shop," Aria told her mother. "And I saw a pair of pretty pink sneakers in one of the shop windows. I definitely want to look for shoes."

After dinner, they first stopped at the perfume shop since it was near the restaurant. The shop had a variety of French perfumes that were not available in the United States. They sampled some of the new perfumes, but Athena purchased a light rose scented perfume which she had previously purchased. "Tried and true," she said to Aria, but Aria purchased a new perfume that smelled spicy.

They strolled along the street and stopped in several clothing shops, but the dresses were not formal enough for the wedding. After the third shop, Athena felt tired. "I am not going to find a dress tonight. Let's go to the bookstore."

They spent a considerable about of time in the bookstore looking at the new and the used books. This bookstore had a large selection of Harry Potter and Tolkien books, and they looked around until the store was ready to close.

They decided to walk to Piccadilly Circus. Since it was dry and warm, many people walked the streets, stood at pubs drinking, and sat in the parks. Piccadilly Circus was crowded, but they stopped and craned their necks to watch several street performers who played music. There were also several living statues which were actors dressed up as Victorian men and women. They stood very still despite people staring at them and trying to make them blink or laugh.

Athena and Aria turned down a side street and headed to a pub for a drink. They were able to get an outdoor table, and they ordered a pitcher of Pimms, a light and refreshing summertime drink that Londoners enjoy. Strawberries, lemon slices, and lime slices are soaked in Pimms over-night, and the alcohol is mixed with lemon-lime soda.

"This is so good," Athena said as she finished her glass and poured another one. "Tomorrow we do some serious dress shopping." Athena drank down half of her glass of Pimms and then topped it off.

"Yes, I agree," Aria said. "Wow. This drink goes down so easy." Athena nodded. "Good thing we are not driving," Aria laughed.

The next day, they headed back to Piccadilly Circus and started shopping. There were several clothing stores on the way up to Selfriges, a large London department store. Athena found a couple of dresses that she liked, but she was still unable to commit to one.

They stopped in several shoe stores and tried on various types of shoes. "Oh, I love these floral sneakers," Aria said as she looked at the shoes in a mirror. "No one has anything like these at home."

"I love this pale blush color." Athena had several pairs in various styles piled on the floor next to her.

They left the shop with two new pairs of shoes each. They saw a shop across the street with gowns in the front window. "Let's stop in there," Athena said. They crossed the street and entered the store.

"Hello. My name is Sophie. Can I help you find something?" the saleswoman asked.

"I am looking for a mother of the bride dress," Athena replied.

"Do you know what shape you are looking for?" she asked. Athena shook her head no. What about color?"

"I am flexible," Athena replied.

The woman looked Athena over. "You are a U.S. size nine?"

"Yes, I am."

Sophie nodded and led them to a small room packed full of dresses. She looked through the racks and pulled out three. "What do you think?" she asked as she placed them on a rack.

Athena and Aria looked over the selection. "These are beautiful," Aria said.

Athena nodded. "Yes, I like them." The three were all champagne colored. Two were tea length, and one was floor length.

"Do you see anything else you would like to try?" Sophie asked.

"I like this pink one, Mom," Aria said, so Sophie took it from her and hung it on the garment rack.

Athena pulled out a sapphire blue dress and a golden rose color dress. Both were tea length.

"Ok. We have enough to start," Sophie said. She pointed Aria to the sofa in front of the podium and took Athena into the dressing room. Athena tried on the pink one first and went out to show Aria.

"Pink isn't the color," Aria shook her head no.

"I was thinking the same," Athena replied. She returned to the dressing room. Next, she came out in the sapphire blue one, but neither of them liked it either.

Athena next came out in the golden rose color dress. "This is a good color," she said as she looked at herself in the mirror. "I'm not sure I like the tea length. What do you think, Aria?"

"I like the color, but it is puffy, and it is definitely too short," Aria said. "You need a full length gown."

Athena nodded. "I agree, and I don't like the noise it makes when I walk," Athena said on her way back to the dressing room.

"What would you like to try next," Sophie asked. She had picked out several more dresses now that she had an idea of what Athena liked and did not like.

Athena looked at the remaining gowns. "This one." Sophie helped her into the dress. Athena smiled. "Oh, I like this."

When Athena came out of the dressing room and Aria saw her, she smiled. "I really like this gown, Mom."

Athena smiled broadly as she looked at herself in the mirror. "Me too."

"I like the golden rose color and the gold embellishments," Aria said.

"This is definitely a unique gown, and it has just the right amount of sparkle." Athena turned from side to side and looked at the dress from all angles in the mirror.

"It looks really good on you, and it definitely fits the Medieval theme." Aria took a picture of her mother in the dress.

Athena nodded her head. "I think this is the one. It doesn't even need to be altered." She continued to look at herself in the mirror. "I will take it," she told Sophie confidently.

"Hurray!" Aria cheered. She looked at her mother and had an idea. Smiling coyly, she said, "wait until Troy sees you in that dress, Mom. He is going to love it."

The comment caught her mother off guard as Aria hoped, and Athena responded without thinking. "He will," she said softly, and then she blushed.

Aria smiled.

"Oh," Athena gasped. She was flustered, and she gathered up the dress and retreated to the dressing room.

Chapter 18

Early one late September morning, Troy stopped for gasoline and coffee in New Jersey just before crossing the border to New York. According to the GPS, he would arrive at Trevor and Aria's house in the mid-afternoon if all went well. After fueling up the truck, he locked it up, and headed into the rest area to freshen up and stretch. He purchased a sandwich, a bottle of water, chips, and two cans of cola then got in the truck and drove back to the highway.

Troy thought about Athena as he drove. Since she went back East, they kept in touch via email and text message. They even video chatted several times; although if he was honest, those video chats were primarily wedding related.

When Trevor and Aria bought a house, his mother wanted to give them some of the family heirlooms for their new home. Trevor also needed help with renovations, so Troy volunteered to drive the items up in a truck and stay to help Trevor remodel knowing it gave him a chance to see Athena again. He opened a can of soda and took a long drink then reached into the bag of corn chips and grabbed a handful. Athena was in Italy right now, and Troy hoped to gain some insight into her from Aria.

His attraction to Athena took him by surprise. He was a bachelor, and although he did date a little, he did not believe he would marry. He enjoyed coming and going as he pleased. He worked long hours, and when he finished working, he often met friends in the local bar for a couple of beers.

"Hum," he mumbled. "When was the last time I took a vacation? When did I get in a routine doing the same thing day after day and week after week? When did my life get so dull?" he grumbled out loud. His life was anything but dull around Athena, he thought. He missed their conversations. Her point of view differed from his often and made him think. She talked about traveling, experiencing new cultures, and making friends. He wanted those experiences too. He missed having a meal with her. He missed seeing her standing barefooted in his kitchen wearing his shirt while he prepared breakfast. Troy let out a sad breath. There was no denying he missed her. He just hoped she missed him as much.

He needed a plan. There was no doubt that he needed to move slowly. He would be patient so as not to scare her off. He had to let Athena make the first move. She always needed to be in charge. That was fine with him if they had the same goals and got to where he wanted to be eventually.

Trevor went outside and sat on the front porch to wait for Troy. It was an unseasonably warm day, and the breeze felt good. Soon, he saw the truck come around the corner. Trevor stood up when Troy pulled into the driveway and brought the truck to a stop. "Hey, glad you made it," he said as Troy opened the door. Trevor walked up to truck. "How was the ride?"

Troy took off his sunglasses, stepped out of the truck, and shook his younger brother's hand. "It was a smooth trip." The two story home was painted a creamy yellow color, and it had brown shutters. The front porch was not as grand as the one on the main house at the ranch, but it was large enough for a couple of chairs and a table.

"Come on inside," Trevor said leading the way. "Want a beer?"

"No thanks, not now."

"Let me show you the house." Trevor took his brother through the first floor and showed him the living room, dining room, kitchen, and downstairs bathroom. He highlighted the architectural features of the home and asked Troy's opinion on the ideas he and Aria had for remodeling. Troy listened and made a few suggestions.

"The kitchen update, flooring, and painting are the primary tasks," Trevor said. They went up the staircase to the landing and then up to the second floor. Trevor showed Troy the two bedrooms and the bathrooms. "We plan to make this third bedroom an office," Trevor explained.

"Hi," Aria called as she climbed the stairs and met up with Trevor and Troy. She hugged Troy and then gave Trevor a kiss hello.

"How was work?" Trevor asked.

"Great," she replied. "I had a couple students at office hour today."

"Do you like your new job, Aria?" Troy asked.

"I love it," she replied. "Teaching in a college is very rewarding."

They walked out into the hallway. "So what colors are you two thinking of painting this hallway and the landing?" Troy asked as he picked up the stack of paint chips that sat on a table.

"I want to paint a warm cream color, but Trevor likes a light mint," Aria explained. She pointed to two chips in Troy's hand. "What do you think?"

Troy looked at them. "Oh, no. I am here to help not to take sides," he laughed, but he also pointed to the cream paint chip. Aria smiled.

They went out to the truck to see the items that Troy brought up. Trevor and Troy stepped up into the back of the truck, and Trevor reached down a hand to help Aria up. Everything was carefully wrapped in blankets and strapped to the sides to minimize movement of the furniture.

"Mom gave us the grandfather clock?!" Trevor exclaimed as he moved the blanket aside and looked at it. "The grandfather clock has been in the family for four generations," he explained to Aria. Trevor never thought his mother would pass the clock on.

"It would look nice on that landing heading up to the second floor," Troy suggested. "Of course, putting it there influences the color selection for that area and the hall. The clock is made of cherry."

Trevor laughed. "Guess Aria wins that color."

They decided to leave the furniture on the truck for the night since the truck did not have to be returned until noon the next day. Troy put the padlock back in place, and they went inside the house.

Trevor laid the drawings for the redesigned kitchen on the table so his brother could look them over. "What do you think?"

Troy looked at the drawings carefully. "This should not be very difficult. It should only take a few weeks."

"I also need help moving some furniture and boxes from my apartment and from Aria's house," Trevor informed his brother.

"No problem. I am here to help. Is everything all set for the wedding?" Troy asked.

"It's been a busy few months," Aria took a breath and let it out, "but everything is on track. I'm getting my veil and majority of the wedding favors in Italy."

Troy nodded. "When do you leave for Italy?"

"Thursday evening. Mom is already there. She presented today at the conference." Aria looked at her watch. "We are video chatting in an hour. Should we head to the house?"

"Yes, the traffic is building. I thought we would take Troy to Sam's for dinner."

"That sounds good," Aria said. "I'll head over now; I want to change my clothes. You two can meet me there."

"We will get ready and meet you there." Trevor leaned over and kissed Aria.

Trevor and Troy arrived at the house a short time later. "Want a tour of the house?" Trevor asked.

Troy shook his head no. "I will wait until Athena returns."

Aria and Trevor looked at each other, and Trevor shrugged. "Well, Mom said to use any tools you need. You can also use grandpa's truck." Aria handed Troy a set of truck keys on an old key chain. She turned on the basement light and started down the stairs.

Trevor and Troy followed her. Troy looked around. The workshop was well equipped, and it was exceptionally clean. Some of the tools were still in boxes, and all the tools were in excellent condition. "Your grandfather's workshop is impressive."

"Yes, he liked to make cabinets and furniture. In fact, we are going to use these in the kitchen." Aria walked over and removed a tarp revealing four kitchen cabinets with glass doors that stood on pallets along the far wall.

Troy took a closer look at them. "They are well crafted. Nice detailing. You said your grandfather made them?"

214

"Yes. Originally, they were going to go in the kitchen upstairs, but he fell ill, and the kitchen was never updated."

"Athena doesn't want to remodel the kitchen now that she owns the home?" Troy asked.

"She said she might remodel at some point, but since we are remodeling our kitchen, we should take them." Aria shrugged her shoulders.

"They will be beautiful that is for certain." Troy looked around and gathered up some of the tools he needed the next day. This was the type of workshop he always dreamed of owning. He liked construction, but what he really wanted to do was make cabinetry and furniture. This workshop had all the tools necessary to make custom pieces.

"Trevor has a key to the house, so you can come get anything else you need," Aria said. She looked at her watch. "Oh, I am going to chat with Mom in five minutes. Take your time and look around." She went upstairs and initiated the video call with her mother.

Trevor and Troy gathered up more tools then went upstairs to join Aria. Troy looked at the fish tank in the dining room. "This is a nice tank," he remarked.

"I need your help moving it to our house."

"So, this is Aria's tank?" Troy looked at the four-foot long, fifty-five gallon aquarium. "Where is this going in the house?"

"She thought about putting it on the landing to the second floor," Trevor explained. "But that's a perfect spot for the grandfather clock, so it will probably go in the foyer."

"I've never had tropical fish." Troy looked in the tank and watched the fish swim. "This is going to be difficult to move."

"Aria will put the fish in bags, empty most of the water, and she will take out some of the gravel and the rocks. It will be much lighter. The tank is on plywood, so in theory, we can pick it up without fear of breaking it."

Troy shook his head. "I hope it works."

They sat down at the kitchen table. Aria was already talking to Athena. "How did your presentation go?" she asked her mother.

"Good, thanks. I had quite an audience. I was concerned because I was presenting on the first day, but I had a good crowd for my presentation. They were interested in my topic, and they asked relevant questions after I spoke. I have my book signing on Wednesday afternoon."

"That's good."

"Actually, I'm glad I am finished presenting. Now, I can relax and attend a few panels," Athena took a sip of mineral water.

"Are you in for the night?" Aria asked. She did not think so because her mother was still dressed up and had jewelry on.

"No, I'm meeting Maura for a late supper shortly."

Trevor and Troy heard her and looked at their watches. "How many hours ahead is Rome?" Troy asked.

"Six."

"She's going out to eat at 10:15 at night?" Troy questioned. Trevor shrugged his shoulders. Aria waved her hand to quiet them.

"What are you doing tonight?" Athena asked her daughter.

"We are taking Troy to Sam's for dinner," Aria replied.

"Oh, good, Troy arrived." Athena tried to sound casual, but she suddenly felt warm. Her voice cracked a little too.

Aria smiled. She thought there was something more than just hanging out between her mother and Troy. She planned to carefully pry Troy for information before she left for Italy. "Yes, he arrived this afternoon." Aria turned the laptop around, so the camera faced Troy and Trevor. "Say hi to Mom," she said to the two men. Trevor and Troy looked a little surprised, but they both waved and said hi. Aria turned the laptop back toward herself.

Athena was smiling, and she cleared her throat. "So, did Troy look at the tools? Does he have everything he needs?"

"He said he does."

"Good. I'm really glad I kept grandpa's tools. Now, they will be put to good use. Did he see the cabinets?"

"Yes, he did."

"Did you give him the truck keys?"

"I did, Mom," Aria sighed.

"Aria, are you certain you do not need a car to the airport? Traffic can be bad, and Trevor is busy with the remodeling."

"I'm sure. Besides, Trevor wants to take me to the airport, so we can spend time together before I leave."

Athena nodded. "I already have the car booked to bring us home when we return. We will have a lot of luggage, and it will be a tight fit with our cars." Aria nodded.

Trevor leaned closer to Troy. "I plan on getting a full-size vehicle next year."

Troy gave Trevor a sideways look. "I don't think it has anything to do with vehicle size," he whispered.

Aria waved at them to be quiet again "Where are you and Maura going, Mom?"

"To Trastevere to her cousin's restaurant. There's a street party tonight too."

Aria nodded. "What time does the conference start tomorrow?"

"Oh, nothing gets going until eleven or so. I'm going to have a leisurely breakfast in the morning."

Aria smiled. "Well, say hi to Maura for me, have fun, and be careful. Good night. I love you."

"We will be careful. I love you too, honey. *Arrivederci*."

Aria waited for her mother to disconnect, and then she closed the laptop.

"Did she say she's going to dinner and then to a party tonight?" Troy asked.

"It's Italy," Aria replied with a shrug of her shoulders. She stood up and picked up her purse.

Trevor was astonished. "It's Monday night! Who has a street party on a Monday night unless it's to watch Monday Night Football?"

"It's Italy," Aria replied again with a bit of annoyance in her voice.

Troy looked at his watch. "Speaking of Monday Night Football, Dallas is on tonight."

"Oh. Well, we better go to dinner then," Trevor said. "Ready, Aria?"

"Hello," Aria called as she entered the house late in the afternoon the next day. Trevor came downstairs and kissed her. Aria looked in the dining room. "You piled all the furniture in that room?"

Trevor nodded, yes.

"Hi, Troy," she said when he came out of the kitchen.

"Hello."

Trevor took the coffee cups she carried, and he set them on the table in the hallway. "We thought it best to put it all in one room, so we can work without moving furniture around. We also returned the rental truck.

We need to get some materials at the home improvement store this evening."

"You better not go in the kitchen, Aria." Troy informed her. She was dressed in black slacks, a print blouse, and a black jacket. "I've started demoing, and there is dust everywhere." He picked up one of the coffee cups and took a drink.

"Trevor told me that you made all the cabinets in your home, Troy." Aria looked for a way to find out what her mother and Troy did together in Texas. "Did Mom get a chance to see them?"

"Yes, Athena saw them. She visited my home a couple times."

Aria smiled. She did not go to Troy's home when they visited in the Spring even though the house was just at the end of the driveway. "It's nice that you gave her a tour. You said she was there a couple times?" Aria tried to sound casual. She did not want to come out and ask what they did, but sometimes being subtle did not get the answers.

"Umm, yes, we hung out together a couple times at my place."

"That's nice. What did you do?" Aria asked.

"Oh, um, we had dinner and breakfast." Troy was nervous. He was not sure what he should tell Aria. "Athena didn't tell you about her stay?"

"She said you two hung out together. But, well, you know, she came home, and we went almost immediately to New York City to meet her editor and to shop for my wedding gown," Aria explained. "We've been so busy wedding planning."

Troy nodded his head and smiled, but he was concerned. Athena and Aria talked about everything, so why didn't Athena tell her daughter about them. He did not expect Athena to discuss intimate details with her daughter, but he did expect Athena to discuss something with her. His heart sank. Maybe she did just want to be friends.

They all seemed tense standing in the hallway. Finally, Trevor spoke up breaking the silence. "Before you leave for Italy, we have to select paint colors," he said to Aria changing the subject.

Thursday morning, Troy painted the stairwell and the landing to the second floor and then continued working in the kitchen. He went back to the home improvement store for supplies, and he stopped to get a couple sub sandwiches for dinner. Trevor spent the day with Aria, and then he took her to the airport. She had an early evening nonstop flight, and Trevor planned to stay there until the plane left and the traffic subsided.

"I'm back," Trevor called as he walked in the door about 7:30 pm.

Troy came out of the dining room. "She's on her way?" Troy asked. Trevor nodded. "The landing is ready for the clock."

"Great. Let's move it."

Troy and Trevor positioned the grandfather clock and started it. "I am very happy to have the clock," Trevor said, "but shouldn't you or Dan get it?"

"Mom asked Dan and I before she gave it to you. We both want you to have it," Troy replied.

Trevor looked at his brother. "Thanks. We'll take good care of it." They went back downstairs. "You got a lot done today, Troy. Thanks."

"I'm happy to help."

"There's a sports bar in town, should we go watch the game and have a couple beers?" Trevor asked.

"Yeah, sounds good."

Chapter 19

Aria walked off the plane and headed to the baggage claim area. The bag she checked was very light. It was primarily for the return trip. She pulled the bag off the conveyor belt and then exited the area. Athena was waiting for her. "Hi," she called excitedly when she saw her mother.

"Hi." Athena waved. She was so happy to have Aria with her in Italy. She gave her daughter a tight hug and took the big bag. "Did you sleep on the plane?"

"I did," Aria replied.

"Good. Let's get you settled in at the hotel and then go out for brunch. We have an appointment for the veil at 12:30."

The two women talked excitedly as they made their way to the train that would take them to downtown Rome. Once at Termini, they exited the station and only had a few blocks to walk to the hotel.

"So, how are things going at the house?" Athena asked as Aria got ready to take a shower.

"Great. Troy is a talented carpenter. He and Trevor knocked out the wall and moved it in half a day. The new garden window is also in. They are working on sheetrock. Daddy said he is going to lend a hand with the remodeling this weekend."

"What?!"

"Daddy said he is going to help. Is that a problem?"

"No. No. Of course not. It's just your dad is not much of a remodeler," Athena commented. Aria headed into the bathroom. "So, your dad was at the house?" Athena called to her through the door.

"Yeah, last night. He, Brook, and Amber came over to see me before I left. Oh, Mom that reminds me. In my purse is an envelope of cash from Dad. I have to convert the money to Euros."

"He gave you cash?"

"He was worried because I never carry cash, so he gave me three hundred dollars."

"Did he meet Troy?" Athena knew it was inevitable that they would meet, but she did not know how she felt about James meeting Troy without her being there.

"Yes, they seemed to get along well."

"How long did they stay?"

"We had dinner. Daddy and Brook brought Chinese."

Athena changed into a pair of slacks and a pink lace blouse. She put on a pair of comfortable shoes and a pair of earrings. Aria emerged from the bathroom a short while later dressed in a pair of leggings and a floral blouse. She slipped on a pair of low-heeled knee-high boots, and they headed out.

They first stopped at the bank and then walked to the restaurant which Athena's friend Laura and her husband owned. "*Ciao!*" Laura exclaimed as they walked in. Laura was a small, very heavy-set woman in her early sixties. She was a fabulous cook, and she and her husband ran the restaurant for over thirty years. "Aria, welcome." She pulled Aria to her and kissed one cheek and then the other. "So, you are getting married.

Wonderful. So wonderful. Come sit. Let me see the ring" Aria held up her left hand. "Beautiful."

In the front of the restaurant were cases filled with a variety of pizzas, pasta dishes, and vegetables. The tables were set with crisp, pure white tablecloths, blue placemats, and white napkins. The walls were painted with images of various fruits and vegetables that were connected with a painted grape vine that wound its way around the room. Laura's husband Giorgio came out of the kitchen wiping his hands. "Welcome Aria," he said, and he too kissed one of Aria's cheeks and then the other.

Laura went into the kitchen and came out carrying a pan of steaming eggplant parmesan. "Your favorite, Aria," she said.

Aria smiled. "Thank you. I love your eggplant."

"Good, eat."

As Athena and Aria ate, Laura and Giorgio came by as customers permitted to catch up and chat. "Is Rosalie making the veil?" Laura asked.

"Yes, we have an appointment at 12:30," Athena replied. "She makes the most beautiful veils, Aria. I took the fabric swatch to her when I arrived, and she will have several choices for you today."

"Rosalie is the best. She made all my girl's veils for communion and wedding."

"I can't wait to see them." Aria buttered another homemade roll and took a bite.

"Have more eggplant, Aria. You are so skinny," Laura said as she scooped up more eggplant and placed it on Aria's plate. Aria looked at her mother who smiled.

Fortunately, Rosalie's shop was not far from the restaurant, so they arrived only a few minutes late. "Ah, Athena. Laura called me to tell me you were on your way." She took Athena's hand in hers. "Good to see you."

"This is Aria, my daughter, the bride."

"*Bellissima.* Such a beautiful bride. Come, I will show you beautiful veils." Rosaline's shop was small and packed with veils and accessories of all sizes and in many shades of white. Aria stopped and looked in a case full of circlets and tiaras. Rosalie walked to the wall where a variety of veils hung on a rod. She pushed all but three back and took out the fabric swatch that Athena left with her. "These are the veils I select for your dress."

Athena and Aria walked over and looked at the three choices. "These are gorgeous," Aria said. The three veils were made of pure white lace and all were Cathedral length. "How do I choose?"

"We try them on and see which one you like best." Rosalie sat Aria on a high stool. She took bobby pins and twisted Aria's hair into a quick updo on the sides and left it long in back as Athena said Aria planned to wear her hair. She attached the first veil then stood Aria up and walked her to the large three sided mirror.

Aria and Athena gasped. This veil had intricate beading along the edge of the veil. Rosalie spread out the veil behind Aria. "It's gorgeous," Athena said. She took a couple pictures and texted one to James.

"Is Daddy up?"

Athena nodded. "He said, wow!"

The second veil had clusters of beading all over. It too was gorgeous, and Athena sent off a picture to James. Athena knew the third veil was the one by Aria's reaction, and she quickly snapped a picture and sent it to James. Aria was speechless. This veil attached at the top of her head with combs. The lace seemed to shimmer and glitter, and the edge of the veil had tiny rhinestones all around. Aria looked in the mirror and turned one way and then the other. She smiled and seemed to glow. "This is it," she said.

Athena nodded yes. She had tears in her eyes. Aria looked so beautiful, and somehow seeing her daughter in a veil made the reality of the wedding all too clear. A text came in, and Athena looked down. It was from James. Just one word, 'Yes'.

"You are so beautiful." Rosalie fussed around Aria. "Let me make a few adjustments."

"I'm going to wear a circlet," Aria explained.

Rosalie nodded and went over to the case in the corner. She selected a circlet and a tiara and brought them to Aria. First, she put the circlet on Aria.

"Oh, that is beautiful," Aria said.

"That is pretty," Athena agreed.

Rosalie then put a glittering tiara on Aria's head just in front of where the veil was attached to her head by the combs. "Oh, this is beautiful too," Aria said.

Athena got up and walked over to Aria. "I have an idea," she began. "Why don't you wear the tiara for the wedding ceremony and then wear the circlet during the reception when you take off the veil," she suggested.

"I like that idea," Aria replied. "We will take both, Rosalie." Rosalie nodded. Aria looked at herself again in the mirror. "Trevor is going to love this."

"I will make the adjustments and have the veil ready Sunday morning. You come make sure it is ok, and I will pack it up."

"Thank you," Aria and Athena said together.

"I have the little girl's veil ready. I will get it to show you." Rosalie went out back.

Aria looked at her mother. "Little girl's veil?"

"I ordered a tiara and veil for Amber." Athena explained.

Aria smiled at her mother. "That is so thoughtful. She will love it."

Athena paid for everything "Well, we are finished for the afternoon." They exited the shop. "Time for a cup of tea."

"And a pastry," Aria added.

They walked down the street to the pastry shop. Trevor messaged Aria several times and sent pictures of the cabinets fully installed. She showed her mother.

"Those cabinets look like they were made for the kitchen," Athena said. "Troy did a very professional job."

"Speaking of Troy," Aria said as casually as she could, "are you looking forward to seeing him again?"

"Yes, I suppose so." Athena tried to keep her voice steady. She did not know what to expect from Troy. She did not know what she wanted from him either.

Early in the evening, Aria video chatted with Trevor before she and Athena went out to dinner. Troy did not want to make noise while they talked, so he took the opportunity to sit down and have a cup of coffee and a snack.

"Did you get that cash your Dad gave you exchanged into Euros?"

"Yes, I did. Mom and I went to the bank and then had lunch at Laura and Giorgio's restaurant. They made me eggplant parmesan." Aria licked her lips. "It was amazing, as usual."

Trevor laughed. "I'm glad."

"I have my veil," Aria teased.

"I guess I cannot see it," Trevor replied.

Athena came out of the bathroom dressed for dinner. "No," she called to him.

Trevor saw Athena in the background. "Where are you two going for dinner?" Troy went behind Trevor to look at the computer screen. He saw Athena dressed in a very skimpy black dress, and his eyes went wide.

"Out with Maura. It's Friday night, so we will probably stop at a few clubs too," Aria replied. "Hi, Troy."

Athena leaned over Aria. "Hi, guys." They waved to her.

"Wow, you two look really nice," Trevor commented as he looked at Aria's black and white strapless dress. "Aria, be careful and text me."

"I will. We are off to Venice early in the morning. I love you."

"I love you too."

Aria clicked off, and Trevor looked up at Troy. Troy looked as nervous as he felt.

The next morning, Athena and Aria boarded an early train for Venice. Train travel in Europe is comfortable and fast, so they went to the dining car for tea and breakfast as soon as the train got underway. It was just under three and a half hours from Rome to Venice. Just enough time for a short nap after they ate.

The sun was shining, and the water was calm when they boarded the vaporetto, water taxi, to the heart of Venice. They stood on deck and the wind blew their hair back as the boat traveled through the canals.

They exited the boat and walked to the Reaulto Bridge. They stopped midway across the bridge and took some pictures. In the water below them, colorful gondolas tied to poles bobbed in the water, and men waited to take riders on a trip through the canals. The water was green and murky, and it lapped up against the buildings and walkways. Unfortunately, on this trip, they did not have time for a gondola ride.

Aria and Athena stopped at several carts and shops as they walked along. "Here we are," Athena said when they reached the glass shop. The window displayed a variety of delicate glassware and intricate hanging lamps.

"*Buon Giorno,*" the woman behind the counter said as they walked in.

"*Buon Giorno.* We placed an order online for jewelry boxes. My name is Aria Romano."

"*Si.* Let me get them," She disappeared in back and returned a few minutes later with a box. She set it on the counter and took one of the jewelry boxes out to show Aria and Athena.

"These are gorgeous," Aria said as she admired one of the boxes.

"*Grazie.*" She removed the other boxes for them to inspect.

"They sparkle and are more beautiful than the pictures online," Aria said, and Athena agreed. The woman wrapped each glass jewelry box carefully and put it in a gift box then she placed the boxes inside a bigger box. She tied the box up with cording and attached a handle so it could be carried easily.

"There is a mask shop down the street," Athena said as she led the way. The shop window was decorated with elaborate masks in a variety of colors and styles. They went in and looked around.

Aria pointed to a pair of masks on the wall. "Those are very nice," she called to her mother. The bride and groom masks were white with delicate black line details, white feathers, and crystals. The saleswoman took down the masks and put them on the counter so they could look at them more closely. "I'll take them," Arian told the saleswoman who nodded.

Athena picked out a rose colored mask with gold details for herself, a pale blue one for Brook, and a light green one for Maria. Neither knew what Shelby planned to wear, so they selected a white mask for her. All the masks had intricate painted details, feathers, and crystals. They next selected an assortment of black masks with feathers and crystals for James, John, Dan, Troy, and the men in the wedding party. For the bridesmaids and maid of honor, who were all wearing red velvet dresses, they selected pale pink masks with red details, white feathers, and crystals.

"Danny is wearing a white tux, right?" Athena asked. Aria nodded yes. "White mask or black for him?"

Aria thought for a moment. "Black," she replied, so they selected a black mask for him and an intricately decorated white one with feathers and lots of crystals for Amber.

"Should we get basic white masks for the women and basic black for the men?" Aria asked, "Or should we get assorted colors?"

Athena looked at the masks. "We could get gold for the women and black for the men," Athena suggested.

"What if we get white, gold, and black masks, and guests can choose whatever color they want?"

"That's a good idea," Athena replied.

While they waited for the shop attendants to pack everything up, Aria texted Trevor several pictures.

Back in Falmouth, James was at the house helping Troy and Trevor for the day. He brought donuts and breakfast sandwiches, and the three men were sitting in the kitchen eating.

"That's Aria," Trevor said when his phone chimed.

Almost at the same time James' phone chimed. "Athena," he chuckled. "Athena and Aria are busy in Venice," James said as he took a bite of a breakfast sandwich.

"They are. Aria has texted me several times." He showed James the picture Aria sent him of her and Athena at the Reaulto Bridge.

"They look like they are also having fun," James said.

"Here's a picture of the bridesmaid's gifts," Trevor showed Troy and James the pictures Aria sent him. Aria sent another picture. Trevor looked at it and then showed Troy. "That's Mom's mask." Another text came in. "That's Shelby's."

"Shelby will like that," Troy said.

"Athena said they are going to do a little shopping after they have lunch." James texted her back. Athena sent him a picture of Amber's mask. He showed Trevor and Troy. "Amber is going to be beautiful." He paused so long they thought something was wrong. "You know," he began, "Athena bought a tiara and veil for Amber too. I was touched. So very touched that she thought of Amber."

When they finally left the shop, Aria and Athena were hungry, so they walked to a café near St. Mark's cathedral for a late lunch and drinks. The square bustled with tourists and vendors selling merchandise. They sat at an outside table and watched people go by while they ate and looked over their lists.

"What do you think about those small glass flowers we saw for favors?" Athena asked.

"I liked them. Can we give flowers to the men too?"

"Guests will be making favor bags, and the glass flowers will be one of the items. They can take one or not."

"What about the small glass masks as a second choice?"

Athena nodded. "That's a good idea. Let's get them after lunch."

Once the favors were purchased, Aria and Athena stopped in several clothing shops. Aria saw a cream colored lace dress in a shop window. "Let's go in." The dress was available in cream and in light pink. Aria took one of each color into the dressing room.

She came out to show her mother. "I like the pink one best," Athena said after Aria tried both on.

"I was thinking the same thing," Aria looked at herself again in the three way mirror.

"That will be nice for a night out in Belize."

"It is dressy yet beachy," Aria replied. She decided to purchase it.

They slowly made their way back to the Reaulto Bridge area. The walkway along the canal was not crowded now. Gondolas floated and moved gently from side to side on the water. Lights were coming on in the shops and along the walk, and they cast a soft glow over the stones and the water.

They stopped at a café on the main canal near the water taxi stop and bought sandwiches to eat on the train. Athena chose a mozzarella, pesto, and tomato on rye bread sandwich, and Aria selected the Italian ham, salami, pepperoni, and cheese on Italian bread sandwich. They also purchased an assortment of pastries for dessert.

They boarded a water taxi to the mainland, and then they walked a short distance to the train station. They did not have to wait long to board the train. They stowed their packages and then sat down. Once the train was underway, Athena went to the dining car for two cups of hot tea. She returned and set the drinks down on the table, and they settled into their seats with their tea and sandwiches. After a successful day of shopping, their feet were tired, and they relaxed as the train returned to Rome.

Troy, Trevor, and James worked steadily breaking only for a half hour for lunch. Trevor and James worked in the upstairs bedrooms putting in closet systems, and then they painted the hallway and one of the bedrooms. Troy finished the kitchen drywall, took up the old kitchen floor, and began prepping for the new flooring.

They were cleaning up when Trevor received a text from Aria. 'Back in Rome. We are going to bed. Good night. I love you.'

"Aria and Athena are in their hotel room. Aria must be exhausted. Her text was short," Trevor told Troy and James.

"They aren't the only ones," James replied. It was almost 6:30 pm. "Let me take you guys out to dinner. We can go to the Wings bar and watch the game."

"Sounds good," Trevor and Troy replied.

Chapter 20

Athena and Aria were late getting back. The car picked them up at the terminal and brought them home to Falmouth. Trevor and Troy were there waiting when the car pulled in the driveway. Trevor opened Aria's door, and she stepped out of the vehicle. He pulled her close, and he kissed her like he had not seen her in months. Troy and Athena had not seen one another in months, yet they stammered a hello, and they barely touched one another's cheek when they kissed.

Troy took one of the big bags and walked to the front door. The driver pulled the other large bag along and set it at the bottom of the steps. He went back for the smaller bags. "Thank you." Athena gave him a tip, and she headed in the house.

"It is good to be home," Athena said as she looked around her kitchen. Now that the conference was over, wedding planning was finished, and the bulk of the wedding items were purchased, she felt she could take some time to relax. Fall was her favorite time of the year, and she wanted to spend some time walking the beach, picking apples, and decorating her home.

The next morning, Athena was preparing breakfast when Aria came downstairs. "Are you going over to the house today to see what has been completed?" Aria inquired. "Trevor said he has to go to the office this morning, so Troy will be there alone." She watched her mother carefully, but Athena's expression did not change.

"I might stop by," Athena said as she made Aria a sandwich for lunch.

"Should we all have dinner together tonight?" Aria asked.

"Yes, I have a pork roast in the freezer. I will defrost it and put it in the crock pot for pulled pork, so we can eat whenever we are ready."

"Yum. That sounds good." Aria put some chips and her water bottle into her lunch bag. "Well, I am off to work."

"Have a good day. I love you."

"You too, Mom. I love you." Aria picked up her tote bag.

Athena closed the door behind Aria, poured a cup of tea, and put a bagel in the toaster for breakfast. She ate standing at the counter while she checked email, and then she went upstairs to shower and get dressed for work. An hour later, she pulled up to Aria's new home. She heard hammering as she approached the front door. She paused, straightened her dress, and rang the doorbell. The hammering stopped, and she heard footsteps approaching the door. It opened, and there stood Troy. He wore a very tight white tee shirt and jeans, and his tool belt hung low on his hips. Athena smiled at him. "Hi."

"Hi. Come on in." He opened the door wider so Athena could get inside.

Troy looked at her as she passed him. She was beautiful, but he dared not say that to her. He had hoped for a warmer welcome when she returned from Italy because they had not seen one another in months.

Athena headed toward the kitchen.

"It's pretty dusty in there," Troy warned. "I'm getting ready to start laying the sub floor. What brings you by?"

Athena stared at him. What brings me by? Really? Although she did not want to show a great deal of affection in front of Aria and Trevor, they were alone in the house now. However, she composed herself quickly. "I just stopped by to say hi and see what progress was made," she said in a cheerful tone. "Is that the flooring they selected?" Athena pointed to the roll of flooring that was in the hallway.

"Yes. I think it will look good. It should bring out the richness of the cabinetry."

She went in the kitchen and looked around. "You really did a fantastic job putting those cabinets in place."

"Thanks," Troy was not going to make the first move, but it was killing him to be so close to Athena and not take her in his arms.

"Well, I probably should be going. I am expected at the agency this morning." Athena headed toward the door even though she did not tell Holly what time she planned to be at the agency. It was apparent that Troy was not going to kiss her or say anything to her about what happened in Texas.

"Oh, ok," he replied with a bit of sadness in his voice that Athena did not catch.

"When is Trevor due back?" she asked.

"Lunch time," Troy replied. "We are going to be working at your house later today. I need to plane wood for the pantry."

"Ok. I will be back in the early afternoon." Athena left the house and returned to her car. She waved good-bye as she drove away, and she saw him close the front door. She let out a huge sad sigh. "Well, I guess that tells me where I stand with him," she said to her reflection in the mirror. It is for the best, she silently consoled herself. She shook her head. What was I thinking? That he would scoop me up into his arms and kiss me? Would I really like that? Well, yes, she answered her own questions.

Athena arrived at the office just before nine o'clock. "Hi," she called as she entered.

Holly got up and greeted her. "Hi. How was Italy?"

"Fantastic as always," Athena replied with a smile.

"Did Aria get her veil?"

Athena nodded. She took out her phone and showed Holly the picture of Aria wearing the veil.

"Wow. That is gorgeous."

They walked into Athena's office. Athena hung up her light jacket and thumbed through the pile of mail on her desk. "So how are things going here?" she asked.

"Slow," Holly replied.

Later that afternoon, Athena returned home. Trevor and Troy were down in the basement working on the pantry cabinet for the kitchen.

"Hi," she called down the stairs to them. "I'm going to change, and I'll be right down." She went upstairs and changed into leggings and a tee shirt, and she put on her indoor/outdoor slippers. She checked her appearance in the mirror, and then she went down to the basement to see how the pantry Troy designed and built was coming along.

"Oh, that looks good," she said looking it over. "You made it match the cabinets my father made," Athena remarked.

"I thought they should match," Troy replied. He watched Athena when she turned to inspect the cabinet.

236

"It is perfect." Athena smiled. "Dad would have been so happy that his cabinets are in Aria and Trevor's home." She continued to look at the cabinet Troy made, but she also glanced at Troy as he worked.

"His workshop made it all possible," Troy replied. He adjusted the glue clamps that held the cabinet together. "I should be able to install the pantry Thursday evening or Friday morning."

Trevor looked at Troy and then at Athena. He decided he should give them some time alone. "I have to check on a couple things for work if you don't need me, Troy."

"No problem. I just have a few small things left to do."

"Good." Trevor turned to Athena, "I will be back by the time Aria gets home. What time is dinner?"

"There's no set time. We can eat when everyone is ready. I'm going to make salad to go with the pulled pork."

"Ok great. I will pick up something for dessert. See y'all later." Trevor went up the stairs and left the house. He got in his car, and they heard him drive away.

In the basement, Athena was not sure what to do. She looked around nervously and thought about heading back upstairs. Troy sensed her discomfort. He did not need help, but he did not want her to run off. "Could you give me a hand?" he asked.

"Certainly," she replied.

Troy had her hold two pieces of wood while he screwed them together. They smiled at one another, but both looked away when their hands touched. Athena withdrew her hand once the pieces of wood were secure. Troy checked the pantry over and made a few minor adjustments. "That should do it," he said. He wiped down the tools he used and started to put everything away. "This really is a well-equipped workshop."

"Dad spent a lot of time down here," she said. "When he passed, several people inquired about the tools, but Mom said she wasn't going to sell them. I feel the same way. I'm very happy they are being used once again."

"Trevor and Aria's home is nice, and it is close by. You must be happy."

Athena looked at him. Did he think she pushed them to purchase a house close to hers? Did he think she would be a meddling kind of mother in law? "What do you mean?" she asked in a defensive tone of voice.

Troy looked up at her. He recognized the defensive tone, and he was unsure why she felt that way. "Just that they have a beautiful home, and it is near where they work and have been living. That's all." He finished putting everything away, rechecked the glue clamps, and then they went upstairs.

Troy was not sure if he should go or stay. He wished he knew what she was thinking. He thought about her every day after she left Texas. He planned to take Trevor up on the offer to visit. Then, Trevor and Aria purchased the house, and his mother wanted to give them furniture. Volunteering to bring up the furniture was not as obvious as a spontaneous vacation.

Athena walked over to the refrigerator. "Would you like something to drink?" she asked.

"Do you have any beer?"

"I do." She opened the door and pulled out a Corona.

Troy smiled. She must have bought those just for him. He was baffled by her conflicting signals. "My favorite," he said as he took the bottle of beer that she offered him. "Are you having one?"

"I think I will." Athena took a bottle out for herself and opened it.

238

Troy leaned against the counter and took a long drink. "This house is in a great location," he said. "Trevor says you can see the ocean from upstairs."

Athena looked surprised. "Didn't he take you on a tour?"

"I only saw the first floor and basement. Trevor and Aria wanted to show me the rest of the house, but I said I would wait for you." Troy shrugged and smiled at Athena.

"Well, let me show you around." Athena took two more bottles of beer out of the refrigerator and handed one to Troy. She led the way to the second floor and showed him the three bedrooms and the upstairs baths then she started up the stairs to the third floor. "This is my favorite room," she said as she went up the small, dark stairway to the attic. Troy followed her, and once they exited the stairwell, the space opened up to a large room with high ceilings that sloped down to the windows. "My dad enlarged the windows, so we had a better view of the ocean," she said. "I have to get the storm windows on soon."

"Wow. This is some view. I see why this is your favorite room." Troy stood at the window and marveled at the view of the ocean.

"Sit down." Athena gestured to the obviously new rocking chairs set in front of the windows. "I spend a lot of time up here."

Troy looked around. Next to one rocking chair was a rolling table on which sat a laptop. Next to the table was another table piled with papers and books. There were two filing cabinets along the back wall and a bookcase overflowing with books. Also, in the room there was a twin bed, a love seat, a coffee table, several end tables, a flat screen TV on a rolling stand, assorted lamps, an exercise bike, and a desk. Piled furthest away were a few stacks of boxes.

They sat in the rocking chairs. From this high up, the water glistened in the sunshine. There were boats on the water and sea gulls flew around. "The view is spectacular," Troy said.

"I want to remodel up here. I slept up here a lot when I was a child. My parents used this room for storage and as a sitting area. I have turned it into an office and den of sorts since moving back in."

"You might consider putting in a sliding door to a small porch. I think you would enjoy sitting on a porch even more."

"Could a porch be added up here?" Athena asked. "I would love to be able to sit outside, write, and look at the ocean."

"Yes, I think so," Troy said. "It needs to be engineered, and you must have structural plans, but it might be worth the expense."

"That would be wonderful if it isn't too expensive."

"A less expensive option is to take out these two windows and replace them with one larger, energy efficient window. It would improve your view and save money. Not to mention no more storm windows."

Athena nodded her head. "I will have to look into it." She loved the idea of a bigger window or a porch.

They sat in the rocking chairs, looked at the ocean, and finished their beers. They chatted about Aria and Trevor's new home, the upcoming wedding, the ranch, and work. Everything but their relationship.

Athena looked at Troy. She truly enjoyed spending time with him, and she really missed him. Of course, she did not feel comfortable telling him how much she missed him. Perhaps he did not miss her.

Troy leaned back in the rocker and looked at Athena. She also leaned back and looked relaxed. Her hair flowed over her right shoulder. Her hands held the beer tightly, but she smiled at him. He wanted her so badly, but she had not indicated she changed her mind, so maybe she really did just want to be friends. Troy stifled a sigh. He did not want to be just friends.

Chapter 21

Sunday morning, Athena got up and went downstairs. Aria joined her a few minutes later. "I am so tired," Aria said.

"Me too." Athena replied. Saturday was an exceptionally busy day for them, but the fish tank was moved, and the remodeling was almost completed. She poured two mugs of hot water for tea. "Let's just go to the apple farm today. I think we all need a restful and relaxing day."

"I agree," Aria said with a deep sigh. She texted Trevor and very quickly received a text back. "Trevor says they are just getting up too. They are both tired."

"Tell them to come over and have breakfast. I will make eggs and pancakes."

"Oh, that sounds good," Aria said as she texted Trevor. "He says they can be here in about a half an hour."

"I'm going to shower then start breakfast." Athena took her mug of tea and headed upstairs.

A little more than a half hour later, Trevor and Troy arrived. Athena whisked up scrambled eggs, bacon cooked in the pan, and the pancake batter was resting. Aria sliced biscuits.

"Wow," Trevor said when he entered the kitchen. He kissed Aria good morning. "What's going on? Your mom never cooks bacon," he whispered very softly in her ear. "And she baked biscuits?"

Aria shrugged her shoulders.

"Good morning. It smells delicious." Troy walked over to the stove where Athena was flipping the bacon.

"Good morning." She smiled at him, and Troy's heart skipped a beat.

"You have your hands full. Can I help with the bacon?"

"Thank you," Athena replied with another smile. "I will start making pancakes."

Troy picked up the wooden fork and began turning the bacon. She had Coronas for him, now she baked biscuits, and was cooking bacon. Maybe she did miss him, Troy thought to himself.

Trevor set the table, and Aria put the orange juice on the table, made a pot of coffee, and put water for tea on to boil. Athena placed a large stack of pancakes and a bowl of scrambled eggs on the table next to the platter of bacon that Troy finished cooking. Trevor and Aria brought over the toasted biscuits, and they all sat down to eat.

"We are going to go apple picking this afternoon," Aria told Troy. "Have you ever had apple cider donuts?"

"No," Troy replied.

"They are incredible," Aria told him. "You will love them."

"The leaves are near peak further north. We could go to the New Hampshire apple farm." Athena suggested. "It's a long ride, but the colors will be pretty."

"Good idea." Trevor turned to Troy, "You will enjoy it. The color will be spectacular." Now, he looked at Athena. "I'll drive." It was almost a question. She smiled and nodded.

Just before noon, Trevor drove over the bridge and turned onto the highway that headed North to New Hampshire. Troy insisted Aria sit up front, and he and Athena sat in the back seat. There was the usual traffic getting around Boston, but once they were past the Rt 128 interchange, the traffic was lighter. The trees were also more colorful.

"The trees are very large, and the leaves really are beautiful," Troy said. He leaned back in the seat and stretched his legs out as far as he could.

He wore a white button down shirt, and Athena thought he suspected that she loved to see him in one. While most of their tans had faded, Troy still had his, and it was accented by the white shirt. He looks so sexy, Athena thought to herself. It made her a little sad to think that he was not showing interest in being with her. She realized she was staring at him when he smiled at her. Her heart pounded, she felt herself flush, and she quickly looked out the window.

The apple farm was very busy when they arrived. Trevor followed the farm hand who directed vehicles and parked his car up a small rise in between two rows of peach trees. The peaches were long harvested, but a few shriveled ones lay on the ground alongside a tree trunk. Troy stood and looked out over the apple orchard. The leaves were a mix of reds, oranges, and yellows. He had been to the northern U.S. before, but he had not seen foliage this vibrant and colorful. He took several pictures.

Trevor and Aria walked hand in hand and led the way to the farm building. "Let's get donuts first," Aria said as she took her place at the end of the long donut line.

Troy looked ahead. "This is the line for donuts?" The three nodded, yes. "Wow," Troy said in disbelief.

Aria took a deep breath. "I love the smell of donuts and apples."

244

Trevor laughed. "You love apple picking." He leaned over and gave Aria a small affectionate kiss. She hooked her arm in his.

While Trevor and Aria stood in line, Athena took Troy into the building to look around. Inside were several tables of fall vegetables and assorted varieties of apples. The coolers along the end wall and the one opposite the tables were full of items such as farm fresh milk, apple cider, ready to bake pies, a variety of cheeses, and butter.

Troy reached in one of the coolers and took out a bottle of soda. Athena looked at the bottle. "Birch beer," she said. "I think you will like it. It has a nutty taste." She took the bottle from Troy and put it and a quart of fresh apple cider on the cashier's counter. On the way back to join Trevor and Aria in line, Athena stopped at the condiments counter and took four small paper cups and a length of paper towel to use as napkins.

"How many donuts should we get?' Aria asked when it was nearly her turn.

Athena looked at the line. It was longer than when they first arrived. "Two dozen?" she suggested. "I don't want to stand in the line again today, do you?"

Aria shook her head no.

When they paid for the donuts, they walked outside, and they sat down at one of the red glossy picnic tables. Athena poured apple cider into the cups and handed everyone a piece of paper towel. "You first," Trevor said to Troy.

Troy reached into the white, foil lined bag and took out a hot donut. The three of them watched as he took a bite. "Delicious. This is really good. But hot." He blew out a breath to cool his mouth.

"Drink some cider," Athena said handing him a cup.

"Wow! This is good." He drank down the rest of the cider, and Athena poured him more. "I've never had cider like this before."

"It's pressed in the barn and as fresh as it can be," Athena told him.

While the four of them were eating, a band set up on stage and began playing country/folk music. Although none of them knew the songs, many people sang along. One couple danced, and several children sat on hay bales at the foot of the stage and looked up at the performers. They ate more donuts and drank more cider while listening to the band.

"Well, ready to pick apples?" Aria asked excitedly. "I'll go get baskets." She ran off to the main building to get them.

"And I will run the rest of the donuts and the cider back to the car," Trevor said as he headed off in the other direction.

Athena and Troy sat and waited at the picnic table. They glanced at one another and smiled nervously. Finally, Troy opened the bottle of birch beer and took a drink. "This is good. Nutty as you said, Athena."

"I loved birch beer when I was young." Troy handed her the bottle, and she took a drink. "It is delicious." She took another drink. "Just like I remember it." She handed the bottle back to Troy who finished the soda.

"There is a homey country feel here," Troy remarked. He noticed that he and Trevor were not the only people wearing cowboy hats and cowboy boots.

When Aria and Trevor came back to the table, the four of them walked over to the edge of the dirt road and waited for the tractor and wagon. It slowly came around the corner of another building and came to a stop right in front of them. People slid down off the flat bed wagon and hoisted up their baskets full of ripe apples. Aria jumped right up on the wagon, and Trevor got up next to her. Athena was shorter and had difficulty getting on. Troy picked her up effortlessly and set her down.

246

"Thank you," Athena said to him, and Troy nodded and sat down next to her.

Once the wagon was loaded with people, the tractor pulled it slowly up a rather steep hill on the way to the orchard. Puffs of dust were kicked up by the tires. The apple trees were so close Troy could extend his arm and brush the dark green leaves on the branches. The sky was clear blue, and the sun shone down and felt warm for early October. Athena pushed up the sleeves of her shirt.

Troy watched her. "Good idea," he said as he unbuttoned the cuffs of his shirt's sleeves and rolled them up.

The tractor turned left at the top of the hill and rolled very slowly along a row of apple trees. At the end of the dirt road, the tractor again turned left and came to a stop. The driver jumped down and addressed the riders who were carefully sliding off the wagon. He told them the types of apples that were ripe and ready for picking, and he told them not to climb any of the trees. He walked over to a nearby apple tree, reached up, and demonstrated the twisting technique for picking apples. Everyone watched him even though almost everyone had been apple picking before and knew the routine. "Enjoy," he said. "Pick up is here or at the bottom of the hill."

While the tractor was parked, a few people jumped up on the wagon. The driver answered a few questions, then he hopped in the tractor's cab, and slowly pulled away.

Athena took pictures of the tractor and wagon, the apples, and the trees. She and Aria posed for their traditional selfie. She took pictures of Aria and Trevor, pictures of Troy, and she had Aria take a couple pictures of her and Troy. She wanted to post about apple picking in New England on her travel blog this evening.

They leisurely walked among the trees and picked a variety of apples. "I will make apple muffins," Athena said as she plucked a ripe Cortland apple from the tree and placed it gently in her basket.

"Oh, yummy," Aria said. She was in the next row picking Golden Delicious apples for her lunch.

They walked a few rows down, and Trevor picked a Macintosh apple off a tree. He polished it on his shirt, and he handed it to Troy. "Taste this." Trevor picked an apple for himself.

Troy took a bite, and apple juice ran down his chin. Athena handed him a piece of paper towel. "These apples are really juicy. And sweet," he said.

"Much better than the ones in the store, right." Trevor bit into his apple.

"Definitely." Troy took another bite.

They walked further down the row to a tree with more apples. It was the peak time for apple picking, and many of the trees only had fruit high up in the tree. Athena stretched to reach an apple far above her head. Troy walked up behind her and lifted her up. "Oh!" she gasped in surprise. She picked several apples, then she turned and smiled at him. "Thanks."

They were so close Troy smelled the floral scent of her shampoo, and he was again overcome with a desire to kiss her. The very gentle breeze played with her long hair, and the sun reflected off her hair's natural red and blonde highlights which seemed to glow around her face. They stared into each other's eyes as he held her.

Troy let Athena down very slowly. He kept his hands at her waist, and they stood only inches apart staring at one another. Athena looked into his dark smoldering eyes and thought she saw desire. Her breathing was shallow, and her heart pounded in her chest.

It was quiet, and they were alone in the row. It was as if time stood still for them. Neither moved. They both waited for the other to either lean in for a kiss or move away. But neither moved for what seemed like minutes.

"Do you have enough apples, Mom?" Aria called from the next row.

Flustered, Athena and Troy both moved apart and looked away from one another. "I do."

"Let me carry that for you." Troy picked up Athena's basket and started walking.

They wandered back to the dirt road, and they sat down at a bright red picnic table and waited for the tractor and wagon to return. Troy took a few more pictures of the landscape and of Trevor, Aria, and Athena, and then he leaned back and looked up. A hawk circled overhead looking for a rodent to eat. The white underside of its feathers stood out against the cloudless sky.

The wagon was crowded on the ride back to the farm building. Aria sat on Trevor's lap, and Troy and Athena each held a basket of apples. Aria hopped off as soon as the wagon came to a stop. "Let's go to the pumpkin patch," she said to Trevor. "We need a pumpkin." Trevor took the apple basket from Athena and caught up to Aria. Troy and Athena followed, and watched as Aria selected a pumpkin.

"Are you going to get a pumpkin, Athena?" Troy asked.

"Not today. I will get one closer to Halloween." She looked around. "I do want to pick up gourds and mini pumpkins for my mantle display though." She walked over to the wooden crates and picked out six mini orange pumpkins and several decorative gourds. "It's too bad you are not staying longer," she said to Troy. "I could take you to Haunted Happenings in Salem, Massachusetts.

Troy smiled. She wanted to take him somewhere. That was a start. "What is Haunted Happenings?"

"It's the Halloween festivities that Salem has every year. There are reenactments of the witch trials, ghost tours, even a Halloween ball."

"It sounds like a fun place to visit," Troy replied.

"Aria and I like to go for a day sometime before Halloween. Trevor came with us last year."

"Is there a candy store there?" Troy remembered the candy Trevor brought them at Thanksgiving the previous year.

Athena laughed. "Yes, he liked the candy store."

They went in the main building and picked up apple cider and cheese on their way to the cash register. It was late in the afternoon, and the sun was going down when they left the apple farm. Aria nodded off in the front seat before they even left New Hampshire. Athena leaned her head back and closed her eyes. Trevor looked in the rear view mirror. He could see his brother watching Athena as she slept peacefully. "Should we get burgers for dinner tonight?" he asked Troy quietly so as not to disturb the sleeping women.

"Yes," Troy whispered.

On Tuesday morning, Athena baked apple muffins. While she waited for them to come out of the oven, she updated her blog with a post on apple picking. She looked through the pictures she took at the apple farm and selected several. She posted a picture of Aria and Trevor eating apples but did not post one of her or Troy.

The smell of baking apples filled the kitchen. She opened the windows to let in some cool air, but there was little breeze, and it was rather warm outside. The sun streamed in the windows, and Athena thought it was a beautiful day for the beach. It was October, and this was one of the last warm beach days of the year. She took the muffins out to cool. It was nearly 7:30 am. She texted Troy, 'How are things going today?'

'Good,' he texted back.

'Have you had breakfast?'

'Just coffee so far.'

'I have fresh baked apple muffins.'

'Sounds good.'

'I will be over soon.'

'Thanks.'

Athena decided to make some scrambled eggs with sausage to go with the muffins. She cooked them and placed them in a covered bowl. She took a stick of butter off the counter, and she placed it and the warm muffins in a wicker basket. She packed everything in a large tote and poured her tea into a travel mug.

A short time later, she pulled into the driveway. Troy came outside as she stepped out of the car. "Hi, Troy."

"Good morning. Let me help you." He took the tote full of food from her and carried it into the house.

While Athena set the food out on the table, Troy took two plates out of the cabinet and two forks out of the drawer.

"It smells delicious," he said as he sat down.

They talked as they ate a leisurely breakfast. "These muffins are very good. I've never had apple muffins before." He took a third muffin, sliced it open, and spread on some warm butter which melted immediately.

"I'm glad you like them." Athena drank her tea and looked at him. She decided to take a chance with him. "Are you busy today?"

"Not especially. The projects are winding down. Some touch up painting and trim work. Why?"

"Do you have lunch plans?"

"No."

"Would you like to have a picnic lunch on the beach with me? It's a beautiful day."

"Yes, I would like to picnic with you." Troy smiled at her, and Athena felt her face get warm.

"Good, about one o'clock?"

"I will be at your house at one o'clock."

Athena cleaned up the dishes and packed up her things. Troy walked her to the door. "See you later."

"Bye."

When she arrived home, Athena went upstairs to write. She was beginning to build a freelance career, and she had an article due at the end of the week for an airline travel magazine. She paused during writing and looked out the window. She really wanted to investigate putting in at least a bigger window, and she hoped she could put on a porch.

Around noon time, Athena began preparing a picnic lunch. She decided to make a green salad with Cesare dressing, and she made Troy a turkey, salami, and provolone sandwich. She took iced tea out of the refrigerator and put it in a thermos then she packed everything up in a picnic basket.

Troy arrived right on time. He carried the basket and Athena carried a tote bag with a large blanket for them to sit on, towels, and of course, her pail for shells. They walked the short distance to the beach. It was deserted, so they selected a spot near the water, and Athena spread out the blanket. They sat down and took off their shoes.

Athena took out a heavy duty paper plate and set it in front of Troy. She opened the container of salad and unwrapped the sandwich. She poured iced tea into two cold cups with lids.

"What a day," Troy leaned back and looked out over the water which was as smooth as glass. The tiniest of waves lapped lightly at the shore. There was no wind at all, and the sun was exceptionally warm. "Is the weather always this nice in October?"

Athena shook her head no. "A couple years ago, it was very cold at this time in October, and we had our first snowfall that stuck to the ground the day before Halloween."

"Oh!" Troy replied.

"That is why I suggested a picnic. A day like today needs to be enjoyed."

"I agree."

After they ate, they stretched out side by side on the blanket and listened to the surf roll ashore. The sea gulls kept coming by to see if there were any scraps of food. Again, they talked about the upcoming wedding, the reception in Texas, winter snow, the holidays, anything but the subject they both wanted to discuss: their relationship.

"Let's walk the beach," Athena suggested.

Troy stood up and reached down to help Athena up. They rolled up their pant legs, and Athena picked up her beach pail then they walked to the edge of the water. The sand was cool but not too cold. A seagull seemed to float along on the water as they walked.

Troy found a fairly large scallop shell and bent down to pick it up. He picked up several smaller scallop shells as well. "I like the orange colored shells," he said as he bent down to pick up a couple more. Athena smiled and picked some up too.

They strolled down the beach and then returned to their blanket and gathered everything up. The sun was getting low in the sky, and the temperature was dropping. "This was an enjoyable afternoon," Troy said as they walked back to her house.

"It was." Athena inserted her key and opened the front door.

"Hi," Aria and Trevor said as they came down the stairs into the kitchen.

"Oh, hi," Athena replied. She was surprised to see them.

"We were wondering where you guys were," Aria looked at the picnic basket. "Oh, were you guys at the beach?"

Athena flushed a little. "It was such a nice day; we had a picnic and spent the afternoon talking, walking the beach, and picking shells." Troy set the basket on the kitchen counter.

"Oh, Troy, the home improvement store called. The sink is in. We can pick it up anytime."

"We can go pick it up now," Troy said. "I will install it tomorrow."

"Let's go." The two men said good-bye and headed to the store.

Thursday morning, Athena opened the front door. "Hi, Jasmine. Come on in."

"Hi, Athena," Jasmine said cheerfully as she walked in the kitchen, took off her black leather jacket, and draped it over the back of a chair. She wore a pair of black jeans and a raspberry colored silky blouse. She sat down at the breakfast bar.

Athena set down two cups of tea and a plate of cookies on the counter. "Oh, raspberry. My favorite." Jasmine picked up a cookie and took a bite. Athena sat down and dunked her tea bag. "So how are things with Troy?" she asked Athena. "Has he made any moves or said anything?"

Athena shook her head no. "Not a word," she said sadly. "He acts like we are just friends." She took a deep breath. "He said yes to a picnic on the beach, but he didn't kiss me or anything." She took a sip of tea.

"Well, that's what you wanted," Jasmine reminded her friend. "Have you said anything to him?"

"No!" Athena quickly replied. "He's a bachelor, and I'm sure he has young women fawning all over him. I told you about the ice cream girl who could not keep her eyes off him. I am just glad I did not say anything to Aria. She doesn't need the stress." Jasmine gave her a sad look. Athena waved her hand. "It's fine. There were no expectations. I enjoy his company, and there is nothing wrong with being friends."

"Potentially a friend with benefits," Jasmine said with a smile.

Athena smiled behind her tea then took a bite of a cookie. "I am going to Nantucket on Saturday to write about the cranberry festival for the magazine. What to come along?"

"I thought Aria was going with you?"

"She was supposed to, but Trevor's boss is having a weekend get a way for the office."

"I can't. It's homecoming weekend." Jasmine thought for a moment. "Why don't you take Troy?" Athena sighed and looked up over her tea mug at Jasmine. "He took you places when you were in Texas, so take him to Nantucket. It's only for the day, right?"

Athena thought about it. "True, and it is only for the day. That's a good idea. I'm sure he would enjoy the boat ride and the island." She texted Troy and asked if he wanted to go to Nantucket on Saturday. 'It is a business trip,' she texted, 'but there will be plenty of time to sight see.'

His reply came less than a minute later. 'Yes. Thanks.' Athena stared at her phone. "He is a man of few words," she said to Jasmine with a roll of her eyes.

They talked for a while, and then Jasmine got up to leave. The two friends hugged. "Let me know how it goes," she said to Athena. Jasmine walked to her car, and Athena waved as she drove off.

Athena looked at her watch. It was still early. She locked the door, picked up her laptop, and went up to the attic to write.

Early Friday evening, after she closed the travel agency for the weekend, Athena brought pizza over to Aria and Trevor's house. Holly had the day off, so Athena spent the entire day at the agency. It was a slow day, so she was able to write between clients. Internet business was good. However, walk in traffic was definitely declining.

"I am here," Athena called as she opened the front door and went inside.

Aria came down the stairs. "Oh good. I'm starving." She and Athena went into the kitchen. "Troy is excited about the trip to Nantucket," Aria said as they set the table.

"He took me places when I visited Texas. I want to return the favor. He has been so busy with the remodel, there hasn't been much time for sightseeing."

"He's a very nice guy," Aria said.

"Yes, he is."

"You two seem to get along well," Aria commented, and Athena nodded her agreement. "You two could date."

Athena stopped and looked at her daughter. "Date? Did Troy say something to you?"

256

"No, why?"

"He is a great guy, and we enjoy one another's company, but I don't think dating is in our future."

"Why not?" Aria asked.

"Well, for one thing, he lives in Texas, and I live here. For another, he has not indicated he wants to be more than friends since he has been here."

"So, he did indicate he was interested when you were in Texas, but now he doesn't seem interested?" This was the breakthrough Aria waited for since her mother returned from Texas.

Athena sighed. She knew she slipped up, but she did not respond. She went back to setting the table and setting the food out.

Aria took a pitcher of water out of the refrigerator and set it on the table. "I'm just letting you know that it's ok if you and Troy are more than just friends. You are both single adults."

Athena stopped again and stared at her daughter. "You wouldn't feel weird with your mother dating your future brother-in-law?"

"No," Aria said seriously. "It's not like he's close to my age. He's your age. It's not like Daddy and Brook."

Athena studied Aria but did not respond immediately. Aria did not accept Brook at first because Brook was only six years older. Fortunately, the problems seemed to subside when Amber was born. "Are you certain you would be comfortable?"

Aria enthusiastically nodded her head yes. "I definitely am fine with you and Troy dating."

"I'm not saying this might happen, but what if we married. Are you going to call him, dad?"

"Do I call Brook, mom?"

Athena let out a sudden laugh. "Maybe you should. I'd love to see the look on her face."

"Mother!" Aria tried to sound stern, but she could not help but burst out laughing too.

Athena smiled at her daughter. She became serious and put her hand on Aria's shoulder. "Really, I'm ok with just being friends with Troy."

Aria raised an eyebrow. "Are you?"

Athena was about to say something to Aria, but further conversation had to wait because they heard the two men come downstairs. Athena changed the subject. "It's almost midsemester," she said inclining her head toward the sound.

"Yes, the semester is flying by. I sent midterm exams to the copy center today," Aria replied as Trevor and Troy came in the kitchen. Trevor took four Coronas out of the refrigerator and set them on the table. Athena opened the pizza boxes, and they all sat down at the table to eat.

"Oh, Troy, thank you so much for putting up the storm windows in the attic." Athena smiled at him.

"You're welcome. I was in the basement working this morning and saw them."

"I really think you should consider putting in a bigger window, Mom," Aria said as she reached for the red pepper flakes. She shook a generous amount on the pizza slice and took a bite.

"I really want to put on the porch," Athena replied. "I am going to talk to James. He has several friends who are architects."

"As long as the structural loads are calculated and plans drawn up to code, I can build it to the specifications," Troy replied.

Athena smiled. "That would be great."

Chapter 22

Troy arrived at Athena's house promptly at six am on Saturday morning. He wore his usual jeans, cowboy boots, and hat, but today, he wore a light blue button down shirt, and he carried a small backpack. "Why did I need to bring extra clothes," he asked.

"We will be going to the beach, and it is supposed to rain later. If you get wet, believe me, there is nothing worse than a wet boat ride back," Athena told him. "Do you have a jacket?" Troy nodded that he did. "Ok, let's go."

Athena drove from Falmouth to Hyannis, and they boarded the ferry. The ship was crowded with passengers, but they were able to get seats near a window. Troy looked nervous.

"Are you ok?" Athena asked. She did not think to ask if he got motion sick.

"Yes, I am fine," Troy replied. He felt a bit awkward because he noticed he was the only one wearing boots and a cowboy hat. Most people wore sneakers, slip on shoes, or even sandals. People in New England certainly dressed differently than people in Texas. At least different from the people he saw day to day.

When the boat was underway, Athena went to the snack bar for tea and coffee. She returned to the table and took a white paper bag out of her tote bag. "Would you like a cinnamon roll?"

"Absolutely."

Athena took one out of the bag and set it on a napkin for Troy. She also took one out for herself. They ate and then settled back in their seats, talked, and looked out the window as the ferry made its way to Nantucket.

As they approached the island, Athena suggested they go up on deck. The sun was shining, but there were clouds on the distant horizon. The wind was light, and the sea was relatively calm. "Nantucket is a small island, only about thirty miles long. It became famous as a whaling town, but today, tourism is its primary industry," she told Troy.

The boat passed a lighthouse on a small jut of land. The houses near the light house were very large. Many of the homes had a dock with a large boat tethered out front. The buildings were all painted a shade of grey and most were multi-storied. Some homes were close to the water, but many had retaining walls.

"Does this area get a lot of hurricanes? Troy asked.

"A hurricane is always a possibility, but most don't hit head on. However, the wind and tidal surge can still be severe."

The ferry made its way through the harbor past motorboats and sailboats of various sizes. Once the ferry docked, people began to disembark. Athena led Troy up a street away from the ship. Most people exited the ferry and turned down the first street, but Athena took them down a different one. On this street, the houses were pristine. All the houses had shutters and window boxes. The window boxes were full of fall flowers. There were yellow, red, orange, and white mums, multi-colored ornamental cabbage, and orange lantern flowers. Most of the window box displays also included gourds or small pumpkins.

They stopped in a few shops as they made their way to the bus stop. Troy took a picture of a carved whale sculpture in front of one shop. Under the whale sculpture, someone had placed three orange pumpkins. They arrived at the bus stop and sat down at the picnic table to wait.

Troy leaned back and looked at Athena. He was surprised but happy when she asked him to accompany her to the island. He was also glad that they were alone. While they walked to the bus stop, Athena smiled and at one point she even took Troy's hand briefly. He did not want to get his hopes up, but he could not help himself.

They rode the bus to the Cranberry Bog stop, and then they followed the crowd and walked down the dirt road to the festival. There were children's activities, a live band, some craft vendors, food, and of course, cranberry harvesting.

"Oh look, the harvesting is ready to begin." Athena took Troy's hand and led him over to the bog.

"Did you know cranberry harvesting began over two hundred years ago on Cape Cod?" Athena told Troy. "People began growing cranberries here on Nantucket in 1857. It was a main crop in this area, and cranberries were even exported to Europe." Athena took many pictures and made a few notes.

"I haven't eaten cranberries very often," Troy told her.

"They are rich in vitamin C. Sailors ate cranberries to prevent scurvy while at sea."

"And I thought cranberries were just for Thanksgiving," Troy said with a laugh.

Athena took more pictures as the cranberries were harvested. The bog was flooded with water, and a machine like an eggbeater went through the bog and agitated the vines. The cranberries floated to the surface. They watched as men and women in thigh high rubber boots moved wooden booms through the bog to corral the cranberries which were then sucked up and loaded onto trucks.

"Let's go over there," Athena led the way to another area. "Wet harvested cranberries are made into juice, sauce, jelly, anything processed. Fresh cranberries that you buy in a store are dry harvested by hand or by machine." Athena took pictures of cranberry vines loaded with cranberries waiting to be harvested.

They walked around and looked at the various exhibits and listened to a guide talk about the history of cranberries and the benefits of eating cranberries.

"All this talk about cranberries is making me hungry. Are you hungry?" Athena asked.

"Yes," Troy replied. "The smoked bar-be-que smells good." They went to the food area, and Troy got a plate of pork bar-be-que for them to share. Athena bought two cranberry muffins, a bottle of beer for Troy, and a water for herself. They found a table and sat down. Athena had a few forkfuls of bar-be-que and half a muffin. She drank the water while she looked through the pictures she took and filled in her notes.

Troy watched her work. He admired her. She was smart, independent, and capable, qualities that gave her confidence which Troy found very appealing. "Do you have enough information for your article?" he asked when she put her camera back in its case and put her notebook back in her bag.

Athena nodded. "Yes, the festival is a small part of the article. This is the third trip I made to the island this year. The article is scheduled to run in April for the next tourist season."

"Would you like more bar be que?"

"No thanks. I'm full."

"Are you sure? You didn't eat much." Athena nodded yes, and Troy finished the meal and drank the beer.

They stayed and listened to the band for a while. They looked at some of the craft vendor booths, and then they walked back to the main road, got on the bus, and went to the beach at the tip of Nantucket. Many of the shops and restaurants were closed for the season, so they crossed the street to one of the restaurants that was open and waited for a table.

The clouds were beginning to build, but there were still large patches of blue sky. The wind was light but had increased since they arrived on the island.

They were seated at a small round table on the patio, and they waited for the tea and coffee they ordered to arrive. "I love the Cape and the Islands, but in the summer, there are so many tourists. The buses are packed with people, and the wait is a lot longer at restaurants. This is a relaxing time of year to visit Nantucket."

"Have you been here often?" Troy asked.

Athena nodded her head yes. "Even though we lived close by, my parents rented a cabin on the Cape for a month every Summer when I was growing up. Most years we visited Nantucket. There wasn't a high speed ferry at that time, so the boat ride was twice as long."

They drank their beverages, and Athena checked her email while they had Wifi. She also checked the ferry schedule. "It looks like the late ferry is cancelled due to forecasted high winds. Should we head back? We could get stuck here and have to spend the night."

Troy contemplated his response. He had been patient, and inviting him on the trip was a start, but it was obvious she was not going to initiate anything. He decided that he could not pass up the opportunity to tell her he wanted to be with her. He put his hand on hers. "I don't mind spending the night if we can get a hotel."

Athena looked up at him. "I wasn't sure you were interested anymore."

Troy leaned closer to her. He took one of her hands in his and kissed it. "I have been thinking about you since you left Texas." He let her hand go and leaned back. "To be honest, I have no idea what you want, but I want to stay and enjoy the weekend with you."

Athena was quiet for a few moments. She let out a breath. "Honestly, for the long term, I don't know." She looked down at her laptop and did a search for a hotel room on Nantucket. "But I'd like to stay here with you tonight," she said while she typed. She looked up at him. "That is if we can get a room we can afford." She resumed her search.

Troy drank his coffee quietly while she worked. "Oh, we got lucky," Athena looked up from her laptop and smiled at Troy. "There was a last minute cancellation, probably because of the weather, and I found us a room that overlooks the ocean at the standard off season room rate."

"You worked your magic." Troy smiled at her.

Athena smiled back. "I guess so." She then texted Aria that everything was fine and that she and Troy decided to stay on Nantucket because the late ferry was cancelled due to high wind.

Aria sent back a text that said, 'Have fun' and added a happy smile emoji. Athena looked at the text for a long time. She suddenly thought that maybe this was not such a good idea. However, she took a deep breath, looked at Troy, and smiled. "Are you ready to walk the beach?"

Troy looked up at the sky which was now mostly cloudy. "Ok," he replied hesitantly. Athena took his hand, and they walked down the path alongside the restaurant to the beach. There were quite a few people sitting on blankets and looking out at the ocean, and some people walked along the water's edge. Two surfers wearing wet suits rode the waves which were considerably bigger than they were in the morning.

Athena kicked off her shoes, and Troy sat down on the bench and removed his boots. She waited for him, and then they walked toward the water. They found a spot, and Athena pulled a very thin, but large, beach blanket from one of her bags, spread it out on the sand, and deposited her bags on it. Troy put his bag and boots down next to her things. Athena rolled up her pant legs, and Troy did the same. She took a child's sand pail out of her bag, hung her camera around her neck, and she put her phone in a plastic phone case because her pants did not have pockets. "Ready?" she asked.

"As ready as I can be," Troy replied.

Athena took his hand and led him to the water's edge. The sand was not as cold as Troy expected, but the water was cold. The waves crashed and rolled up the beach and covered Troy's feet. "Oh, that is chilly," he said as he jumped further away from the water.

"Oh, look!" Athena exclaimed.

Troy followed her finger, and he saw a seal in the water right in front of them. The seal rolled in the surf. He definitely did not mind the cold water. The seal playfully dove under the surface and then came up again.

"Wow!" Troy exclaimed. "I never saw a seal in the wild before; the only seals I ever saw were at aquariums." They watched as the seal rolled on its back and ate and then dove back under the water.

Athena took her camera out, and she snapped quite a few pictures. "This will be fantastic for the article." She took more pictures, and then they walked further along the beach. Athena stopped here and there to pick up seashells or a rock. There were several clusters of scallop shells in neat piles, and she picked them up.

Troy looked out over the dark ocean to the horizon. He understood why Athena loved it here. The surf roared in his ears, and the waves crashed ashore over and over again. The waves were rhythmic and soothing, but also terrifying in their power.

As they walked along, sea gulls swooped around them, and others sat in the water riding up and down on the waves. The seal continued to play in the rolling surf just offshore. Troy took Athena's hand, and they walked further up the beach.

They were a long way from their blanket when they turned around and headed back. "Is the tide going out or coming in," Troy asked. Athena looked at her watch. "Going out," she said.

Most people had left the beach because the clouds were dark and thick, and the wind increased, but the seal still played in the surf, so they stopped to watch him for a while.

Athena's sand pail overflowed with seashells, and when she returned to the blanket, she dumped them in a zip bag she brought with her. "Let's go sit on the bench, and we can put our shoes back on," she suggested. They carried everything back to the bench. Athena took out a small bottle of baby powder and sprinkled it on her feet. To Troy's surprise, the sand came right off. She handed him the bottle, and he used it to dust off his feet before putting on his boots.

"We should head back to town," Athena said as they walked back up the path to the road. They timed it perfectly, and the bus arrived very quickly. "There's a grocery store near the bus stop where we can pick up a few things for our stay."

The ride back was quick, and they walked a short distance to the very busy grocery store. People were buying water and bread to prepare for the storm Troy presumed, but many more people were purchasing beer and wine. They purchased a couple of toothbrushes, several bottles of water, and a bottle of wine. "The hotel is not far, just up the hill and over a block," Athena told Troy. "Let's check in and then go to dinner. The restaurant on the wharf has delicious food."

After checking in and putting their things in their room, they walked from the hotel to the restaurant. The evening air was cool and damp, and as they waited for a table, it started to rain, so they were seated inside near the fireplace. The fire was inviting and cast a warm, orange glow over everything. The walls were decorated with fishing nets and buoys. One wall had a mural of sea life, and the centerpieces on the tables consisted of a bowl of seashells with a candle in the middle.

Troy looked over the menu which was shaped like a fish. He usually had fried fish on the rare occasions he went to a seafood restaurant, and he only had clam chowder once before. "I leave the ordering in your capable hands," he said to Athena when the waitress came to take their order. Athena ordered the fried fishermen's platter for two. She also ordered two cups of New England clam chowder and shrimp cocktail for appetizers, and of course, Cape Codders to drink.

When the shrimp and the chowder arrived, Athena waited while Troy tried the chowder. "Delicious." He took another spoonful. "Much better than canned," he laughed.

"Definitely. Although there are a couple of brands of canned chowder available in New England that are very good." She put a few oyster crackers into her chowder and passed them to Troy who added some to his cup.

"I haven't spent much time at the ocean, but I can see why you love it, Athena."

"I find the sounds of the ocean very soothing." She knew she would not be happy living away from the ocean for a long period of time, and she was certain Troy felt the same about the ranch and Texas.

Troy seemed to sense what she was thinking. He leaned back and looked around. "I could get used to the ocean," he said. "I would want to be at the ranch at times, but I definitely could live near the ocean."

Athena smiled at him. She appreciated the gesture, but was it right to ask him to leave the ranch and move here? She was not comfortable asking him for that sacrifice.

A waiter came by, and they ordered another round of drinks, and within minutes, the platters of food arrived.

"Wow! That's a lot of food." Troy's eyes were wide as he looked at the oval platter overflowing with fried fish, clams, shrimp, and scallops. There was a separate platter of French fries and onion rings.

"You are in for a treat." Athena took out her phone and snapped a couple pictures of the food then she scooted her chair close to Troy and had him lean in for a selfie. "Do you mind if I post this online?"

Troy shook his head no. "I don't mind at all." Actually, he thought it was quite a breakthrough. Although he was ready to announce he loved

Athena to the world, he knew that she did not want anyone, especially Aria it seemed, to know about them. He was willing to wait. If she wanted a secret relationship, then that was what they would have. At least for now.

"Try a scallop," Athena said breaking him from his thoughts.

Troy picked up a fork and speared a scallop. He dipped it in the creamy white tartar sauce and then put it in his mouth. "This is really good. I don't think I have ever had scallops."

Athena nodded and ate one. "Scallops are my favorite. Try a clam strip," she suggested.

They ordered another round of drinks and finished the entire platter down to the last French fry.

"I'm so stuffed." Athena leaned back and picked up her drink.

"That was delicious." Troy picked up his drink, leaned back, and admired Athena. She looked relaxed as she sat there sipping her drink. Her long hair flowed over her left shoulder. Her eyes were dark and captivating. He never looked at anyone the way he looked at her. She completed him, and he knew they could be very happy together if she could just let go. How could she be so confident in so many aspects of life yet so indecisive about love? He reached over and took her hand. He wanted to say the words, but he knew he needed to tread lightly. He leaned forward and kissed her hand instead.

"You are beautiful, Athena."

She smiled at him. "Thank you." Troy kissed her hand again.

They took a cab back to the hotel because it was pouring outside, and the wind was blowing hard. Troy held Athena's hand as they walked up the stairs to their room. They took off their shoes, and Troy opened the bottle of wine. Athena held the two water glasses while Troy poured the wine.

"To storms," he said as he touched his glass to hers. Athena smiled and drank.

Troy turned on the gas fireplace, and Athena walked to the window, opened the curtains, and then turned off all the lights so they could look out at the ocean. "We were very lucky to get this room. What a view." she said.

Troy looked out at the rain and the rolling sea. Lightning illuminated the sky. Waves rolled ashore, and spray flew into the air. The wind whistled and roared. It was powerful and yet beautiful. He wrapped his arms around Athena's waist, and she leaned back into him. He smelled her light floral perfume. He filled his lungs with it, so he would remember it always. He moved her hair to the side, and he kissed her neck. She turned and kissed him as she ran her hands up his back and over his shoulders. The tension melted away as Athena brought Troy down to her. She kissed him and pulled him close. She wanted him, and from his response, she knew he wanted her as badly. They both had been waiting months to once again be in each other's arms.

They continued to kiss while slowly undressing one another. Troy's hands rubbed Athena's arms, and then very slowly, he moved his hands to her waist. He slid his hands inside the shirt, and he very gently lifted it up. She raised up her arms, and he slid it off her body. His mouth instantly found hers again. The passion built as Athena unbuttoned Troy's shirt and slid her hands up his chest and down his arms removing it. The shirt dropped to the floor. Desperate to feel her skin against his, Troy undid the clasp of her bra and pulled it off. Athena's breath caught as he pressed his bare chest to hers and kissed her deeply.

He kissed her neck and whispered sweet words in her ear. Athena sighed as he kissed his way lower to her breasts. He had to taste all of her,

270

and she arched her back in pleasure. As he kissed his way down her abdomen, he undid her jeans and pushed them down over her hips and off her body. He hooked a finger in the little black lace panty she wore and pushed it down as well. He kissed his way back up to her mouth and pulled her naked body to him.

Athena wrapped her arms around his head and tangled her fingers in his hair. "Troy," she moaned in his mouth as his mouth devoured hers.

With very little effort, he picked her up into his arms and set her carefully on the bed. He took a moment to look at her hair fanned out over the pillow. Desire flared in her eyes as he undid his jeans and took them off. He slid his naked body over hers. He sucked in her bottom lip as his hand went down and explored her body. Her eyes closed as she reached her climax, and his name left her lips in a whisper.

"Look at me, Athena." His voice was rough. With difficulty, her eyes fluttered open. "Keep looking at me."

Athena's eyes were glazed, but she stared into his eyes as their bodies joined once again. As the storm raged outside, their passion increased, and they made love into the early morning hours, satisfying one another until they fell into a blissful sleep.

Light coming in the window woke Athena up the next morning. Troy walked over to the bed and kissed her gently. "Good morning. Did you sleep well?"

"I did. Did you?"

Troy kissed her again. "Yes, I did. I went downstairs and got us some tea, coffee, and pastries." Athena got up and slipped on a tee shirt, and they sat down at the small table near the window to eat breakfast.

The sky was cloudy, but the rain had stopped. The wind was still blowing, but not with the intensity of during the night. They quietly ate pastries while looking out at the ocean beyond.

The sea was rough, and Athena wondered if they would be able to get a ferry back today. "I should check the ferry schedule." She stood up to get her laptop.

Troy stood up and grabbed her around the waist. His action caught her by surprise, and she gasped, but then Athena looked at him and smiled.

"Don't worry about the ferry," he said as he steered her toward the bed. He laid down, pulled Athena on top of him, and kissed her. She loved how he made her feel. They were so in tune with one another that it felt like they had been lovers for years. Troy looked into her eyes "We don't need to hurry back."

"We definitely do not need to hurry back, Troy." Athena closed her eyes. She felt tingly all over as he kissed his way down her neck and chest.

Fortunately, the hotel was not full, so they were lax about check out time. It was just before noon when Troy and Athena left. They decided to go back to the seafood restaurant on the wharf for lunch. Troy enjoyed the clam strips, so he ordered a basket with fries, and Athena ordered scallops and onion rings. "Would you like a mimosa?" she asked.

"Yes, thank you."

Last night's storm had brought in much cooler air, but the restaurant had outdoor heaters, so they sat on the patio overlooking the water and ate lunch. A sea gull sat nearby and watched them eat. Troy noticed the do not feed the gulls sign, but he knew people must feed them because the bird sat patiently waiting for a morsel.

"What boat should we take back to the mainland?" Athena asked.

"Are you in a hurry to get back?"

Athena smiled. "No."

Troy reach across the table and put his hand on top of hers. "You are so much more relaxed when we are alone." He rubbed his thumb over the back of her hand.

"Am I?"

Troy nodded yes. "I like when you are relaxed. I feel like we have a chance."

Athena smiled at him, and he gave her hand a gentle squeeze. This was not the time to discuss the future.

After lunch, they strolled along one of the main shopping streets. Troy bought Danny a toy fishing boat. Athena bought some beach plum jelly and saltwater taffy. She planned to make a welcome gift basket for the family when they came up from Texas for the wedding.

By the time they finished shopping, the sky had cleared, so they walked up the hill to an historic church. "From the tower there is a great view of the island," Athena explained as she paid their entrance fees.

They climbed the steps to the first level, and they looked at the historic photos of the island that hung on the walls. There were two rocking chairs in front of a large picture window, so they sat down, rocked, and looked at the view for a while.

"I am surprised it isn't busier here this morning," Athena remarked. "Many people must have left the island because of the storm." She reached over and took Troy's hand.

"This is what you need in your attic room," Troy said.

"Yes, this window is wonderful," Athena agreed. She squeezed his hand. After a while, they got up and went up the tiny staircase to the upper level. There was a guide up there answering questions and telling visitors about the history of the island and the church. Athena took many photos. Troy took a few photos and looked at the photographs on the walls while they chatted with the guide.

As they started down the staircase, Troy stopped, turned back to Athena, and kissed her. "You are at the perfect height," he said kissing her again.

There was plenty of time before their ferry was scheduled to leave, so they walked down to the beach and walked along the water's edge picking up more seashells and bits of driftwood and sea glass. When Athena's pail was full, they returned to their blanket nestled in the grass up the dune. Further down the beach, a couple laid together on a blanket, but aside from the two couples, the beach was deserted.

They stayed at the beach until it was time to board the ferry back to the mainland. The temperature was cold, but they stood on the deck as the boat pulled out of the harbor, and they were rewarded with a beautiful sunset. There were a few clouds on the horizon to reflect the intense orange and red glow of the setting sun, and the water shimmered and reflected the vibrant colors. It was a spectacular sight, and Athena knew it was the perfect photo to end her article.

Troy leaned toward Athena, and she looked into his eyes, and they kissed.

"Let's take a selfie," she said.

"I'll take a picture of you two," an older man walking on deck taking pictures said.

"Thank you." She handed him her camera.

"Happy to do it," he replied with a smile.

Troy and Athena stayed in each other's arms and watched as the sun sank below the horizon before going inside and getting warm.

274

They returned to Hyannis and slowly walked hand in hand to the car. "Aria and Trevor are away until Monday evening," Athena told Troy as they put their bags in the trunk.

Troy nodded his head. "Yes," he said. He wanted to stay with her the entire weekend, but he did not want to presume that she wanted him to stay at her house.

They got in the car, she started it, and began driving. Athena looked over at him. "Troy, would you like to stay with me tonight?"

"Athena, I want to stay with you every night."

She smiled, but it was a nervous smile. Troy reached over and took her hand.

Chapter 23

Troy needed trim molding, and since Trevor and Aria were still away, he and Athena headed to the home improvement store early Monday morning.

They first went to the lumber area. Troy was very selective about the molding. Athena watched him as he took out a piece of molding and looked at it carefully. The pieces had to be straight, so it took quite some time to get all the materials he needed.

"I need a box of finish nails for the nail gun," he said. "Is there anything you need here?"

"I was going to look at the house plants while we were here," Athena said. "I want to get a plant for their garden window."

"Why don't you head to the garden area, and I will get the nails and meet you there."

"Ok." Athena headed toward the indoor plant section.

She was looking over the plants when she heard her name. She looked around to see who called her and saw David. He waved and headed toward her.

"Hi, Athena. How are you?"

"I am well, David. How are you?"

"I'm good. Did you get my message?"

"Oh, yes. I'm sorry. I was away over the weekend doing research on Nantucket." Athena saw Troy. He walked toward them much faster than he normally walked.

"Hello," Troy said in a deep, almost booming, voice as he approached.

The two men eyed each other. It was awkward, but Athena straightened up, cleared her throat, and began the introductions. "Troy, this is David, an old friend. David, this is Troy. He is Trevor's brother. He's here remodeling Aria and Trevor's new home."

Troy sighed. He was back to being just Trevor's brother. The two men tentatively shook hands.

"Yeah, Athena and I have been friends since Junior High," David said with a fake smile that did not mask his feelings for Troy. "You know what they say, Old Friends are the Best Friends."

Troy looked David up and down. "It is nice that after all these years, you and Athena are still Just friends," he said with a smile.

David glared at Troy for a long moment. He then turned to Athena. "The reason I called last week was to ask when I should come over and put in the storm windows. The nights are getting colder."

"Oh." Athena blushed. "Thank you, David, but Troy already put the storm windows in for me."

"He did?" David was clearly annoyed. "That's nice." He looked at Troy. "So, Troy, how long are you visiting? I imagine you are anxious to get back to warm Texas."

Troy gave a little laugh. "I don't mind the cold at all," he said. "And Texas isn't always warm. Parts of Texas even get snow."

David continued to glare at Troy. "Well, I should get back to work," he finally said. "Athena, I will call you, and maybe we can get together for coffee, or in your case tea. I know you prefer tea," he said smugly. Athena gave a weak nod.

"Bye. It was nice to meet one of Athena's Friends," Troy emphasized the word friends. He turned to Athena, and although he was not certain it was a good idea, he placed his hand at the small of her back and directed her attention to a bromeliad. He casually glanced over his shoulder and saw David looking at them. David glared at Troy for a moment, and then he turned and walked away.

Athena and Troy made their purchases and got back into the truck.

"Is he invited to the wedding?" Troy asked as he drove back to the house.

Athena smiled. Troy was jealous. "No," she said slowly. "We kept the guest list small and with primarily Trevor and Aria's friends."

"Good." Athena distinctly heard Troy say even though he said it softly.

As Troy feared, once Aria and Trevor returned from their trip, Athena distanced herself from him. Troy was frustrated. He really did not understand why she was so afraid, but in a way, he also understood. I will give her time, he thought to himself.

Troy and Trevor were working in the kitchen, and Athena and Aria were upstairs painting the bedroom walls. "It's too bad Troy has to go back so soon," Aria said.

Athena stood on a ladder painting. "It is, but I'm sure he has work to do."

"I'm glad he was able to go apple picking and to Nantucket."

"Yes, he really was able to get a taste of New England." Athena did not look at Aria. She was reluctant to discuss Troy, Nantucket, or Texas. She did not know what she wanted, but she knew she did not want to worry her daughter.

"I'm going to stay at Trevor's tonight," Aria said. "We have a few things left to pack, so they can move the last of the boxes and furniture tomorrow."

"Ok," Athena really was not listening closely.

"Mom?"

"Oh, sorry. Umm, I thought we could get rotisserie tonight." Athena stepped down off the ladder. They painted the room a soft coral color with an accent wall of cream. "I like this color combination."

Aria nodded. "The room has a vibrant feel, and I love it."

Trevor came in to see how they were doing. "You two did a great job," he said, and he kissed Aria. "Troy said he needs to make several cuts on the mitre saw at your house," he said to Athena.

"Hey, the room looks good," Troy said as he came into the room. "Would you come to your house with me, Athena?" he asked.

"Absolutely," she said in a higher than normal voice. "Let me wash up and get my purse, and I will meet you downstairs."

She left the room, and Aria turned to Troy. "You don't need to rush back," she said. Troy looked at her. "I just thought you two might like some time alone. To talk."

"Why don't we meet you and Athena at her house in a couple hours for dinner?" Trevor suggested. "We will clean up here, and we have to get a few empty boxes."

"We will stop and pick up chicken and a couple of sides for dinner," Aria added. "I'll go tell Mom the plan." Aria left the room and went to find her mother.

Troy looked at Trevor. He appreciated time alone with Athena, but they were being obvious which was likely to backfire with Athena.

"Aria is trying to help," Trevor said with a shrug.

"Is Aria ok with me and Athena?" Troy asked.

"Sure, why wouldn't she be?"

"Athena seems convinced that Aria might have a problem with her and I being in a relationship."

"Actually, Aria is upset that Athena has not told her everything."

"Are you ok with Athena and I?" Although Troy really did not believe it was anyone's business, he was curious how Trevor felt.

"Yes," Trevor said quickly. "You are both single adults." Troy looked at Trevor. He had not spent much time with his youngest brother in recent years, and Trevor really grew up in that time. "We'll text before heading over to the house," Trevor said with a smile that quickly faded with a look from Troy.

That was exactly the reaction Troy thought Athena feared.

Athena woke up before her alarm went off. She sat up suddenly when she realized Troy was not next to her. He came out of the bathroom and slid into bed. "Good morning," he said as he kissed her.

"Good morning." She felt a little sad; this was their last day together. She knew when they stayed on Nantucket that it was only a temporary affair. Long distance relationships do not work, she reminded herself. But right now, she did not care.

He saw the nervousness in her eyes. "Are you ok?"

Athena nodded. "I'm fine." She smiled. "I was just thinking it is your last day here."

Troy wrapped his arms around her, and he kissed her repeatedly. He wanted to fill his senses with her scent, her touch, her taste. Troy was not sure when it happened, but he was in love with her. And he hoped she was falling in love with him too.

"Troy," she moaned softly.

"Athena, this feels so right."

Athena moaned as Troy kissed her neck. She knew she was falling in love with him, but still something held her back. She took a deep breath. No matter how much she resisted, it did feel right.

"I want you," Troy whispered as he kissed his way down her body. He wanted to get back to the house before Trevor and Aria got there, but he was reluctant to leave Athena. He wanted to stay with her as long as possible.

Aria was disappointed when she and Trevor arrived at the house to see Troy working on the trim.

"Good morning," Trevor said.

Aria texted her mother, 'Where are you?'

'On my way with breakfast,' she texted back, and within a few minutes she pulled into the driveway. Aria helped Athena bring the food inside.

"I'm starving," Trevor said. He reached in the bag and pulled out a breakfast sandwich. Troy sat down and drank some coffee, and Trevor handed him a sandwich.

When the ladies left for work, Trevor and Troy made a list of what needed to be completed, and they worked steadily all morning.

"This kitchen is very functional now," Trevor said as he watched Troy wipe down the cabinets. "Thanks. I don't know what I would have done without you."

"You're welcome," Troy replied. "I enjoyed it, especially making the pantry."

"I think you could make a lot of money making custom cabinets."

Troy finished and stood back to admire the kitchen. "I actually prefer cabinetry and finish work to framing and sheet rock."

"I know James was impressed with your work. He knows a lot of people who might be interested in custom cabinetry in their homes." Trevor looked around. "Well, I think we are finished." He looked at his watch. It was almost noon. "Let's go get the last of the boxes at my apartment and then go have lunch. We can put the tools away later."

"Sounds good."

"We are back," Trevor announced as he and Troy walked through the front door.

"Hi," Aria called. She was stretched out on the sofa with her tablet in her hand. There was a half empty glass of water with two lemon slices on the coffee table. Trevor sat down at the end of the sofa near her feet. Troy sat in an armchair. "I was thinking," Aria began.

"Oh no," Trevor said. "What do you want to change?"

"I was just thinking the mantle is not very fancy," Aria said pointing to the gas fireplace mantle.

"Troy, have you done much masonry?" Trevor asked with a laugh.

"A bit," he replied. "I'd be glad to come back." He stood up. "I think I will go gather up my things since I leave in the morning." He looked at his brother. Trevor rubbed Aria's feet and leaned toward her. She reached down and ran her fingers through his hair. Troy smiled. It was nice to see them so in love.

He did not have much to pack, just some clothes and another pair of boots. He bought some maple sugar candy and a boat for Danny, some apple crisp mix for his mother, and saltwater taffy for the whole family to enjoy. Athena said she was going to box up some apples for him to bring back to Texas.

He heard Athena arrive. He hoped to get some time alone with her before he flew back. He zippered his suitcase and went back downstairs.

Trevor made reservations for a table near a window overlooking the wharf at his favorite restaurant in Boston. James, Brook, and Amber joined them there. Troy sat next to Athena. She was stunning in a deep blue lace dress that had short sleeves and was slightly off the shoulders. Her long hair was pulled back in the front, which showed off her diamond stud earrings, and then it flowed over her shoulders. Around her neck, she wore a thin silver chain with a single diamond. Troy caught himself staring at her several times throughout dinner, and when their eyes locked, she smiled. He took her hand under the table, and she laced her fingers in his.

Troy ordered clam chowder and the seafood basket. Athena, of course, ordered her favorite, scallops. She also ordered clam fritters for an appetizer, and she passed a couple to Troy to try.

"These are good," he said taking another bite.

"I will make a New Englander of you," Athena laughed. Aria noticed how much her mother smiled, and she was glad to see her mother so happy.

After dinner, James, Brook, and Amber headed right home. Amber hugged Aria and then she turned to Athena. "Good night, Aunt Athena."

"Good night, Amber."

James shook Troy's hand a couple of times and thanked him for all his hard work. "I hope you enjoyed your stay, Troy."

"I did," Troy replied. He looked over at Athena.

"Brook is itching to remodel our kitchen," James said. "I'll be in touch." They shook hands again.

Once they left, Trevor, Aria, Troy, and Athena walked along the wharf, up the greenway, and past the carousel which was closed at this time of night. There was a slight breeze, and Troy noticed Athena pulled her jacket a little tighter. He wanted to put his arm around her, but he stopped. When Aria was around, Athena did not even take his hand except when it could not be seen.

"It's nice that Amber calls you Aunt Athena," Troy said as they walked.

"I prefer she call me, Athena. I am not her aunt."

"It is a sign of respect."

"I get it, but I think it confuses children." Troy gave a huff. Athena looked at him. "You disagree?"

"Yes, I do. There is nothing wrong with children showing respect to adults. You are Aria's mother, and Amber and Aria are half-sisters."

"But I am not her aunt, and I think it is important for children to understand the family tree."

Troy leaned closer to Athena. "You do realize as Aria's mother you are in the family tree."

Athena conceded that fact. It was Troy's last night visiting, and she was not going to spend it arguing about the family tree and what she should be called. They walked on the path under the arch to the Christopher Columbus statue.

284

Troy stopped and read the plaque. "The park is beautiful," he said.

"It is," Athena replied. "It is one of my favorite places to walk, and at Christmas time, the arch is lit up with blue lights."

"I am stuffed," Trevor said as he and Aria walked over to them hand in hand.

"Troy, did you like the mix of Manhattan and New England clam chowder?" Aria asked. "That's Mom's favorite way to have chowder."

Troy nodded. "I liked it. The tangy tomato and the creamy chowder worked well together."

"I'm glad you liked it," Athena said with a smile.

It was getting late, but they slowly wandered back to the car. Aria hooked her arm in Trevor's. "It's chilly tonight."

"It is." Athena shivered a little.

When they got in the car, Trevor turned on the heat and drove out of the city. At this time of night, the drive back was quick and easy. Trevor and Troy walked Athena and Aria in the house. Athena turned on the gas fireplace in the living room and then made tea and coffee.

About 12:30 am, Trevor and Troy decided to go back to the house. "Good night," Athena said. "Why don't you two come over for breakfast before we take Troy to the airport."

"Ok," they replied. Aria kissed Trevor good night, and then she and Athena went upstairs to bed.

Athena was in the kitchen cooking breakfast when Aria came downstairs. "Good morning, honey. How did you sleep?"

"Good. How about you, Mom?"

"I was a little restless."

Aria thought her mother looked sad as she cooked a big breakfast of bacon, eggs, and waffles. Perhaps she was going to miss Troy, Aria thought to herself. She wanted to ask her mother some questions, but she knew she had to tread lightly.

Trevor and Troy arrived around 8:30 am. Troy put the truck in the garage, came inside, and hung the keys on the key rack by the door. "Good morning," he said.

"Breakfast is ready," Athena told them as she placed the platter of eggs on the table.

"It smells and looks delicious." Troy held the chair for Athena, and she sat down. He sat beside her, and they all started to fill their plates.

At 10:30 am, they left to take Troy to the airport. Athena checked Troy in online the day before and printed his boarding pass. Since he did not have bags to check, they walked directly to the security area.

"Thanks very much for all your help," Trevor said to Troy. "We could not have done it without you."

"It was my pleasure," Troy replied shaking his brother's hand and giving him a hug. "Any time you need help, just call." He truly meant it. He enjoyed spending time with Trevor and getting to know him again.

"I'll see you next month," Trevor said.

"Mom is excited to have you visit for a few days," Troy told him.

"Thank you, Troy," Aria said. "You did a great job on our home." She hugged him and then wrapped her arm around Trevor. They moved back a little without being obvious so that Troy and Athena could say good-bye.

Athena was uncharacteristically nervous. She looked at Troy. "It was nice to see you again."

Troy took her hand. "I will miss you, Athena," he whispered.

She nodded. "I will miss you too." They hugged. "Have a good flight home, Troy." They shared a quick non-passionate kiss on the cheek.

"Take care y'all," Troy said.

"Bye," they replied and waved.

Troy turned and walked toward the security line entrance. Suddenly, he stopped, turned, and went back to Athena. She started to ask if everything was ok, but before she said anything, he put his bags down, pulled her into a tight embrace, and kissed her passionately. She wrapped her arms around him and kissed him back.

Aria and Trevor stared in complete surprise. In fact, several people stopped and watched. Troy released her, picked up his bags, and got in the security line.

Athena watched him go. She did not turn around to look at her daughter until Troy waved before going into the screening area. She waved back then turned around. Aria and Trevor were smiling, but they very wisely did not say anything.

Later that night, Aria joined Athena at the kitchen table for a cup of tea. "What are you thinking about, Mom?"

"Nothing in particular."

"Are you and Troy in a relationship now?"

Athena looked at her daughter. "No," she shook her head. "We enjoy hanging out together, but there can't be a relationship. Our lives are thousands of miles apart."

"It looked like there was something between you two at the airport," Aria said. Although she and her mother were extremely close, if her mother did not want to talk about something, the subject was closed.

"We had fun on Nantucket. We enjoy each other's company. That's all."

"It can be more, Mom. I told you, I am ok with you and Troy being together. It's actually really nice to see you both happy."

Athena smiled at Aria and placed her hand over her daughter's hand. "Thank you. However, there is nothing serious between us. I don't want you to worry."

"I'm not worried, Mom. But you seem to be."

Athena shook her head. "No, I'm not worried," she said. "We had fun together. That is all there is to it."

"Is that all you want?"

Athena nodded her head. "I think that is all there can be."

"Why?"

Athena patted her daughter's hand. "Don't worry about it," she said again, and Aria knew her mother would not say more.

Athena changed the subject. "The shower is the week Trevor is away, and then we can just settle in for a quiet Thanksgiving before it is time for fittings, the end of the semester, and Christmas, ok?"

Aria sighed and nodded her head. "Ok."

Chapter 24

Troy was out riding when he saw a car turn in the driveway to the ranch. He knew it was Trevor, so he picked up the pace to get back to greet his brother. He hurriedly put the horse back in the stable and went to the main house. Trevor sat on the porch next to Dan. "Hi, Trevor. Good to see you," he said as he shook his brother's hand. He sat down and stretched his legs out.

Maria came out on the porch and brought them beer, tortilla chips, and a bowl of salsa. She sat down in one of the rocking chairs.

"It's good to be home," Trevor said.

John walked up on the porch. "Glad you are here, Trevor. How was the conference?"

"You know how they can be. Long." Trevor laughed.

"How's work?" John sat down opposite his sons.

"Everything is going well at work. I'm in line for a promotion in the coming year."

"Oh, that's great," they all replied.

"The house looks fantastic. Troy saved us," Trevor said as he dipped a chip in salsa and put it in his mouth. He washed it down with a long drink of beer. "The furniture looks good. I have some pictures on my phone." He took out his phone and opened the gallery to show his mother the pictures.

Maria scrolled through them, and John leaned over to look as well. "The house looks beautiful. I like where you put the clock." She stood up. "Well, you boys catch up while I cook dinner." She handed Trevor's phone to Dan so he could look at the pictures. Seeing her sons together on her porch made her very happy.

"I'm going to go wash up." John said, and he followed Maria inside.

"So, tell me, how are Aria and Athena?" Dan asked. Troy gave Dan a stern look, but Dan did not look up from the pictures.

"They are both good. Busy with the wedding details. Aria likes her new job," Trevor replied.

Dan handed the phone back to Trevor. "The clock does look good in your house."

"It does." He paused and looked at his brothers. "Mom asked if I wanted the cradle too."

"Are you two planning to have kids right away?" Dan asked.

Trevor was silent for a few short moments. "No, I don't think so."

Dan looked sternly at his brother. "You don't think so?" Dan made a face. "Well, you had better well find out," he replied.

Troy looked at Trevor. "Haven't you two discussed children?" At their age, children seemed like a logical discussion for two people in a relationship and about to get married.

Trevor shook his head slightly. "No. Not really."

"Not really?!" Dan and Troy exclaimed in unison.

"I am sure we must have discussed children at some point," Trevor said; although, he could not immediately recall a discussion about having

290

children. They discussed birth control, so he guessed that was a discussion about children.

"Shelby was pregnant a month after we married," Dan told him.

Trevor pursed his lips and looked up at Dan and Troy. "No. No. I am certain Aria does not want children right away. She just started teaching full time at the college. She is building her career. No. No, I am certain she doesn't want them now."

"He's trying to convince himself," Dan said smugly to Troy.

Trevor looked thoughtful. "In fact, I don't think I have seen Aria even hold a baby."

"None of her friends have babies?" Dan asked.

"A couple. But I have never seen her hold one of them, and she hasn't talked about children."

"I know Mom is looking for more grandchildren. She is very happy that Shelby and I are settling our differences," Dan informed his brothers.

"Are you and Shelby back together?" Trevor asked.

"We are working on it."

"Trevor, just talk to Aria when you get home," Troy suggested.

Trevor still contemplated the idea. "I am certain she is not ready for children," he mumbled mostly to himself.

"He's really worried," Dan laughed. He enjoyed Trevor's predicament. "Trevor, has Athena hinted about wanting grandchildren?"

Trevor looked up and shook his head no. "No. No. I have never even heard Athena mention the word grandchildren. Has she said anything to you, Troy?"

Troy gave his brothers a very stern look, and both leaned back a little in their chairs. "No," he said firmly. "The topic has never come up." He

291

looked at Trevor. "Look, you and Aria are both young. You have plenty of time to come to a decision about children together."

Trevor sighed. "Yeah, you're right. There is plenty of time."

Trevor's phone rang. "Hi, Aria," he said. Trevor got up and walked by the railing while listening to Aria talk.

Dan looked at Troy and laughed. "Perfect timing."

"That sounds like a plan. Why don't you open their gifts last, and I can thank everyone too?" Trevor listened to Aria. "I'm sitting on the porch with Dan and Troy."

"Aria and Athena say hi," he said to Dan and Troy. They waved, and Trevor said, "they say hi."

Trevor blocked his other ear. "Are you in the limo? It's hard to hear," he said loudly into the phone. Dan and Troy heard a loud pop and laughing.

"Ok. Have fun tonight. I love you and miss you too. Bye." He pushed end and sat back down. "Athena rented a limo and a bunch of them are taking Aria out tonight," Trevor explained to Dan and Troy.

"A Bachelorette party?" Dan asked. "Sounds like they are having a lot of fun."

Trevor sighed and stared at his phone. "Yeah, they are going to some clubs in Boston."

"Really? I wonder if there will be male strippers." Dan looked at the nervous expressions on his brothers' faces and burst out laughing.

On Saturday morning, Troy, Dan, Trevor, and John went out for a ride. It was a warm day for November, and it had been a hot and dry Summer and Fall. Trevor was surprised at how low the river was this year. As they rode alongside the fence at the edge of their ranch and checked it, they chatted about the weather, the lack of rain, and the cattle. They rode for a couple of hours, and as they approached the house, they saw Maria sitting on the porch. John stayed in the stable and finished some chores, and Dan went upstairs to see what Shelby and Danny were doing. Trevor and Troy went up on the porch and sat down in the chairs next to their mother.

"Did they tell you about the gazebo, Trevor?" she asked. Trevor nodded, yes. "I've always wanted a gazebo, and now I have a reason to build one. Troy and Dan are going to start building it this week."

"It's a win, win," Trevor laughed.

"We have started to get the RSVPs back for the reception here. Looks like most people are coming. We are going to get a bar-be-que pig and maybe make some smoked beef ribs."

"That sounds good."

"We can also cook hamburgers and hotdogs on the grill." Maria pulled a small notepad out of her apron pocket and looked it over. "Oh, Trevor. I wanted to ask you. Should we get a DJ?"

"A DJ will keep the party going."

"Ok. I'll have Shelby look for one."

"We have everything set for the family when y'all come up for the wedding," Trevor explained.

"Do any of you have a vehicle large enough for the family?" Maria asked.

Trevor shook his head no. "Athena booked a rental."

"Good," Maria replied.

"James has a great house rental for you," Trevor added.

"I can imagine." Troy chuckled. He looked at his mother. "James seems to do everything big."

293

"Yes, Athena sent me the information. It's a beautiful house." Maria rocked in the chair. "The wedding looks like it is going to be grand."

Trevor smiled. "It will be grand. As Troy said, when James does something, he does it big, and Athena is that way too, especially when it involves Aria."

Maria stood up. "Trevor, let me know when you have Aria on webcam. I'm going to fix some sandwiches." She went into the kitchen. Trevor followed her inside, picked up his laptop, and sat down at the dining room table.

Troy sat back daydreaming when he heard, bar be que. He walked into the dining room. "Did I hear bar be que?"

Shelby nodded yes. "It's delicious. Go get some." Troy hurried in the kitchen to get sandwiches.

After lunch, Trevor opened the video chat program. "Mom, I have Aria on," he called. Maria came bustling into the dining room. She took off her apron and sat down next to him. Shelby sat on the other side of Trevor, and the others gathered around the table.

"Hi," Aria said happily. She picked up Shelby's gift first. It was wrapped in paper covered with umbrellas and flowers. She tore back the paper carefully and smiled. "Oh, thank you, Shelby," she said. "Trevor, look." Aria held a cappuccino maker up for him to see.

Trevor turned to Shelby and Dan, "Thank you."

Next, Aria opened Maria's gift which was wrapped in the same paper. "Oh, Maria, thank you. It is beautiful." She held up a Swarovski crystal vase for Trevor to see.

Trevor looked at his mother. "Wow, Mom." He took her hand, "It is beautiful."

"I'm so glad you both like it," Maria said.

So the guests could see Trevor on the webcam, Aria turned the laptop around. "Thank you everyone for your generosity. We will see y'all at the wedding," he said as he gave the crowd a wave.

Aria looked into the webcam and blew him a kiss. "I love you."

"I love you too."

Danny climbed up on Trevor's lap. "Hi Aria," he waved and shouted at the computer.

"Danny, you can speak normally. She can hear you," Trevor explained to him.

"Hi, Danny," Aria said.

Athena leaned over Aria, so he could see her. "Hi, Danny." Troy heard Athena's voice, and he got up, walked around the table, and leaned over Trevor. "Hi, Troy." Athena said. She gave him a big smile.

"Hi. How are you?" He wanted to ask her about last night, but he knew he could not with everyone sitting right there.

"I'm well. We are having a fun girl's weekend."

"Hi," Maria said as she edged in front of Troy and leaned in toward the laptop."

"Hang on," Trevor said. He took the webcam off the top of the computer and passed it around so everyone could say hi.

"Oh, I wish I was there," Shelby said. "I can't wait for the wedding."

Aria smiled. "I wish you and Maria could be here too."

Trevor put the webcam back on the laptop, and Danny leaned in close again. "Danny, I will see you soon," Aria said.

"Bye," Danny said as he waved to her.

"What are you ladies doing next?" Trevor asked. Then he heard loud popping sounds, and someone handed Aria a glass of champagne. "Ok," he laughed, "have a great time."

"We will. Love you." She blew him a kiss.

"I love you too." Trevor closed the laptop. "Looks like a good party," he said to the others.

Chapter 25

The next month was so busy that Athena and Aria, who were normally night owls, were in bed before eleven o'clock many nights. Aria had several gown fittings. She and Athena were the only ones at the fittings, and they brought the veil and the shoes to see the complete look. The length of the gown was perfect, but the body needed some alterations.

Despite all she had to do, Athena's house was beautifully decorated. Outside, the shrubs next to the house had multiple strands of lights. There was a lighted wreath on the door, and a small lighted tree next to the door. She had lighted garlands around the archways from the kitchen to the dining room and from the dining room to the living room. The kitchen also had garlands and lights at the top of the cabinets. The hutch in the dining room had a lighted and decorated garland. The living room had a large tree by the fireplace, and the mantle was decorated with lights, a variety of Santa Claus figures, and stockings. There was a small lighted tree in the kitchen decorated with coastal ornaments and another lighted tree decorated with small glass ornaments in the entry hall. The banister to the second floor had a lighted garland, and there was a small tree on the second floor landing decorated with assorted seashells and glass ornaments. Athena even had a lighted ceramic tree in the attic room.

On the countertop in the kitchen were stacks of plastic containers containing an assortment of cookies for the holiday, and there were more containers of cookies in the freezer for the wedding reception. Athena made several varieties of Italian cookies, traditional chocolate chip and peanut butter cookies, brownies, and many, many spritz cookies.

Christmas morning, Athena, Aria, and Trevor popped champagne, made Mimosas, and toasted, "Merry Christmas." They clinked glasses and drank. Athena made cranberry muffins and baked egg and sausage cups for breakfast, she set up a buffet on the coffee table, and then the three of them sat around the tree and opened presents.

"Oh Aria, this is beautiful," Athena said when she opened a package with a bracelet and an owl charm.

Aria laughed. "Mom, we think alike." She had just opened a package containing a similar bracelet with a penguin charm. "I love it."

Christmas music played softly, and a very light snow was falling outside. Athena thought it was a perfect Christmas, and she could think of only one thing that would make it even better, Troy.

Later that morning, Trevor turned on his laptop and connected with the family in Texas. They took turns wishing one another Merry Christmas. "Danny, are you excited about flying up here tomorrow?" Trevor asked as he and Aria watched Danny open their present to him: a Star Wars rolling bag for the flight the next day.

"I guess so," he mumbled.

"Flying is fun, Danny," Trevor told him.

"Maybe you will be able to say hi to the pilot," Aria said, which made Danny smile.

Troy leaned toward the camera. "Merry Christmas. I am looking forward to visiting again and maybe having some chowder, Athena." He smiled at her when she appeared on the screen.

Athena blushed, and her heart raced. "I think that can be arranged." She smiled at Troy. "Have a safe flight." She stepped back and then hurried to the kitchen and took a calming breath while Trevor said good-bye.

"Can't wait until tomorrow, Mom," Trevor said. "Dress warm. The forecast is for cold weather. Love you." Athena closed her eyes. She could not wait for tomorrow.

Early, the morning after Christmas, Athena checked on the flight, confirmed the rental car, and met James at the rental house to stock the kitchen with food and to get the keys. "I like this house," Athena said as she looked around. "The kitchen is huge." The kitchen had a center island with a cooktop and there was an island to sit at as well. She liked that it had double ovens and a microwave that was also a convection oven. James helped her put the perishables in the refrigerator and put the groceries in the empty cabinets.

"What time does their flight land?"

"1:36 pm," Athena replied. "Trevor, Aria, and I are heading to the airport shortly. Would you like to come too? They want to meet you."

"I will meet them tonight at dinner. I must get home. Amber has dance class this afternoon." Athena nodded. "The reservation is for seven o'clock at Luigi's," James reminded her.

Athena put a vase of fresh flowers on the counter. Next to it, she placed a gift basket of local foods, a box of chocolates, and a tray of cookies. She also set a gift bag containing several cars on the counter for

Danny. When everything was set, they walked out the kitchen door and headed toward their cars parked in the driveway.

Suddenly, James stopped. "What's wrong?" Athena asked.

James turned and looked at her with sad eyes. "Our baby is getting married," he said.

Athena put her hand on his arm. "I know. The time went fast. It seems like not so long ago Aria was just a little girl in dance class." She gave James a hug.

Athena, Aria, and Trevor arrived at the airport and parked. "I'll ride with the family," Trevor said. "This way I can direct them to the house in case we get separated." As they walked, Aria hooked her arm in Trevor's. Soon after they reached the terminal, the plane landed, so they did not have to wait long for the family.

"Hi!" Maria called and waved as she exited the baggage claim area. She carried a large bag on each arm. Troy and Dan each pulled two large suitcases and had smaller bags on their shoulders. John pulled two rolling bags each topped with a smaller bag. Shelby and Danny both had rolling bags with a smaller bag on top. Trevor ran up to Maria, kissed her, and took her bags.

It took quite some time for everyone to say hello and get the car rented and loaded.

When they arrived at the rental house, the men started to unload the luggage. Troy left his luggage in the car because he planned to stay with Trevor while he worked on a few small projects at the house.

"What a gorgeous place," Shelby said when she walked inside the rental house. She looked around at the furnishings and turned to Danny, "No running, no playing, and no touching anything."

Danny opened his present. "Wow, cars!" he said as he started to run the cars over the countertop. Shelby grabbed his arm.

"There is a rec room downstairs where Danny can play," Athena told Shelby.

"Let's go see the playroom, Danny," Shelby said leading Danny away.

After unpacking, they all went over to Aria and Trevor's home. "Beautiful," Maria said as she looked at the cabinets in the kitchen. "Troy they are just beautiful."

Trevor and Aria took the family on a tour of the rest of the house, and then they sat in the living room by the fireplace, drank iced tea, and talked.

About 5:30 pm, Athena and Aria decided to go home to get ready for dinner.

"Yes, we should get back to the house and get ready too," Maria said. They put on their coats and started to leave.

"Dad, Troy and I will get ready and then come to the rental and drive with you to the restaurant."

"Ok." John nodded. "I'll use the GPS to get back."

Aria and Athena got in their car and drove home. Aria breathed a sigh of relief. "I think that went well."

"It went very well," Athena replied.

They quickly showered and dressed. It was very cold outside and there was a brisk wind, so Athena took her long wool coat out of the closet. She also took out her white scarf and mittens.

"I'm going to start the car and warm it up," Aria called up the stairs.

Athena went downstairs and was changing over her purse to a dressier black one when Aria came back inside. "It's snowing," she said with a shiver, and she went upstairs to get out her long winter coat.

They all met at the restaurant just before seven pm. Trevor made the introductions then they sat down around the two long tables that were pushed together. Troy sat down next to Athena, and Aria sat on the other side of her. They seated Amber and Danny side by side, but the two children did not seem interested in talking. Danny kept going to the window to look out at the snow.

"Do you think we can make a snowman?" he asked.

Trevor laughed. "We might get enough to make a tiny one."

"Can we do it tonight, Uncle Trevor? Can we?

"We can try. There isn't much snow."

The dinner conversation flowed easily as they all got to know one another. James and John talked about real estate. John told James that he leased land for a wind farm.

"Yes. Diversify," James said to him. "It is the only way to keep a business afloat these days."

Troy took Athena's hand under the table. She gave his hand a little squeeze. He took the opportunity, while everyone was involved in different conversations, to whisper, "I missed you" in her ear. She smiled at him and squeezed his hand again.

Wednesday morning, Athena prepared blueberry pancakes, bacon, scrambled eggs, and toast. She poured mugs of tea for herself and Aria and put on a pot of coffee. Trevor and Troy arrived for breakfast. "Good morning," they said as they came in the door and took off their boots.

"Good morning," Athena replied. "Aria is in her room," she said to Trevor, and he went upstairs. This was the first opportunity Troy had to be alone with Athena, and he walked over to her, took her hand, and kissed it. They heard footsteps, and when Trevor and Aria entered the kitchen, Troy was pouring coffee for himself and Trevor, and Athena was taking bacon out of the pan.

Aria looked at Trevor and shook her head. Trevor shrugged his shoulders, and they sat down at the table. He put two pancakes on his plate, and poured on some warm, pure, maple syrup. Troy did the same.

Aria turned to Trevor, "Is the family ok on their own for a while today?"

Trevor nodded yes and swallowed his mouthful of pancakes. "I gave them directions, and they have a GPS. They are going to the mall. Shelby and Mom want to do some shopping, and Dan and Dad are taking Danny to the movies." He served himself more pancakes.

"I need to go to the home improvement store," Troy said.

"You can take the truck again, Troy," Athena said. "Or I can drive you," she added quickly.

"What are you doing today, Mom?" Aria asked. Athena was smiling and intently watching Troy as he took two more pancakes. "Mom?"

"What? Oh. I have a few odds and ends to do," she replied.

Aria looked at Trevor and glanced at the door with her eyes. "We should get going soon, Trevor. We have a lot to do. I am going to get my boots on." Aria got up and went upstairs.

Trevor finished his pancakes and cleaned up his and Aria's plates. Aria came back downstairs and took her heavy coat out of the closet. "I will text you when we are finished and heading back to the house, Mom," Aria said.

"Ok, honey." Athena gave her daughter a hug. "I made lasagna for dinner tonight. Be careful. Call or text if you need anything." Aria nodded, and she and Trevor left the house.

As soon as they closed the door behind them, Troy flicked the lock on the door, pulled Athena to him, and kissed her so passionately she could hardly breathe. She wrapped her arms around his neck, and he picked her up and carried her upstairs to her bedroom. He gently set her feet on the floor, and he closed the bedroom door. Then he took her in his arms again, and they continued kissing while frantically removing one another's clothing.

"I missed you, Troy," Athena said breathlessly. She slipped off his shirt and ran her hands up his muscular chest as she kissed him.

Troy finished removing her clothing and looked at her. She was so beautiful. He wanted to take her immediately, but he controlled the impulse. He effortlessly picked her up and carried her to the bed. He set Athena down carefully and laid by her side. He kissed her and caressed her body until she was writhing beneath him in pleasure. A soft moan passed her lips as he covered her mouth with his.

He leaned back and smoothed her hair with his fingers. Athena opened her eyes and smiled at him. Troy looked pleadingly into her dark eyes. Eyes that swallowed him. "Athena, you are all I have thought of since I left."

"I missed you too, Troy." Athena feverishly kissed him. "Troy," she breathed, "make love to me." She pulled him closer. She kissed him. "Now, Troy. Now."

Troy slid his hands beneath her and buried himself inside her.

It was nearly lunchtime when they showered and went downstairs.

"Troy?" He looked at her. "I really missed you, and I know it sounds strange given what we just did; but can we take it slow and not tell the others just yet?"

Troy smiled. "Of course, Athena. I understand. We have the wedding and guests." He did not want to do anything to take away from Aria and Trevor's day. He took her hand. "Ready to go to the home improvement store?"

"Yes." Athena kissed him. "Thanks for understanding."

Aria and Trevor arrived at their house at 3:30 pm. Athena and Troy were in the kitchen. Athena held pieces of wood together while Troy secured them.

"What are you making, Troy?" Aria asked.

Troy looked up at her. "Drawer dividers. Athena wanted to purchase some for your kitchen drawers, but I thought custom wooden ones to match the cabinets would look nicer. I had plenty of leftover wood." He took the unit from Athena and showed Aria and Trevor.

"Nice," Trevor said.

Troy picked up the other unit and then put them in the cabinet drawers. Athena looked at the dividers. "I need these for my drawers too," she said to Troy.

"Yes, I have seen the pile of utensils in your drawers," he replied with a smile.

Athena looked at him and rolled her eyes. "Well, I better get home and get the lasagna in the oven," she said.

"I will come home with you, Mom."

"Troy and I will bring everyone over at 5:30, or as soon as they are ready." Trevor said as he leaned over and kissed Aria goodbye.

"Welcome. Come in," Athena said as she opened the door. "Aria and I are so happy to have you at our home." She and Aria took their coats and hung them up in the hall closet.

"This is a beautiful home," Maria said. "And your decorations are so festive."

"Thank you. Would you like a tour?"

"Oh yes."

Athena led the way while Aria, Trevor, and Troy started to set out drinks and munchies for everyone. "This is my office, den, sitting room," Athena said when she brought them up to the attic room.

"Oh, I see you did get rocking chairs." Maria sat down in one of the two matching white rocking chairs in front of the windows.

"I did. I loved the rockers on your porch, and I knew I had to have two for my room."

"Is that the ocean?" John asked. He could see light reflected off the water in the distance.

"Yes, you have to come over during the day," Athena told him. "Troy suggested that I put in a sliding door to a small porch, and I am seriously considering it. He said as long as he has structural plans, he can build it for me."

Maria smiled and sighed softly.

"This is a great room," Shelby said. Danny climbed up on the exercise bike that stood along the back wall. "Be careful, Danny," Shelby warned.

"That is a recent addition too," Athena told Shelby. "My old one squeaked terribly."

They went back downstairs. Troy handed Dan and John a beer each. "Shelby, would you like one?"

"No thanks, Troy."

"I made a pitcher of Sangria and a pitcher of Pimms," Athena said.

"What is Pimms?" Maria asked.

"It's English. They primarily drink it in the summer, but it is light and refreshing, and Aria and I like it at holiday time too."

"Oh, I will try it," Maria said.

"Shelby?" Athena asked. Shelby shook her head no.

"I have flavored seltzer water and soda," Athena informed her.

"I think I'll try a seltzer," she replied.

The dining room table was covered in a rich, red velvet tablecloth. In the center of the table there was a tall arrangement of white spider chrysanthemums and velvety red roses. White taper candles in holders decorated with holly were on either side of the arrangement. Athena and Aria began setting out bowls of olives, plates of deviled eggs, pineapple salad, and a large bowl of Greek salad made with cucumbers, tomatoes, onions, and Kalamata olives. Trevor filled everyone's glass with wine, and Danny's with grape juice. He thought it was odd that Shelby asked for juice instead of wine, but he nodded and filled hers with juice as well.

Athena set the lasagna in the center of the table, and Aria put out a plate of stuffed mushrooms. When Athena took the hot, crispy, garlic bread out of the oven, they sat down to dinner. Athena raised her glass, "To many more holiday dinners together," she said. "Merry Christmas."

"Merry Christmas," they all cheered and began to eat.

"Oh, your lasagna is so delicious," Maria said to Athena.

"Thank you," Athena replied. "It's my grandmother's recipe."

While they ate, soft holiday music played in the background. Athena looked around the table. Everyone looked happy. They were all laughing and talking. She thought it was so nice having a large family gathered around the table again. It reminded her of holidays when she was young, and her extended family visited.

After dinner, Athena made tea, coffee, and hot chocolate. She whipped up half and half, topped each mug with the frothy cream, and then sprinkled on a garnish of cinnamon or shaved chocolate. For dessert, Athena put out a tray of homemade cookies.

"What are these?" Danny asked holding up a thin waffle like cookie.

"Those are Pizzelles, Danny," Aria explained.

Danny took a bite. "Umm, good."

Troy ate several slices of Italian brown cookies and then ate a couple of brownies. "These are delicious," he said to Athena when she sat down at the table next to him.

"Thank you. I am glad you like them." She broke a slice of brown cookie in half and took a bite.

Athena was at home alone Thursday morning. Trevor and the groomsmen went to the tux shop to get their tuxes. Dan and Shelby accompanied Danny. Aria went with the bridesmaids to pick up their gowns. Athena took out her own gown and accessories and tried everything on. She looked in the mirror. Mother of the Bride, she thought to herself and sighed. She stood staring at her reflection until a text broke her concentration.

'How are you doing?' Ellen texted.

'Good' Athena texted back. 'Trying on my dress.'

'I'm taking the early train tomorrow morning. I will be there by noon.'

Athena sent back a smile emoji.

'How is Troy?' Ellen asked.

'Very good. I am meeting him at Trevor and Aria's house at eleven o'clock. We are going out to lunch.'

'Have fun' Ellen texted back with a smiley face and a heart emoji.

Athena shook her head. She confided in her friends Ellen and Jasmine about Troy and her feelings for him. They were both supportive and pushed her to pursue a relationship with him. She liked Troy very much, but the other considerations still worried her and made her pull back. She took off the dress and hung it and her accessories up on the outside of the closet door. She dressed in a pair of jeans, a pink sweater, and black boots. She then got in her car and drove to Aria and Trevor's home.

"Hello," she called as she opened the door and walked in.

Troy came out of the kitchen. "Hello," he said with a smile. He had a paint brush in his hand. Athena could not deny that just seeing him made her heart flutter.

"What are you painting?"

"The downstairs half bath. Aria complained it was a dark room. I just finished."

They walked into the kitchen, and Troy began cleaning his paint brush while Athena looked in the bathroom. "Oh, I like the color," she said. "This room is small and doesn't have a window, but the yellow painted walls make the room brighter."

The doorbell rang. "That's Mom and Dad," Troy said.

Athena left the room, she looked out the side window out of habit, and then opened the door. "Hi," she smiled at Maria and John. "Come on in."

John carried a box and Maria carried a large shopping bag. "I bought some linens for their downstairs bath," Maria said as Athena led them to the kitchen. Maria took several sets of towels out of the bag she carried. "Those blue towels just do not go with the new color."

John set the box he carried on the counter and sat down on one of the bar stools. Maria opened the box and pulled out a yellow and white artificial flower arrangement.

"What a pretty arrangement, Maria," Athena said. "It will brighten the bathroom." Maria nodded and went in the bathroom and arranged the items. Athena followed her. "It's perfect."

"Thank you," Maria replied. "Have you been here long?" she asked.

"Maybe ten minutes," Athena replied politely.

Troy looked in and nodded his approval. "Looks good." He went back in the kitchen, and when Maria and Athena came in, he asked, "ready for lunch?"

Athena looked at him. She did not mind the four of them going to lunch, but he failed to tell her his plan. "Athena, you can leave your car here. I'll drive." Troy locked up the house, and they got into the rented vehicle. John sat upfront with Troy, and Athena and Maria sat in the middle seat.

"Where are we going for lunch?" Maria asked.

"Sam's. It is a seafood restaurant. You will love the clam chowder," Troy said looking in his rear view mirror, so he could see his mother. "It's Athena's favorite restaurant."

Maria nodded her head and gave a weak smile.

Chapter 26

Multiple cars caravanned to The Castle early in the afternoon on Friday to avoid the rush hour traffic. They walked around the museum and discussed the wedding decorations while waiting for the rehearsal to begin. Once everyone was present, the priest and the venue's wedding coordinator went through the procedure for the ceremony the next day.

Troy, Dan, and those people who were not part of the ceremony brought in boxes of arrangements, candy, favors, and other items. Athena directed the placement of the boxes for the staff, so they could set the items out the next day. She moved around the room and put notes with directions on the tables and made certain everything was in order.

Meanwhile, the wedding party ran through the ceremony twice. Once they were confident they knew what to do the next day, they went to the rehearsal dinner at a restaurant near the wedding venue. In addition to the traditional bridal party and immediate family, Ellen, and several guests who came in from out of town were also invited.

John made the first toast. "Maria and I would like to thank y'all for coming tonight as we prepare to celebrate the wedding of our son Trevor to the very lovely Aria. We wish you both a long, healthy, and very happy life together."

"Cheers," everyone said, and Trevor and Aria kissed.

Dinner was served buffet style, so people walked around, talked, and mingled. Athena wore a burgundy long sleeved lace dress with a keyhole back and black high heels. Troy leaned against the bar and watched her as she moved around the room greeting and talking to people.

Dan walked up beside him. "She looks good," he said. He could not resist. Troy glared at his brother but said nothing. He straightened up and walked over to Athena.

She smiled as he approached. He wore black slacks and a white button down dress shirt that hugged his body very well. She reached out and took his hand. "Ellen, this is Troy. Troy this is Ellen, my editor," she said.

Troy extended his hand. "It's nice to meet you." He was very happy that Athena did not introduce him as Trevor's brother.

"It is very nice to meet you, Troy." Ellen smiled at him. "I saw pictures of the work you did at Aria and Trevor's home. You did a fantastic job."

"Thank you," Troy replied.

The evening was very casual, and Troy stayed by Athena's side while she talked to other guests.

Just before the party broke up, Ellen saw Athena in the ladies' room. She checked to be sure they were alone. "Troy is hot. He's even better looking in person," she said to Athena.

Athena smiled. "He is."

"I have known you for quite a while, Athena, and I have never seen you so relaxed and happy."

"Well, it is a wedding," Athena replied stifling a laugh.

"You know what I mean." Ellen put her hand on Athena's shoulder. "Seriously, he's good for you."

Athena smiled. "He is."

The morning of the wedding, the bridesmaids came to Athena's house. She put out tea, coffee, hot chocolate, and an assortment of muffins and breakfast sandwiches for the girls to eat before the stylists arrived.

The stylists planned to do all the women's nails at the house and style the bridesmaids' and Athena's hair. At the wedding venue, the stylists planned to do Aria's hair as well as Brook, Shelby, Maria, and Amber's hair. They would also do all the women's make up.

Once the girls were talking excitedly and having breakfast, Athena retreated to her bathroom to shower. She stood in the shower and let the hot water run over her. She was happy, and if she was honest, a little sad too. Things would be different now. She washed and conditioned her hair then soaped up and rinsed. She turned off the water, stepped out, and dried herself. She walked into her bedroom, and she could hear the girls laughing in Aria's room down the hall. She realized how much she enjoyed having the girls visit her home. Now they would go to Aria's home. Athena looked at herself in the mirror. Change was inevitable, and the changes both excited her and made her a little sad. However, today was a day for happiness, so she put on a button front shirt and jeans and went in to join the girls.

By coincidence, all the women had longish hair, so their hair was going to be styled in similar fashion. A stylist curled the ends of Athena's hair then she pulled back the front in a braid and secured it at the back of Athena's head with an elaborate, gold, filigree, double hair comb. She sprayed Athena's hair to keep it in place.

At noon, the limo arrived to take them to The Castle. The driver helped load everything into the vehicle. Athena locked up the house and got in. "Does everyone have everything?" she asked. They all did a quick check, and then Athena told the driver they were ready.

The limo pulled away from the curb, and Brittany popped a bottle of champagne. They each held out a glass. Brittany poured the champagne, and then she cleared her throat. "To Aria. You and I have been friends since we were in college. I wish you well as you begin your life with Trevor. I love you. Happy Wedding Day!" They all gave a cheer and drank.

When they arrived at the venue, James, Troy, and Dan helped them get the gowns and accessories to the room where they were dressing. Brook and Amber were already there, and one hair stylist worked on Brook's hair and the other on Amber's hair.

Athena went out into the foyer. "Where are Maria and Shelby?" she asked Dan, but just then Maria came out to help too. "That is a beautiful gown, Maria. The color looks great on you."

"Thank you," Maria replied. "Athena, you better get into your gown soon."

"I will. The stylists are ready for you and Shelby."

Shelby heard her name and came out of a side room. "Oh good, I really could use some hair help," she said. Athena directed her and Maria to the room with the stylists then she went to finish checking on the wedding and reception arrangements.

The chapel, where the ceremony would take place, had a stone altar and tall stained glass windows. At the end of each pew was a large white bow accented with red roses and baby's breath. Two large urns full of white gladiolas, roses, baby's breath, and white bows stood on either side of the altar.

The room for the reception was grand. Because it was also a museum, there were suits of armor lining the railing of the upper gallery. There were large hanging banners at the edges of the room, and several gold chandeliers hung down from the high ceiling for illumination. The round tables were covered with white tablecloths. There were brocade circles in the center of each table on which tall centerpieces with Ostridge feathers, masks, and white roses were placed. Each place card had either a white, gold, or black mask, and there were several extra masks on the tables so guests could select the color they wanted. The florist brought extra vases full of red and white roses, and Athena placed one on the DJ table, one on the guest book table, and two on the candy and favor table.

Troy walked along and helped her, but mostly he watched. She checked the entry and even went into the ladies' and men's rooms to inspect them. Satisfied that all was in order, Athena returned to the room to put on her gown. The bridesmaids were getting into their gowns and the stylists were getting Aria ready.

Aria's hair was the longest and both stylists worked on her hair. First, they curled the hair, and then they pulled the front sections of hair back and wove an intricate pattern of hair at the back of her head which was accented with pearls, rhinestones, and baby's breath. The makeup artist applied subtle makeup.

The photographer arrived, and she took some photos of the women getting ready. She arranged and then photographed Aria's gown and shoes. The flowers were photographed as well. Athena, Brook, Maria, and Shelby had white rose wristlets with ribbons to match their gowns. Amber's flower basket was trimmed with red and white streamers and filled with white rose petals. The bridesmaids carried bouquets of large white roses accented with red alstroemeria and trimmed with thin white and red ribbon streamers. Aria's bouquet was a mix of large red and white roses and baby's breath.

James knocked at the door. "Are we on schedule?" he asked Athena.

"Yes, Aria is almost ready. Come in."

James went in, and the sight of Aria in her gown took his breath away. He took out a handkerchief and dabbed at his eyes. He walked over to his daughter and kissed her lightly. "You are so beautiful." He dabbed his eyes again. The photographer was right there snapping pictures.

When it was time for the ceremony, the groomsmen seated the guests. Once everyone was seated, Trevor and Tyler, the best man, took their places at the front of the altar, and the priest came out and signaled to the organist who began playing Pachelbel's Cannon D. The curtain parted, and Maria and John came down the aisle and took their places. Athena was escorted by Jason, one of the groomsmen.

Troy stared at her as she walked down the aisle. Her floor length gown was a rich golden color with a hint of rose that complimented her skin tone and hair. The top of the gown was an off the shoulder style and embellished with many crystals. It had a drop waist also edged with crystals. Her hair flowed over her bare shoulders and down her back. The gown glittered in the light, and Troy thought she looked radiant.

Athena took her place in the aisle across from him, and he could not take his eyes off her. She smiled at him and then turned to watch as the bridesmaids and groomsmen walked down the aisle. Dan noticed Troy continued to stare at Athena and nudged him lightly. Troy straightened up and turned to see Brittany coming down the aisle. She was followed by Danny who did not smile. He looked serious and a little stiff as he held the pillow with the rings out in front of him. Amber was more relaxed. She slowly walked down the aisle sprinkling white rose pedals. She wore a small tiara on her head with a short veil attached. She smiled and posed a few times while a guest took her picture.

Once the wedding party was in place, the music changed to Mendelssohn's Wedding March, and everyone rose. Aria and James stood at the back of the chapel, and then they slowly started to make their way down the aisle to the altar.

Trevor smiled when he saw Aria. She was gorgeous and looked like a princess, and he dabbed his eyes. Troy looked at Athena and saw her dab her eyes with a tissue.

People took pictures as Aria and James passed them. Aria's pure white gown had a sweetheart neckline. The bodice was an intricate textured brocade that was fitted to the drop waist where it flared out and fell in layers. The gown had an attached cape and a very long train. On her head, she wore a rhinestone tiara. The cathedral length veil flowed down past the train and reflected the light of the chandeliers. The lace seemed to shimmer, and the edge of the veil glimmered with tiny rhinestones all around as Aria glided down the aisle. When they reached the altar, James shook Trevor's hand. He kissed Aria and placed her hand in Trevor's hand then took his place in the pew between Athena and Brook.

Aria and Trevor stood before the priest, and he began the ceremony.

After the ceremony, the photographer gathered the families and took many photographs while the other guests enjoyed hor d'oeuvres. One by one, the family members rejoined the guests until the DJ announced the arrival of the attendants and the bride and groom. "Let's all welcome Mr. and Mrs. Young!" he shouted, and everyone clapped enthusiastically and cheered. Aria and Trevor slowly made their way in. They waved and stopped to say hello to guests as they wound their way to the head table.

Tyler picked up his champagne glass, and everyone quieted down for the best man's toast. "Let's all raise our glasses to the happy couple. I hope your days are happy and your love lasts forever. To Aria and Trevor. Cheers!"

"Cheers!" everyone shouted and then they sat down to enjoy an elegant dinner. The food was delicious and plentiful, and liquor flowed freely. Troy sat next to Athena. James sat on the other side of her when he was not walking around with a bottle of champagne talking to people and refilling glasses.

A couple of times, Troy took Athena's hand under the table. He lightly ran his thumb in the palm of her hand, and she twined her fingers with his.

"Let's go get a beer at the bar," Dan whispered to Troy after dinner. "I'm not big on champagne."

Troy nodded his head. He looked at his father who took only tiny sips of champagne during toasts. He caught his father's attention, and the three men stood up. Athena looked up at him. "I'll be right back. We are going to the bar."

The bar tender poured them each a beer. "Ah, beer drinkers," James said jovially when he stopped at the bar for another bottle of champagne. "Having a good time?"

"Yes," they replied in unison.

When Troy and Dan returned to the table, Athena was up talking with some of the guests. Troy's heart fluttered as he watched her laugh and toss her head back. Dan sat down, nudged Shelby, and inclined his head toward Troy. She smiled and took Dan's hand.

The DJ asked for everyone's attention, and people gathered around. Aria and Trevor took to the dance floor wearing their masks for their first dance.

"Where did he learn to dance?" Dan asked Troy.

"I don't know, but he's pretty good," Troy replied.

"I gave them dancing lessons for an engagement present," Athena whispered to them.

"Really?" they both replied.

"Yes," Athena replied. "Trevor didn't mention it?"

As the song ended, Aria and Trevor took off their masks and kissed to loud applause.

The DJ started another song. "Let's have the father of the bride and the bride, and the mother of the groom and the groom on the floor, please," he said, and the guests gathered around to watch. James and Aria talked while they danced, and James dabbed his eyes several times. The DJ transitioned to another song and said, "let's have the bride and groom, the father of the bride and the mother of the groom, and the mother of the bride and the father of the groom on the floor, please."

John took Athena's hand and led her out to the dance floor. "This is a beautiful wedding, Athena. Thank you for all your hard work."

Athena smiled at him. "Thank you, John. It was a lot of work, but I am so pleased at the outcome. Everyone seems to be having such a good time." Troy watched Athena dance and talk with his father. John said something to her, and she laughed.

"Ok, let's get the flower girl and ring bearer on the floor. Brook and Shelby pushed the two kids out onto the dance floor. Everyone oohed and ahhed as they twirled around. "Aren't they adorable," the DJ said, and the crowd cheered and clapped. Amber smiled and curtsied, but Danny just stood there waiting for permission to leave. "Let's get everyone out on the dance floor now. Come on folks. This is a party!" He cranked up the music.

Many people stepped on the dance floor and started to dance. Some of the guests wore a mask and others did not.

Troy strode across the room and tapped his father on the shoulder. John smiled and placed Athena's hand in Troy's. He pat Troy on the back, and then turned and left to find Maria.

Troy held Athena's right hand and put his left hand on her waist. He looked into her eyes. "You are incredibly beautiful in that dress."

"Thank you." Athena smiled at him. Troy was definitely the type of man she wanted. Oh, she could talk to him, and she enjoyed spending time with him, but there was more to it. He was confident and assertive without being overbearing. But most importantly, he had eyes only for her, no matter who else was around. She knew she could be very happy with him.

Troy felt Athena's body relax as she moved closer to him. He slipped his hand around her back. They spent most of the evening together. They danced to several more songs and then took a break. Athena occasionally introduced him as Trevor's brother, which made Troy sigh, but sometimes she just said, this is Troy. They stopped and talked to Ellen and Jasmine for a while, and when Athena went to make sure everything was ready for the cake cutting, the two women gave Troy the thumbs up. He smiled and nodded his appreciation.

Later, Troy asked the DJ to play several slow songs in a row. He got Athena back out on the dance floor, and he held her tight as they danced.

Just after eleven pm, Aria went up to her mother. "Mom, you look happy."

"Thank you. And you look radiant," Athena said as she kissed her daughter.

"Thank you for everything. You made my day so special." They hugged, and they both had tears in their eyes.

"I love you so much," Athena hugged Aria again.

"I love you too, Mom."

Trevor came up to them, and Athena hugged him too.

James walked over and put his arms around Athena and Aria. "Thanks, Dad," Aria said.

"Your happiness is everything to me and your mother," he replied, and they all hugged again. He shook Trevor's hand. "Take care of each other," he said.

"We will. Thank you."

"Are you two ready to leave?" James asked.

"We are," Aria and Trevor said together.

"The limo is outside. Let me tell the DJ."

Troy came over and shook Trevor's hand and gave Aria a hug. Maria, John, and the rest of the family also said their good-byes. Brook came over too after she passed a sleeping Amber to another family member.

James came back. "The DJ will tell the guests to line up to see you two off as soon as we give the signal."

Athena and Aria hugged again. "I'll call you in the morning before we go to the airport, Mom."

"Have a great time in Belize," Athena said.

"I'll see you in Texas."

"Yes. Be safe."

Aria and Trevor went into a side room to get ready to leave. Trevor helped Aria fasten her winter cloak over her gown, and he put on his coat.

The wait staff brought out buckets full of plastic swords and wands decorated with a bell and ribbons. "Ok ladies and gentlemen, the bride and groom are getting ready to leave on the honeymoon. Everyone, grab a sword or a wand, and let's give them a rousing send off." The staff lined up the guests mixing swords and ribbon wands.

James signaled the DJ when they were ready, and the DJ announced the bridal couple's departure. Aria hugged her mother again then she took Trevor's hand, and they made their way to the door. The guests waved the ribbon wands and the bells jingled, and the swords formed a tunnel for them to walk through while the DJ wished them a great honeymoon.

Athena's eyes filled with tears as the limo pulled away. Troy reached up and wiped the tears off her cheek. "Are you ok?" he whispered. Athena nodded as she took his hand, and they went back inside and danced. Troy held her close and slowly he felt her body relax. She laid her head on his shoulder and he closed his eyes.

After a couple of dances, Troy joined Dan and his father at the bar, and Athena mingled and then stopped to talk to Ellen and Jasmine.

"Well?" Athena said to her friends.

"He has my vote," Jasmine laughed.

"Mine too," Ellen added quickly. "The way he looks at you, Athena. Like you are the only woman in the world."

"He's a keeper," Athena said as her eyes locked on Troy's across the room.

James walked up to her. "Athena, let's dance." He took her hand and led her out on the dance floor.

"Everything went very well," James said as they moved around.

"It did," Athena agreed.

"I can't believe Aria is married." He dabbed his eyes again. "Next thing I know, Amber will be getting married."

Athena patted him on the shoulder. "I know. The time goes fast." She thought for a moment. "But I am looking at it as just the next phase in life," she said confidently.

"That's true," James replied. "Oh, I told the other limo drivers to pick us up about midnight. Do you think that is ok?"

Athena nodded her head, yes. "Oh, James, some of the guests are getting ready to leave. I'm going to make the rounds and thank everyone." She headed off toward a few guests who were gathering up their things.

"I'll join you soon," James called. He turned and walked toward Troy who stood alone near the cookie table. James knew he might not get another opportunity to talk to him. He walked up and shook Troy's hand. "I wanted to talk to you alone."

Troy looked at him. "What about?"

"Athena." Troy gave James a stern look. This was none of his business. James recognized the look and added quickly, "let me just say, I think you and Athena would be good together." Troy relaxed a little, but still looked at James suspiciously.

James continued. "I see how you two look at one another. There's something there. But if I know Athena, she's overthinking it." Troy did not respond. James shook his head. "She's putting up barriers. She deserves to be happy, but she has a lot of trouble allowing herself to be happy. Just hang in there. She will come around." He shook Troy's hand again, waved to some people leaving, and headed toward them.

"What was that about?" Dan asked as he approached Troy.

"Apparently, he approves of Athena and I," Troy replied without emotion.

"Good to know," Dan said. "Let's go get another beer."

The limos arrived right at midnight. The DJ was packing up, and the wait staff was busy clearing the room. It was snowing lightly outside. They loaded the leftover favors, cookies, candy, and centerpieces into the second limo. Maria and Athena took one last look around to make certain they had everything.

James carried Amber to the limo and laid her on the back seat. Brook got inside. Troy carried out a centerpiece and got in the limo. Brittany followed him in.

Dan, Shelby, and Danny got into the first limo. Danny laid down and fell instantly asleep. Maria and John joined them.

James walked over to Athena. "Are you all set?"

"I am. Thank you, James," she replied.

"Thank you. You did most of the work. I mostly paid."

"That's a lot. And you thought of this beautiful venue."

James kissed her lightly on the cheek.

They looked in the first limo and said good night to John, Maria, Dan, and Shelby, and then the driver drove off to bring the family to the rental house.

James and Athena got into the second limo. First, the driver dropped off James, Brook, and Amber. "Are you three going to be ok bringing the stuff in the house?" James asked.

"Don't worry. We can manage," Troy replied.

"I could come to the house and then have the driver bring me back."

"We will be fine," Athena said. "Good night."

"Good night." James closed the door, and the driver went to Athena's house. The driver, Troy, and Brittany helped Athena bring the items inside. Athena handed Brittany a centerpiece. "Thanks for all your help."

Brittany hugged Athena, "I had a fantastic time. Bye Troy." Brittany walked to her car.

"Text me when you get home," Athena called to her. Brittany waved as she drove away.

The limo driver waited for Troy to bring him to Trevor and Aria's house. While inside the house, Athena took Troy's hand. She pulled him to her and kissed him. "Can you stay with me tonight?" she whispered in his ear.

He kissed her. "Yes, I can. If that's what you want." he whispered back. Athena nodded yes. Troy went outside to the limo, made sure everything was out of the vehicle, tipped the driver, and sent him away. He went back into the house, and he closed and locked the door. Athena handed him a glass of champagne.

"What should we drink to?" he asked.

"To life's possibilities," she said, and he touched his glass to hers and they drank. Athena picked up the bottle of champagne, took his hand, and walked into the living room.

Troy refilled the glasses and set the bottle down on the coffee table. Athena kicked off her heels and laid down on the sofa. Troy removed his jacket and tie and took off his boots. They drank more champagne and watched the fire crackling in the fireplace. Athena's phone vibrated. Brittany was home safe, so she texted Brittany back then set her phone on the coffee table. Troy looked over at Athena. Her curled hair was spread out on the sofa pillow. She smiled at him, and he felt his heart beating very fast.

Athena reached up, took his hand, and then pulled him down to her. She put her arms around his broad shoulders and kissed him. She poured everything into the kiss.

Troy eagerly kissed her back, but then he leaned back a little. "Are you sure you want this?" Troy wanted to be with her more than he ever wanted anything in the world, but she gave off conflicting signals, and he needed to be assured that she wanted him as well.

She looked into his eyes. "I definitely want you here with me tonight," she whispered. She pushed him back against the sofa, slid her body on top of his, and kissed him very passionately.

Troy slowly unzipped Athena's dress. She sat up, and he gently slid the dress down and off her shoulders. Troy kissed his way down her neck then he stood and pulled Athena up. The dress fell to the floor, and she carefully stepped out of it. Troy picked it up and laid it neatly on the coffee table. She wore a lace nude colored bra and panty set which he removed as he kissed her body.

Athena tangled her fingers in Troy's hair and sighed as he kissed first one breast and then the other. Her hands moved to his shirt, and she unbuttoned it then slid it off his body. She ran delicate kisses along his shoulder as he molded her body to his.

Athena reached between them and undid his pants. She pushed them down over his narrow hips. "Troy, make love with me," she breathed in his ear.

He stepped out of the pants, then picked her up, and carried her across the room and up the stairs to her bedroom. They fell together in a tangle on the bed.

"Athena are you truly mine?" he whispered while his hands claimed her.

She responded by devouring his mouth with hers. She rolled on top of him, and he wrapped his arms around her hips.

"No one has ever made me feel as I feel when I am with you, Troy." She lifted her head and looked into his eyes. She saw desire in his eyes, and she relished in the thought of how much he wanted her. No one had ever looked at her the way he did, and she wanted him. There was no doubt, she wanted him.

He saw the desire in her eyes. She was his tonight. He would have to settle for the night, but it was a start.

As they stared into one another's eyes, as each saw passion in the other, Troy rolled over and slid into her at the same time. They stayed still merging and melding into one. Athena wrapped her legs around Troy's back, and he wrapped his arms around her and pulled her close.

They started to move, and they both gave everything they had to the other. Tomorrow was another day. But tonight, they were together, and they were one.

Chapter 27

Troy and Athena slept until almost ten o'clock then went downstairs and prepared breakfast. Athena still was not one hundred percent sure this was a good idea, but she could not deny that she felt wonderful when she was with Troy. She never let herself get completely lost in love, but Troy broke down barriers that she did not even know existed. Troy was truly her soul mate.

Ellen texted. 'I had a great time. On the train back to NYC. TTYS.' Athena sent a short text back to Ellen.

"Everyone had a great time yesterday," she said to Troy.

He scrambled up four eggs while Athena made coffee and tea. "I have never been to a wedding like it," he replied. "It was beautiful."

Athena cooked up a few breakfast sausages, put down several slices of toast, and set an assortment of cookies on a plate. Troy brought the eggs to the table, and they sat down. Athena watched Troy as he cut up a piece of sausage. His hair was rumpled. His shirt was open, and he wore only underwear. It would be nice to wake up by his side every morning, she thought to herself.

The phone rang and broke her out of her thoughts. "Hi, honey. How are you two doing?" Athena said into the phone. Troy got up and went into the living room because he was not sure if Athena wanted Aria to know he stayed the night.

"Thanks again, Mom," she said. "Everything was perfect, and everyone looked like they had a fantastic time."

"It was perfect, Aria. And you were such a beautiful bride. Have a great honeymoon, honey."

"We are leaving the hotel for the airport. I love you."

"I love you too." Athena ended the call, and then went to join Troy in the living room. He stood by the fireplace and stared into the fire. Athena walked up and slid her arms around his waist.

"I need to pack up my things today. I'm staying at the rental house tonight. We will go to the airport together since we are leaving so early in the morning." Troy took Athena's hand in his and kissed it. He hoped Athena would fly to Texas with them, but she planned to fly down a couple days before the Texas wedding reception.

That afternoon, Athena showered and did her hair. She put on a silky party dress and heels. She took a pair of boots with her, and then she drove to James and Brook's home at six o'clock. Troy and the family arrived just after she did, and they all walked in together.

This was not the house Athena and James lived in together, so Athena did not feel uncomfortable visiting. James and Brook had a New Year's Eve open house every year. They served a splendid buffet dinner, and this year, Brook's brother was the DJ. Athena had not been to one of their parties in several years because she and Aria usually spent New Year's Eve out of the country. Last year, she and Aria went to London the day after Christmas and stayed into the new year. Trevor surprised Aria by showing up at their hotel very early in the morning of New Year's Eve.

"I'm glad you could come this year, Athena," Brook said when Athena went in the kitchen to help prepare the food.

"Me too. You put on a great party, Brook."

Maria came in the kitchen. "Can I help?" she asked.

"I can always use help," Brook replied with a smile.

The three women worked together to get the food ready for the guests.

Later in the evening, Athena sat on the sofa having a cup of tea and talking with Troy and several other people when Amber and Danny walked over to her. "Athena, are you my aunt now?" Danny asked.

Athena looked at Danny and then at Troy. She cleared her throat. "What do you mean, Danny?" she asked apprehensively.

"Aria is my aunt, so are you my aunt too?" he asked.

"Oh," she stuttered. "Oh, no, I'm not your aunt, Danny. Aria married your Uncle Trevor so that makes her your aunt."

"See, I told you," Amber replied smugly.

"Is she related to me now?" Danny asked quietly as he pointed to Amber.

Shelby leaned in and whispered, "Danny, that is not nice. Amber is your Aunt Aria's stepsister."

Danny looked at his mother and asked, "so is she related to me now?" Shelby shook her head no, and Danny let out a sigh of relief.

"It's confusing for the kids," Shelby said. Athena nodded her agreement. It was one of the things that worried her about having a relationship with Troy. What if she and Troy married, and Aria and Trevor had a baby? She would be the baby's grandmother, and Troy would be the uncle, and the baby's grandmother and uncle would be married. How confusing for the child. Oh my god, what am I doing? she thought to herself, and she felt her heart race and the blood drain out of her head.

"Are you ok?" Troy asked, and she jumped.

"Yes. Yes, I am fine. Excuse me." She stood up and very quickly went to the bathroom. Maria saw Athena moving quickly away from Troy, and she shook her head and narrowed her eyes. She did not know what was going on, but she worried that her son was the one who would get hurt.

The rest of the evening, Troy could tell something was wrong. Athena became distant to him. She quickly let go of his hand when we took it, and she was jittery. Noticeably jittery.

"Is Athena ok, Troy?" John asked.

"I don't know," he said sadly. "Dad, you were right. She spooks easily. I don't know why, but for some reason, she's worried about what other people will think if she is involved with her daughter's brother-in-law. No one but her seems to think it's a problem."

"Give her some time," John said. He laid a hand on Troy's shoulder.

At midnight, everyone counted down. "Happy New Year," they shouted. People were toasting and laughing. Troy leaned over and kissed Athena on the cheek. "Happy New Year."

She gave him a nervous smile. "Happy New Year."

"Well, we hate to leave, but we have an early flight," John said to James and Brook while the others got their coats on. "Happy New Year," Brook said to John. "It was very nice to meet all of you." She shook his hand and went to say good-bye to other guests who were leaving.

Athena came over to say good-bye. John took her hand. "Thank you again, Athena. You did a beautiful job with the wedding, and we had a very good time here."

"You are welcome, John," Athena said. "You will all have to come back for a relaxing visit."

"Yes, we need to come back." John turned to James. "Could you make certain Troy knows the best way back to the house?"

"Certainly." James shook John's hand and walked over to Troy.

John did not like to meddle, but he wanted to speak to Athena alone. "You know, Athena," he paused, "we play many roles in life: mother, daughter, sibling, spouse." Athena nodded. "Sometimes those roles seem to conflict with one another. But if you follow your heart, you will find a way. And in the end, you will be happy."

Athena closed her eyes and took a deep breath then she looked at John. "Will everything turn out alright?"

"No one knows for certain. But you won't know the possibilities unless you try." He smiled at her, pat her arm, and walked away.

Maria saw John talking to Athena and wondered what he was saying to her. She walked over to Athena and was going to ask, but she decided not to. John would tell her later. She smiled at Athena. "You will be arriving on the Tuesday before Trevor and Aria return from Belize?"

"Yes. I arrive in the early afternoon. Please let me know if you need me to bring anything else to Texas." Athena and Maria hugged.

Troy walked over, and Athena gave him a hug. "Take care," she said.

Troy looked into her eyes. "You take care too. I will see you soon." Athena gave a tiny smile and nodded yes.

The next morning, even though it was still dark, Athena looked out at the ocean. She returned from the party about one am and went upstairs to her attic room. She wrapped up in a blanket, sat in a rocking chair, and stayed up there through the night. She barely slept, and she was tired from crying. She missed Troy already, and she feared she was making a terrible mistake.

To her surprise, the doorbell rang. She looked at her watch; it was six am. She opened her doorbell video APP. She gasped. It was Troy.

Athena ran downstairs and opened the door. "Hi. Is everything ok?"

"I'm sorry if I woke you, but I wanted to see you alone before I left."

"Come in." Athena moved back so Troy could get inside the house.

"I only have a few minutes; the taxi is waiting for me. Athena, I have something to say." Troy took a deep breath. "I don't know what happened yesterday to change your mind, again. I think it happened when Danny asked if you were his aunt. Who cares what people think? If two people love each other, nothing else should matter."

She started to speak, but Troy cut her off. "I need to finish, Athena. I do not want to be just your in-law, or just your friend, or even just your lover. I want to be with you. I think about you all the time. I'm not naïve. I know there are things we have to work out, but I am willing to work them out to be with you if you will only give us a chance." He paused and looked at her. There were tiny tears at the corners of her eyes. "I am in love with you, Athena. And I think… I think you love me too. But you won't give yourself permission to love."

Athena closed her eyes. He said he loved her. There were so many reasons why a relationship was not a good idea. Yet, she loved him too, but she could not say it. Larger tears welled up in her eyes.

He lifted her chin. "Athena, look at me," he said softly. She opened her eyes and the tears escaped. He tenderly wiped them away. "I'm saying I want us to be together, but you have to want it too. If you don't want me, I will never bother you again, but if you do, I am ready to do whatever it takes to make our relationship work. It is up to you."

Her Unexpected Adventure

Troy pulled Athena into his arms and kissed her. All the love he had for her he poured into the kiss. It may well be the last time he kissed her, and he wanted to remember how she felt and how she tasted, forever.

He released her, turned, and went outside to the waiting taxi. Athena could not catch her breath, and when she finally did, he was gone. She watched the taxi drive away as tears rolled down her cheeks.

Chapter 28

Late in the day, Athena got dressed and went to the travel agency. She kept the closed sign on the door and locked it. She made a cup of tea and sat down at her desk. She needed to be away from her home and the memory of Troy because she had some decisions to make. When she was with Troy, she was not only happy, but she did not feel like she had to be the one in control all the time. What did that mean? It worried and excited her at the same time because she never felt that way before. She trusted him, and trust was something she was cautious with in her relationships.

Athena picked up her new planner and looked it over. The start of the new year was typically a very slow time of year. No one had money after the holidays, so they were not booking vacations. Holly did a great job managing the agency while she was away and then busy with wedding planning. In the past few months, Athena came to rely heavily on Holly, and Holly proved she was up to the challenge.

A message came in on her phone. It was Ellen.

'Want to video chat', Athena texted back. A few minutes later, Athena looked at Ellen. "Are you in your office?"

Ellen nodded her head yes. "Are you in the office too?"

"Yes," Athena replied with a laugh.

"Only you and I would be in the office on January 1st," Ellen said.

"Because we are both workaholics."

"Good news. Since the release date for your book is February 8th, I booked you at the Vacation Expo the third weekend in March for a book signing here in the city."

"Ok, sounds good." Athena replied. "I have a booth for the agency at that expo." She paused for a few moments. "I think it is time to let Holly take the reins. I'll oversee some of it, but Holly can do most of the planning, and she can run the booth."

"You are delegating?!" Ellen could not believe her ears. "Athena, are you ok?"

"I'm ok, yes." She paused. "No." She let out a huge sigh.

"Just because Aria is married doesn't mean you won't still be close to her. My daughter and I are very close. Maybe more so now that she had the baby."

Athena smiled. "I'm not worried about me and Aria."

"What is it then?"

"I'm thinking of staying longer in Texas."

"That's not a problem."

"I'm not sure how long I will stay."

"This is about Troy, isn't it?"

"Am I crazy?"

"It's not crazy to be in love with someone. What is the problem? The distance?"

"Well yes, distance is a consideration. I can't live in Texas all year, and I doubt he will want to live here all year."

"That can be worked out. Something else is bothering you."

Athena took a deep breath. "I'm worried about children."

"You think he wants children?!"

"No. I don't think he does. I'm worried about Aria's children. They will be confused. I will be their grandmother and Troy their uncle, but we would be together."

Ellen was quiet for a few moments. Athena waited for her to say something. Finally, Ellen said, "Ok, now I know you are in love with him because that is the lamest excuse possible." Athena did not respond. "Honestly, you are worried that potential children would be confused? In today's society, there are all kinds of families, so that is not an issue. And isn't it more important to show children that a loving relationship is more important than labels?"

"True," Athena mumbled.

"How does he make you feel?"

"Happy. Complete. I can't find the words. When I am with him, I let my guard down and that scares me."

"That's love, Athena. It is being vulnerable to someone and trusting someone. Don't let your past relationships ruin this one."

Athena nodded. "Thanks Ellen."

"Anytime. I just want you to be happy."

"I'm going to change my ticket to an open return. I will keep in touch." Athena actually smiled. "I feel better. Thanks."

"Maybe your third book should be about romantic getaways. Venice, Santorini, Rome, Paris."

Athena laughed. "He's never been to any of those places."

"That could help you see the destinations differently. He will put you in a romantic state of mind. That piece you wrote on Nantucket made me want to take Mark there. Your writing has always focused on the best value

337

for the money, but this was different. It was practical with a romantic slant. It appeals to a larger audience."

"Thanks. I took a different approach to the article after Troy and I spent the weekend there because of the bad weather." She gasped, "Oh, Ellen. I am so sorry. I meant to tell you. I received an email the morning of the wedding. My article was selected as a cover story, and my photo will be on the cover."

"Oh, congratulations! Your first cover. See he's good for you."

"Well, I better get working on changing my ticket. I also have to talk to Holly, make certain the two houses are secure, and then start packing." She paused and smiled. "Thanks Ellen. You are more than my editor; you are my friend. Happy New Year."

"Be well, and Happy New Year."

Dan and Troy were busy setting up speakers around the new gazebo. Maria and John were out picking up food and checking on orders. Trevor and Aria were due in the next day, and the party was on Friday.

"Are you ok?" Dan asked Troy as they worked. "You're quiet, even for you."

"I don't know. Why did Athena change her plans? She was supposed to be here yesterday," Troy grumbled.

"You said it yourself. She is a busy businesswoman. She said she had a couple things she had to take care of before coming here. It's the new year." Dan tried to sound upbeat despite his concern that something was wrong.

"Yes, but she's renting a car. I could have picked her up at the airport," Troy complained. "Unless she doesn't want to be alone with me. She may have decided she doesn't want a relationship with me."

Dan stopped working and looked at Troy. He watched the color drain out of his brother's face, and he knew Troy was very worried. Troy would be devastated if Athena decided she did not want a relationship. They sometimes fought, but they were brothers, and Dan wanted Troy to be happy. "Look, I'm sure she just wants a car so she can be independent." Dan tried to sound positive.

Troy nodded. Her independence and her ability to take charge were some of the things he loved about Athena.

"She should be here very soon." Dan looked at his watch and then looked down the driveway and out toward the road.

Troy nodded. Sometimes Dan made him mad, but he appreciated his brother's support. They continued to work on the gazebo. A short while later, they heard a car approach the ranch. "That must be Athena," Dan said.

Troy suddenly found his mouth was so dry he could not speak. His hands felt cold and clammy, and he rubbed them together. He nodded his head. Dan saw Troy taking deep breaths and letting them out slowly to calm his nerves. When the car approach, Troy took a very deep breath and let it out.

"Good luck," Dan said, and Troy waved acknowledgment as he walked over to the road. He did not know what he was going to say to Athena. Maybe she would give him a clue as to her feelings, or maybe she would just tell him flat out there was never going to be a relationship. Troy's head swam with possibilities.

Athena stopped the car opposite the gazebo. "Hi Troy," she said with a smile. He looked good in a very tight black tee shirt that showed off his body, jeans, and of course, boots, a cowboy hat, and a tool belt slung low on his hips.

"Hi, Dan," she called. Dan waved hello.

"Hi, Athena." Troy liked the sunny yellow blouse she wore because it lit up her face, and it was a hopeful color.

"The gazebo looks good. Am I in the same cabin?"

Troy nodded, yes. "I will help you with your bags."

Athena pulled up to the cabin and parked. She popped the trunk and got out of the car.

"I was surprised you changed your arrival date," Troy said as he approached.

"It couldn't be avoided. There were a couple things I absolutely had to do before I came down here."

Troy nodded. She smiled, and she seemed happy to see him. He thought maybe he worried for nothing. He opened the trunk wider. "Two big suitcases?" Troy remarked as he pulled the heavy suitcases from the trunk one at a time.

"Well, I wanted to be prepared on this trip," she said with a laugh.

Troy pulled the two suitcases toward the cabin. "When must you fly back?" He wanted to know right now where he stood with her. He could not continue to wonder and worry.

"I have a book signing the third weekend of March in New York City," Athena replied as casually as she could keeping the excitement and the nerves she felt out of her voice. She pulled her rolling bag out of the trunk and closed it, and then she walked around and took her personal bag off the passenger's seat.

Troy stopped, put the bags down, and turned toward her. "What are you saying?"

"I changed my ticket to an open return ticket. I can go back tomorrow, or anytime within ninety days.

She set her personal bag on top of the rolling bag, opened it, and pulled out a gift bag. "For you." She held it out for him.

Puzzled, he opened the bag and looked inside. He pulled out a covered glass jar that was packed full of small orange scallop shells. They stared at each other and neither of them moved or spoke for what seemed like several minutes.

Dan smiled and watched from a distance.

Maria and John came home, and they walked over to him. "Dan, what are you staring at?" Maria asked.

Dan pointed toward the cabin. Maria gasped, and John smiled. "I think you may be gaining a third daughter soon, Mom."

Athena and Troy stood facing one another. Troy looked down at the jar in his hands. Was it possible she decided she wanted to be with him? He took a breath to steady his nerves. "Are you saying you want to try?"

Athena took a deep breath. "No," she said, and Troy's heart seemed to stop for a moment. She took another breath and continued, "I am saying, I will do whatever it takes to make this work."

"And you're certain of this decision?" Troy asked.

Athena nodded yes.

Troy closed his eyes and let out a sigh of relief. "I love you, Athena." He lifted her up and twirled her around several times. He looked into her eyes and kissed her.

When he stopped kissing her, she put her hands on either side of his face and kissed him. "I love you too, Troy."

Finally, Troy put Athena down. He put the jar back in the bag and grabbed the luggage handles. Instead of walking up to the cabin's porch, he turned, and started walking down the driveway.

"Where are you going?" Athena asked. "I thought I was in this cabin?"

"I'm taking your luggage to your new Texas home," Troy said as he continued walking.

"Wait for me!" Athena picked up her bags and ran quickly to Troy's side, and together they walked home.

The End

Thank you for reading *Her Unexpected Adventure*. If you enjoyed the story, please leave a favorable review on Amazon or Goodreads. Posting a review is the best way to thank an author for a story that you enjoyed.

Cheryl A. Hunter writes in several genres including Contemporary Fiction, Historical Fiction, and Paranormal Fiction. Visit her Amazon Author's Page for a list of books available and to read excerpts. https://www.amazon.com/Cheryl-A-Hunter/e/B07K657RKJ/ref=aufs_dp_fta_dsk

Sign up for Cheryl's newsletter and receive a free bonus chapter from *Her Unexpected Adventure*, as well as chapters from her other books. When you sign up, you will also be the first to learn about new releases, bonus chapters, and special promotions.

Visit Cheryl's website: http://www.cherylahunter.com/

Follow Cheryl on social media

Facebook: https://www.facebook.com/CherylAHunter101

Twitter: @CherylAHunter4**Visit Cheryl's website:** http://www.cherylahunter.com/

When you sign up for her newsletter, you will receive news of upcoming releases, promotions, and free content including a bonus chapter of *Her Unexpected Adventure*. There are also giveaways and coupons good in her ETSY and online shops.

Follow her on Facebook: CherylAHunter

Follow her on Twitter: @CherylAHunter4